KU-094-094

Past readers of Spillane books h ....ed
'the direct and audacious speech
characters', 'the action and the sweeping
twists the stories take as they progress',
and 'they transport us to a world where
violence and constant excitement are
normal conditions of life.' All these things
are true of *Vengeance is Mine*.

Mickey Spillane, one of the world's top
mystery story writers, is read in fourteen
languages every minute of every day. Since
I, The Jury was published in 1947, his books
have sold more than 55,000,000 copies
throughout the world. People like them.

BAAFI · 11001
B.LH · O 16

Also by MICKEY SPILLANE

I, THE JURY
THE DELTA FACTOR
ONE LONELY NIGHT
THE BIG KILL
THE LONG WAIT
KISS ME, DEADLY
THE DEEP
ME, HOOD!
THE GIRL HUNTERS
THE FLIER
RETURN OF THE HOOD
KILLER MINE
THE SNAKE
DAY OF THE GUNS
BLOODY SUNRISE
THE DEATH DEALERS
THE TWISTED THING
THE BY-PASS CONTROL
THE BODY LOVERS
SURVIVAL . . . ZERO!
MY GUN IS QUICK
THE ERECTION SET

and published by CORGI BOOKS

Mickey Spillane

Vengeance is Mine

CORGI BOOKS
A DIVISION OF TRANSWORLD PUBLISHERS LTD

To
JOE and GEORGE
who are always ready for
a new adventure
And to
WARD . . .
who used to be

CHAPTER ONE

THE guy was dead as hell. He lay on the floor in his pyjamas with his brains scattered all over the rug and my gun was in his hand. I kept rubbing my face to wipe out the fuzz that clouded my mind, but the cops wouldn't let me. One would pull my hand away and shout a question at me that made my head ache even worse and another would slap me with a wet rag until I felt like I had been split wide open.

I said, 'Goddamn it, stop!'

Then one of them laughed and shoved me back on the bed.

I couldn't think, I couldn't remember, I was wound up like a spring and ready to bust. All I could see was the dead guy in the middle of the room and my gun. My gun! Somebody grabbed at my arm and hauled me upright and the questions started again. That was as much as I could take. I gave a hell of a kick and a fat face in a fedora pulled back out of focus and started to groan, all doubled up. Maybe I laughed, I don't know. Something made a coarse, cackling sound.

Somebody said, 'I'll fix the bastard for that!' but before he could the door opened and the feet coming in stopped all the chatter except the groan and I knew Pat was there.

My mouth opened, and my voice said, 'Good old Pat, always to the rescue.'

He didn't sound friendly. 'Of all the damn fool times to be drunk. Did anyone touch this man?' Nobody answered. The fat face in the fedora was slumped in a chair and groaned again.

'He kicked me. The son of a bitch kicked me . . . right here.'

Another voice said, 'That's right, Captain. Marshall was questioning him and he kicked him.'

Pat grunted an answer and bent over me. 'All right, Mike, get up. Come on, get up.' His hand wrapped around my wrist and levered me into a right angle on the edge of the bed.

'Cripes, I feel lousy,' I said.

'I'm afraid you're going to feel a lot worse.' He took the wet rag and handed it to me. 'Wipe your face off. You look like hell.'

I held the cloth in my hands and dropped my face into it. Some of the clouds broke up and disappeared. When the shaking stopped I was propped up and half pushed into the bathroom. The shower was a cold lash that bit into my skin, but it woke me up to the fact that I was a human being and not a soul floating in space. I took all I could stand and turned off the faucet myself, then stepped out. By that time Pat had a container of steaming coffee in my hand and practically poured it down my throat. I tried to grin at him over the top of it, only there was no humour in the grin and there was less in Pat's tone.

His words came out in a disgusted snarl. 'Cut the funny stuff, Mike. This time you're in a jam and a good one. What the devil has gotten into you? Good God, do you have to go off the deep end every time you get tangled with a dame?'

'She wasn't a dame, Pat.'

'O.K., she was a good kid and I know it. There's still no excuse.'

I said something nasty. My tongue was still thick and unco-ordinated, but he knew what I meant. I said it twice until he was sure to get it.

'Shut up,' he told me. 'You're not the first one it's happened to. What do I have to do—smack you in the teeth with the fact that you were in love with a woman that got killed until you finally catch on that there's nothing more you can do about it?'

'Nuts! There were two of them.'

'All right, forget it. Do you know what's outside there?'

'Sure, a corpse.'

'That's right, a corpse. Just like that. Both of you in the same hotel room and one of you dead. He's got your gun and you're drunk. What about it?'

'I shot him. I was walking in my sleep and I shot him.'

This time Pat said the nasty word. 'Quit lousing me up, Mike. I want to find out what happened.'

I waved my thumb towards the other room. 'Where'd the goons come from?'

'They're policemen, Mike. They're policemen just like me and they want to know the same things I do. At three o'clock the couple next door heard what they thought was a shot. They attributed it to a street noise until the maid walked in this morning and saw the guy on the floor and passed out in the doorway. Somebody called the cops and there it was. Now, what happened?'

'I'll be damned if I know,' I said.

'You'll be damned if you don't.'

I looked at Pat, my pal, my buddy. Captain Patrick Chambers, Homicide Department of New York's finest. He didn't look happy.

I felt a little sick and got the lid of the bowl up just in time.

Pat let me finish and wash my mouth out with water, then he handed me my clothes. 'Get dressed.' His mouth crinkled up and he shook his head disgustedly.

My hands were shaking so hard I started to curse the buttons on my shirt. I got my tie under my collar, but I couldn't knot it, so I let the damn thing hang. Pat held my coat and I slid into it, thankful that a guy can still be a friend even when he's teed off at you.

Fat Face in the fedora was still in the chair when I came out of the bathroom, only this time he was in focus and not groaning so much. If Pat hadn't been there he would have laid me out with the working end of a billy and laughed while he did it. Not by himself, though.

The two uniformed patrolmen were from a police car and the other two were plain-clothes men from the local precinct. I didn't know any of them and none of them knew me, so we were even. The two plain-clothes men and one cop watched Pat with a knowledge behind their eyes that said, 'So it's one of those things, eh?'

Pat put them straight pretty fast. He shoved a chair under me and took one himself. 'Start from the beginning,' he said. 'I want all of it, Mike ; every single detail.'

I leaned back and looked at the body on the floor. Someone had had the decency to cover it with a sheet. 'His name is Chester Wheeler. He owns a department store in Columbus, Ohio. The store's been in his family a long time. He's got a wife and two kids. He was in New York on a buying tour for his business.' I looked at Pat and waited.

'Go on, Mike.'

'I met him in 1945, just after I got back from overseas. We were in Cincinnati during the time when hotel rooms were scarce. I had a room with twin beds and he was sleeping in the lobby. I invited him up to share a bed and he took me up on it. Then he was a captain in the Air Force, some kind of a purchasing agent, working out of Washington. We got drunk together in the morning, split up in the afternoon, and I didn't see him again until last night. I ran into him in a bar where he was brooding into a beer feeling sorry for himself and we had a great reunion. I remember we changed bars about half a dozen times, then he suggested we park here for the night, and we did. I bought a bottle and we finished it after we got up here. I think he began to get maudlin before we hit the sack, but I can't remember all the details. The next thing I knew somebody was beating my head trying to get me up.'

'Is that all?'

'Every bit of it, Pat.'

He stood up and looked around the room. One of the plain-clothes men anticipated his question and remarked, 'Everything is untouched, sir.'

Pat nodded and knelt over to look at the body. I would liked to have taken a look myself, but my stomach wouldn't stand it. Pat didn't speak to anyone in particular when he said, 'Wound self-inflicted. No doubt about it.' His head jerked up in my direction. 'You know, you're going to lose your licence over this, Mike.'

'I don't know why. I didn't shoot him,' I said sourly.

Fat Face sneered, 'How do you know you didn't, wise guy?'

'I never shoot people when I'm drunk,' I snarled, 'unless they push me around and make like they're tough.'

'Wise guy.'

'Yeah, real wise.'

'Cut it out, the both of you,' Pat snapped. Fat Face shut up and let me alone with my hangover. I slouched across the room to a chair in the corner and slid down into it. Pat was having a conference over by the door that wound up with everyone but Fat Face leaving. The door hadn't closed shut before the coroner came in, complete with wicker basket and pall-bearers.

The little men in my head started up with their hammers and chisels, so I closed my eyes and let my ears do the work. The medical examiner and the cops reached the same conclusion. It was my gun that shot him. A big round .45 fired at very close range. The fingerprint boys picked my prints off the rod and the other guy's too. His were on top.

A call came in for Pat right then and while he was on the phone I heard Fat Face suggest something to the M.E. that brought me straight up in the chair.

Fat Face said, '. . . Murder just as easy. They were drunk and had an argument. Bright eyes plugged him and put the gun in his hand to make it look like suicide. Then he soused himself up with liquor to make it look good.'

The M.E. bobbed his head. 'Reasonable enough.'

'You dirty fat slob, you!' I came out of the chair like a shot and spun him round on his heels. Cop or no cop, I would have caved his nose in for him if Pat hadn't dropped the phone and stepped in between us. This time he took my arm and didn't let go until he finished his phone call. When the body had been hoisted into the basket and carted off Pat unbuttoned his coat and motioned for me to sit on the bed.

I sat.

He had his hands in his pockets and he spoke as much to the plain-clothes man as to me. His words didn't come easy, but he didn't stumble over them exactly. 'I've been waiting for this, Mike. You and that damn gun of yours were bound to get in trouble.'

10

'Stow it, Pat. You know I didn't shoot the guy.'

'Do I?'

'Hell, you ought to . . .'

'Do you know you didn't?'

'It was a closed room and I was so far gone I didn't even hear the gun go off. You'll get a paraffin test on the body that will prove it anyway. I'll go for one myself and that will settle that. What are we jawing about?'

'About you and that rod, that's what! If the guy was a suicide you'll be up the creek without a licence. They don't like for people to be carrying firearms and a load of liquor too.'

He had me cold on that one. His eyes swept the room, seeing the clothes on the backs of the chairs, the empty whisky bottles on the windowsill, the stubs of cigarettes scattered all over the floor. My gun was on the desk along with a spent casing, with the white powder clotting in the oil showing the prints.

Pat closed his eyes and grimaced. 'Let's go, Mike,' he said.

I put on my coat over the empty holster and squeezed between the two of them for the ride down to headquarters. There was a parking-lot ticket in my pocket, so I didn't worry about my heap. Fat Face had that look in his eyes that said he was hoping I'd make a break for it so he could bounce me one. It was rough having to disappoint the guy.

For once I was glad to have a friend in the department. Pat ran the tests off on me himself and had me stick around downstairs until the report was finished. I had the ashtray half filled before he came back down. 'What did it show?' I asked him.

'You're clean enough. The corpse carried the powder burns all right.'

'That's a relief.'

His eyebrows went up. 'Is it? The D.A. wants to have a little talk with you. It seems that you managed to find an awfully fussy hotel to play around in. The manager raised a stink and carried it all the way upstairs. Ready?'

I got up and followed him to the elevators, cursing my luck for running into an old buddy. What the hell got into the guy anyway? It would have been just as easy for him to jump out the damn window. The elevator stopped and we got out. It would have been better if there was an organ playing a dirge. I was right in the spirit for it.

The D.A. was a guy who had his charming moments, only this time there weren't any photographers around. His face wore a tailor-made look of sarcasm and there was ice in his words. He told me to sit down then perched himself on the edge of the desk. While Pat was running through the details he never took his eyes off me nor let his expression change one bit. If he thought he was getting under my skin with his professional leer he had another think coming. I was just about to tell him he looked like a frog when he beat me to it.

'You're done in this town, Mr Hammer; I suppose you know that.'

What the hell could I say? He held all the cards.

He slid off the desk and stood at parade rest so I could admire his physique, I guess. 'There were times when you proved yourself quite useful . . . and quite trying. You let yourself get out of hand once too often. I'm sorry it happened this way; but it's my opinion that the city is better off without you or your services.' The D.A. was getting a big whang out of this.

Pat shot him a dirty look, but kept his mouth shut. I wasn't a clam. 'Then I'm just another citizen again?'

'That's right, with no licence and no gun. Nor will you ever have one again.'

'Are you booking me for anything?'

'I can't very well. I wish I could.'

He must have read what was coming in the lopsided grin I gave him because he got red from his collar up. 'For a D.A. you're a pain in the behind,' I said. 'If it wasn't for me the papers would have run you in the comic section long ago.'

'That will be enough, Mr Hammer!'

'Shut your yap or arrest me, otherwise I'll exercise my rights as a citizen, and one of 'em happens to be objecting to the actions of any public official. You've been after my hide ever since you walked into this office because I had sense enough to know where to look for a few killers. It made nice copy for the Press and you didn't even get an honourable mention. All I have to say is this . . . it's a damn good thing the police are civil service. They have to have a little bit of common sense to get where they are. Maybe you were a good lawyer . . . you should have kept at it and quit trying to be king of the cops.'

'Get out of here!' His voice was a short fuse ready to explode any second. I stood up and jammed on my hat. Pat was holding the door open. The D.A. said, 'The very first time you so much as speed down Broadway, I'm going to see to it personally that you're slapped with every charge in the book. That will make good Press copy too.'

I stopped with my hand on the knob and sneered at him, then Pat jerked my sleeve and I closed the door. In the hallway he kept his peace until we reached the stairs; it was as long as he could hold it. 'You're a fool, Mike.'

'Nuts, Pat. It was his game all the way.'

'You could keep your trap closed, couldn't you?'

'No!' I licked the dryness from my lips and stuck a cigarette in my mouth. 'He's been ready for me too long now. The jerk was happy to give me the shaft.'

'So you're out of business.'

'Yeah ; I'll open up a grocery store.'

'It isn't that funny, Mike. You're a private investigator and a good cop when you have to be. There were times when I was glad to have you around. It's over now. Come on in my office . . . we might as well have a drink on it.' He ushered me into his sanctum sanctorum and waved me into a chair. The bottom drawer of his desk had a special niche for a pint bottle and a few glasses, carefully concealed under a welter of blank forms. Pat drew two and handed one over to me. We toasted each other in silence, then spilled them down.

'It was a pretty good show while it lasted,' Pat said.

'Sure was,' I agreed, 'sure was. What happens now?'

He put the bottle and glasses away and dropped into the swivel chair behind his desk. You'll be called in if there's an inquest. The D.A. is liable to make it hard on you out of meanness. Meanwhile, you're clear to do what you please. I vouched for you. Besides, you're too well known to the boys to try to drop out of sight.'

'Buy your bread and butter from me, will you?'

Pat let out a laugh. 'I wish you wouldn't take it so lightly. You're in the little black book right now on the special S-list.'

I pulled out my wallet and slid my licence out of the card case and threw it on his desk. 'I won't be needing that any more.'

He picked it up and examined it sourly. A large envelope on the filing cabinet held my gun and the report sheet. He clipped the card to the form and started to put it back. On second thought he slid the magazine out of the rod and swore. 'That's nice. They put it in here with a full load.' He used his thumb to jack the shells out of the clip, spilling them on the desk.

'Want to kiss old betsy goodbye, Mike?'

When I didn't answer he said, 'What are you thinking of?'

My eyes were squinted almost shut and I started to grin again. 'Nothing,' I said, 'nothing at all.'

He frowned at me while he dumped the stuff back in the envelope and closed it. My grin spread and he started to get mad. 'All right, damn it, what's so funny? I know that look. . . . I've seen it often enough. What's going through that feeble mind of yours?'

'Just thoughts, Pat. Don't be so hard on a poor unemployed pal, will you?'

'Let's hear those thoughts.'

I picked a cigarette out of the container on his desk, then put it back after reading the label. 'I was just thinking of a way to get that ticket back, that's all.'

That seemed to relieve him. He sat down and tugged at his tie. 'It'll be a good trick if you can work it. I can't see how you can.'

I thumbed a match and lit up a smoke. 'It won't be hard.'

'No? You think the D.A. will mail it back to you with his apologies?'

'I wouldn't be a bit surprised.'

Pat kicked the swivel chair all the way around and glared at me. 'You haven't got your gun any more, you can't hold him up.'

'No,' I laughed, 'but I can make a deal with him. Either he *does* mail it back with his apologies or I'll make a sap out of him.'

His palms cracked the desk and he was all cop again. This much wasn't a game. 'Do you know anything, Mike?'

'No more than you. Everything I told you was the truth. It'll be easy to check and your laboratory backs up my statements. The guy was a suicide. I agree with you. He shot himself to pieces and I don't know why or when. All I know is where and that doesn't help. Now, have you heard enough.'

'No, you bastard, I haven't.' This time he was grinning back at me. I shoved my hat on and left him there still grinning. When I closed the door I heard him kick the desk and swear to himself.

I walked out into the glaring brightness of midday, whistling through my teeth, though by rights I should have been in a blue funk. I hopped in a cab at the corner and gave him my office address. All the way uptown I kept thinking about Chester Wheeler, or what was left of him on the rug. An out-an-out suicide and my gun in his mitt, they said. Private citizen Michael Hammer, that's me. No ticket, no gun and no business, even my hangover was gone. The driver let me out in front of my building and I paid him off, walked in and pushed the bell for the elevator.

Velda was curled up in my big leather chair, her head buried in the paper. When I walked in she dropped it and looked at me. There were streaks across her face from wiping away the tears and her eyes were red. She tried to say something, sobbed and bit her lip.

'Take it easy, honey.' I threw my coat on the rack and pulled her to her feet.

'Oh, Mike, what happened?' It had been a long time since I'd seen Velda playing woman like this. My great big beautiful secretary was human after all. She was better this way.

I put my arms around her, running my fingers through the sleek midnight of her hair. I squeezed her gently and she put her head against my cheek. 'Cut it, sugar, nothing is that bad.

14

They took away my ticket and made me a Joe Doe. The D.A. finally got me where he wanted me.'

She shook her hair and gave me a light tap in the ribs. 'That insipid little squirt! I hope you clobbered him good!'

I grinned at her G.I. talk. 'I called him a name, that's what I did.'

'You should have clobbered him!' Her head went down on my shoulder and sniffed. 'I'm sorry, Mike. I feel like a jerk for crying.'

She blew her nose on my fancy pocket handkerchief and I steered her over to the desk. 'Get the sherry, Velda. Pat and I had a drink to the dissolution of the Mike Hammer enterprise. Now we'll drink to the new business. The S.P.C.D., Society for the Prevention of Cruelty to Detectives.'

Velda brought out the makings and poured two short ones. 'It isn't that funny, Mike.'

'I've been hearing that all morning. The funny part is that it's *very* funny.'

The sherry went down and we had another. I lit a pair of smokes and stuck one between her lips. 'Tell me about it,' she said. The tears were gone now. Curiosity and a little anger were in her eyes, making them snap. For the second time today I rehashed what I knew of it, bringing the story right through the set-to in the D.A.'s office.

When I finished she said some very unladylike curses and threw her cigarette at the waste basket. 'Damn these public officials and their petty grievances, Mike. They'll climb over anybody to get to the top. I wish I could do something instead of sitting here answering your mail. I'd like to turn that pretty boy inside out!' She threw herself into the leather chair and drew her legs up under her.

I reached out a toe and flipped her skirt down. On some people legs are just to reach the ground. On Velda they were a hell of a distraction. 'Your days of answering the mail are over, kid.'

Her eyes got wet again, but she tried to smile it off. 'I know. I can always get a job in a department store. What will you do?'

'Where's your native ingenuity? You used to be full of ideas.' I poured another glass of sherry and sipped it, watching her. For a minute she chewed on her fingernail, then raised her head to give me a puzzled frown.

'What are you getting at, Mike?'

Her bag, a green-leather shoulder-strap affair, was lying on the desk. I raised it and let it fall. It hit the polished wood with a dull clunk. 'You have a gun and a licence to carry it, haven't you? And you have a private operator's ticket

15

yourself, haven't you? O.K., from now on the business is yours. I'll do the legwork.'

A twitch pulled her mouth into a peculiar grin as she realized what I meant. 'You'll like that, too, won't you?'

'What?'

'The legwork.'

I slid off the edge of the desk and stood in front of her. With Velda I didn't take chances. I reached out a toe again and flipped her dress up to the top of her sheer nylons. She would have made a beautiful calendar. 'If I went for any I'd go for yours, but I'm afraid of that rod you use for ballast in your handbag.'

Her smile was a funny thing that crept up into her eyes and laughed at me from there. I just looked at her, a secretary with a built-in stand-off that had more on the ball than any of the devil's helpers I had ever seen and could hold me over the barrel without saying a word.

'You're the boss now,' I said. 'We'll forget about the mail and concentrate on a very special detail . . . getting my licence and my gun back where it belongs. The D.A. made me out a joker and put the screws on good. If he doesn't send 'em back with a nice, sweet note, the newspapers are going to wheel out the chopping block for the guy.

'I won't even tell you how to operate. You can call the signals and carry the ball yourself if you want to. I'll only stick my nose in during the practice sessions. But if you're smart, you'll concentrate on the body of Chester Wheeler. When he was alive he was a pretty nice guy, a regular family man. All the grisly details are in the paper there and you can start from that. Meanwhile, I'll be around breaking ground for you and you'll spot my tracks here and there. You'll find some signed blank cheques in the drawer for your expense account.'

I filled the sherry glass up again and drained it in one gulp. It was a beautiful day, a real dilly. My face cracked into a smile that was followed by a short rumble of pleasure.

Once more Velda said, 'It *isn't* funny, Mike.'

I lit another cigarette and pushed my hat back on my head. 'You'll never know how real funny it actually is, kid. You see, only one bullet killed Chester Wheeler. I always carry six in the clip and when Pat emptied it out there were only four of them.'

Velda was watching me with the tip of her tongue clenched between her teeth. There wasn't any kitten-softness about her now. She was big and she was lovely, with the kind of curves that made you want to turn around and have another look. The lush fullness of her lips had tightened into the faintest kind of snarl and her eyes were the carnivorous eyes you could

16

expect to see in the jungle watching you from behind a clump of bushes.

I said it slowly. 'If you had that gun in your hand pointed at somebody's belly, could you pull the trigger and stand ready to pull it again if you had to?'

She pulled her tongue back and let her teeth close together. 'I wouldn't have to pull it twice. Not now I wouldn't.'

She was watching me as I walked across the office. I looked over my shoulder and waved so-long, then closed the door fast. She still hadn't bothered to pull her dress back down, and like I'd said, I wasn't taking any chances.

Some day she wasn't going to get so smart with me.

Or maybe she would.

CHAPTER TWO

THE papers were full of it that night. The tabloids had me splashed all over the front pages and part of the middle section. The same guys that hung on my tail when they had wanted a story took me apart at the seams in their columns. Only one bothered to be sentimental about it. He wrote me an epitaph. In rhyme. The D.A. was probably laughing his head off.

In another hour he'd be crying in his beer, the jerk.

I finished off an early supper and stacked the dishes in the sink. They could wait. For fifteen minutes I steamed under a shower until my skin turned pink, then suffered under a cold spray for a few seconds before I stepped out and let a puddle spread around my feet. When I finished shaving I climbed into a freshly pressed suit and transferred a few hundred bucks from the top drawer to my wallet.

I took a look in the mirror and snorted. I could have been a man of distinction except for my face and the loose space in my jacket that was supposed to fit around a rod. That at least I could fix. I strapped on a mighty empty holster to fill out the space under my arm and felt better about it. I looked in the mirror again and grimaced. It was a hell of a shame that I wasn't handsome.

Last night was a vague shadow with only a few bright spots, but before I started to backtrack there was something I wanted to do. It was just past seven o'clock when I found a parking place near the hotel that had caused all the trouble. It was one of those old-fashioned places that catered to even older-fashioned people and no fooling around. Single girls couldn't even register there unless they were over eighty. Before I went in I snapped the back off my watch, pushed out the works and dropped it in my shirt pocket.

The desk clerk wasn't glad to see me. His hand started for the telephone, stopped, then descended on the desk bell three times, loud and clear. When a burly shouldered individual who kept the lobby free of loiterers appeared the clerk looked a little better. At least his shaking stopped.

There wasn't any need to identify myself, 'I lost the works out of my watch last night. I want 'em back.'

'But . . . the room hasn't been cleaned yet,' he blurted.

'I want 'em now,' I repeated. I held out a thick, hairy wrist

18

and tapped the empty case. The burly guy peered over my shoulder interestedly.

'But . . .'

'Now!'

The house dick said, 'I'll go up with 'im and we can look for it, George.'

Evidently the clerk was glad to have his decisions made for him, because he handed over the keys and seemed happy at last.

'This way.' The dick nudged me with his elbow and I followed him. In the elevator he stood with his hands behind his back and glared at the ceiling. He came out of it at the fourth floor to usher me down the hall where he put the key in the lock of number 402.

Nothing had changed. The blood was still on the floor, the beds unmade and the white powder sprinkled liberally around. The dick stood at the door with his arms crossed and kept his eyes on me while I poked around under the furniture.

I went through the room from top to bottom, taking my time about it. The dick got impatient and began tapping his fingernails against the wall. When there was no place left to look the dick said, 'It ain't here. Come on.'

'Who's been here since the cops left?'

'Nobody, feller, not even the cleaning girls. Let's get going. You probably lost that watch in a bar somewhere.'

I didn't answer him. I had flipped back the covers of the bed I slept in and saw the hole right in the edge of the mattress.

Mattress filling can stop a slug like a steel plate and it couldn't have gone in very far, but when I probed the hole with my forefinger all I felt was horsehair and coil springs. The bullet was gone. Someone had beaten me to it. Beaten me to a couple of things . . . the empty shell case was gone too.

I put on a real bright act when I made like I found my watch works under the covers. I held it up for the guy to see then shoved it back in the case. He grunted. 'All right, all right. Let's get moving.' I gave him what was supposed to be a smile of gratitude and walked out. He stuck with me all the way down and was even standing in the doorway to see me go down the street to my car.

Before long he was going to catch all kinds of hell.

So would the desk clerk when the cops got wise to the fact that Chester Wheeler was no more of a suicide than I was. My late friend of the night before had been very neatly murdered.

And I was due for a little bit of hell myself.

I found a saloon with an empty parking place right out in front and threw a buck on the bar. When my beer came I took a nickel from the change and squeezed into a phone-booth

19

down the end. It was late, but Pat wasn't a guy to leave his office until things were cleaned up and I was lucky this time.

I said, 'Michael Q. Citizen, speaking.'

He laughed into the receiver. 'How's the grocery business?'

'Booming, Pat, really booming. I have a large order for some freshly murdered meat.'

'What's that?'

'Just a figure of speech.'

'Oh!'

'By the way, how clear am I on the Wheeler death?'

I could almost see the puzzled frown on his face. . . . 'As far as I can see you can't be held for anything. Why?'

'Just curious. Look, the boys in blue were in that room a long time before I came back to the land of the living. Did they poke around much?'

'No, I don't think so. It was pretty obvious what happened.'

'They take anything out with them?'

'The body,' he said. 'Your gun, a shell casing, and Wheeler's personal belongings.'

'That was all?'

'Uh-huh.'

I paused a moment, then : 'Don't suicides generally leave a note, Pat?'

'Generally, yes. That happens when they're sober and there isn't a witness. If they've thought about it awhile they usually try to explain. In a fit of passion they rarely waste the time.'

'Wheeler wasn't a passionate man, I don't think,' I told him. 'From all appearances he was an upright, business man.'

'I thought of that. It *was* peculiar, wasn't it? Did he look like a suicide type to you?'

'Nope.'

'And he didn't mention anything along that line beforehand. Hmmm!'

I let a few seconds go by. 'Pat . . . how many slugs were left in my rod?'

'Four, weren't there?'

'Correct. And I hadn't shot it since I was on the target range with you last week.'

'So . . .?' His voice had an uneasy tinge to it.

Real softly I said, 'That gun never has less than six in it, chum.'

If he had been a woman he would have screamed. Instead he bellowed into the phone and I wouldn't answer him. I heard him shouting, 'Mike, goddamn it, answer me. . . . *Mike!*'

I laughed just once to let him know I was still there and hung up.

All he needed was five minutes. By that time he'd have the

D.A. cornered in his office like a scared rabbit. Sure, the D.A. was big stuff, but Pat was no slouch either. He'd tell that guy off with a mouthful of words that would make his hair stand on end and the fair-haired boy of the courts wouldn't dare do a thing.

It was getting funnier all the time. I went back to the bar and drank my beer.

The after-supper crowd began drifting in and taking places at the bar. At eight-thirty I called Velda, but she wasn't home. I tried again an hour later and she still wasn't there. She wasn't at the office either. Maybe she was out hiring a signpainter to change the name on the door.

When I finally shifted into the corner up against the cigarette machine I started to think. It didn't come easy because there hadn't been any reason to remember then and we had let the booze flow free. Last night.

Famous last words.

Last night the both of us had thrown five years to the wind and brought the war back to the present. We were buddies again. We weren't the kind of buddies you get to be when you eat and sleep and fight with a guy, but we were buddies. We were two-strong and fighting the war by ourselves. We were two guys who had met as comrades-in-arms, happy to be on the right side and giving all we had. For one night way back there we had been drinking buddies until we shook hands to go finish the war. Was that the way it was supposed to be? Did some odd quirk of fate throw us together purposely so that later we'd meet again?

Last night I had met him and drank with him. We talked, we drank some more. Was he happy? He was, after we ran into each other. Before that he had been curled over a drink at the bar. He could have been brooding. He could have been thinking. But he was happy as hell to see me again! Whatever it was he had been thinking about was kicked aside along with those five years and we had ourselves one hell of a drinking bout. Sure, we fought the war again. We did the same thing anybody else did when they caught up with someone they knew from those days. We talked it and we fought it and we were buddies again decked out in the same uniform ready to give everything for the other guy on our side whether we knew him or not. But the war had to give out sometime. The peace always has to come when people get too tired of fighting. And yet, it was the end of our talk that brought the cloud back to his eyes. He hadn't wanted it to stop or be diverted into other channels. He told me he had been in town a week and was getting set to go home. The whole deal was a business trip to do some buying for his store.

21

Yeah, we were buddies. We weren't buddies long, but we were buddies good. If we had both been in the jungle and some slimy Jap had picked him off I would have rammed the butt of a rifle down the brown bastard's throat for it. He would have done the same for me, too. But we weren't in any damn jungle. We were right here in New York City where murder wasn't supposed to happen and did all the time. A guy I liked comes into my own city and a week later he's dead as hell.

One week. What did he do? What happened? Who was he with? Where was the excuse for murder, here or in Columbus, Ohio? A whole damn week. I slapped my hat on the stool to reserve it and took another few nickels from my change and wormed into the phone-booth again. There was one other question. What was I going to do about it? My face started to go tight again and I knew the answer.

I dialled two numbers. The second got my man. He was a private investigator the same as I used to be except that he was essential, honest and hard-working. His name was Joe Gill and he owed me a favour that he and his staff could begin repaying as of now.

I said, 'This is Mike, Joe. Remember me?'

'Hell,' he laughed, 'with all your publicity how could I forget you? I hope you aren't after a job.'

'Not exactly. Look, you tied up right now?'

'Well . . . no. Something on your mind?'

'Plenty, friend. You still doing insurance work?'

Joe grunted an assent. 'That's *all* I'm doing. You can keep your guns and your tough guys. I'll track down missing beneficiaries.'

'Care to do me a favour, Joe?'

He only hesitated a second. 'Glad to, Mike. You've steered me straight plenty of times. Just name it.'

'Swell. This guy that died in the hotel room with me— Chester Wheeler—I want some information on him. Not a history . . . I just want him backtracked over the past week. He's been in town doing some buying for his store in Columbus, Ohio, and I want a record of what he'd done since he hit town. Think it can be done?'

I could hear his pencil rasping on paper. 'Give me a few hours. I'll start it myself and put the chain gang out on the details. Where can I reach you?'

I thought a moment, then told him. 'Try the Greenwood Hotel. It's a little dump on a side street up in the Eighties. They don't ask questions there.'

'Right! See you later.'

I cradled the receiver and picked my way back through the crowd to the bar. My hat was hanging over a pin-up lamp on the wall and my seat was occupied and the guy was spending my money for beer.

I didn't get mad, though. The guy was Pat.

The bartender put down another beer and took some more of my change. I said, 'How's tricks, kid?'

Pat turned around slowly and looked at me for the first time. His eyes were clouded and his mouth had a grim twist to it. He looked tired and worried. 'There's a back room, Mike. Let's go sit down. I want to talk to you.'

I gulped my beer down and carried a full one back to the booth. When I slid my deck of Luckies across the table to him he shook his head and waited until I lit up. I asked, 'How did you find me?'

He didn't answer. Instead, he popped one of his own, very softly, very forcefully. He wasn't kidding around. 'What's it all about, Mike?'

'What's what?'

'You know.' He leaned forward on his arms, never taking his eyes off my face. 'Mike, I'm not going to get excited this time. I'm not going to let you talk me into losing a lot of sleep any more. I'm a police officer, or at least I'm supposed to be. Right now I'm treating this like it might be something important and like you know more about it than I do. I'm asking questions that are going to be answered. What's going on?'

Smoke drifted into my eyes and I squinted them almost shut. 'Supposing I told you Chester Wheeler was murdered, Pat.'

'I'd ask how, then who.'

'I don't know how and I don't know who.'

'Then why, Mike? Why is it murder?'

'Two shots were fired from my gun, that's why.'

He gave the table a rap with his knuckles. 'Damn you, Mike, come out with it! We're friends ; but I'm tired of being hamstrung. You're forever smelling murder where murder isn't and making it come out right. Play it square!'

'Don't I always?'

'With reservations!'

I gave a sour laugh. 'Two shots out of that rod. Isn't that enough?'

'Not for me it isn't. Is that all you have?'

I nodded and dragged in on the butt.

Pat's face seemed to soften and he let the air out of his lungs slowly. He even smiled a little. 'I guess that's that, Mike. I'm glad I didn't get sweated up about it.'

I snubbed the cigarette out on the table top. 'Now you've got me going. What are you working up to?'

'Precedent, Mike. I'm speaking of past suicides.'

'What about 'em?'

'Every so often we find a suicide with a bullet in his head. The room has been liberally peppered with bullets, to quote a cliché. In other words, they'll actually take the gun away from the target, but pull the trigger anyway. They keep doing it until they finally have nerve enough to keep it there. Most guys can't handle an automatic anyway and they fire a shot to make sure they know how it operates.'

'And that makes Wheeler a bona-fide suicide—right?'

He grinned at the sneer on my face. 'Not altogether. When you pulled your little razzmatazz about the slugs in your gun I went up in the air and had a handful of experts dig up Wheeler's itinerary and we located a business friend he had been with the day before he died. He said Wheeler was unusually depressed and talked of suicide several times. Apparently his business was on the down-grade.'

'Who was the guy, Pat?'

'A handbag manufacturer, Emil Perry. Well, if you have any complaints, come see me, but no more scares, Mike. O.K.?'

'Yeah,' I hissed. 'You still didn't say how you found me.'

'I traced your call, friend citizen. It came from a bar and I knew you'd stay there awhile. I took my time at the hotel checking your story. And, er . . . yes, I did find the bullet hole in the mattress.'

'I suppose you found the bullet, too?'

'Why, yes, we did. The shell case, too.' I sat there rigid, waiting. 'It was right out there in the hall where you dropped it, Mike. I wish you'd quit trying to give this an element of mystery just to get me in on it.'

'You chump!'

'Can it, Mike! The house dick set me straight.'

I was standing up facing him and I could feel the mad running right down into my shoes. 'I thought you were smart, Pat. You chump!'

This time he winked. 'No more games, huh, Mike?' He grinned at me a second and left me standing there watching his back. Now I was playing games. Hot dog!

I thought I was swearing under my breath until a couple of mugs heard their tomatoes complain and started to give me hell. When they saw my face they told their dames to mind their business and went on drinking.

Well, I asked for it. I played it cute and Pat played it cuter. Maybe I was the chump. Maybe Wheeler did kill himself. Maybe he came back from the morgue and tried to slip out with the slug and the shell too.

I sure as a four-letter word didn't. I picked up my pack of butts and went out on the street for a smell of fresh air that wasn't jammed with problems. After a few deep breaths I felt better.

Down on the corner a drugstore was getting rid of its counter customers and I walked in past the tables of novelties and cosmetics to a row of phone-booths in the back. I pulled the Manhattan directory out of the rack and began thumbing through it. When I finished I did the same thing with the Brooklyn book. I didn't learn anything there, so I pulled up the Bronx listing and found an Emil Perry who lived in one of the better residential sections of the community.

At ten minutes after eleven I parked outside a red-brick, one-family house and killed the motor. The car in front of me was a new Cadillac sedan with all the trimmings and the side door bore two gold initials in Old English script, E.P.

There was a brass knocker on the door of the house, embossed with the same initials, but I didn't use it. I had the thing raised when I happened to glance in the window. If the guy was Emil Perry, he was big and fat with a fortune in jewels stuck in his tie and flashing on his fingers. He was talking to somebody out of sight and licking his lips between every word.

You should have seen his face. He was scared silly.

I let the knocker down easy and eased back into the shadows. When I looked at my watch ten minutes had gone by and nothing happened. I could see the window through the shrubs and the top of the fat man's head. He still hadn't moved. I kept on waiting and a few minutes later the door opened just far enough to let a guy out. There was no light behind him so I didn't see his face until he was opposite me. Then I grinned a nasty little grin and let my mind give Pat a very soft horse-laugh.

The guy that came out only had one name—Rainey. He was a tough punk with a record as long as your arm and he used to be available for any kind of job that needed a strong arm.

I waited until Rainey walked down the street and got in a car. When it pulled away with a muffled roar I climbed into my own heap and turned the motor over.

I didn't have to see Mr Perry after all. Anyway, not tonight. He wasn't going anywhere. I made a U-turn at the end of the street and got back on the main drag that led to Manhattan. When I reached the Greenwood Hotel a little after midnight the night clerk shoved the register at me, took cash in advance and handed me the keys to the room. Fate with a twisted sense of humour was riding my tail again. The room was 402.

If there was a dead man in it tomorrow it'd have to be me.

I dreamt I was in a foxhole with a shelter half-dragged over me to keep out the rain. The guy in the next foxhole kept calling to me until my eyes opened and my hand automatically reached for my rifle. There was no rifle; but the voice was real. It came from the hall. I threw back the covers and hopped up, trotting for the door.

Joe slid in and closed it behind him. 'Cripes,' he grunted, 'I thought you were dead.'

'Don't say that word. I'm alone tonight. You get it?'

He flipped his hat to the chair and sat on it. 'Yeah, I got it. Most of it anyway. They weren't very co-operative at the hotel seeing as how the cops had just been there. What did you do to 'em?'

'Gave him a steer. Now the honourable Captain of Homicide, my pal, my buddy who ought to know better, thinks I'm pulling fast ones on him as a joke. He even suspects me of having tampered with some trivial evidence.'

'Did you?'

'It's possible. Of course, how would I know what's evidence and what's not. After all, what does it matter if it *was* a suicide?'

Joe gave a polite burp. 'Yeah,' he said.

I watched him while he felt around in his pocket for a fistful of notes. He tapped them with a forefinger. 'If I charged you for this you'd of shelled out a pair of C's. Six men lost their sleep, three lost their dates and one caught hell from his wife. She wants him to quit me. And for what?'

'And for what?' I repeated.

He went on: 'This Wheeler fellow seemed pretty respectable. By some very abstract questioning here and there we managed to backtrack his movements. Just remember, we had to do it in a matter of hours, so it isn't a minute-by-minute account.

'He checked in at the hotel immediately upon arriving eight days ago. His mornings were spent visiting merchandising houses here in the city where he placed some regular orders for items for his store. None of these visits were of unusual importance. Here are some that may be. He wired home to Columbus, Ohio, to a man named Ted Lee asking for five thousand bucks by return wire. He received it an hour later. I presume it was to make a special purchase of some sort.

'We dug up a rather sketchy account of where he spent his evenings. A few times he returned to the hotel slightly under the influence. One night he attended a fashion show that featured a presentation of next year's styles. The show was followed by cocktails and he may have been one of the men who helped one of a few models who had a couple too many down the elevator and into a cab.'

I started to grin. 'Models?'

He shook his head. 'Forget it,' he told me, 'it wasn't a smoker with a dirty floor show for dessert.'

'O.K., go on.'

'From then on he was in and out of the hotel periodically and each time he had a little more of a jag on. He checked in with you and was dead before morning. The hotel was very put out. That's it.'

He waited a second and repeated, 'That's it, I said.'

'I heard you.'

'Well?'

'Joe, you're a lousy detective.'

He shot me an impatient glance tainted with amazement. '*I'm* a lousy detective? You without a licence and *I'm* the lousy detective? That's a hell of a way of thanking me for all my trouble! Why, I've found more missing persons than you have hairs on that low forehead of yours and . . .'

'Ever shoot anybody, Joe?'

His face went white and his fingers had trouble taking the cigarette out of his mouth. 'Once . . . I did.'

'Like it?'

'No.' He licked his lips. 'Look, Mike . . . this guy Wheeler . . . you were there. He *was* a suicide, wasn't he?'

'Uh-uh. Somebody gave him the business.'

I could hear him swallow clear across the rooom. 'Uh . . . you won't need me again, will you?'

'Nope. Thanks a lot, Joe. Leave the notes on the bed.'

The sheaf of papers fell on the bed and I heard the door close softly. I sat on the arm of the chair and let my mind weave the angles in and out. One of them had murder in it.

Some place there was a reason for murder big enough to make the killer try to hide the fact under a cloak of suicide. But the reason has to be big to kill. It has to be even bigger to try to hide it. It was still funny the way it came out. I was the only one who could tag it as murder and make it stick. Some place a killer thought he was being real clever. Clever as hell. Maybe he thought the lack of one lousy shell in the clip wouldn't be noticed.

I kept on thinking about it and I got sore. It made me sore twice. The first time I burned up was because the killer took me for a sap. Who the hell did he think I was—a cheap uptown punk who carried a rod for effect? Did he think I was some goon with loose brains and stupid enough to take it lying down?

Then I got mad again because it was my friend that died. My friend, not somebody else's. A guy who was glad to see me even after five years. A guy who was on the same side with me and

27

gave the best he could give to save some bastard's neck so that bastard could kill him five years later.

The army was one thing I should have reminded Pat of. I should have prodded his memory with the fact that the army meant guns and no matter who you were an indoctrination course in most of the phases of handling lethal weapons hit you at one time or another. Maybe Chester Wheeler *did* try to shoot himself. More likely he tried to fire it at someone or someone fired it at him. One thing I knew damn well: Chet had known all about automatics and if he did figure to knock himself off he wasn't going to fire any test shot just to see if the gun worked.

I rolled into bed and yanked the covers up. I'd sleep on it.

CHAPTER THREE

I STOOD on the corner of Thirty-third Street and checked the address from Joe's notes. The number I wanted was halfway down the block, an old place recently remodelled and refitted with all the trimmings a flashy clientele could expect. While I stared at the directory a covey of trim young things clutching hatboxes passed behind me to the elevator and I followed them in. They were models, but their minds weren't on jobs. All they talked about was food. I didn't blame them a bit. In the downstairs department they were shipshape from plenty of walking, but upstairs it was hard to tell whether they were coming or going unless they were wearing falsies. They were pretty to look at, but I wouldn't give any of them bed room.

The elevator slid to a stop at the eighth floor and the dames got out. They walked down the corridor to a pair of full-length, frosted plate-glass doors etched with ANTON LIPSEK AGENCY and pushed in. The last one saw me coming and held the door open for me.

It was a streamlined joint if ever there was one. The walls were a light pastel tint with a star-sprinkled ceiling of pale blue. Framed original photos of models in everything from nylon step-ins to low-slung convertibles marched around the walls in a double column. Three doors marked PRIVATE branched off the anteroom, while a receptionist flanked by a host of busy stenos pounding typewriters guarded the entrance to the main office.

I dumped my cigarette into an ash tray and grinned at the receptionist. Her voice had a forced politeness, but her eyes were snooty. 'Yes?'

'The Calway Merchandising Company had a dinner meeting the other night. Several models from this agency were present for the fashion show that came later. I'm interested in seeing them . . . one of them, at least. How can I go about it?'

She tapped her pencil on the desk. Three irritable little taps. Evidently this was an old story to her. 'Is this a business or . . . personal inquiry, sir?'

I leaned on the edge of the desk and gave her my real nasty smile. 'It could be both, kid, but one thing it's not and that's *your* business.'

'Oh! . . . oh!' she said. 'Anton—Mr Lipsek, I mean—he handles the assignments. I'll . . . call him.'

Her hands flew over the intercom box, fumbling with the keys. Maybe she thought I'd bite, because she wouldn't take her eyes off my face. When the box rattled at her she shut it off and said I could go right in. This time I gave her my nice smile, the one without the teeth. 'I was only kidding, sugar.'

She said 'Oh!' again and didn't believe me.

Anton Lipsek had his name on the door in gold letters and under it the word MANAGER. Evidently he took his position seriously. His desk was a roll-top affair shoved in a corner, bulging with discarded photographs and sketches. The rest of the room was given over to easels, display mounts and half-finished sketches. He was very busy managing, too.

He was managing to get a whole lot of woman, dressed in very little nothing, in place amid a bunch of props so the camera would pick up most of the nothing she was wearing and none of the most she was showing. At least that's what it looked like to me.

I whistled softly. 'Ve-ry nice.'

'Too much skin,' he said. He didn't even turn around.

The model tried to peer past the glare of the lamps he had trained on her. 'Who's that?'

Anton shushed her, his hands on her nice bare flesh giving a cold professional twist to her torso. When she was set just right he stepped back behind the camera, muttered a cue and the girl let a ghost of a smile play with her mouth. There was a barely audible click and the model turned human again.

They could make me a manager any day.

Anton snapped off the lights and swivelled his head around.

'Ah, yes! Now, sir, what can I do for you?'

He was a tall, lanky guy with eyebrows that met above his nose and a scrimy little goatee that waggled when he talked and made his chin come to a point. 'I'm interested in finding a certain model. She works here.'

The eyebrows went up like a window shade. 'That, sir, is a request we get quite often. Yes, quite often.'

I said very bluntly, 'I don't like models. Too flat-chested.'

Anton was beginning to look amazed when she came out from behind the props, this time with shoes on, too. ' 'Tain't me you're talkin' about, podner.' An unlit cigarette was dangling from her mouth. 'Got a light?'

I held a match under her nose, watching her mouth purse around the cigarette when she drew in the flame. 'No, you're exceptional,' I said.

This time she grinned and blew the smoke in my face.

Anton coughed politely. 'This, er, model you mentioned. Do you know her?'

'Nope. All I know is that she was at the Calway Merchandising affair the other night.'

'I see. There were several of our young ladies present on that assignment, I believe. Miss Reeves booked that herself. Would you care to see her?'

'Yeah, I would.'

The girl blew another mouthful of smoke at me and her eyelashes waved hello again. 'Don't you ever wear clothes?' I asked her.

'Not if I can help it. Sometimes they make me.'

'That's what I'd like to do.'

'What?'

'Make you.'

Anton choked and clucked, giving her a push. 'That will be enough. If you don't mind, sir, this way.' His hand was inviting me to a door in the side of the room. 'These young ladies are getting out of hand. Sometimes I could . . .'

'Yeah, so could I.' He choked again and opened the door.

I heard him announce my name, but I didn't catch what he said because my mind couldn't get off the woman behind the desk. Some women are beautiful, some have bodies that make you forget beauty ; here was a woman who had both. Her face had a supernatural loveliness as if some master artist had improved on nature itself. She had her hair cut short in the latest fashion, light tawny hair that glistened like a halo. Even her skin had a creamy texture, flowing down the smooth line of her neck into firm, wide shoulders. She had the breasts of youth—high, exciting, pushing against the high neckline of the white jersey blouse, revolting at the need for restraint. She stood up and held her hand out to me, letting it slip into mine with a warm, pleasant grip. Her voice had a rich vibrant quality when she introduced herself, but I was too busy cursing the longer hemlines to get it. When she sat down again with her legs crossed I stopped my silent protests of long dresses when I saw how tantalizingly nice they could mould themselves to the roundness of thighs that were more inviting when covered. Only then did I see the nameplate on the desk that read JUNO REEVES.

Juno, queen of the lesser gods and goddesses. She was well named.

She offered me a drink from a decanter in a bar set and I took it, something sweet and perfumy in a long-stemmed glass.

We talked. My voice would get a nasty intonation then it would get polite. It didn't seem to come out of me at all. We could have talked about nothing for an hour, maybe it was just minutes. But we talked and she did things with her body deliberately as if I were a supreme test of her abilities as a woman and she laughed, knowing too well that I was hardly conscious of what I was saying or how I was reacting.

She sipped her drink and laid the glass down on the desk, the dark polish of her nails in sharp contrast against the gleaming crystal. Her voice eased me back to the present.

'This young lady, Mr Hammer . . . you say she left with your friend?'

'I said she *may* have. That's what I want to find out.'

'Well, perhaps I can show you their photographs and you can identify her.'

'No, that won't do it. I never saw her myself either.'

'Then why . . .'

'I want to find out what happened that night, Miss Reeves.'

'Juno, please.'

I grinned at her.

'Do you suppose they did . . .' she smiled obliquely, 'anything wrong?'

'I don't give a damn what they did. I'm just interested in knowing. You see, this pal of mine . . . he's dead.'

Her eyes went soft. 'Oh, I'm awfully sorry. What happened?'

'Suicide, the cops said.'

Juno folded her lower lip between her teeth, puzzled. 'In that case, Mr Hammer . . .'

'Mike,' I said.

'In that case, Mike, why bring the girl into it? After all . . .'

'The guy had a family,' I cut in. 'If a nosy reporter decides to work out an angle and finds a juicy scandal lying around, the family will suffer. If there's anything like that I want to squelch it.'

She nodded slowly, complete understanding written in her face. 'You *are* right, Mike. I'll see the girls as they come in for assignments and try to find out who it was. Will you stop by tomorrow sometime?'

I stood up, my hat in my hand. 'That'll be fine, Juno. To-morrow then.'

'Please.' Her voice dropped into a lower register as she stood up and held her hand out to me again. Every motion she made was like liquid being poured and there was a flame in her eyes that waited to be breathed into life. I wrapped my hand around hers just long enough to feel her tighten it in subtle invitation.

I walked to the door and turned around to say goodbye again. Juno let her eyes sweep over me, up and down, and she smiled. I couldn't get the words out. Something about her made me too warm under my clothes. She was beautiful and she was built like a goddess should be built and her eyes said that she was good when she was bad.

They said something else, too, something I should know and couldn't remember.

When I got to the elevators I found I had company. This company was waiting for me at the far end of the hall, comfortably braced against the radiator smoking a cigarette.

This time she had more clothes on. When she saw me coming she ground the butt under her heel and walked up to me with such deliberate purpose that my eyes began to undress her all over again.

'Make me,' she said.

'I need an introduction first.'

'Like you do.' The light over the elevator turned red and I heard the car rattling in the well.

When we hit the ground floor she linked her arm in mine and let me lead her out to the street. We reached Broadway before she said, 'If you *really* need an introduction, my name is Connie Wales. Who're you?'

'Mr Michael Hammer, chick. I used to be a private investigator. I was in the papers recently.'

Her mouth was drawn up in a partial smile. 'Wow, am *I* in company.'

We reached Broadway and turned north. Connie didn't ask where we were going, but when we passed three bars in a row without stopping I got an elbow in the ribs until I got the hint. The place I did turn into was a long, narrow affair with tables for ladies in the rear. So we took a table for ladies as far down as we could get, with a waiter mumbling under his breath behind us.

Both of us ordered beer and I said, 'You're not very expensive to keep, are you?'

'Your change'll last longer this way,' she laughed. 'You aren't rich, or are you?'

'I got dough,' I said, 'but you won't get it out of me, girlie,' I tacked on.

Her laugh made pretty music and it was real. 'Most men want to buy me everything I look at. Wouldn't you?' She sipped her brew, watching me over the rim of the glass with eyes as shiny as new dimes.

'Maybe a beer, that's all. A kid I knew once told me I'd never have to pay for another damn thing. Not a thing at all.'

She looked at me soberly. 'She was right.'

'Yeah,' I agreed.

The waiter came back with his tray and four more beers. He sat two in front of each of us, picked up the cash and shuffled away. As he left, Connie stared at me for a full minute. 'What were you doing in the studio?'

I told her the same thing I told Juno.

She shook her head. 'I don't believe you.'

'Why?'

'I don't know. It just doesn't sound right. Why would any reporter try to make something out of a suicide?'

She had a point there; but I had an answer. 'Because he didn't leave a farewell note. Because his home life was happy. Because he had a lot of dough and no apparent worries.'

'It sounds better now,' she said.

I told her about the party and what I thought might have happened. When I sketched it in I asked, 'Do you know any of the girls that were there that night?'

Her laugh was a little deeper this time. 'Golly, no, at least not to talk to. You see, the agency is divided into two factions, more or less— the clotheshorses and the no-clotheshorses. I'm one of the sugar pies who fill out panties and nighties for the nylon trade. The clotheshorses couldn't fill out a paper sack by themselves so they're jealous and treat us lesser-paid kids like dirt.'

'Nuts,' I said. 'I saw a few and they can't let their breaths out all the way without losing their falsies.'

She almost choked on her drink. 'Very cute, Mike, very cute. I'll have to remember all your acid witticisms. They'll put me over big with the gang.'

I finished the last of the beer and shoved the empties to the edge of the table. 'Come on, kid, I'll take you wherever you want to go then I'll try to get something done.'

'I want to go back to my apartment with you.'

'You'll get a slap in the ear if you don't shut up. Come on.'

Connie threw her head back and laughed at me again. 'Boy, oh, boy, what ten other guys wouldn't give to hear me say that!'

'Do you say that to ten other guys?'

'No, Mike.' Her voice was a whisper of invitation.

There wasn't an empty cab in sight so we walked along Broadway until we found a hack-stand with a driver grabbing a nap behind the wheel. Connie slid in and gave him an address on Sixty-second Street then crowded me into the corner and reached for my hand.

She said, 'Is all this very important, Mike? Finding the girl and all, I mean.'

I patted her hand. 'It means plenty to me, baby. More than you'd expect.'

'Can I . . . help you some way? I want to, Mike. Honest.'

She had a hell of a cute face. I turned my head and looked

down into it and the seriousness in her expression made me nod before I could help myself. 'I need a lot of help, Connie. I'm not sure my friend went out with this girl; I'm not sure she'll admit it if she did and I can't blame her; I'm not sure about anything any more.'

'What did Juno tell you?'

'Come back tomorrow. She'll try to find her in the meantime.'

'Juno's quite a . . . she's quite a . . .'

'Quite,' I finished.

'She makes that impression on everybody. A working girl doesn't stand a chance around that woman.' Connie faked a pout and squeezed my arm. 'Say it ain't so, Mike.'

'It ain't so.'

'You're lying again,' she laughed. 'Anyway, I was thinking. Suppose this girl *did* go out with your friend. Was he the type to try for a fast affair?'

I shoved my hat back on my head and tried to picture Chester Wheeler. To me he was too much of a family man to make a decent wolf. I told her no, but doubtfully. It's hard to tell what a guy will or won't do when he's in town without an overseer or a hard-working conscience.

'In that case,' Connie continued, 'I was thinking that if this girl played games like a lot of them do, she'd drag him around the hot spots with him footing the bill. It's a lot of fun, they tell me.'

She was getting at something. She shook her head and let her hair swirl around her shoulders. 'Lately the clotheshorses have been beating a path to a few remote spots that cater to the model-and-buyer crowd. I haven't been there myself, but it's a lead.'

I reached over and tipped her chin up with my forefinger. 'I like the way you think, girl.' Her lips were full and red. She ran her tongue over them until they glistened wetly, separated just a little to coax me closer. I could have been coaxed, only the cab jolted to a stop against the kerb and Connie stuck out her tongue at the driver. She made a wry face and held on to my hand just to be sure I got out with her. I handed the driver a bill and told him to keep the change.

'It's the cocktail hour, Mike. You will come up, won't you?'

'For a while.'

'Damn you,' she said, 'I never tried so hard to make a guy who won't be made.'

The place was a small-sized apartment house that made no pretence at glamour. It had a work-it-yourself elevator that wasn't working and we hoofed it up the stairs to the third floor where Connie fumbled in her pocket until she found her key. I snapped on the light like I lived there permanently and threw my hat on a chair in the living-room and sat down.

Connie said, 'What'll it be, coffee or cocktails?'

'Coffee first,' I told her. 'I didn't eat lunch. If you got some eggs put them on too.' I reached over the arm of the chair into a magazine rack and came up with a handful of girlie mags that were better than the postcards you get in Mexico. I found Connie in half of them and decided that she was all right. Very all right.

The smell of the coffee brought me into the kitchen just as she was sliding the eggs on to a plate and we didn't bother with small talk until there was nothing left but some congealed egg yolk. When I finally leaned back and pulled out my deck of Luckies she said, 'Good?'

'Uh-huh.'

We had the cocktails in the living-room. The hands on my watch went round once, then twice. Every so often the shaker would be refilled and the ice would make sharp sounds against the metal surface. I sat there with a glass in my hand and my head back, dreaming my way through the haze. I ran out of matches and whenever I put a cigarette in my mouth Connie would come across the room with a light for me.

A nice guy who was dead.

Two shots gone.

One bullet and one shell case found in the hall.

Suicide.

Hell.

I opened my eyes and looked at Connie. She was curled up on a studio couch watching me. 'What's the programme, kid?'

'It's almost seven,' she said. 'I'll get dressed and you can take me out. If we're lucky maybe we can find out where your friend went.'

I was too tired to be nice. My eyes were heavy from looking into the smoke that hung in the air and my belly felt warm from the drinks. 'A man is dead,' I said slowly. 'The papers said what the cops said, he died a suicide. I know better. The guy was murdered.'

She stiffened, and the cigarette bent in her fingers. 'I wanted to find out why so I started tracing and I found he might have been with a babe one night. I find where that babe works and start asking questions. A very pretty model with a very pretty body starts tossing me a line and is going to help me look. I start getting ideas. I start wondering why all the concern from a dame who can have ten other guys yet makes a pass at a guy who hasn't even got a job and won't buy her more than beer and takes her eggs and coffee and her cocktails.'

Her breath made a soft hissing noise between her teeth. I

saw the cigarette crumple up in her hand and if she felt any pain it wasn't reflected in her face. I never moved while she pushed herself up. My hands were folded behind my head for a cushion and stayed there even while she stood spraddle-legged in front of me.

Connie swung so fast I didn't close my eyes for it. Not a flat palm, but a small, solid fist sliced into my cheek and cracked against my jaw. I started to taste the blood inside my mouth and when I grinned a little of it ran down my chin.

'I have five brothers,' she said. Her voice had a snarl in it. 'They're big and nasty, but they're all men. I have ten other guys who wouldn't make one man put together. Then you came along. I'd like to beat your stupid head off. You have eyes and you can't see. All right, Mike, I'll give you something to look at and you'll know why all the concern.'

Her hand grabbed her blouse at the neckline and ripped it down. Buttons rolled away at my feet. The other thing she wore pulled apart with a harsh tearing sound and she stood there proudly, her hands on her hips, flaunting her breasts in my face. A tremor of excitement made the muscles under the taut flesh of her stomach undulate, and she let me look at her like that as long as it pleased me.

I had to put my hands down and squeeze the arms of the chair. My collar was too tight all of a sudden, and something was crawling up my spine.

Her teeth were clamped together. Her eyes were vicious.

'Make me,' she said.

Another trickle of blood ran down my chin, reminding me what had happened. I reached up and smacked her across the mouth as hard as I could. Her head rocked, but she still stood there, and now her eyes were more vicious than ever. 'Still want me to make you?'

'Make me,' she said.

CHAPTER FOUR

WE ate supper in a Chinese joint on Times Square. The place was crowded but nobody had eyes for the meal ; they were all focused on Connie, including mine, and I couldn't blame them any. If low-cut gowns were daring, then she took the dare and threw it back at them.

I sat across the table wondering if skin could really be that soft and smooth, wondering how much less could be worn before a woman would be stark naked. Not much less.

The meal went that way without words. We looked, we smiled, we ate. For the first time I saw her objectively, seeing a woman I had and not just one I wanted. It was easy to say she was beautiful, but not easy to say why.

But I knew why. She was honest and direct. She wanted something and she let you know it. She had spent a lifetime with five men who treated her as another brother and expected her to like it. She did. To Connie, modelling was just a job. If there was glamour attached to it she took it without making the most of it.

It was nearly nine o'clock when we left, straggling out with full bellies and a pleasant sensation of everything being almost all right. I said, 'Going to tell me the schedule?'

Her hand found mine and tucked it up under her arm. 'Ever been slumming, Mike?'

'Some people think I'm always slumming.'

'Well, that's what we're going to do. The kids all have a new craze on an old section of the town. They call it The Bowery. Sound familiar?'

I looked at her curiously. 'The Bowery?'

'You ain't been around recently, bub. The Bowery's changed. Not all of it, but a spot here and there. Not too long ago a wise guy spotted himself a fortune and turned a junk joint into a tourist trap. You know, lousy with characters off the street to give the place atmosphere, all the while catering to a slightly upper crust who want to see how the other half lives.'

'How the hell did they ever find that?'

A cab saw me wave and pulled to the kerb. We got in and I told him where to go and his hand hit the flag. Connie said, 'Some people get tired of the same old thing. They hunt up these new deals. The Bowery is one of them.'

'Who runs the place?'

Connie shrugged, her shoulders rubbing against mine. 'I don't know, Mike. I've had everything second hand. Besides, it isn't only one place now. I think there're at least a dozen. Like I said, they're model-and-buyer hangouts, and nothing is cheap, either.'

The cab wound through traffic, cut over to a less busy street and made the running lights that put us at the nether end of Manhattan without a stop. I handed the driver a couple of bills and helped Connie out of the door.

The Bowery, a street of people without faces. Pleading voices from the shadows and the shuffle of feet behind you. An occasional tug at your sleeve and more pleading that had professional despair in the tone. An occasional woman with clothes too tight giving you a long, steady stare that said she was available cheap. Saloon doors swung open so frequently they seemed like blinking lights. They were crowded, too. The bars were lined with the left-overs of humanity keeping warm over a drink or nursing a steaming bowl of soup.

It had been a long time since I had made the rounds down here. A cab swung into the kerb and a guy in a tux with a red-head on his arm got out laughing. There was a scramble in his direction and the redhead handed out a mess of quarters, then threw them all over the pavement to laugh all the louder when the dive came.

The guy thought it was funny, too. He did the same thing with a fin, letting it blow out of his hand down the street.

Connie said, 'See what I mean?'

I felt like kicking the bastard. 'Yeah, I see.'

We followed the pair with about five feet between us. The guy had a Mid-Western drawl and the dame was trying to cover up a Brooklyn accent. She kept squeezing the guy's arm and giving him the benefit of slow, sidewise glances he seemed to like. Tonight he was playing king all right.

They turned into a bar that was the crummiest of the lot on the street. You could smell the stink from outside and hear the mixture of shrill and raucous voices a block away. A sign over the doorway said NEIL'S JOINT.

The characters were there in force. They had black eyes and missing teeth. They had twitches and fleas and their language was out of the gutter. Two old hags were having a hair-pull over a joker who could hardly hold on to the bar.

What got me was the characters who watched them. They were even worse. They thought it was a howl. Tourists. Lousy, money-heavy tourists who thought it was a lot of fun to kick somebody else around. I was so damn mad I could hardly speak. A waiter mumbled something and led us to a table in the back room that was packed with more characters. Both kinds.

Everybody was having a swell time reading the dirty writing on the walls and swapping stories with the other half. The pay-off was easy to see. The crowd who lived there were drinking cheap whisky on the house to keep them there while the tourists shelled out through the nose for the same cheap whisky and thought it was worth it.

It sure was fun. Nuts!

Connie smiled at a couple of girls she knew and one came over. I didn't bother to get up when she introduced us. The girl's name was Kate and she was with a crowd from upstate. She said, 'First time you've been here, isn't it, Connie?'

'First . . . and last,' she told her. 'It smells.'

Kate's laugh sounded like a broken cowbell. 'Oh, we're not going to stay here long. The fellows want to spend some money, so we're going over to the Inn. Feel like coming along?'

Connie looked at me. I moved my head just enough so she'd know it was O.K. by me. 'We'll go, Kate.'

'Swell, come on over and meet the gang. We're meeting the rest later on. They wanted to see all the sights including . . .' she giggled, 'those houses where . . . you know.' She giggled again.

Connie made a mouth and I grunted.

So we got up and met the gang. If it weren't that I had Connie with me they would have treated me like another character, too. Just for a minute, maybe, then a few fat guts would have been bounced off the walls. There was Joseph, Andrew, Homer, Martin and Raymond and not a nickname in the pack. They all had soft hands, big diamonds, loud laughs, fat wallets and lovely women. That is, all except Homer. He had his secretary along, who wasn't as pretty as she was ready, willing and able. She was his mistress and made no bones about it.

I liked her best. So did Connie.

When I squeezed their hands until they hurt we sat down and had a few drinks and dirty jokes, then Andrew got loud about bigger and better times elsewhere. The rest threw in with him and we picked up our marbles and left. Martin gave the waiter a ten-spot he didn't deserve and he showed us to the door.

Connie didn't know the way so we just followed. The girls did all the steering. Twice we had to step around drunks and once we moved into the gutter to get out of the way of a street brawl. They should have stayed in the gutter where they belonged. I was so hopping mad I could hardly speak and Connie rubbed her cheek against my shoulder in sympathy.

The Bowery Inn was off the main line. It was a squalid place with half-boarded-up windows, fly-specked beer-signs and an outward appearance of something long ago gone to seed.

That was from the outside. The first thing you noticed when you went in was the smell. It wasn't. It smelled like a bar should smell. The tables and the bar were as deliberately aged with worm holes and cigarette burns as the characters were phoney. Maybe the others couldn't see it, but I could.

Connie grimaced, 'So this is The Inn I've heard so much about.'

I could hardly hear her over the racket. Everybody was running forward to greet everybody else and the dames sounded like a bunch of pigs at a trough. The fat bellies stood back and beamed. When the racket eased off to a steady clamour everybody checked their coats and hats with a one-eyed bag behind a booth, who had a spittoon on the counter to collect the tips.

While Connie was helloing a couple of gaunt things from her office I sidled over to the bar for a shot and a beer. I needed it bad. Besides, it gave me a chance to look around. Down at the back of the room was a narrow single door that hung from one hinge and had a calendar tacked to it that flapped every time it opened.

It flapped pretty often because there was an unending stream of traffic coming and going through that door and the only characters inside there had on evening gowns and tuxes with all the spangles.

Connie looked around for me, saw me spilling down the chaser and walked over. 'This is only the front, Mike. Let's go in where the fun is. That's what they say, anyway.'

'Roger, baby, I need fun pretty bad.'

I took her arm and joined the tail-end of the procession that was heading for the door on one hinge and the calendar.

We had quite a surprise. Quite a surprise! The calendar door was only the first. It led into a room with warped walls and had to close before the other door would open. The one hinge was only a phony. There were two on the inside frame nicely concealed. The room was a soundproof connexion between the back room and the bar and it was some joint, believe me.

Plenty of thousands went into the making of the place and there were plenty of thousands in the wallets that sat at the fancy chrome-trimmed bar or in the plush-lined seats along the wall. The lights were down low and a spot was centred on a completely naked woman doing a striptease in reverse. It was nothing when she was bare, but it was something to watch her get dressed. When she finished she stepped out of the spot and sat down next to a skinny bald-headed gent who was in one hell of a dither having a dame alongside him he had just seen in the raw. The guy called for champagne.

Now I saw why the place was a popular hangout. The walls

were solid blocks of photographs, models by the hundreds in every stage of dress and undress. Some were originals, some were cut from magazines. All were signed with some kind of love to a guy named Clyde.

Connie and I tipped our glasses together and I let my eyes drift to the pictures. 'You up there?'

'Could be. Want to look around?'

'No. I like you better sitting where I can see you personally.'

A band came out and took their places behind the stand. Homer excused himself and came around the table to Connie and asked her to dance. That left me playing kneeses with his mistress until she looked at the floor anxiously and practically asked me to take her out there.

I'm not much for dancing, but she made up for it. She danced close enough to almost get behind me and had a hell of an annoying habit of sticking her tongue out to touch the tip of my ear. Homer did all right for himself.

It took an hour for the party to get going good. At eleven-thirty the place was jammed to the rafters and a guy couldn't hear himself think. Andrew started talking about spending money again and one of the girls squalled that there was plenty of it to throw away if the boys wanted some sporting propositions. One of them got up and consulted with a waiter, who came back in a minute and mumbled a few words and nodded towards a curtained alcove to one side.

I said, 'Here we go, kid.'

Connie screwed up her face. 'I don't get it, Mike.'

'Hell, it's the same old fix. They got gambling tables in the back room. They give you the old peephole routine to make it look good.'

'Really?'

'You'll see.'

Everybody got up and started off in the direction of the curtain. The pitch was coming in fast now. I began to think of Chester Wheeler again, wondering if he made this same trip. He had needed five grand. Why? To play or to pay off? A guy could run up some heavy sugar in debts on a wheel. Suicide? Why kill yourself for five grand? Why pay off at all? A word to the right cop and they'd tear this place down and you could forget the debts.

One of the girls happened to look over her shoulder and screamed, 'Oh, there's Clyde! Hello, Clyde! Clyde . . . hello!'

The lean guy in the tux turned his cold smile on her and waved back, then finished making his rounds of the tables. I felt my mouth pulling into a nasty grin and I told Connie to go ahead.

I walked over to Clyde.

'If it ain't my old pal Dinky,' I said.

Clyde was bent over a table and the stiffness ran through his back, and he didn't stop talking until he was damned good and ready. I stuck a Lucky between my lips and fired it just as the lights went down and the spot lit up another lewd nude prancing on the stage.

Then Clyde swung his fish eyes on me. 'What are you doing here, shamus?'

'I was thinking the same thing about you.'

'You've been here too long already. Get out!' The stiffness was still in his back. He threaded through the tables, a quick smile for someone here and there. When he reached the bar a bottle was set up in front of him and he poured himself a quick shot.

I blew a stream of smoke in his face. 'Nice layout.'

His eyes were glassy with hate now. 'Maybe you didn't hear me right.'

'I heard you, only I'm not one of your boys to jump when you speak, Dink.'

'What do you want?'

I blew some more smoke at him and he pulled out of the way. 'I want to satisfy my curiosity, Dink. Yeah, that's what I want to do. The last time I saw you was in a courtroom taking the oath from a wheel-chair. You had a bullet in your leg. I put it there, remember? You swore that you weren't the guy who drove a getaway car for a killer, but the bullet in your leg made you out a liar. You did a stretch for that. Remember now?'

He didn't answer me.

'You sure came a long way, kid. No more wheel spots for you. Maybe now you do the killing?'

His upper lip curled over his teeth. 'The papers say you don't carry a gun any more, Hammer. That's not so good for you. Keep out of my way.'

He went to raise his drink to his mouth, but I swatted his elbow and the stuff splattered into his face. His face went livid. 'Take it easy, Dink. Don't let the cops spot you. I'll take a look around before I go.'

My old friend Dinky Williams, who called himself Clyde, was reaching for the house phone on the end of the bar when I left.

To cross the room I had to walk around behind the spot and it took me a minute to find the curtain in the semi-darkness. There was another door behind the curtain. It was locked. I rapped on the panel and the inevitable peephole opened that showed a pair of eyes over a nose that had a scar down the centre.

43

At first I thought I wasn't going to get in, then the lock clicked and the door swung in just a little.

Sometimes you get just enough warning. Some reflex action shoves you out of the way before you can get your head split open. My hand went up in time to form a cushion for my skull and something smashed down on my knuckles that brought a bubbling yell up out of my throat.

I kept on going, dove and rolled so that I was on my back with my feet up and staring at the ugly face of an oversize pug who had a billy raised ready to use. He didn't go for the feet, but he didn't think fast enough to catch me while I was down.

I'm no cat, but I got my shoes under me in a hurry. The billy swung at my head while I was still off balance. The guy was too eager. He missed me. I didn't miss. I was big, he was bigger. I had one bad hand and I didn't want to spoil the other. I leaned back against the wall and kicked out and up with a slashing toe that nearly tore him in half. He tried to scream. All I heard was a bubbling sound. The billy hit the floor and he doubled over, hands clawing at his groin. This time I measured it right. I took a short half-step and kicked his face in.

I looked at the billy, picked it up and weighed it. The thing was made for murder. It was too bulky in my pocket so I dropped it in the empty shoulder holster under my arm and grunted at the guy on the floor who was squirming unconsciously in his own blood.

The room was another of those rooms between rooms. A chair was tilted against the wall beside the door, the edge of it biting into the soundproofing. Just for kicks I dragged the stupe over to the chair, propped him in it and tilted it back against the wall again. His head was down and you could hardly see the blood. A lot could go on before he'd know about it, I thought.

When I was satisfied with the arrangement I snapped the lock off the door to accommodate the customers and tried the other door into the back room. This one was open.

The lights hit me so hard after the semi-darkness of the hall that I didn't see Connie come over. She said, 'Where've you been, Mike?'

Her hand hooked in my arm and I gave it an easy squeeze 'I got friends here, too.'

'Who?'

'Oh, some people you don't know.'

She saw the blood on the back of my hand then, the skin of the knuckles peeled back. Her face went a little white. 'Mike . . . what did you do?'

44

I grinned at her. 'Caught it on something.'

She asked another question, one I didn't hear. I was too busy taking in the layout of the place. It was a gold mine. Over the babble you could hear the click and whirr of the roulette wheels, the excited shrieks when they stopped. There were tables for dice, faro spreads, bird cages and all the games and gadgets that could make a guy want to rip a bill off his roll and try his luck.

The place was done up like an old-fashioned Western gambling hall, with gaudy murals on every wall. The overhead lights were fashioned from cartwheels and oxen yokes, the hanging brass lanterns almost invisible in the glare of the bright lights inside them. Along one wall was a fifty-foot bar of solid mahogany complete with brass rail, never-used cuspidors and plate-glass mirrors with real bullet holes.

If ever I had a desire to be surrounded by beauty, I would have found it there. Beauty was commonplace. It was professional. Beauty was there under a lot of make-up and too much skin showing. Beauty was there in models who showed off what they liked to advertise best. It was like looking into the dressing-room of the Follies. There was so much of it you tried to see it all at once and lost out with your hurry.

It was incredible as hell.

I shook my head. Connie smiled, 'Hard to believe, isn't it?'

That was an understatement. 'What's the pitch?'

'I told you, Mike. It's a fad. It caught on and spread like the pox. Pretty soon it'll get around, the place will be jammed and jumpin', then the whole deal will get boring.'

'So they'll move on to something else.'

'Exactly. Right now it's almost a club. They're fawned over and fought over. They make a big splash. Wait till it all catches up with them.'

'And all this in the Bowery. Right in the middle of the Bowery! Pat would give his right arm for a peep at this. Maybe I'll let him give me a left arm too.'

I stopped and peered around again. Beauty. It was starting to get flat now. There were too many big bellies and bald heads in the way. They spoiled the picture. I spotted Homer and Andrew in the crowd having a big time at the crap table. Evidently Homer was winning because his babe was stuffing the chips he handed her into a bag that wouldn't take too many. The ones she had left over got tied up in her handkerchief.

We made a complete tour of the place before picking out a leather-covered corner-spot to watch the shindig and drink at the same time. A waiter in a cowboy outfit brought us highballs and crackers and said it was on the house. As soon as he left Connie asked, 'What do you think, Mike?'

'I don't know, sugar. I'm wondering if my pal would have gone for this.'

'Wasn't he like the rest?'

'You mean, was he a man?'

'Sort of.'

'Hell, he probably would. What guy wouldn't take in a hot spot with a babe. He's alone in the city, no chaperon and bored stiff. His work is done for the day and he needs a little relaxation. We'll leave it at that. If he did get persuaded to come it didn't take much persuasion.'

I lit a cigarette and picked up my drink. I had a long swallow and was following it with a drag on the butt when the crowd split apart for a second to let a waiter through and I had a clear view of the bar.

Juno was sitting there laughing at something Anton Lipsek just said.

The ice started to rattle against my glass and I had that feeling up my spine again. I said to Connie, 'Get lost for a little while, will you?'

'She's truly beautiful, isn't she, Mike?'

I blushed for the first time since I wore long pants. 'She's different. She makes most of them look sick.'

'Me, too?'

'I haven't seen her with her clothes off. Until then, you're the best.'

'Don't lie, Mike.' Her eyes were laughing at me.

I stood up and grinned back at her. 'Just in case you really want to know, she's the best-looking thing I ever saw. I get steamed up watching her from fifty feet away. Whatever a dame's supposed to have on the ball, she's got it. My tongue feels an inch thick when I talk to her and if she asked me to jump I'd say, "How high?" and if she asked me to poop I'd say, "How much?". But here's something you can tuck away if it means anything to you. I don't like her and I don't know why I don't.'

Connie reached over and took a cigarette from my pack. When it was lit she said, 'It means plenty to me. I'll get lost, Mike. But just for a little while.'

I patted her hand and walked over to where the queen of the gods and goddesses was holding court. When she saw me her smile made sunshine and the funny feeling started around my stomach.

She held out her hand and I took it. 'Mike, what are you doing here?'

Juno guided me to a stool on Olympus, letting go my hand

almost reluctantly. More eyes than Anton Lipsek's watched me enviously. 'I was side-tracked into a flirtation when I left your office.'

Anton wiggled his beard with an 'Ah, hah!' He caught on fast.

'I guess it pays to be physical,' Juno smiled. Her eyes drifted over the crowd. 'There aren't many men here who are. You're rather an attraction.'

So was she. You might say she was overclothed by comparison, but not overdressed. The front of the black gown came up to her neck and the sleeves came down to meet her gloves. The width of her shoulders, the regal taper of her waist was sheathed in a shimmering silk that reflected the lights and clung tenaciously to her body. Her breasts rose full and high under the gown, moving gently with her breathing.

'Drink?'

I nodded. The music of her voice brought the bartender to life and he put a highball in front of me. Anton joined us in a toast, then excused himself and walked over to the roulette wheel. I deliberately swung around on the stool, hoping she'd follow me so I could have her to myself.

She did, smiling at me in the mirrors that had the bullet holes.

'I have news for you, Mike. Perhaps I should let it keep so I could see you again tomorrow.'

My hand started to tighten around the glass. One of the bullet holes was in the way so I turned my head to look at her. 'The girl . . .'

'Yes. I found her.'

Ever have your inside squeeze up into a knot so hard you thought you'd turn inside out? I did. 'Go on,' I said.

'Her name is Marion Lester. I presume you'll want to see her yourself, of course. Her address is the Chadwick Hotel. She was the third one I spoke to this afternoon and she readily admitted what had happened, although she seemed a little frightened when I told her the full story.'

'All right, all right, what did she say?' I took a quick drink and pushed the glass across the bar.

'Actually . . . nothing. Your friend *did* help her into a cab and he saw her home. In fact, he carried her upstairs and tucked her into bed with her clothes on, shoes and all. It seems as if he was quite a gentleman.'

'Damn,' I said, 'damn it all to hell anyway!'

Juno's fingers found mine on the bar rail and her smile was replaced by intense concern. 'Mike, please! It can't be that bad. Aren't you glad it was that way?'

I cursed under my breath, something nice and nasty I had

to get out. 'I guess so. It's just that it leaves me climbing a tree again. Thanks anyway, Juno.'

She leaned towards me and my head filled with the fragrance of a perfume that made me dizzy. She had grey eyes. Deep grey eyes. Deep and compassionate. Eyes that could talk by themselves. 'Will you come up tomorrow anyway?'

I couldn't have said no. I didn't want to. I nodded and my lip worked into a snarl I couldn't control. Even my hands tightened into fists until the broken skin over my knuckles began to sting. 'I'll be there,' I said. I got that funny feeling again. I couldn't figure it, damn it, I didn't know what it was

A finger tapped my shoulder and Connie said, 'I'm losted, Mike. Hello, Juno.'

Olympus smiled another dawn.

Connie said, 'Can we go home now?'

I slid off the stool and looked at the goddess. This time we didn't shake hands. Just meeting her eyes was enough. 'Good night, Juno.'

'Good night, Mike.'

Anton Lipsek came back and nodded to the both of us. I took Connie's arm and steered her towards the door. Joseph, Andrew, Martin, Homer and Raymond all yelled for us to join the party then shut up when they saw the look on my face. One of them muttered, 'Sour sort of fellow, isn't he?'

The joker with the bashed-in face wasn't in his chair where I had left him. Two other guys were holding the fort and I knew what they were doing there. They were waiting for me. The tall skinny one was a goon I knew and who knew me and licked his lips. The other one was brand, spanking new. About twenty-two maybe.

They looked at Connie, wondering how to get her out of there so she wouldn't be a witness to what came next. The goon I knew licked his lips again and rubbed his hands together. 'We been waiting for you, Hammer.'

The kid put on more of an act. He screwed up his pimply face to make a sneer, pushing himself away from the wall trying to make shoulders under his dinner jacket. 'So you're Mike Hammer, are ya? Ya don't look so tough to me, guy.'

I let my hand fool with the buttons on my coat. The billy in the empty holster pushed against the fabric under my arm and looked real as hell. 'There's always one way you can find out, sonny,' I said.

When the kid licked his lips a little spit ran down his chin. Connie walked ahead of me and opened the door. I walked past the two of them and they never moved. In a little while they'd be out of a job.

Not an empty table showed in this first back room. The

show was over and the tiny dance floor was packed to the limit. The late tourist crowd was having itself a fling and making no bones about it. I scanned the sea of heads looking for Clyde. It was a hell of a change from Dinky Williams. But he wasn't around. We picked up our stuff from the hag at the check-room and I tossed a dime in the spittoon. She swore and I swore back at her.

The words we used weren't unusual for the front section of the Bowery Inn, and no heads turned except two at the bar. One was Clyde's. I waved my thumb towards the back. 'Lousy help you hire, Dink.' His face was livid again.

I didn't even look at the babe. It was Velda.

CHAPTER FIVE

I WAS sitting in the big leather chair in the office when Velda put her key in the lock. She had on a tailored suit that made her look like a million dollars. Her long black page-boy hair threw back the light of the morning sunshine that streamed through the window and it struck me that of all the beauty in the world I had the best of it right under my nose.

She saw me then and said, 'I thought you'd be here.' There was frost in her voice. She tossed her handbag on the desk and sat in my old chair. Hell, it was her joint now anyway.

'You move pretty fast, Velda.'

'So do you.'

'Referring to my company of last night, I take it.'

'Exactly. Your legwork. They were very nice, just your type.'

I grinned at her. 'I wish I could say something decent about your escort.'

The frost melted and her voice turned soft. 'I'm the jealous type, Mike.'

I didn't have to lean far to reach her. The chair was on casters that moved easily. I wound my fingers in her hair, started to say something and stopped. Instead, I kissed the tip of her nose. Her fingers tightened around my wrist. She had her eyes half-closed and didn't see me push her handbag out of reach. It tipped with the weight of the gun in it and landed on the floor.

This time I kissed her mouth. It was a soft, warm mouth. It was a light kiss, but I'll never forget it. It left me wanting to wrap my arms around her and squeeze until she couldn't move. No, I didn't do that. I slid back into my chair and Velda said, 'It was never like that before, Mike. Don't treat me like the others.'

My hand was shaking when I tried to light another cigarette. 'I didn't expect to find you down the Bowery last night, kid.'

'You told me to get to work, Mike.'

'Finish it. Let's hear it all.'

Velda leaned back in the chair, her eyes on mine. 'You said to concentrate on Wheeler. I did. The papers carried most of the details and there was nothing to be learned here. I hopped the first plane to Columbus, visited with his family and business associates and got the next plane back again.'

She picked her handbag off the floor and extracted a small black loose-leaf pad, flipping the cover back to the first page. 'Here is the essence of what I learned. Everyone agreed that Chester Wheeler was an energetic, conscientious husband, father and business man. There has never been any family trouble. Whenever he was away he wrote or called home frequently. This time they had two picture postcards from him, a letter and one phone call. He phoned as soon as he arrived in New York to tell them he'd had a successful trip. He sent one card to his son, a plain penny postcard. The next card was post-marked from the Bowery and he mentioned going to a place called the Bowery Inn. Then he wrote a letter to his wife that was quite commonplace. A postscript to his twenty-two-year-old daughter mentioned the fact that he had met an old high-school friend of hers working in the city. That was the last they heard until they were notified of his death.

'When I dug up his business friends I got nowhere. His business was fine, he was making a lot of money, and he had no worries at all.'

I clamped my teeth together. 'Like hell you got nowhere,' I said softly. My mind drifted back over that little conversation with Pat. A little talk about how a guy named Emil Perry said Wheeler had been depressed because business was rotten. 'You're sure about his business?'

'Yes. I checked his credit rating.'

'Nice going. Continue.'

'Well . . . the only lead I saw was this place called the Bowery Inn. I did some fast quizzing when I got home and found out what it was all about. The man who runs the place you seemed to know. I put on an act and he fell for it. Hard. He didn't seem to like you much, Mike.'

'I can't blame him. I shot him once.'

'After you left he couldn't talk for five minutes. He excused himself and went into the back room. When he returned he seemed satisfied about something. There was blood on his hands.'

That would be Dinky, all right. He liked to use his hands when he had a couple of rods backing him up. 'That all?'

'Practically. He wants to see me again.'

I felt the cords in my neck pull tight. 'The bastard! I'll beat the pants off him for that!'

Velda shook her head and laughed. 'Don't you get to be the jealous type too, Mike. You don't wear it so well. Is it important that I see him again?'

I agreed reluctantly. 'It's important.'

'Is it still murder?'

'More than ever, sugar. I bet it's a big murder, too. A great big beautiful murder with all the trimmings.'

'Then what do you suggest I do next?'

I gave it a thought first, then looked at her a moment. 'Play this Clyde. Keep your eyes open and see what happens. If I were you I'd hide that P.I. ticket and leave the gun home. We don't want him putting two and two together and getting a bee in his bonnet.

'If you follow me on this you'll see the connexion. First we have Wheeler. We have the fact that he *might* have taken a model out that night and he *might* have gone to the Inn where he *might* have run into something that meant murder. If Clyde didn't enter into this I'd skip the whole premise, but he makes it too interesting to pass up.

'There's only one hitch. Juno found the girl he left with the night of the party. She didn't go out with him!'

'But, Mike, then . . .'

'Then I'm supposing he *might* have gone with somebody else some other time. Hell of a lot of mights in this. Too many. At least it's something to work on, and if you stick around this Clyde character long enough something will turn up one way or another.'

Velda rose, her legs spread apart, throwing out her arms in a stretch that made her jacket and skirt fill up almost to bursting. I had to bend my head down into a match to get my eyes off her. Clyde was going to get a hell of a deal for his money. I slapped my hat on and opened the door for her.

When we reached the street I put her in a taxi and watched until she was around the corner. It was just nine-thirty, so I headed for the nearest phone-booth, dropped a nickel in the slot and dialled police headquarters. Pat had checked in, but he couldn't be located at present. I told the switchboard operator to have him meet me in a spaghetti joint around the corner from headquarters in a half-hour and the guy said he'd pass the message on. I found my heap and climbed in. It was going to be a busy day.

Pat was waiting for me over a half-finished cup of coffee. When he saw me come in he signalled for another coffee and some pastry. I threw my leg over the chair and sat down. 'Morning, officer. How's every little thing in the department?'

'Going smoothly, Mike.'

'Oh, too bad.'

He set his coffee cup down again. His face was absolutely blank. 'Don't start anything, Mike.'

I acted indignant. 'Who, me? What could I start that's not already started?'

The waiter brought my coffee and some Danish and I

52

dunked and ate two of them before either of us spoke again. Curiosity got the best of Pat. He said, 'Let's hear it, Mike.'

'Are you going to be stupid about it, Pat?'

His face was still frozen. 'Let's hear it, Mike.'

I didn't make any bones about trying to keep it out of my eyes or the set of my jaw. My voice came up from my chest with a nasty rumble and I could feel my lip working into a snarl that pulled the corners of my mouth down.

'You're a smart cop, Pat. Everybody knows it, but most of all I know it and you know it yourself. You know something else besides. I'm just as smart. I said Wheeler was murdered and you patted me on the head and told me to behave.

'I'm saying it again, Pat. Wheeler was murdered. You can get in this thing or I can do it alone. I told you I wanted that ticket back and I'm going to get it. If I do, a lot of reputations are going to fall by the wayside including yours and I don't want that to happen.

'You know me and you know I don't kid around. I'm beginning to get ideas, Pat. They think good. I've seen some things that look good. Things that put more taste in the flavour of murder. I'm going to have me another killer before long and a certain D.A. is going to get his nose blown for him.'

I don't know what I expected Pat to do. Maybe I expected him to blow his top or start writing me off as a has-been in the brain department. I certainly didn't expect to see his face go cold and hear him say, 'I gave you the benefit of the doubt a long time ago, Mike. I think Wheeler was murdered, too.'

He grinned a little at my expression and went on, 'There's a catch. Word reached the D.A. and he looked into it and passed his professional opinion in conjunction with the Medical Examiner. Wheeler was, beyond doubt, a suicide. I have been told to concentrate my efforts on more recent developments in the wide field of crime.'

'Our boy doesn't like you either now, eh?'

'Ha!'

'So?'

'What do you know, Mike?'

'Just a little, pal. I'll know more before long and I'll drop it in your lap when there's enough of it to get your teeth in. I don't suppose your prestige suffered from the D.A.'s tirade.'

'It went up if anything.'

'Good! Tonight I'll buzz you with all the details. Meanwhile you can look up the whereabouts of one former torpedo called Rainey.'

'I know him.'

'Yeah?'

'We had him on an assault and battery charge a while back. The complainant failed to complain and he was dismissed. He called himself a fight promoter.'

'Street brawls,' I said sourly.

'Probably. He was loaded with jack, but he had a room in the Bowery.'

'*Where*, Pat?' My eyes lit up and Pat went grim.

'The Bowery. Why?'

'Interesting word. I've been hearing a lot about it these days. See if you can get a line on him, will you?'

Pat tapped a cigarette on the table. 'This is all on the table, isn't it?'

'Every bit of it, chum. I won't hold back. I'm curious about one thing, though. What changed your mind from suicide to murder?'

Pat grinned through his teeth. 'You. I didn't think you'd chase shadows. I said I wouldn't get excited this time, but I couldn't help myself. By the time I reached the office I was shaking like a punk in his first hold-up and I went down to take a look at the body. I called in a couple of experts and though there were few marks on the body it was the general opinion that our lad Wheeler had been through some sort of a scuffle prior to taking a bullet in the head.'

'It couldn't have been much of a fuss. He was pretty damn drunk.'

'It wasn't,' he said, 'just enough to leave indications. By the way, Mike . . . about that slug and shell we found in the hall. Was that your work?'

I let out a short, sour laugh. 'I told you that once. No. Somebody had a hole in his pocket.'

He nodded thoughtfully. 'I'll check the hotel again. It had to be either a resident or a visitor, then. It's too bad you didn't lock the door.'

'A lock won't stop a killer,' I said. 'He had all the time in the world and could make as much noise as he wanted. Most of the guests were either half-deaf or dead to the world when the gun went off. It's an old building with thick walls that do a nice job of muffling sound.'

Pat picked up the cheque and laid a dollar on top of it. 'You'll contact me tonight then?'

'You bet! See you later and tell the D.A. I was asking for him.'

It took fifteen minutes to get to the Chadwick Hotel. It was another side-street affair with an essence of dignity that stopped as soon as you entered the lobby. The desk clerk was the Mom type until she spoke, then what came out made you

54

think of other things. I told her I wanted to see a certain Marion Lester and she didn't bother to question or announce me. She said, 'Room 312 and go up the stairs easy. They squeak.'

I went up the stairs easy and they squeaked anyway. I knocked on the door of 312, waited and knocked again. The third time I heard feet shuffling across the floor and the door opened just far enough to show wide blue eyes, hair curlers and a satin negligée clutched tightly at the throat. I jumped the gun before she could ask questions with 'Hello, Marion. Juno told me to see you.'

The wide eyes got wider and the door opened the rest of the way. I closed it behind me and made like a gentleman by sweeping off my hat. Marion licked her lips and cleared her throat. 'I . . . just got up.'

'So I see. Rough night?'

'. . . No.'

She took me through the miniature hall into a more minia-ture living-room and waved for me to sit down. I sat. She said, 'It's so early . . . if you don't mind, I'll get dressed.'

I told her I didn't mind and she shuffled into the bedroom and began pulling drawers out and opening closets. She wasn't like the other girls I knew. She was back in five minutes. This time she had a suit on and the curlers were out of her hair. A little make-up and her eyes didn't look so wide either.

She sat down gracefully in a straight-backed chair and reached for a cigarette in a silver box. 'Now, what did you want to see me about, Mr . . .'

'Mike Hammer. Just plain Mike.' I snapped a match on my thumbnail and held it out to her. 'Did Juno tell you about me?'

Marion nodded, twin streams of smoke sifting out through her nostrils. Her voice had a tremor in it and she licked her lips again. 'Yes. You . . . were with Mr Wheeler when he . . . he died.'

'That's right. It happened under my nose and I was too drunk to know it.'

'I'm afraid there's little I can . . . tell you, Mike.'

'Tell me about that night. That's enough.'

'Didn't Juno tell you?'

'Yeah, but I want to hear you say it.'

She took a deep drag on the butt and squashed it in a tray. 'He took me home. I had a few too many drinks, and . . . well, I was feeling a little giddy. I think he rode around in a cab with me for a while. Really, I can't remember every-thing exactly . . .'

'Go on.'

'I must have passed out, because the next thing I knew I

woke up in my bed fully clothed and with an awful hangover. Later I learned that he had committed suicide, and frankly, I was very much upset.'

'And that's all?'

'That's all.'

It's too bad, I thought. She's the type to show a guy a time if she wanted to. It was just too damn bad. She waited to see what I'd say next, and since it was still early I asked, 'Tell me about it from the beginning. The show and all, I mean.'

Marion smoothed out her hair with the flat of her hand and looked up at the ceiling. 'The Calway Merchandising Company made the booking through Miss Reeves . . . Juno. She . . .'

'Does Juno always handle those details?'

'No, not always. Sometimes they go through Anton. You see, Juno is really the important one. She makes all the contacts and is persuasive enough to throw quite a few accounts to the agency.'

'I can see why,' I admitted with a grin.

She smiled back. 'Our agency is perhaps the most exclusive in town. The models get paid more, are more in demand than any others, and all through Miss Reeves. A call from her is equal to a call from the biggest movie studio. In fact, she's managed to promote several of the agency models right into pictures.'

'But to get back to the show . . .' I prompted.

'Yes . . . the call came in and Juno notified us at once. We had to report to Calway Merchandising to pick up the dresses we had to show and be fitted. That took better than two hours. One of the managers took us to the dinner where we sat through the speeches and what have you, and about an hour beforehand we left to get dressed. The show lasted for fifteen minutes or so; we changed back to our street clothes and joined the crowd. By that time drinks were being served and I managed to have a couple too many.'

'About meeting Wheeler, how'd you manage that?'

'I think it was when I left. I couldn't make the elevator any too well. We got on together and he helped me down and into a cab. I told you the rest.'

There it was again. Nothing.

I pushed myself out of the chair and fiddled with my hat. 'Thanks, kid. That cooks it for me, but thanks anyway. You can go back to bed now.'

'I'm sorry I couldn't help you.'

'Oh, it helps a little. At least I know what not to look for. Maybe I'll be seeing you around.'

She walked ahead of me to the door and held it open. 'Perhaps,' she said. 'I hope the next time is under more pleasant circumstances.' We shook hands briefly and her forehead wrinkled. 'Incidentally, Juno mentioned reporters. I hope . . .'

'They can't make anything out of it as long as things stand that way. You can practically forget about it.'

'I feel better now. Goodbye, Mr Hammer.'

'So long, kid. See ya.'

I crouched behind the wheel of my car and made faces at the traffic coming against me. It was a mess to start with and got messier all the time. Murder doesn't just happen. Not the kind of murder that gets tucked away so nicely not a single loose end stuck out.

Damn it anyway, where *was* a loose end? There had to be one! Was it money? Revenge? Passion? Why in hell did a nice guy like Wheeler have to die? Stinking little rats like Clyde ran around and did what they damn well pleased and a nice guy had to die!

I was still tossing it around in my mind when I parked along that residential street in the Bronx. The big sedan was in the driveway and I could make out the E.P. in gold Old English script on the door. I pulled the key out of the ignition and walked up the flagstone path that wound through the bushes.

This time I lifted the embossed knocker and let it drop.

A maid in a black-and-white uniform opened the door and stood with her hand on the knob. 'Good morning. Can I help you?'

'I want to see Mr Perry,' I said.

'Mr Perry left orders that he is not to be disturbed. I'm sorry, sir.'

'You go tell Mr Perry that he's gonna get disturbed right now. You tell him Mike Hammer is here and whatever a guy named Rainey can do I can do better.' I grabbed the handle and pushed the door and she didn't try to stop me at all when she saw my face. 'You go tell him that.'

I didn't have long to wait. She came back, said, 'Mr Perry will see you in his study, sir,' waved her hand towards the far end of the hall and stood there wondering what it was all about as I walked past.

Mr Perry was the scared fat man. Now he was really scared. He didn't sit—he occupied a huge leather chair behind a desk and quivered from his jowls down. He must have been at peace with himself a minute before because an opened book lay face-down and a cigar burned in an ash tray.

I threw my hat on the desk, cleared away some of the fancy junk that littered it and sat on the edge. 'You're a liar, Perry,' I said.

The fat man's mouth dropped open and the first chin under it started to tremble. His pudgy little fingers squeezed the arms of his chair trying to get juice out of it. He didn't have much voice left when he said, 'How dare you to . . . in my own home! How dare you . . .'

I shook a butt out of the pack and jammed it in the corner of my mouth. I didn't have a match so I lit it from his cigar. 'What did Rainey promise you, Perry—a beating?' I glanced at him through the smoke. 'A slug in the back, maybe?'

His eyes went from the window to the door. 'What are you . . .'

I finished it for him. 'I'm talking about a hood named Rainey. What did he promise you?'

Perry's voice faded altogether and he looked slightly sick. I said, 'I'll tell you once then I want an answer. I told you whatever Rainey can do I can do better. I can beat the hell out of you worse. I can put a slug where it'll hurt more and I'll get a large charge out of it besides.

'I'm talking about a guy you said you knew. His name was Wheeler, Chester Wheeler. He was found dead in a hotel room and the verdict was suicide. You informed the police that he was despondent . . . about business, you said.'

Emil Perry gave a pathetic little nod and flicked his tongue over his lips. I leaned forward so I could spit the words in his face. 'You're a damned liar, Perry. There was nothing the matter with Wheeler's business. It was a stall, wasn't it?'

The fear crept into his eyes and he tried to shake his head.

'Do you know what happened to Wheeler?' I spoke the words only inches away from him. 'Wheeler was murdered. And you know something else . . . you're going to be in line for the same thing when the killer knows I'm on your tail. He won't trust your not talking and you, my fat friend, will get a nice nasty slug imbedded somewhere in your intestines.'

Emil Perry's eyes were like coals in a snowbank. He held his breath until his chin quivered, his cheeks went blue and he passed out. I sat back on the edge of the desk and finished my cigarette, waiting for him to come around.

It took a good five minutes and he resembled a lump of clay someone had piled in the chair. A lump of clay in a business suit.

When his eyes opened he made a pass at a perspiring decanter on the desk. I poured out a glass of ice water and handed it to him. He made loud gulping sounds getting it down.

I let my voice go flat. 'You didn't even know Wheeler, did you?'

His expression gave me the answer to that one.

'Want to talk about it?'

58

Perry managed a fast negative movement of his head. I got up and put my hat on and walked to the door. Before I opened it I looked back over my shoulder. 'You're supposed to be a solid citizen, fat boy. The cops take your word for things. You know what I'm going to do? I'm going out and find what it is that Rainey promised you and really lay it on.'

His face turned blue and he passed out before I closed the door. The hell with him. He could get his own water this time.

CHAPTER SIX

The sky had clouded over, putting a bite in the air. Here and there a car coming in from out of town was wearing a top hat of snow. I pulled in to a corner restaurant and had two cups of coffee to get the chill out of my bones, then climbed back in the car and cut across town to my apartment, where I picked up my topcoat and gloves. By the time I reached the street there were grey feathers of snow in the air slanting down through the sheer walls of the buildings to the street.

It was twelve-fifteen before I found a parking lot with room to rent. As soon as I checked my keys in the shack I grabbed a cab and gave the driver the address of the Anton Lipsek Agency on Thirty-third Street. Maybe something could be salvaged from the day after all.

This time the sweet-looking receptionist with the sour smile didn't ask questions. I told her, 'Miss Reeves, please,' and she spoke into the intercom box. The voice that came back was low and vibrant, tinged with an overtone of pleasure. I didn't have to be told that she was waiting for me.

The gods on Olympus could well be proud of their queen She was a vision of perfection in a long-sleeved dress striding across the room to meet me. The damn clothes she wore. They covered everything up and let your imagination fill in the blanks. The sample she offered was her hands and face, but the sample was enough because it made you want to undress her with your eyes and feel the warm flesh of a goddess. There was a lilt to her walk and a devil in her eyes as we shook hands, a brief touch that sent my skin crawling up my spine again.

'I'm so glad you came, Mike.'

'I told you I would.' The dress buttoned up snug at the neck and she wore but one piece of jewellery, a pendant. I flipped it into the light and it threw back a shimmering green glow. I let out a whistle. The thing was an emerald that must have cost a fortune.

'Like it?'

'Some rock.'

'I love beautiful things,' she said.

'So do I.' Juno turned her head and a pleased smile flashed at me for a second and disappeared. The devils in her eyes laughed their pleasure, too, and she walked to her desk.

That was when the grey light from the window seeped into the softness of her hair and turned it a gold that made my heart beat against my chest until I thought it would come loose.

There was a bad taste in my mouth.

My guts were all knotted up in a ball and that damnable music began in my head. Now I knew what that creepy feeling was that left my spine tingling. Now I knew what it was about Juno that made me want to reach out and grab her.

She reminded me of another girl.

A girl that happened a long time ago.

A girl I thought I had put out of my mind and forgotten completely in a wild hatred that could never be equalled. She was blonde, a very yellow, golden blonde. She was dead and I made her that way. I killed her because I wanted to and she wouldn't stay dead.

I looked down at my hands and they were shaking violently, the fingers stiffened into talons that showed every vein and tendon.

'Mike . . . ?' The voice was different. It was Juno and now that I knew what it was I could stop shaking. The gold was out of her hair.

She brought her coat over to me to hold while she slipped into it. There was a little piece of mink fur on her hat that matched the coat. 'We *are* going to lunch, aren't we?'

'I'm not here on business.'

She laughed again and leaned against me as she worked the gloves over her fingers. 'What were you thinking of a minute ago, Mike?'

I didn't let her see my face. 'Nothing.'

'You aren't telling the truth.'

'I know it.'

Juno looked at me over her shoulder. There was a pleading in her eyes. 'It wasn't me . . . something I did?'

I forced a lopsided smile. 'Nothing you did, Juno. I just happened to think of something I shouldn't have.'

'I'm glad, Mike. You were hating something then and I wouldn't want you to hate me.' She reached for my hand almost girlishly and pulled me to the door at the side of the room. 'I don't want to share you with the whole office force, Mike.'

We came out around the corner of the corridor and I punched the bell for the elevator. While we waited she squeezed my arm under hers, knowing that I couldn't help watching her. Juno, a goddess in a fur coat. She was an improvement on the original.

And in that brief second I looked at her the light filtered through her hair again and reflected the sheen of gold. My whole head rocked with the fire and pain in my chest and I felt Charlotte's name trying to force itself past my lips. Good God! Is this what it's like to think back? Is this what happened when you remember a woman you loved then blasted into hell? I ripped my eyes away and slammed my finger against the buzzer on the wall, holding it there, staring at it until I heard metal scraping behind the doors.

The elevator stopped and the operator gave her a princely nod and a subdued murmur of greeting. The two other men in the car looked at Juno, then back to me jealously. She seemed to affect everyone the same way.

The street had taken on a slippery carpet of white that rippled under the wind. I turned up my coat collar against it and peered down the road for a cab. Juno said, 'No cab, Mike. My car's around the corner.' She fished in her pocket and brought out a gold chain that ran through two keys. 'Here, you drive.'

We ducked our heads and went around the block with the wind whipping at our legs. The car she pointed out was a new Caddy convertible with all the trimmings that I thought only existed in show windows. I held the door open while she got in, slammed it shut and ran around the other side. Stuff like this was really living.

The engine was a cat's purr under the hood wanting to pull away from the kerb in a roar of power. 'Call it, Juno. Where to?'

'There's a little place downtown that I discovered a few months ago. They have the best steaks in the world if you can keep your mind on them. The most curious people in the world seem to eat there . . . almost fascinating people.'

'Fascinating?'

Her laugh was low, alive with humour. 'That isn't a good word. They're . . . well, they're most unusual. Really, I've never seen anything like it. But the food is good. Oh, you'll see. Drive down Broadway and I'll show you how to go.'

I nodded and headed towards the Stem with the windscreen wipers going like metronomes. The snow was a pain, but it thinned out traffic somewhat and it was only a matter of minutes before we were downtown. Juno leaned forward in the seat, peering ahead at the street corners. I slowed down so she could see where we were and she tipped her finger against the glass.

'Next block, Mike. It's a little place right off the corner.'

I grinned at her. 'What are we doing . . . slumming? Or is it one of those Village hangouts that have gone uptown?'

'Definitely not uptown. The food is superb.' Her eyes flashed just once as we pulled into the kerb. I grinned back and she said, 'You act all-knowing, Mike. Have you been here before?'

'Once. It used to be a fag joint and the food was good then, too. No wonder you saw so many fascinating people.'

'Mike!'

'You ought to get around a little more, woman. You've been living too high in the clouds too long. If anybody sees me going in this joint I'm going to get whistled at. That is . . . if they let me in.'

She passed me a puzzled frown at that. 'They tossed me out one time,' I explained. 'At least they started to toss me out. The reinforcements called for reinforcements and it wound up with me walking out on my way anyway. I had my hair pulled. Nice people.'

Juno bit her lip trying to hold back a laugh. 'And here I've been telling all my friends where to go to find wonderful steaks! Come to think of it a couple of them were rather put out when I mentioned it to them a second time.'

'Hell, they probably enjoyed themselves. Come on, let's see how the third side lives.'

She shook the snow out of her hair and let me open the door for her. We had to go through the bar to the hat-check booth and I had a quick look at the gang lined up on the stools. Maybe ten eyes met mine in the mirror and tried to hang on, but I wasn't having any. There was a pansy down at the end of the bar trying to make a guy who was too drunk to notice and was about to give it up as a bad job. I got a smile from the guy and he came close to getting knocked on his neck. The bartender was one of them, too, and he looked put out because I came in with a dame.

The girl at the hat-check booth looked like she was trying hard to grow a moustache and wasn't having much luck at it. She gave me a frosty glare, but smiled at Juno and took her time about looking her over. When the babe went to hang up the coats Juno looked back at me with a little red showing in her face and I laughed at her.

'Now you know, huh?' I said.

Her hand covered the laugh. 'Oh, Mike, I feel so very foolish! And I thought they were just being friendly.'

'Oh, very friendly. To you, that is. I hope you noticed the cold treatment I got and I usually get along with any kind of dame.'

The dining-room was a long, narrow room with booths along the sides and a few tables running down the middle. Nobody was at the tables, but over half the booths were filled, if you can call two people of the same sex sitting along the same side filled. A waiter with a lisp and hair that curled around his neck came over and curtsied then led us to the last booth back.

I ordered a round of cocktails to come in front of the steaks and the waiter gave me another curtsy that damn near had a kiss in it. Juno opened a jewelled cigarette-case and lifted out a king size. 'I think he likes you, Mike,' she said. 'Smoke?'

I shook my head and worked the next-to-last one out of my crumpled pack. Outside at the bar somebody stuck a nickel in the jukebox and managed to hit a record that didn't try to take your ears off. It was something sweet and low-down with a throaty sax carrying the melody, the kind of music that made you want to listen instead of talk. When the cocktails came we picked them up together. 'Propose a toast, Mike.'

Her eyes shone at me over the glass. 'To beauty,' I said. 'To Olympus. To a goddess that walks with the mortals.'

'With very . . . wonderful mortals,' Juno added.

We drained the glasses.

There were other cocktails and other toasts after that. The steaks came and were the best in the world like she said. There was that period when you feel full and contented and can sit back with a cigarette curling sweet smoke and look at the world and be glad you're part of it.

'Thinking, Mike?'

'Yeah, thinking how nice it is to be alive. You shouldn't have taken me here, pretty lady. It's getting my mind off my work.'

Her face knitted in a frown. 'Are you *still* looking for a reason for your friend's death?'

'Uh-huh. I checked on that Marion babe, by the way. She was the one. Everything was so darned aboveboard it knocked the props out from under me. I was afraid it would happen like that. Still trying though, still in there trying.'

'Trying?'

'Hell, yes. I don't want to wind up a grocery clerk.' She didn't get what I meant. My grin split into a smile and that into a laugh. I had no right to feel so happy, but way back in my head I knew that the sun would come up one day and show me the answer.

'What brought that on? Or are you laughing at me?'

'Not you, Juno. I couldn't laugh at you.' She stuck out her tongue at me. 'I was laughing at the way life works out. It gets pretty complicated sometimes, then all of a sudden it's as simple as hell, if hell can be simple. Like the potbellies with all the bare-backed babes in the Bowery. You know something . . . I didn't think I'd find you there.'

She shrugged her shoulders gracefully. 'Why not? A great many of your "potbellies" are wonderful business contacts.'

'I understand you're tops in the line.'

I could see that pleased her. She nodded thoughtfully. 'Not without reason, Mike. It has meant a good deal of exacting work both in and out of the office. We only handle work for the better houses and use the best in the selections of models. Anton, you know, is comparatively unknown as a person, simply because he refuses to take credit for his photography, but his work is far above any of the others. I think you've seen the interest he takes in his job.'

'I would, too,' I said.

Her tongue came out again. 'You would, too. I bet nothing would get photographed.'

'I bet a lot would get accomplished.'

'In that case you'd be running headlong into our code of ethics.'

'Nuts! Pity the poor photographer. He does all the work and the potbellies have all the fun.' I dragged on my cigarette and squinted my eyes. 'You know, Clyde has a pretty business for himself.'

My casual reference to the guy brought her eyebrows up. 'Do you know him?'

'Sure, from way back. Ask him to tell you about me some day.'

'I don't know him that well myself. But if I ever get the chance I will. He's the perfect underworld type, don't you think?'

'Right out of the movies. When did he start running that place?'

Juno tapped her cheek with a delicate forefinger. 'Oh . . . about six months ago, I think. I remember him stopping in the office to buy photographs in wholesale lots. He had the girls sign all the pictures and invited them to his opening. It was all very secret, of course. I didn't get to go myself until I heard the girls raving about the place. He did the same thing with most of the agencies in town.'

'He's got a brain, that boy,' I drawled. 'It's nice to have your picture on the wall. He played the girls for slobs and they never knew it. He knew damn well that a lot of them travelled with the moneybags and would pull them into his joint. When word got around that there was open gambling to boot, business got better and better. Now he gets the tourists too. They think it's all very smart and exciting . . . the kind who go around hoping for a raid so they can cut their pictures out of the papers and send them home to the folks for laughs.'

She stared at me, frowning.

'I wonder who he pays off?' I mused.

'Who?'

'Clyde. Somebody is taking the long green to keep the place going. Clyde's shelling out plenty to somebody with a lot of influence, otherwise he would have had the cops down his throat on opening night.'

Juno said impatiently, 'Oh, Mike, those tactics went out with the Prohibition era . . .,' then her voice got curious. 'Or didn't they?'

I looked across the table at this woman who wore her beauty so proudly and arrogantly. 'You've only seen the best side of things so far, kid. Plenty goes on you wouldn't want to look at.'

She tossed her head. 'It seems incredible that those things still happen, Mike.'

I started to slap my fist against my palm gently. 'Incredible, but it's happening,' I said. 'I wonder what would happen if I shafted my old buddy, Dinky Williams?' My mouth twisted into a grin. 'Maybe it's an angle. Maybe . . .' I let my sentence trail off and stared at the wall.

Juno signalled the waiter and he came back with another round of cocktails. I checked my watch and found myself in the middle of the afternoon. 'We'll make these our last, oke?'

She leaned her chin on her hands, smiling. 'I hate to have you leave me.'

'It's not a cinch for me, either.' She was still smiling and I said, 'I asked another beautiful girl who could have had ten other guys why she picked me to hold hands with. She gave me a good answer. What's yours, Juno?'

Her eyes were a fathomless depth that tried to draw me down into them. Her mouth was still curved in a smile that went softer and softer until only a trace of it was left. Full, lovely lips that barely had to move to form the words. 'I detest people who pamper me. I detest people who insist upon putting me on a pedestal. I think I like to be treated rough and you're the only one who has tried it.'

'I haven't tried anything.'

'No. But you've been thinking of it. Sometimes you don't even speak politely.'

She was a mind reader like all good goddesses should be and she was right. Quite right. I didn't know what the hell was going on in my head, but sometimes when I looked at her I wanted to reach across the table and smack her right in the teeth. Even when I thought of it I could feel the tendons in the back of my hand start twitching. Maybe a goddess was just too damn much for me. Maybe I'd been used to my own particular kind of guttersnipe too long. I kicked the idea out of my mind and unlocked the stare we were holding on each other.

'Let's go home,' I said. 'There's still some day and a long night ahead of me.'

She was wanting me to ask her to continue this day and not break it off now, but I didn't let myself think it. Juno pushed back her chair and stood up. 'The nose. First I must powder the nose, Mike.' I watched her walk away from me, watched the swing of her hips and the delicate way she seemed to balance on her toes. I wasn't the only one watching, either. A kid who had artist written all over her in splotches of paint was leaning against the partition of the booth behind me. Her eyes were hard and hot and followed Juno every step of the way. She was another one of those mannish things that breed in the half-light of the so-called aesthetical world. I got a look that told me I was in for competition and she took off after Juno. She came back in a minute and her face was pulled tight in a scowl and I gave her a nasty laugh. Some women, yes. Others, nix.

My nose got powdered first, and I waited by the door for her after throwing a good week's pay to the cashier.

The snow that had slacked off started again in earnest. A steady stream of early traffic poured out of the business section, heading home before the stuff got too deep. Juno had snow tyres on the heap so I wasn't worried about getting caught, but it took us twice the time to get back uptown as it did to come down.

Juno decided against going back to the office and told me to go along Riverside Drive. At the most fashionable of the cross-streets I turned off and went as far as the middle of the block. She indicated a new grey-stone building that stood shoulder-to-shoulder with the others, boasting a doorman in a maroon uniform and topcoat. She leaned back and sighed, 'We're home.'

'Leave the car here?'

'Won't you need it to get where you're going?'

'I couldn't afford to put gas in this buggy. No, I'll take a cab.'

I got out and opened the door. The maroon uniform walked over and tipped his hat. Juno said, 'Have the car taken to the garage for me, please?'

He took the keys. 'Certainly, Miss Reeves.'

She turned to me with a grin. The snow swirling around her clung to the fur of her collar and hat, framing her face with a sprinkling of white. 'Come up for a drink?' I hesitated. 'Just one, Mike, then I'll let you go.'

'O.K., baby, just one and don't try to make it any more.'

Juno didn't have a penthouse, but it was far enough up to make a good Olympus. There was no garishness about the place, big as it was. The furnishings and the fixtures were matched in the best of taste, designed for complete, comfortable living.

I kept my coat and hat on while she whipped up a cocktail, my eyes watching the lithe grace of her movements. There was an unusual symmetry to her body that made me want to touch and feel. Our eyes met in the mirror over the sofa and there was the same thing in hers as there must have been in mine.

She spun around with an eloquent gesture and held out the glasses. Her voice was low and husky again. 'I'm just a breeze past thirty, Mike. I've known many men. I've had many men, too, but none that I really wanted. One day soon I'm going to want you.'

My spine chilled up suddenly and the crazy music let loose in my head because she had the light in her hair again. The stem of the glass broke off in my fingers, tearing into my palm. The back of my neck got hot and I felt the sweat pop out of my forehead.

I moved so the light would be out of her hair and the gold would be gone from it, covering up the insane hatred of memory by lifting my hands to drink from the bowl of the broken glass.

It spoiled the picture for me, a picture that should be beautiful and desirable, scarred by something that should be finished but kept coming back.

I put the pieces of the glass down on the windowsill and she said, 'You looked at me that way again, Mike.'

This time I forced the memory out of my mind. I slipped my hand over hers and ran my fingers through her hair, sifting its short silky loveliness. 'I'll make it up to you sometime, Juno. I can't help thinking and it hasn't got anything to do with you.'

'Make it up to me now.'

I gave her ear a little pull. 'No.'

'Why?'

'Because.'

She pouted and her eyes tried to convince me.

I couldn't tell her that it was because there was a time and place for everything, and though this was the time and place she wasn't the person. I was only a mortal. A mortal doesn't undress a goddess and let his eyes feast and his hands feel and his body seek fulfilment.

Then, too, maybe that wasn't the reason at all. Maybe she reminded me of something else I could never have.

Never.

She said it slowly. 'Who was she, Mike? Was she lovely?'

I couldn't keep the words back. I tried, but they wouldn't

stay there. 'She was lovely. She was the most gorgeous thing that ever lived and I was in love with her. But she did something and I played God; I was the judge and I the jury and the sentence was death. I shot her right in the gut and when she died I died too.'

Juno never said a word. Only her eyes moved. They softened, offered themselves to me, trying to convince me that I wasn't dead . . . not to her.

I lit a cigarette and stuck it in my mouth, then got the hell out of there before her eyes became too convincing. I felt her eyes burning in my back because we both knew I'd be back.

Juno, goddess of marriage and births, queen of the lesser gods and goddesses. Why wasn't she Venus, goddess of beauty and love? Juno was a queen and she didn't want to be. She wanted to be a woman.

Darkness had come prematurely, but the reflected lights on the whiteness of the snow made the city brighter than ever. Each office building discharged a constant stream of people clutching their collars tight at the throat. I joined the traffic that pressed against the sides of the buildings trying to get away from the stinging blast of air, watching them escape into the mouths of the kiosks.

I grabbed a cab, stayed in it until I reached Times Square, then got out and ducked into a bar for a quick beer. When I came out there were no empty cabs around so I started walking up Broadway towards Thirty-third. Every inch of it was a fight against the snow and the crowd. My feet were soaked and the crease was out of my pants. Halfway there the light changed suddenly and the cars coming around the corner forced the pedestrians back on the kerb.

Somebody must have slipped because there was a tinkle of glass then a splintering crash as the front came out of a store showcase on the corner. Those who jumped out of the way were crammed in by others who wanted to see what happened. A cop wormed in through the mêlée and stood in front of the window and I got out through the path he left behind him.

When I reached Thirty-third I turned east hoping to find a taxi to get over to the parking lot and decided to give it up as a bad job and walk the rest of the way after one more look.

I stepped out on the kerb to look down the street when the plate glass in a window behind me twanged and split into a spider web of cracks. Nobody had touched it this time, either. A car engine roared and all I saw was the top half of a face looking out from the back window of a blue sedan and it was looking straight at me for a long second before it pulled out of sight.

My eyes felt tight and my lips were pulled back over my teeth. My voice cut into the air and faces turned my way. 'Twice the same day,' I said, 'right on Broadway, too. The crazy bastard, the crazy son-of-a-bitch!'

I didn't remember getting to the car lot or driving out through traffic. I must have been muttering to myself because the drivers of cars that stopped alongside me at red lights would look over and shake their heads like I was nuts or something. Maybe I was. It scares me to be set up as a target right off the busiest street in the world.

That first window. I thought it was an accident. The second one had a bullet hole in the middle of it just before it came apart and splashed all over the pavement.

The building where I held down an office had a parking space in the basement. It was empty. I drove in and rolled to a corner and locked up. The night man took my keys and let me sign the register before letting me take the service elevator up to my floor.

When I got out I walked down the corridor, looking at the darkened glass of the empty offices. Only one had a light behind it and that one was mine. When I rattled the knob the latch snapped back and the door opened.

Velda said, 'Mike! What are you doing here?'

I brushed right past her and went to the filing cabinet where I yanked at the last drawer down. I had to reach all the way in the back behind the rows of well-stuffed envelopes to get what I wanted.

'What happened, Mike?' She was standing right beside me, her lip caught between her teeth. Her eyes were on the little ·25 automatic I was shoving in my pocket.

'No bastard is going to shoot at me,' I told her. My throat felt dry and hoarse.

'When?'

'Just now. Not ten minutes ago. The bastard did it right out in the open. You know what that means?'

That animal snarl crossed her face and was gone in a second. 'Yes. It means that you're important all of a sudden.'

'That's right, important enough to kill.'

She said it slowly, hoping I had the answer. 'Did you . . . see who it was?'

'I saw a face. Half of it. Not enough to tell who it was except that it was a man. That face will try again and when it does I'll blow the hell out of it.'

'Be careful, Mike. You don't have a licence any more. The D.A. would love to run you in on a Sullivan charge.'

I got up out of my crouch and gave her a short laugh. 'The

70

law is supposed to protect the people. If the D.A. wants to jug me I'll make a good time out of it. I'll throw the constitution in his face. I think one of the first things it says is that the people are allowed to bear arms. Maybe they'll even have to revoke the Sullivan Law and then we'll really have us a time.'

'Yeah, a great whizbang, bang-up affair.'

For the first time since I came in I took notice of her. I don't know how the hell I waited so long. Velda was wearing a sweeping, black, evening gown that seemed to start halfway down her waist, leaving the top naked as sin. Her hair, falling around her shoulders, looked like onyx and I got a faint whiff of a deep, sensual aroma.

There was no fullness to the dress. It clung. There was no other word for it. It just clung, and under it there wasn't the slightest indication of anything else. 'Is that all you got on?'

'Yes.'

'It's cold outside, baby.' I know I was frowning, but I couldn't help it. 'Where you going?'

'To see your friend Clyde. He invited me out to supper.'

My hand tightened into a fist before I could stop it. Clyde, the bastard! I forced a grin through the frown. It didn't come out so well. 'If I knew you would look like that I'd have asked you out myself.'

There was a time when she would have gotten red and slammed me across the jaw. There was a time when she would have broken any kind of a date to put away a hamburger in a diner with me. Those times had flown.

She pulled on a pair of elbow-length gloves and let me stand there with my mouth watering, knowing damn well she had me where it hurt. 'Business, Mike, business before pleasure always.' Her face was blank.

'I let my tone get sharp. 'What were you doing here before I came in?'

'There's a note on your desk explaining everything. I visited the Calway Merchandising Company and rounded up some photographs they took of the girls that night. You might want to see them. You take to pretty girls, don't you?'

'Shut up.'

She glanced at me quickly so I wouldn't see the tears that made her eyes shine. When she walked to the desk to get her coat I started swearing under my breath at Clyde again because the bastard was getting the best when I had never seen it. That's what happens when something like Velda is right under your nose.

I said it again. This time there was no sharpness in my voice. 'I wish I had seen you like that before, Velda.'

She took a minute to put on her coat and it was so quiet in

71

that room I could hear her breathing. She turned around, the tears were still there. 'Mike . . . I don't have to tell you that you can see me any way you like . . . any time.'

I had her in my arms, pressing her against me, feeling every warm, vibrant contour of her body. Her mouth reached for mine and I tasted the wet sweetness of her lips, felt her shudder as my hands couldn't keep off the whiteness of her skin. My fingers dug into her shoulders leaving livid red marks. She tore her mouth away with a sob and spun around so I couldn't see her face, and with one fast motion that happened too quickly she put her hands over mine and slid them over the flesh and on to the dress that clung and down her body that was so warmly alive, then pulled away and ran to the door.

I put a cigarette in my mouth and forgot to light it. I could still hear her heels clicking down the hall. Absently I reached for the phone and dialled Pat's number out of habit. He said hello three times before I answered him and told him to meet me in my office.

I looked at my hands and the palms were damp with sweat. I lit my cigarette and sat there, thinking of Velda again.

CHAPTER SEVEN

It took Pat thirty minutes to get there. He came in stamping the snow off his shoes and blowing like a bull moose. When he shed his coat and hat he threw a briefcase on the desk and drew up a chair.

'What are you looking so rosy about, Mike?'

'The snow. It always gets me. How'd you make out today?'

'Fine,' Pat said, 'just fine and dandy. The D.A. made a point of telling me to keep my nose clean again. If he ever gets boosted out of office I'm going to smack him right in the sneezer.' He must have read the surprise on my face. 'O.K., O.K., it doesn't sound like me. Go ahead and say it. I'm getting tired of being snarled up in red tape. You had it easy before you threw away your ticket and you didn't know it.'

'I'll get it back.'

'Perhaps. We have to make murder out of suicide first.'

'You almost had another on your hands today, chum.'

He stopped in the middle of a sentence and said, 'Who now?'

'Me.'

'You!'

'Little me. On a crowded street, too. Somebody tried to pop me with a silenced gun. All they got was two windows.'

'I'll be damned! We got a call on one of those windows, the one on Thirty-third. If the slug didn't poke a hole through all the scenery and land where it could be found it would have passed for an accident. Where was the other one?'

I told him and he said he would be damned again. He reached for the phone and buzzed headquarters to have them go through the window for the slug. When he hung up I said, 'What's the D.A. going to do when he hears about this?'

'Quit kidding. He isn't hearing anything. You know the rep you have . . . the bright boy'll claim it's one of your old friends sending a greeting card for the holidays.'

'It's too early for that.'

'Then he'll grab you on some trumped-up charge and get himself a big play in the papers. The hell with him!'

'You aren't talking like a good cop now, feller.'

Pat's face darkened and he leaned out of his chair with his teeth bared to the gums. 'There's a time when being a good cop won't catch a killer. Right now I'm teed off, Mike. We're both on a hot spot that may get hotter and I don't like it. It might be that I'm getting smart. A little favourable publicity never hurts anybody and if the D.A. tries to trim my corns I'll have a better talking point if I have something I can toss at him.'

I laughed. Cripes, how I laughed! For ten years I had sung that song to him and now he was beginning to learn the words.

It was funnier now than it was in the beginning.

I said, 'What about Rainey? You find him?'

'We found him.'

'Yeah?'

'Yeah what! He was engaged in the so-called legitimate profession of promoting fights. Some arena on the island. We couldn't tap him for a thing. What about him?'

There was a bottle of booze in the desk and I poured out two shots. 'He's in this, Pat. I don't know just how he fits, but he's there.' I offered a silent toast and we threw them down. It burned a path to my stomach and lay there like a hot coal. I put down the glass and sat on the windowsill. 'I went out to see Emil Perry. Rainey was there and had the guy scared silly. Even I couldn't scare him worse. Perry said Wheeler had spoken of suicide because business was bad; but a check showed his outfit to be making coin hand over fist. Riddle me that one.'

Pat whistled slowly.

I waited for him to collect his thoughts. 'Remember Dinky Williams, Pat?'

Pat let his head move up and down. 'Go on.' His face was getting that cop look on it.

I tried to make it sound casual. 'What's he doing now? You know?'

'No.'

'If I were to tell you that he was running a wide-open gambling joint right here in the city, what would you do?'

'I'd say you were crazy, it's impossible, then put the vice squad on it.'

'In that case I won't tell you about it.'

He brought his hand down on the desk so hard my cigarettes jumped. 'The hell you won't! You'll tell me about it right now! Who am I supposed to be—a rookie cop for you to play around with?'

It was nice to see him get mad again. I eased down off the windowsill and slumped in my chair. His face was red as a beet. 'Look, Pat. You're still a cop. You believe in the integrity and loyalty of the Force. You may not want to, but you'll be duty-bound to do just what you said. If you do a killer gets away.'

He went to talk, but I stopped him with a wave of my hand. 'Keep still and listen. I've been thinking that there's more to this than you or I have pictured. Dink's in it, Rainey's in it,

74

guys like Emil Perry are in it too. Maybe lots more we don't know about . . . yet. Dinky Williams is cleaning up a pretty penny right this minute running wheels and bars without a licence. Because I told you that don't go broadcasting it around. It may hurt you to be reminded of the fact, but just the same it has to be . . . if Dinky Williams runs a joint, then somebody is getting paid off. Somebody big. Somebody important. Either that or a whole lot of small somebodies who are mighty important when you lump 'em all together. Do you want to fight that set-up?'

'You're damned well told I do!'

'You want to keep your badge? You think you can buck it?' His voice was a hoarse whisper. 'I'll do it.'

'You have another think coming and you know it. You'd just *like* to do it. Now, listen to me. I have an inside track on this thing. We can play it together or not, but we're doing it my way or you can stick your nose in the dirt and root up the facts yourself. It won't be easy. If Dinky *is* paying off we can get the whole crowd at once, not just Dinky. Now call it.'

I think if I had had a licence it would have been gone right there, friend or no friend. All I had was a name on the door that didn't mean anything now. Pat looked at me with disgust and said, 'What a great Captain of Homicide *I* am! The D.A. would give his arm for a recording of this little conversation. O.K. Inspector, I'm waiting for my orders.'

I gave him a two-fingered salute. 'First, we want a killer. To get him we need to know why Wheeler was killed. If you were to mention the fact that a certain guy named Clyde was heading for trouble you might get results. They won't be pretty results, but they might show us where to look.'

'Who's Clyde?' There was an ominous tone in his voice.

'Clyde is Dinky's new monicker. He got fancy.'

Pat was grinning now. 'The name is trouble, Mike. I've heard it mentioned before.' He stood up and pulled a cigarette from my deck of Luckies. I sat there and waited. 'We're getting into Ward politics now.'

'So?'

'So you're a pretty smart bastard. I will say you should've been a cop. You'd be Commissioner by now or dead. One or the other. You might still be dead.'

'I almost was this afternoon.'

'Sure, I can see why. This Clyde guy has all the local monkeys by their tails. He gets everything fixed, everything from a parking ticket to a murder rap. All you have to do is mention the name and somebody starts bowing and scraping. Our old friend Dinky has really come up in the world.'

'Nuts! He's a small-time heel.'

'Is he? If it's the same guy we're talking about he's able to pull a lot of strings.'

Pat was too calm. I didn't like it. There were things I wanted to ask him and I was afraid of the answers. I said, 'How about the hotel? You checked there, didn't you?'

'I did. Nobody registered the day of the killing, but there were quite a few guests admitted to other rooms that same night. They all had plausible alibis.'

That time I let out a string of dirty words. Pat listened and grinned again. 'Will I see you tomorrow, Mike?'

'Yeah. Tomorrow.'

'Stay away from store windows.'

He put on his hat and slammed the door. I went back to looking at the pictures Velda had left on my desk. The girl named Marion Lester was laughing into the camera from the folds of a huge fur-collared coat. She looked happy. She didn't look like she'd be drunk in another couple of hours and have to be put to bed by a friend of mine who died not long after.

I slid all the photos in the folder and stuffed them in the desk drawer. The bottle was still half full and the glass empty. I cured that in a hurry. Pretty soon it was the other way around, then there was nothing in either of them and I felt better. I pulled the phone over by the cord and dialled a number that I had written on the inside of a matchbook cover.

A voice answered and I said, 'Hello, Connie . . . Mike.'

'My ugly lover! I thought you'd forgotten me.'

'Never, child. What are you doing?'

'Waiting for you.'

'Can you wait another half-hour?'

'I'll get undressed for you.'

'You get dressed for me because we may go out.'

'It's snowing.' She sounded pained. 'I don't have galoshes.'

'I'll carry you.' She was still protesting when I stuck the receiver on its arms.

There was a handful of ·25 shells in the drawer that I shovelled into my pocket, little bits of insurance that might come in handy. Just before I left I pulled out the drawer and hauled out the envelope of photographs. The last thing I did was type a note for Velda telling her to let me know how she made out.

The guy in the parking lot had very thoughtfully put the skid chains on my buggy and earned himself a couple of bucks. I backed out and joined the line of cabs and cars that pulled their way through the storm.

Connie met me at the door with a highball in her hand and shoved it at me before I could take off my hat. 'My hero,' she said, 'my big, brave hero coming through the raging blizzard to rescue poor me.'

It was a wonderful highball. I gave her back the empty and kissed her cheek. Her laugh was little bells that tinkled in my ear. She closed the door and took my coat while I went inside and sat down. When she joined me she sat on the sofa with her legs crossed under her and reached for a smoke. 'About tonight . . . we are going where?'

'Looking for a killer.'

The flame of the match she held trembled just a little. 'You . . . know?'

I shook my head. 'I suspect.'

There was real interest in her face. Her voice was soft. 'Who?'

'I suspect a half-dozen people. Only one of them is a killer. The rest contributed to the crime somehow.' I played with the cord on the floor lamp and watched the assorted expressions that flickered across her face.

Finally she said, 'Mike . . . is there some way I can help? I mean, is it possible that something I know might have a meaning?'

'Possibly.'

'Is that . . . the only reason you came here tonight?'

I turned the light off and on a few times. Connie was staring at me hard, her eyes questioning. 'You don't have much faith in yourself, kid,' I grinned. 'Why don't you look in the mirror sometime? You got a face that belongs in the movies and a body that should be a crime to cover. You have an agile mind, too. I'm only another guy. I go for all that.

'The answer is yes, that's all I came here for tonight. If you were anybody else I still would have come, but because you're you it makes it all the nicer and I look forward to coming. Can you understand that?'

Her legs swung down and she came over and kissed my nose, then went back to the couch. 'I understand, Mike. Now I'm happy. Tell me what you want.'

'I don't know, Connie. I'm up a tree. I don't know what to ask for.'

'Just ask for anything you want.'

I shrugged. 'O.K., do you like your work?'

'Wonderful.'

'Make a lot of jack?'

'Oodles.'

'Like your boss?'

'Which one?'

'Juno.'

Connie spread her hands out in a non-committal gesture.

'Juno never interferes with me. She had seen my work and was impressed with it. When I had a call from her I was thrilled to the bones because I hit the top. Now all she does is select those ads that fit me best and Anton takes care of the rest.'

'Juno must make a pile,' I said observingly.

'I guess she does! Besides drawing a big salary she's forever on the receiving end of gifts from over-generous clients. I'd almost feel sorry for Anton if he had the sense to care.'

'What about him?'

'Oh, he's the arty type. Doesn't give a hoot for money as long as he has his work. He won't let a subordinate handle the photography, either. Maybe that's why the agency is so successful.'

'He married? A wife would cure that.'

'Anton married? That's a laugh. After all the women he handles, and I do mean handles, what mere woman would attract that guy. He's positively frigid. For a Frenchman that's disgraceful.'

'French?'

Connie nodded and dragged on her smoke. 'I overheard a little secret being discussed between Anton and Juno. It seems that Juno met him in France and brought him over here, just in time for him to escape some nasty business with the French court. During the war he was supposed to have been a collaborator of a sort . . . taking propaganda photos of all the bigwig Nazis and their families. As I said, Anton doesn't give a hoot about money or politics as long as he has his work.'

'That's interesting but not very helpful. Tell me something about Clyde.'

'I don't know anything about Clyde except that looking like a movie gangster he is a powerful attraction for a lot of jerks from both sexes.'

'Do the girls from the studio ever give him a play?'

She shrugged again. 'I've heard rumours. You know the kind. He hands out expensive presents to everybody during the holidays and is forever treating someone to a lavish birthday party under the guise of friendship when it's really nothing but good business practice. I know for a fact that the crowd has stuck to the Bowery longer than they ever have to another fad. I'm wondering what's going to happen when Clyde gets ordinary people.'

'So am I,' I said. 'Look, do something for me. Start inquiring around and see who forms his clientele. Important people. The kind of people who have a voice in the city. It'll mean getting yourself invited to the Inn, but that ought to be fun.'

'Why don't you take me?'

'I'm afraid that Clyde wouldn't like that. You shouldn't have any trouble getting an escort. How about one of those ten other guys?'

'It can be managed. It would be more fun with you though.'

'Maybe some other time. Has one of those ten guys got dough?'

'They all have.'

'Then take the one with the most. Let him spend it. Be a little discreet if you start to ask questions and don't get too pointed with them. I don't want Clyde to get sore at you too. He can think of some nasty games to play.' I had the group of photos behind my back and I pulled them out. Connie came over to look at them. 'Know all these girls?'

She nodded as she went through them. 'Clotheshorses, every one. Why?'

I picked out the one of Marion Lester and held it out. 'Know her well?'

She made a nasty sound with her mouth. 'One of Juno's pets,' she said. 'Came over from the Stanton Studio last year when Juno offered her more money. She's one of the best, but she's a pain.'

'Why?'

'Oh, she thinks she's pretty hot stuff. She's been playing around a lot besides. One of these days Juno will can her. She's got a tramp complex that will lose the agency some clients one of these days.' She riffled through some of the others and took out two, one a shot of a debutante type in a formal evening gown that was almost transparent. 'This is Rita Loring. You wouldn't think it, but she saw thirty-five plenty of years ago. One of the men at the show that night hired her at a fabulous sum to model exclusively for him.'

The other photo was a girl in a sports outfit of slacks, vest and blouse, touched with fancy gimcracks that women like. She was photographed against a background that was supposed to represent a girl's dormitory. 'Little Jean Trotter, our choice teen-age type. She eloped the day before yesterday. She sent Juno a letter and we all chipped in to buy her a television set. Anton was quite perturbed, since she left in the middle of a series. Juno had to pat his hand to calm him down. I never saw him get so mad.'

She handed the pictures back to me and I put them away. The evening was early so I told her to get busy on the phone and arrange herself a date. She didn't like it, but she did it so I'd get jealous. She did the damndest job of seduction over a telephone I'd ever heard. I sat there and grinned until she got mad and took it out on the guy on the other end. She said she'd meet him in a hotel lobby downtown to save time, and hung up.

'You're a stinker, Mike,' she said.

I agreed with her. She threw my coat at me and climbed into her own. When we reached the street entrance I did like I said and carried her out to the car. She didn't get her feet wet, but the snow blew up her dress and that was just as bad. We had supper in a sea-food place, took time for a drink and some small talk, then I dumped her in front of the hotel where she was to meet her date. I kissed her so-long and she stopped being mad.

Now I had to keep me a couple of promises. One was a promise to outdo a character named Rainey. I followed a plough up Broadway for a few blocks, dragging along at a walk. To give it time to get ahead of me I pulled to the kerb on a side street and walked back to a corner bar. This time I went right to the phone and shoved in a nickel.

I had to wait through that nickel and another one before Joe Gill finally pulled himself out of the tub and came to the phone. He barked a sharp hello and I told him it was me.

'Mike,' he started, 'if you don't mind, I'd rather not . . .'

'What kind of a pal are you, chum? Look, you're not getting into anything. All I want is another little favour.'

I heard him sigh. 'All right. What is it now?'

'Information. The guy is Emil Perry, a manufacturer. He has a residence in the Bronx. I want to know all about him, socially and financially.'

'Now you're asking a toughie. I can put some men on his social life, but I can't go into his financial status too deeply. There're laws, you know.'

'Sure, and there're ways to get around them. I want to know about his bank accounts even if you have to break into his house to get them.'

'Now, Mike!'

'You don't *have* to do it, you know.'

'What the hell's the use of arguing with you. I'll do what I can, but this time we're even on all past favours, understand? And don't do me any more I'll have to repay.'

I laughed at him. 'Quit being a worrier. If you get in trouble I'll see my pal the D.A. and everything will be okeydoke.'

'That's what I'm afraid of. Keep in touch with me and I'll see what I can do.'

'Roger. 'Night, Joe.'

He grunted a goodbye and the phone clicked in my ear. I laughed again and opened the door of the booth. Soon I ought to know what Rainey had on the ball to scare the hell out of a big shot like Perry. Meanwhile I'd find out if I could be scared a little myself.

The *Globe* presses were grinding out a late edition with a racket that vibrated throughout the entire building. I went in through the employees' entrance and took the elevator up to the rewrite room where the stutter of typewriters sounded like machine guns. I asked one of the copy boys where I could find Ed Cooper and he pointed to a glass-enclosed room that was making a little racket all its own.

Ed was the sports editor on the *Globe* with a particular passion for exposing the crumbs that made money the easy way, and what he didn't know about his business wasn't worth knowing. I opened the door and walked into a fullscale barrage that he was pouring out of a mill as old as he was.

He looked up without stopping, said, 'Be right with you, Mike.'

I sat down until he finished his paragraph and played with the .25 in my jacket pocket.

My boy must have liked what he wrote because he had a satisfied leer on his face that was going to burn somebody up. 'Spill it, Mike. Tickets or information?'

'Information. A former hood named Rainey is a fight promoter. Where and who does he promote?'

Ed took it right in stride. 'Know where the Glenwood Housing project is out on the island?'

I said I did. It was one of those cities-within-a-city affairs that catered to ex-G.I.s within an hour's drive from New York.

'Rainey's in with a few other guys and they built this arena to get the trade from Glenwood. They put on fights and wrestling bouts, all of it stinko. Just the same, they pack 'em in. Lately there's been some talk of the fight boys going in the tank so's a local betting ring can clean up. I got that place on my list if it's any news to you.'

'Fine, Ed. There's a good chance that Rainey will be making the news soon. If I'm around when it happens I'll give you a buzz.'

'You going out there tonight?'

'That's right.'

Ed looked at his watch. 'They got a show on. If you step on it you might catch the first bout.'

'Yeah,' I said. 'It oughta be real interesting. I'll tell you about it when I get back to the city.' I put on my hat and opened the door. Ed stopped me before I got out.

'Those guys I was telling you about—Rainey's partners—they're supposed to be plenty tough. Be careful.'

'I'll be very careful, Ed. Thanks for the warning.'

I went out through the clatter and pounding beat of the

presses and found my car. Already the snow had piled up on the hood, pulling a white blind over the windows. I wiped it off and climbed in.

One thing about the city: it was mechanized to the point of perfection. The snow had been coming down for hours now, yet the roads were passable and getting better every minute. What the ploughs hadn't packed down the cars did, with big black eyes of manhole covers steaming malevolently on every block.

By the time I reached the arena outside the Glenwood area I could hear the howling and screaming of the mob. The parking place was jammed and overflowed out on to the street. I found an open spot a few hundred yards down the street that was partially protected by a huge oak and rolled in.

I had missed the first bout, but judging from the stumble-bums that were in there now I didn't miss much. It cost me a buck for a wall seat so far back I could hardly see through the smoke to the ring. Moisture dripped from the cinder-block walls and the seats were nothing more than benches roughed out of used lumber. But the business they did there was terrific.

It was a usual crowd of plain people hungry for entertainment and willing to pay for it. They could do better watching television if they stayed home. I sat near the door and let my eyes become accustomed to the semi-darkness. The last few rows were comparatively empty, giving me a fairly full view of what went on in the aisles.

There was a shout from the crowd and one of the pugs in the ring was counted out. A few minutes later he was carted up the aisle and out into the dressing-room. Some other gladiators took their places.

By the end of the fourth bout everybody who was going to be there was there. The two welters who had waltzed through the six rounds went past me into the hall behind the wall trailing their managers and seconds. I got up and joined the procession. It led to a large, damp room lined with cheap metal lockers and wooden, plank benches with a shower-room spilling water all over the floor. The whole place reeked of liniment and sweat. Two heavies with bandaged hands were playing cards on the bench, keeping score with spit marks on the floor.

I walked over to one of the cigar-smoking gents in a brown striped suit and nudged him with a thumb. 'Where's Rainey?'

He shifted the cigar to the other side of his mouth and said, 'Inna office, I guess. You gotta boy here tonight?'

'Naw,' I told him. 'My boy's in bed wita cold.'

'Tough. Can't maka dime that way.'

'Naw.'

He shifted the cigar back, bringing an end to that. I went

82

looking for the office that Rainey was inna. I found it down at the end of the hall. A radio was playing inside, tuned to a fight that was going on in the Garden. There must have been another door leading to the office because it slammed and there was a mumble of voices. One started to swear loudly until another told him to shut up. The swearing stopped. The voices mumbled again, the door slammed, then all I heard was the radio blaring.

I stood there a good five minutes and heard the end of the fight. The winner was telling his story of the battle over the air when the radio was switched off. I opened the door and walked in.

Rainey was sitting at a table counting the receipts for the night, stacking bills in untidy piles and keeping tally in a small red book. I had my hand on the knob and shut the door as noiselessly as I could. There was a barrel bolt below the knob and I slid it into the hasp.

If Rainey hadn't been counting out loud he would have heard me come in. As it was, I heard him go into the five thousand mark before I said, 'Good crowd, huh?'

Rainey said, 'Shut up,' and went on counting.

I said, 'Rainey.'

His fingers paused over a stack of fives. His head turned in slow motion until he was looking at me over his shoulder. The padding in his coat obscured the lower half of his face and I tried to picture it through the back window of a sedan racing up Thirty-third Street. It didn't match, but I didn't care so much either.

Rainey was a guy you could dislike easily. He had one of those faces that looked painted on, a perpetual mixture of hate, fear and toughness blended by a sneer that was a habit. His eyes were cold, merciless marbles hardly visible under thick, fleshy lids.

Rainey was a tough guy.

I leaned against the door jamb with a cigarette hanging from my lips, one hand in my pocket around the grip of the little .25. Maybe he didn't think I had a gun there. His lip rolled up into a snarl and he reached under the table.

I rapped the gun against the door jamb and even through the cloth of the coat you could tell that it was just what it was. Rainey started to lose that tough look. 'Remember me, Rainey?'

He didn't say anything.

I took a long shot in the dark. 'Sure, you remember me, Rainey. You saw me on Broadway today. I was standing in front of a plate-glass window. You missed.'

His lower lip fell away from his teeth and I could see more

of the marbles that he had for eyes. I kept my hand in my pocket while I reached under the table and pulled out a short-nosed ·32 that hung there in a clip.

Rainey finally found his voice. 'Mike Hammer,' he said. 'What the hell got into you?'

I sat on the edge of the table and flipped all the bills to the floor. 'Guess.' Rainey looked at the dough then back to me.

The toughness came back in a hurry. 'Get out of here before you get tossed out, copper.' He came halfway out of his seat.

I palmed that short-nosed ·32 and laid it across his cheek with a crack that split the flesh open. He rocked back into his chair with his mouth hanging, drooling blood and saliva over his chin. I sat there smiling, but nothing was funny.

I said, 'Rainey, you've forgotten something. You've forgotten that I'm not a guy that takes any crap. Not from anybody. You've forgotten that I've been in business because I stayed alive longer than some guys who didn't want me that way. You've forgotten that I've had some punks tougher than you'll ever be at the end of a gun and I pulled the trigger just to watch their expressions change.'

He was scared, but he tried to bluff it out anyway. He said, 'Why don'tcha try it now, Hammer? Maybe it's different when ya don't have a licence to use a rod. Go ahead, why don'tcha try it?'

He started to laugh at me when I pulled the trigger of the ·32 and shot him in the thigh. He said, 'My God!' under his breath and grabbed his leg. I raised the muzzle of the gun until he was looking right into the little round hole that was his ticket to hell.

'Dare me some more, Rainey.'

He made some blubbering noises and leaned over the chair to puke on the money that was scattered around his feet. I threw the little gun on the table. 'There's a man named Emil Perry. If you go near him again I'll put the next slug right where your shirt meets your pants.'

I shouldn't have been so damn interested in the sound of my own voice. I should have had the sense to lock the other door. I should've done a lot of things and there wouldn't have been anybody standing behind me saying, 'Hold it, brother, just hold it right there.'

A tall, skinny guy came around the table and took a long look at Rainey, who sat there too sick to speak. The other one held a gun in my back. The skinny one said, 'He's shot! You bastard, you'll catch it for this!' He straightened up and back-handed me across the mouth nearly knocking me off the table. 'You a heist artist? Answer me, damn you!' The hand lashed out into my mouth again and this time I did go off the table.

The guy with the gun brought it down across the back of my neck throwing a spasm of pain shooting through my head and shoulders. He stood in front of me this time, a short pasty-faced guy with the urge to kill written all over him. 'I'll handle this, Artie. These big boys are the kind of meat I like.'

Rainey retched and moaned again. I picked myself up slowly and Rainey said, 'Gimme the gun. Lemme do it. God-damn it, gimme that gun!' The skinny guy put his arms around his waist and lifted him to his feet so he could hobble over to the wall where I was.

The guy with the automatic in his hand grinned and took a step nearer. It was close enough. I rammed my hand against the slide and shoved it back while his finger was trying like hell to squeeze the trigger. It didn't take much effort to rip it right out of his hand while I threw my knee between his legs into his groin. He hit the floor like a bag of wet sand and lay there gasping for breath.

Some day the people who make guns will make one that can't be jammed so easily. The skinny guy holding Rainey let go and made a dive for the ·32 on the table.

I shot him in the leg too.

That was all Rainey needed. The toughness went out of him and he forgot about the hole in his thigh long enough to stagger back to his chair and hold his hands up in front of him, trying to keep me away. I threw the automatic on the table with the ·32.

'Somebody told me you boys were pretty rough,' I said. 'I'm a little disappointed. Don't forget what I told you about Emil Perry.'

The other guy with the hole in his leg sobbed for me to call a doctor. I told him to do it himself. I stepped on a pack of ten-dollar bills and they tore under my shoe. The little guy was still vomiting. I opened the door and looked back at the three tough guys and laughed. 'A doctor'll have to report those gun-shot wounds,' I reminded them. 'It would be a good idea to tell him you were cleaning a war souvenir and it went off.'

Rainey groaned again and clawed for the telephone on the table. I was whistling when I shut the door and started back towards my car. All that time gone to waste, I thought. I had been playing it soft when I should have played it hard.

There had been enough words. Now the fun ought to start.

CHAPTER EIGHT

I WAS in bed when Joe called. The alarm had been set for eleven-thirty and was five minutes short of going off. I drawled a sleepy hello and Joe told me to wake up and listen.

'I'm awake,' I said. 'Let's hear it.'

'Don't ask me how I got this stuff. I had to do some tall conniving, but I got it. Emil Perry has several business accounts, a checking account for his wife and a large personal savings account. All of them except his own personal account was pretty much in order. Six months ago he made a cash withdrawal of five thousand bucks. That was the first. It's happened every other month since then, and yesterday he withdrew all but a few hundred. The total he took out in cash was an even twenty thousand dollars.'

'Wow,' I said, 'Where did it go!'

'Getting a line on his personal affairs wasn't as easy as I thought. Item one, he has a wife and family he loves almost as much as his standing in the community. Item two, he likes to play around with the ladies. Item three, put item one and two together and what do you have?'

'Blackmail,' I said. 'All the set-up for blackmail. Is that all?'

'As much as I had time for. Now, if there's nothing else on your mind, and I hope there isn't, I'll be seeing you never again.'

'You're a real pal, Joe. Thanks a million.'

'Don't do me any more favours, Mike—hear?'

'Yeah, I hear. Thanks again.'

There was too much going on in my head to stay in bed. I crawled under the shower and let it bite into my skin. When I cried off I shaved, brushed my teeth and went out and had breakfast. Fat little Emil scared to death of Rainey. Fat little Emil making regular and large withdrawals from the bank. A good combination. Rainey had to get dough enough to throw in the kitty to build that arena some way.

I looked out the window at the grey sky that still had a lot of snow in it, thinking that it was only the beginning. If what I had in mind worked out there ought to be a lot more to come.

The little .25 was still in the pocket of my jacket and it slapped against my side as I walked out to the elevator. The streets were clear and I told the boy to take off the chains and toss them in the trunk. He made himself another couple of bucks. When I backed out of the garage I drove across to Broadway and turned north pointing for the Bronx.

This time the big sedan with the gold initials was gone. I drove around the block twice just to be sure of it. All the blinds on the upper floor were drawn and there was a look of desertion about the place. I parked on the corner and walked back, turning in at the entrance.

Three times I lifted the heavy bronze knocker, and when that didn't work I gave the door a boot with my foot. A kid on a bicycle saw me and shouted, 'They ain't home, mister. I seen 'em leave last night.'

I came down off the stoop and walked over to the kid. 'Who left?'

'The whole family, I guess. They was packing all kinds of stuff in the car. This morning the maid and the girl that does the cleaning left, too. They gimme a quarter to take some empty bottles back to the store. I kept the deposit, too.'

I fished in my pocket for another quarter and flipped it to him. 'Thanks, son. It pays to keep your eyes open.'

The kid pocketed the coin and took off down the street, the siren on the bike screaming. I walked back up the path to the house. A line of shrubs encircled the building and I worked my way behind them, getting my shoes full of snow and mud. Twice I stopped and had a look around to be sure there weren't any nosy neighbours ready to yell cop. The bushes did a good job. I felt all the windows, trying them to see if they were locked. They were.

I said the hell with it and wrenched a stone out of the mud and tapped the glass a good one. It made a racket, but nobody came around to investigate. When I had all the pieces picked out of the frame I grabbed the sill and hoisted myself into the room.

If sheet-covered chairs and closed doors meant what it looked like, Emil Perry had flown the coop. I tried the lamp and it didn't work. Neither did the phone. The room I was in seemed to be a small study, something where a woman would spend a lot of time. There was a sewing machine in the corner and a loom with a half-finished rug stretched out over nails in the framework.

The room led into a hallway of doors, all closed. I tried each one, peering into the yellow light that came through the blinds. Nothing was out of place, everything had been recently cleaned, and I backed out a little madder each time.

The hallway ran into a foyer that opened to the breezeway beside the house. On one side I could see the kitchen through a small window in the wall. On the other side a heavily carpeted flight of stairs led to the next floor.

It was the same thing all over again. Everything neat as a pin. Two bedrooms, a bathroom, another bedroom and a study. The last door faced the front of the house and it was locked.

It was locked in two places, above and below the knob.

It took me a whole hour to get those damn things open.

No light at all penetrated this room. I flicked a match on my thumbnail and saw why. A blackout shade had been drawn over the other shade on each of the two windows. It didn't hurt to lift them up because nobody could see in through the outermost shade.

I was in Emil Perry's own private cubicle. There were faded pictures on the wall and some juicy calendar pin-ups scattered around on the tables and chairs. A day bed that had seen too many years sagged against one wall. Under one window was a desk and a typewriter, and alongside it a low, two-drawer filing cabinet. I wrenched it open and pawed through the contents. Most of it was business mail. The rest were deeds, insurance papers and some personal junk. I slammed the drawers shut and started taking the place apart slowly.

I didn't find a damn thing.

What I did find was in the tiny fireplace and burned to a crisp. Papers, completely burned papers that fell to dust as I touched them. Whatever they were, he had done a good job of burning them. Not one corner or bit showed that was anything but black.

I swore to myself and went back to the filing cabinet where I slid out an insurance policy on Perry's wife. I used the policy as a pusher to get all the bits into the envelope, then sealed the flap and put the policy back in the drawer.

Before I went out I tried to make sure everything was just like he had left it. When I gave a few things an extra adjustment I closed the door and let the two locks click into place.

I went out the same way I came in, making a rough attempt at wiping out the tracks I had left in the snow and mud behind the bushes. When I climbed in behind the wheel of my car I wasn't feeling too bad. Things were making a little more sense. I turned on the key, let the engine warm up and switched back to Manhattan.

At Fifty-ninth Street I pulled over and went into a drugstore and called the Calway Merchandising Outfit. They gave me Perry's business address and I put in a call to them too. When I asked for Mr Perry the switchboard operator told me to wait a moment and put through a connexion.

A voice said, 'Mr Perry's office.'

'I'd like to speak to Mr Perry, please.'

'I'm sorry,' the voice said, 'Mr Perry has left town. We don't know when he'll be back. Can I help you?'

'Well . . . I don't know. Mr Perry ordered a set of golf clubs and wanted them delivered today. He wasn't at home.'

'Oh . . . I see. His trip was rather sudden and he didn't leave word here where he could be reached. Can you hold the parcel?'

'Yeah, we'll do that,' I lied.

Emil Perry had very definitely departed for parts unknown. I wondered how long he'd be away.

When I got back in my car I didn't stop until I had reached my office building. I had another package waiting for me. If I hadn't gone in through the basement it would have been a surprise package. The elevator operator gave a sudden start when I stepped in the car and looked at me nervously.

I said, 'What's the matter with you?'

He clicked his tongue against the roof of his mouth. 'Maybe I shouldn't tell you this, Mr Hammer, but some policemen went up to your office a little while ago. Real big guys they were. Two of 'em are watching the lobby besides.'

I stepped out of that car fast. 'Anybody in my office now?'

'Uh-huh. That pretty girl who works for you. Is there any trouble, Mr Hammer?'

'Plenty, I think. Look, forget you saw me. I'll make it up to you later.'

'Oh, that's all right, Mr Hammer. Glad to help.'

He closed the door and brought the elevator upstairs. I walked over to the phone on the wall and dropped in a nickel, then dialled my own number. I heard the two clicks as both Velda's phone and the extension were lifted at the same time.

Velda sounded nervous when she said good morning. I held my handkerchief over the mouthpiece and said, 'Mr Hammer, please.'

'I'm sorry, but he hasn't come in yet. Can I take a message?'

I grunted and made like I was thinking, then, 'Yes if you please. He is to meet me at the Cashmore Bar in Brooklyn in an hour from now. I'll be a few minutes late, so if he calls in, remind him.'

'Very well,' Velda replied. Her voice had a snicker in it now, 'I'll tell him.'

I stood there by the phone and let ten minutes go by slowly, then I put in another nickel and did the same thing over again. Velda said, 'You can come up now, Mike. They're gone. Brooklyn is a long way off.'

She had her feet up on the desk, paring her nails with a file, when I walked in. She said, 'Just like you used to do, Mike.'

'I don't wear dresses you can see up, though.'

Her feet came down with a bang and she got red. 'How'd you find out'—her head nodded towards the door—'about them?'

'The elevator operator put me wise. He goes on our bonus list. What did they want?'

'You.'

'What for?'

'They seemed to think you shot somebody.'

'That snivelling little bastard had the nerve to do it!' I threw my hat at the chair and ripped out a string of curses. I swung around, mad as hell. 'Who were they?'

'They let me know they were from the D.A.'s office.' A little worried frown drew lines across her forehead. 'Mike . . . is it bad?'

'It's getting worse. Get me Pat on the phone, will you?'

While she was dialling I went to the closet and got out the other bottle of sherry. Velda handed me the phone as I finished pouring two glasses.

I tried to make my voice bright but there was too much mad in it. I said, 'It's me, Pat. Some of the D.A.'s boys just paid me a visit.'

He sounded amazed. 'What are you doing there, then?'

'I wasn't here to receive them. A dirty dog sent them on a wild-goose chase to Brooklyn. What goes on?'

'You're in deep, Mike. This morning the D.A. sent out orders to pick you up. There was a shooting out on the Island last night. Two guys caught a slug and one of them was a fellow named Rainey.'

'Sounds familiar. Was I identified?'

'No, but you were seen in the vicinity and overheard threatening this Rainey fellow just a short time before.'

'Did Rainey say all this himself?'

'He couldn't very well. Rainey is dead.'

'What!' My voice sounded like an explosion.

'Mike . . .'

My mouth couldn't form an answer.

Pat said it again. 'Mike . . . did you kill him?'

'No,' I got out. 'I'll be in the bar up the street. Meet me there, will you. I have things to talk about.'

'Give me an hour. By the way, where were you last night?'

I paused. 'Home. Home in bed sound asleep.'

'Can you prove it?'

'No.'

'O.K., I'll see you in a little while.'

Velda had drained both glasses while I was talking and was filling them up again. She looked like she needed them.

'Rainey's dead,' I told her. 'I didn't kill him but I wish I had.'

Velda bit her lip. 'I figured as much. The D.A. is tagging you for it, isn't he?'

'Right on the nose. What happened last night?'

She handed me a glass and we lifted them together. Hers went down first. 'I won some money. Clyde got me slightly drunk and propositioned me. I didn't say no ; I said later. He's still interested. I met a lot of people. That's what happened.'

'A waste of time.'

'Not entirely. We joined a party of visiting firemen and some very pretty young ladies. The life of the party was Anton Lipsek and he was quite drunk. He suggested they go up to his apartment in the Village and some of them did. I wanted to go, but Clyde made a poor excuse of not being able to break away from his business. One other couple refused, too, mainly because the boy friend was ahead on the roulette wheel and wanted to go back to it. The girl with him was the same one you had that night.'

'Connie?'

'Is that her name?' she asked coldly.

I grinned and said it was.

Velda rocked back in her seat and sipped the sherry. 'Two of the girls that went along with Anton worked with Connie. I heard them talking shop a few minutes before your girl friend made some catty remarks that brought the conversation to a halt.'

She waited until I had finished my drink. 'Where were *you* last night?'

'Out to see a guy named Rainey.'

Her face went white. 'But . . . but you told Pat . . .'

'I know. I said I didn't kill him. All I did was shoot him in the leg a little bit.'

'Good heavens! Then *you* did . . .'

I rocked my head from side to side until she got the idea. 'He wasn't hurt bad. The killer did me one better and plugged him after I left. That's the way it had to be. I'll find out the details later.' I stuck a cigarette in my mouth and let my eyes find hers while I lit it. 'What time did you meet Clyde last night?'

Her eyes dropped and her lips went into a pout. 'He made me wait until twelve o'clock. He said he was tied up with some work. I got halfway stood up, Mike, and right after you telling me how nice I looked.'

The match burned down to my fingers before I put it out. 'That gave him a chance to get out to Rainey, kill him and get back. That just about does it!' Velda's eyes popped wide-open

91

and she swallowed hard. 'Oh, no, Mike . . . no! I—I was with him right after . . .'

'On Dinky it wouldn't show if he just killed a guy. Not on Dinky. He's got too many of 'em under his belt.'

I picked my hat from the chair where I had tossed it and straightened out the wrinkles in the crown. 'If the police call again stall 'em off. Don't mention Pat. If the D.A. is there call him a dirty name for me. I'll be back later.'

When I stepped out the door I knew I wasn't going to be anywhere later. A big burly character in high-top shoes got up off the top step where he was sitting and said, 'Lucky the boys left a couple of us here after all. They're gonna be mad when they get back from Brooklyn.' Another character just as big came from the other end of the hall and joined in on the other side.

I said, 'Let's see your warrant.'

They showed it to me. The first guy said, 'Let's go, Hammer, and no tricks unless you want a fist in your face.' I shrugged and marched over to the elevator with them.

The operator caught wise right off and shook his head sadly. I could see he was thinking that I should've known better. I squeezed over behind him as some others got on and by the time we hit the lobby I felt a little better. When the operator changed his uniform tonight he was going to be wondering where that .25 automatic came from. Maybe he'd even turn it into the cops like a good citizen. They'd have a swell time running down that toy.

There was a squad car right outside and I got in with a cop on either side of me. Nobody said a word and when I pulled out a pack of butts one of the cops slapped them out of my hands. He had three cigars stuffed in the breast pocket of his overcoat and when I faked a stretch my elbow turned them into mush. I got a dirty look for that. He got a better one back.

The D.A. had his office all ready for me. A uniformed cop stood by the door and the two detectives ushered me to a straight-backed chair and took their places behind it. The D.A. was looking very happy indeed.

'Am I under arrest?'

'It looks that way, doesn't it?'

'Yes or no?' I gave him the best sarcasm I could muster. His teeth grated together.

'You're under arrest,' he said. 'For murder.'

'I want to use the telephone.'

He started smiling again. 'Certainly. Go right ahead. I'll be glad to speak to you through a lawyer. I want to hear him try to tell me you were home in bed last night. When he does I'll drag in the super of your apartment, the doorman and the people who live on both sides of you who have already sworn that they heard nothing going on in your place last night.'

I picked up the phone and asked for outside. I gave the number of the bar where I was supposed to meet Pat and watched the D.A. jot it down on a pad. Flynn, the Irish bartender, answered and I said, 'This is Mike Hammer, Flynn. There's a party there who can vouch for my whereabouts last night. Tell him to come up to the D.A.'s office, will you?'

He was starting to shout the message down the bar when I hung up. The D.A. had his legs crossed and kept rocking one knee up and down. 'I'll be expecting my licence back some time this week. With it I want a note of apology or you might not win the next election.'

One of the cops smacked me across the back of my head.

'What's the story?'

The D.A. couldn't keep still any longer. His lips went thin and he got a lot of pleasure out of his words. 'I'll tell you, Mr Hammer. Correct me if I'm wrong. You were out to the Glenwood Arena last night. You argued with this Rainey. Two men described you and identified you from your picture. Later, they were all in the office when you opened the door and started shooting. One was hit in the leg, Rainey was hit in the leg and head. Is that right?'

'Where's the gun?'

'I give you credit enough to have gotten rid of it.'

'What happens when you put those witnesses on the stand?'

He frowned and grated his teeth again.

'It sounds to me,' I told him, 'that they might make pretty crummy witnesses. They must be sterling characters.'

'They'll do,' he said. 'I'm waiting to hear who it is that can alibi you.'

I didn't have to answer that. Pat walked in the office, his face grey around the mouth, but when his eyes lit on the smirking puss of the D.A. it disappeared. Bright boy gave him an ugly stare. Pat tried for a little respect and didn't make it. I've heard him talk to guys in the line-up the same way he did to the D.A. '*I* was with him last night. If you had let the proper department handle this you would have known it sooner. I went up to his apartment about nine and was there until 4 a.m. playing cards.'

The D.A.'s face was livid. I could see every vein in his hand as he gripped the ends of the desk. 'How'd you get in?'

Pat looked unconcerned. 'Through the back way. We parked around the block and walked through the buildings. Why?'

'What was so interesting at this man's apartment that made you go there?'

Pat said, 'Not that it's any of your business, but we played cards. And talked about you. Mike here said some very un-complimentary things about you. Shall I repeat them for the record?'

Another minute of it and the guy would have had apoplexy. 'Never mind,' he gasped, 'never mind.'

'That's what I mean about having witnesses with sterling characters, mister,' I chipped in. 'I take it the charges are dropped?'

His voice barely had enough strength to carry across the room. 'Get out of here. You, too, Captain Chambers.' He let his eyes linger on Pat. 'I'll see about this later.'

I stood up and fished my other deck of Luckies. The cop with the smashed cigars still sticking out of his pockets watched me with a sneer. 'Got a light?' He almost gave me one at that until I realized what he was doing. I smiled at the D.A., a pretty smile that showed a lot of teeth. 'Remember about my licence. I'll give you until the end of the week.'

The guy flopped back in his chair and stayed there.

I followed Pat downstairs and out to his car. We got in and drove around for ten minutes going nowhere. Finally Pat muttered, 'I don't know how the hell you do it.'

'Do what?'

'Get in so much trouble.' That reminded me of something. I told him to stop and have a drink, and from the way he swung around traffic until we found a bar I could see that he needed it.

I left him at the bar to go back to the phone-booth where I dialled the *Globe* office and asked for the city editor. When Ed came on I said, 'This is Mike, Ed. I have a little favour to ask. Rainey was knocked off last night.'

He broke in with, 'Yeah, I thought you were going to tell me if anything happened. I've been waiting all day for you to call.'

'Forget it, Ed, things aren't what you're thinking. I didn't bump the bastard. I didn't know he was going to get bumped.'

'No?' His tone called me a liar.

'No,' I repeated. 'Now listen . . . what happened to Rainey is nothing. You can do one of two things. You can call the D.A. and say I practically forecasted what was going to happen last night or you can keep quiet and get yourself a scoop when the big boom goes off. What'll it be?'

He laughed, a typical soured reporter's laugh. 'I'll wait, Mike. I can always call the D.A., but I'll wait. By the way, do you know who Rainey's two partners were?'

'Tell me.'

'Petey Cassandro and George Hamilton. In Detroit they have quite a rep, all bad. They've both served stretches and they're as tough as they come.'

'They're not so tough.'

'No . . . you wouldn't think so now, would you? Well, Mike, I'll be waiting to see what gives. It's been a long time since I had a scoop on the police beat.'

Pat wanted to know what I did and I told him I called the office. I straddled the stool and started to work on the high-ball. Pat had his almost finished. He was thinking. He was worried. I slapped him on the back, 'Cheer up, will you? For Pete's sake, all you did was make the D.A. eat his words. That ought to make you feel great.'

Pat didn't see it that way. 'Maybe I'm too much cop, Mike. I don't like to lie. If it wasn't that I smelt a frame I would have let you squirm out of it yourself. The D.A. wants your hide nailed to his door and he's trying hard to get it.'

'He came too damn close to getting it to suit me. I'm glad you got the drift of the situation and knew your way around my diggings well enough to make it sound good.'

'Hell, it *had* to sound good. How the devil would you be able to prove you were home in bed all night? That kind of alibi always looks mighty foolish on a witness stand.'

'I'd never be able to prove it in a million years, chum,' I said.

The drink almost fell out of his hand when it hit him. He grabbed my coat and spun me around on the stool. 'You *were* home in bed like you said, weren't you?'

'Nope. I was out seeing a guy named Rainey. In fact, I shot him.'

Pat's fingers loosened and his face went dead-white. 'God!'

I picked up my glass. 'I shot him, but it wasn't in the head. Somebody else did that. I hate like hell to put you on the spot, but if we're going to tie into a killer the both of us'll do better than just one.'

Pat rubbed his face. It still didn't have its normal colour back. I thought he was going to get sick until he gulped down his drink and signalled for another. His hands shook so bad he could hardly manage it without the ice chattering against the glass.

'You shouldn't have done it, Mike,' he said. 'Now I'll have to take you in myself. You shouldn't've done it.'

'Sure, take me in and have the D.A. eat your tail out. Have him get you booted off the Force so some incompetent jerk can take your place. Take me in so the D.A. can get his publicity at the expense of the people. Let a killer go around laughing his head off at us. That's what he wants.

'Hell, can't you see the whole thing smells? It reeks from here to there and back again.' Pat stared into his glass, his head shaking in outrage. 'I went to see Emil Perry. Rainey was there. Perry tied up with Wheeler because he gave an excuse

95

for Wheeler's suicide when actually he didn't even know the guy except to say hello to at business affairs. Perry ties in with Wheeler and Rainey ties in with Perry.

'Every month Perry had been pulling five grand out of his bank. Smell it now. Smells like blackmail, doesn't it? Go on, admit it. If you won't, here's something that will *make* you admit it. Yesterday Perry withdrew twenty grand and left town. That wasn't travelling expenses. That was to buy up his blackmail evidence. I went out to his house and found what was left of it in his fireplace.'

I reached inside my coat for the envelope and threw it down in front of him. He reached for it absently. 'Now I'll tell you what started the Rainey business. When I first saw Perry I told him I was going to find out what it was that Rainey had on him and lay the whole thing in the open. It scared him so much he passed out. Right away he calls Rainey. He wants to buy it back and Rainey agrees. But meanwhile Rainey has to do something about it. He took a shot at me right on Broadway and if I had caught a slug there wouldn't have been a single witness, that's the way people are.

'When I went out to see him I put it to him straight, and just to impress him I ploughed a hole in his leg. I did the same thing to one of his partners.'

I didn't think Pat had been listening, but he was. He turned his head and looked at me with eyes that had cooled down to a sizzle. 'Then how did Rainey stop that other bullet?'

'Let me finish. Rainey wasn't in this alone by a long shot. He wasn't that smart. He was taking orders and somewhere along the line he tried to take off on his own. The big boy knew what was cooking and went out to take care of Rainey himself. In the meantime he saw me, figured I'd do it for him, and when I didn't he stepped in and took over by himself.'

Pat was picturing the thing in his mind, trying to visualize every vivid detail. 'You've got somebody lined up, Mike. Who?'

'Who else but Clyde? We haven't tied Rainey to him yet, but we will. Rainey isn't hanging out in the Bowery because he likes it. I'll bet ten to one he's on tap for Clyde like a dozen other hard cases he keeps handy.'

Pat nodded. 'Could be. The bullets in Rainey's leg and head were fired from the same gun.'

'The other guy was different. I used his pal's automatic on him.'

'I don't know about that. The bullet went right through and wasn't found.'

'Well, I know about it. I shot him. I shot them both and left the guns right there on the table.'

96

The bartender came down and filled up our glasses again. He shoved a bowl of peanuts between us and I dipped into them. Pat popped them into his mouth one at a time. 'I'll tell you what happened down there, Mike. The one guy who wasn't shot dragged his partner outside and yelled for help. He said nobody came so he left Rainey where he was figuring him to be dead and pulled his buddy into a car and drove to a doctor over in the Glenwood development. He called the cops from there. He described you, picked out your picture and there it was.'

'There it is is right. Right there you have a pay-off again. The killer came in after I left and either threatened those two guys or paid 'em off to put the bee on me and keep still as to what actually did happen. They both have records in Detroit and one carried a gun. It wouldn't do either one of 'em any good to get picked up on a Sullivan charge.'

'The D.A. has their affidavits.'

'You're a better witness for me, kid. What good is an affidavit from a pair of hoods when one of the finest sticks up for you?'

'It would be different under oath, Mike.'

'Nuts! As long as you came in when you did it never gets that far. The D.A. knew when he was licked. In one way I'm glad it happened.'

Pat told me to speak for myself and went back to his thinking. I let him chase ideas around for a while before I asked him what he was going to do. He said, 'I'm going to have those two picked up. I'm going to find out what really happened.'

I looked at him with surprise and laughed. 'Are you kidding, Pat? Do you really think either one of those babies will be sticking around after that?'

'One has a bullet hole in his leg,' he pointed out.

'So what?' I said. 'That's nothing compared to one in the head. Those guys are only so tough . . . they stop being tough when they meet somebody who's just a little bit tougher.'

'Nevertheless, I'm getting out a tracer on them.'

'Good! That's going to help *if* you find them. I doubt it. By the way, did you check on the bullets that somebody aimed at me?'

Pat came alive fast. 'I've been meaning to speak to you about that. They were both .38 specials, but they were fired from different guns. There's more than one person who wants you out of the way.'

Maybe he thought I'd be amazed just to be polite, at least. He was disappointed. 'I figured as much, Pat. It still works down to Rainey and Clyde. Like I said, when I left Perry, he

97

must have called Rainey. It was just before lunch-time and maybe he figured I'd eat at home. Anyway, he went there and when I stopped to pick up my coat and gloves he started tailing me. I wasn't thinking of a tail so I didn't give it a thought. He must have stuck with me all day until I was alone and a good target.'

'That doesn't bring Clyde into it.'

'Get smart, Pat. If Rainey was taking orders from Clyde then maybe Clyde followed *him* around, too, just to be sure he didn't miss.'

'So Clyde took the second shot at you himself. You sure made a nice package of it. All you need is a photograph of the crime.'

'I didn't see enough of his face to be sure it was him, but it was a man in that car, and if he shot at me once he'll shoot at me again. That'll be the last time he'll shoot anyone.'

I finished my drink and pushed it across the bar for more. We both ordered sandwiches and ate our way through them without benefit of conversation. There was another highball to wash them down. I offered Pat a Lucky and we lit up, blowing the smoke at the mirror behind the bar.

I looked at him through the silvered glass. 'Who put the pressure on the D.A., Pat?'

'I've been wondering when you were going to ask that,' he said.

'Well! . . .'

'It came from some odd quarters. People complaining about killers running loose and demanding something be done about it. Some pretty influential people live out in Glenwood. Some were there when the questioning was done.'

'Who?'

'One's on the Board of Transportation, another is head of a political club in Flatbush. One ran for state senator a while back and lost by a hair. Two are big-business men—and I do mean big. They both are active in civic affairs.'

'Clyde has some fancy friends.'

'He can go higher than that if he wants to, Mike. He can go lower where the tougher ones are, too, if it's necessary. I've been poking around since I last saw you. I got interested in old Dinky Williams and began asking questions. There weren't too many answers. He goes high and he goes low. I can't figure it, but he's not a small-timer any more.'

I studied the ice in the glass a minute. 'I think, pal, that I can make him go so low he'll shake hands with the devil. Yeah ; I think it's about time I had a talk with Clyde.'

CHAPTER NINE

I DIDN'T get to do what I wanted to do that night because when I went back for my car I checked into the office long enough to find Velda gone and a note on my desk to call Connie. The note was signed with a dagger dripping blood. Velda was being too damn prophetic.

Dagger or no dagger, I lifted the phone and dialled her number. Her voice didn't have a lilt in it today. 'Oh, Mike,' she said, 'I've been so worried.'

'About me?'

'Who else? Mike . . . what happened last night? I was at the club and I heard talk . . . about Rainey . . . and you.'

'Wait a minute, kitten, who did all this talking?'

'Some men came in from the fights on the Island and they mentioned what happened. They were sitting right behind me talking about it.'

'What time was that?'

'It must have been pretty late. Oh, I don't know, Mike. I was so worried I had Ralph take me home. I . . . I couldn't stand it. Oh, Mike . . . ' Her voice broke and she sobbed into the phone.

I said, 'Stay there. I'll be up in a little while and you can tell me about it.'

'All right, . . . but please hurry.'

I hurried. I passed red lights and full-stop intersections and heard whistles blowing behind me twice, but I got up there in fifteen minutes. The work-it-yourself elevator still wasn't working so I ran up the stairs and rapped on the door.

Connie's eyes were red from crying and she threw herself into my arms and let me squeeze the breath out of her. A lingering perfume in her hair took the cold out of my lungs and replaced it with a more pleasant sensation. 'Lovely, lovely,' I said. I laughed at her for crying and held her at arm's length so I could look at her. She threw her head back and smiled.

'I feel so much better now,' she said. 'I had to see you, Mike. I don't know why I was so worried, but I was and couldn't help it.'

'Maybe that's because I remind you of your brothers.'

'Maybe, but that's not it.' Her lips were soft and red. I kissed them gently and her mouth asked for more.

'Not in the doorway, girl. People will talk.' She reached around behind me and slammed it shut. Then I gave her more. Her body writhed under my hands and I had to push her away to walk into the living-room.

She came in behind me and sat down at my feet. She looked more like a kid who hated to grow up than a woman. She was happy and she rubbed her cheek against my knees. 'I had a lousy time last night, Mike. I wish I could have gone with you.'

'Tell me about it.'

'We drank and danced and gambled. Ralph won over a thousand dollars then he lost it all back. Anton was there and if we had gone with him he wouldn't have lost it.'

'Was Anton alone again?'

'He was while he stayed sober. When he got a load on he began pinching all the girls and one slapped his face. I didn't blame her a bit. She didn't have anything on under the dress. Later he singled out Lillian Corbet—she works through the agency—and began making a pass at her in French. Oh, the things he was saying!'

'Did she slap him too?'

'She would have if she understood French. As it was the dawn began to break and she gave him the heave-ho. Anton thought it was all very funny so he switched back to English and started playing more games with Marion Lester. She didn't have any objections, the old bag.'

I reached down and ran my fingers through her hair. 'So Marion was there too?'

'You should have seen her switching her hips on the dance floor. She got Anton pretty well worked up and he isn't a man to work up easily. A guy about a half a head shorter than she was moved in on Anton and outplayed him by getting him soused even worse. Then he took Marion over and Anton invited everyone up to his place. What a time they must have had.'

'I bet. What did you do then?'

'Oh, some more gambling. I wasn't having much fun. Ralph would rather gamble than dance or drink any day. I sat and talked to the bartender until Ralph lost the money he had won, then we went back to a table and had a couple of champagne cocktails.'

Her head jerked up and that look came back on her face. 'That was when those men came in. They talked about the shooting and about Rainey and you. One said he read about you in the papers not so long ago and how you were just the type to do something like that and they started betting that the cops would have you before morning.'

'Who lost the bet?'

'I don't know. I didn't turn around to look. It was bad enough sitting there hearing them talk about it. I . . . I started to get sick and I guess I cried a little. Ralph thought it was something he did to me and began pawing me to make up for it. I made him take me home. Mike . . . why didn't you call me?'

'I was busy, sugar. I had to explain all that to the cops.'

'You didn't shoot him, did you?'

'Only a little bit. Not enough to kill him. Somebody else did that.'

'Mike!'

I rocked her head and laughed at her. 'You got there early, didn't you?' Connie nodded Yes. 'Did you see Clyde at all during that time?'

'No . . . come to think of it, he didn't show up until after midnight.'

'How'd he look?'

Connie frowned and bit her thumb. Her eyes looked up into mine after a while and she grimaced. 'He seemed . . . strange. Nervous, sort of.'

Yes, he would seem nervous. Killing people leaves you like that sometimes. 'Did anyone else seem interested in the conversation? Like Clyde?'

'I don't think he heard about it. There was just those men.'

'Who else was there, Connie? Anybody that looked important?'

'Quit kidding? Everybody is important. You don't just walk into the Bowery Inn. Either you're pretty important or you're with somebody who is.'

I said, 'I got in and I'm a misfit.'

'Any beautiful model is better than the password,' she grinned.

'Don't tell me they have a password.'

'Clyde used to . . . to the back rooms. A password for each room. It's gotten so you don't need it now. That's what those little rooms are for between the larger rooms. They're sound-proof and they're lined with sheet steel.'

I tightened my fingers in her hair and pulled her head back so I could look into her face. 'You found out a lot in a hurry. The first time you were there was with me.'

'You told me I had brains, too, Mike. Have you forgotten already? While I sat on my fanny at the bar while Ralph gambled, the bartender and I had a very nice discussion. He told me all about the layout including the alarm and escape system. There are doors in the wall that go off with the alarm in case of a raid and the customers can beat it out the back. Isn't that nice of Clyde?'

101

'Very thoughtful.'

'I gave the hassock she was sitting on a push with my foot.
'Gotta go, sugar, gotta go.'

'Ah, Mike, not yet, please.'

'Look, I have things to do much as I'd like to sit here. Some
place in this wild wild city there's a guy with a gun who's going
to use it again. I want to be around when he tries.'

She tossed her hair like an angry cat and said, 'You're mean.
I had something to show you, too.'

'Yeah?'

'Will you stay long enough to see it?'

'I guess I can.'

Connie stood up, kissed me lightly on the cheek and shoved
me back in the chair. 'We're doing a series for a manufacturing
house. Their newest number that they're going to advertise
arrived today and I'm modelling it for a full-page, four-colour
spread in the slick mags. When the job is done I get to keep it.'

She walked out of the room with long-legged strides and into
the bedroom. She fussed around in there long enough for me
to finish a cigarette. I had just squashed it out when she called
out, 'Mike . . . come here.'

I pushed open the door of the bedroom and stood there feeling my skin go hot and cold then hot again. She was wearing a
floor-length nightgown of the sheerest, most transparent white
fabric I had ever seen. It wasn't the way the ad. would be
taken. Then the lights would be in front of her. The one in the
room was behind her and she didn't have anything on under it.

When she turned the fabric floated out in a billowy cloud
and she smiled into my eyes with a look that meant more than
words.

The front of it was wide open.

'Like me, Mike?'

My forefinger moved, telling her to come closer. She floated
across the room and stood in front of me, challenging me with
her body. I said, 'Take it off.'

All she did was shrug her shoulders. The gown dropped to
the floor.

I looked at her, storing up a picture in my mind that I could
never forget. She could have been a statue standing there, a
statue moulded of creamy white flesh that breathed with an
irregular rhythm. A statue with dark, blazing eyes that spoke
of the passion that lay within. A statue that stood in a daring
pose that made you want to reach out to touch and pull so
close the fire would engulf you too.

The statue had a voice that was low and desiring. 'I could
love you so easily, Mike.'

'Don't,' I said.

102

Her lips parted, her tongue wet them. 'Why?'

My voice had a rough edge to it. 'I can't take the time.'

The coals in her eyes jumped into flame that burned me. I grabbed her by the shoulders and pulled her against my chest, bruising her lips against mine. Her tongue was a little spear that flicked out, stabbing me, trying to wound me enough so I wouldn't be able to walk away.

I didn't let it stab me deep enough. I shoved her back, tried to talk and found that my voice wasn't there any more.

So I walked away. I walked away and left her standing there in the doorway, standing on a white cloud stark naked, the imprints of my fingers still etched in red on her shoulders.

'You'll get the person you're after, Mike. Nothing can stop you. Nothing.' Her voice was still husky, but there was a laugh behind it, and a little bit of pride, too. I was closing the door when I heard her whisper, 'I love you, Mike. Really and truly, I do.'

Outside, the snow had started again. There was no wind, so it drifted down lazily sneaking up on the city to catch it by surprise. What few stragglers were left on the street stuck close to the kerb and looked back over their shoulders for taxis.

I got in the car and started the wipers going, watching them kick angrily through the snow that had piled up on the windscreen. At least the snow made all cars look alike. If anybody with a gun was waiting for me he'd have a fine time picking out my heap from the others.

Thinking about it made me mad. One gun was in an exhibit folder at police headquarters and the other was probably hanging in a locker if it hadn't been thrown away. It gave me an empty, uneasy feeling to be travelling without a rod slung under my arm. Sullivan Law? Hell, let me get picked up. It was all right for some harmless citizen to forget there were kill-crazy bastards loose, but one of them was looking for me.

There was a .30-calibre Luger sitting home in the bottom drawer of my dresser with a full clip of shells. It was just about the same size as a .45, too, just the right size to fit in my holster.

A plough was going by in front of my apartment house when I got there, so I figured it would be another hour at least before it would be around again and safe enough to park there.

I took the stairs instead of waiting for the elevator and didn't bother to shuck my coat when I opened the door. I felt for the light switch, batted it up, but no light came on. I cursed the fuse system and groped for a lamp.

What is it that makes you know you're not alone? What vague radiation emanates from the human body just strongly enough to give you one brief, minute premonition of danger that makes you act with animal reflexes? I had my hand around the base of the lamp when I felt it and I couldn't suppress the half-scream, half-snarl, that came out of my throat.

I threw the lamp as hard as I could across the wall, letting the cord rip loose from the socket as it smashed into a thousand pieces against the wall. There were two muffled snorts and a lance of flame bit into the darkness, bracketing me.

I didn't let it happen again. I dove towards the origin of the snorts and crashed into a pair of legs that buckled with a hoarse curse and the next moment a fist was smashing against my jaw driving my head against the floor. Somehow I got out of the way of that fist and slugged out with my forearm trying to drive him off me.

My feet got tangled in the table and kicked it over. The two vases and the bar set splintered all over the room with a hellish racket and somebody in the next apartment shouted to somebody else. I got one arm under me then and grabbed a handful of coat. The guy was strong as a bull and I couldn't hold it. That fist came back and worked on my face some more with a maniacal fury I couldn't beat off. I was tangled in my coat and there were lights in the room now that didn't come from the lamps.

All I knew was that I had to get up . . . had to get my feet under me and heave to get that thing off my back. Had to get up so I could use my hands on any part of him I could grab. I did it without knowing it and heard him ram into a chair and knock it on its side.

My teeth must have been bared to the gums and I screamed when I went in for the kill because I had him cold.

Then my legs got tangled in the lamp cord and I went flat on my face. My head hit something with a sharp crack that was all noise and no pain because there's a point at which pain stops and unconsciousness takes over, and in that second between I knew the killer was deciding between killing me or making a break for it. Doors started to slam and he decided to run and I let my eyes close and drew in the darkness like a blanket around me and slept an unnatural sleep that was full of soft golden hair and billowy white nightgowns I could see through and Connie in a dress she was more out of than in.

The man bending over me had a serious round face with an oval-shaped mouth that worked itself into funny shapes. I began to laugh and the serious face got more serious and the mouth worked more furiously than before. I laughed at that funny little mouth going through all those grotesque distortions for quite a while before I realized he was talking.

He kept asking me my name and what day it was. At last I

had sense enough to stop laughing and tell him my name and what day it was. The face lost its seriousness and smiled a little bit. 'You'll be all right,' it said. 'Had me a bit worried for a minute.' The head turned and spoke to somebody else. 'A slight concussion, that's all.'

The other voice said it was too bad it wasn't a fracture. I recognized the voice. In another minute or two the face came into focus. It was the D.A. He had his hands in his coat pockets trying to look superior like a D.A. should look because there were people around.

I wormed into a sitting position and sent knives darting through my brain. The crowd was leaving now. The little man with the funny mouth, carrying his black bag, the two women with their hair in curlers, the super, the man and woman who seemed to be slightly sick. The others stayed. One had a navy-blue uniform with bright buttons, two wore cigars as part of their disguise. The D.A., of course. Then Pat. My pal. He was there, too, almost out of sight in the only chair still standing on its own legs.

The D.A. held out his palm and let me look at the two smashed pellets he was holding. Bullets. 'They were in the wall, Mr Hammer. I want an explanation. Now.'

One of the cigars helped me on my feet and I could see better. They all had faces with noses now. Before they had been just a blur. I didn't know I was grinning until the D.A. said, 'What's so funny? I don't see anything funny.'

'You wouldn't.'

It was too much for the bright boy. He reached out and grabbed me by the lapels of my coat and pushed his face into mine. Any other time I would have kicked his pants off for that. Right now I couldn't lift my hands.

'What's so funny, Hammer? How'd you like . . .'

I turned my head and spat. 'You got bad breath. Go 'way.'

He half threw me against the wall. I was still grinning. There was white about his nostrils and his mouth was a fine red line of hate. 'Talk!'

'Where's your warrant?' I demanded easily. 'Show me your warrant to come in my house and do that, then I'll talk, you yellow-bellied little bastard. I'm going to meet you in the street not long from now and carve that sissified pasty face of yours into ribbons. I'll be all right in a few minutes and you better be gone by then and your stooges with you. They're not cops. They're like you . . . with the guts of a bug and that's not a lot of guts. Go on, get out, you crummy hophead.'

The two detectives had to stop him from kicking me in the face. His legs, his knees, his whole body shook with coarse tremors. I'd never seen a guy as mad as he was. I hoped it'd be permanent. They took him out of there and with their rush they never noticed that Pat stayed on, still comfortably sunk in the chair.

'I guess that's telling him,' I said. 'A man's home is his castle.'

'You'll never learn,' Pat said sadly.

I fumbled for a butt and pushed it between my lips. The smoke bit into my lungs and didn't want to let go. I got a chair upright and eased into it so my head wouldn't spin. Pat let me finish the butt. He sat back with his hands folded in his lap and waited until I was completely relaxed. 'Will you talk to me, Mike?'

I looked at my hands. The knuckles were skinned all to hell and one nail was torn loose. A piece of fabric was caught in it. 'He was here when I came in. He took two shots at me and missed. We made such a racket he ran for it after I fell. If I hadn't fallen the D.A. would have had me on a murder. I would have killed the son-of-a-bitch. Who called him in?'

'The neighbours called the precinct station,' Pat told me. 'Your name was up and when it was mentioned the desk man called the D.A. He rushed right over.'

I grunted and kneaded my knuckles into my palm. 'Did you see the slugs he had?'

'Uh-huh. I dug 'em out myself.' Pat stood up and stretched 'They were the same as the ones in the windows on Broadway. That's twice you've been missed. They say the third time you aren't so lucky.'

'They'll be matching the bullets from one of those rods.'

'Yeah, I expect they will. According to your theory, if they match the one from the Broadway window, the guy who attacked you was Rainey. If they fit the one from the Thirty-third Street incident it's Clyde.'

I rubbed my jaw, wincing at the lump and the scraped flesh. 'It couldn't be Rainey.'

'We'll see.'

'See hell! What are you waiting for? Let's go down and grab that louse right now!'

Pat smiled sorrowfully. 'Talk sense, Mike. Remember that word *proof*? Where is it? Do you think the D.A. will support your pet theory . . . now? I told you Clyde could pull strings. Even if it was Clyde he didn't leave any traces around. No more traces than the guy who shot Rainey and the other punk at the arena. He wore gloves, too.'

'I guess you're right, kiddo. He could even work himself up a few good alibis if he had to.'

'That's still not the answer,' Pat said. 'If we were working on a murder case unhampered it would be different. On the

106

books Wheeler is still a suicide and we'd be bucking a lot of opposition to make it look different.'

I was looking at my hand where my thumb and forefinger pinched together. I was still holding a tiny piece of fabric. I held it out to him. 'Whoever he was left a hunk of his coat on my fingernail. You're a specialist. Let the sciences of your lab. work that over.'

Pat took it from my fingers and examined it closely. When he finished he pulled an envelope from his pocket and dropped it in. I said, 'He was a strong guy if ever I met one. He had a coat on and I couldn't tell if he was just wiry-strong or muscle-strong, but one thing for sure, he was a powerhouse.

'Remember what you said, Pat . . . about Wheeler having been in a scuffle before he died? I've been thinking about it. Suppose this guy was tailing Wheeler and walked into the room. He figured Wheeler would be in bed, but instead he was up going to the bathroom or something. He figured to kill Wheeler with his hands and let it look like we had a drunken brawl. Because Wheeler was up it changed his plans. Wheeler saw what was going to happen and made a grab for my gun that was hanging on the chair.

'Picture it, Pat. Wheeler with the gun . . . the guy knocks it aside as he fires and the slug hits the bed. Then the guy forces the gun against Wheeler's head and it goes off. A scrap like that would make the same kind of marks on his body, wouldn't it?'

Pat didn't say anything. His head was slanted a little and he was going back again, putting all the pieces in their places. When they set just right he nodded. 'Yes, it would at that.' His eyes narrowed. 'Then the killer picked up one empty shell and dug the slug out of the mattress. A hole as small as it left wouldn't have been noticed anyway. It would have been clean as a whistle if you didn't know how many slugs were left in the rod. It would have been so pretty that even you would have been convinced.'

'Verily,' I said.

'It's smooth, Mike. Lord, but it's smooth. It puts you on the spot because you were the only one looking for a murderer. Everyone else was satisfied with a suicide verdict.' He paused and frowned, staring at the window. 'If only that damn hotel had some system about it . . . even a chambermaid with sense enough to keep on her toes ; but no. The killer walks out in the hall and drops his slug and shell that we find hours later.'

'He was wearing an old suit.'

'What?'

'It must have been old if it had a hole in the pockets.'

Pat looked at me and the frown deepened. His hand fished

107

for his notebook and he pulled out several slips of paper stapled together. He looked through them, glanced up at me, then read the last page again. He put the book back in his pocket very slowly. 'The day before Wheeler died there were only two registered guests,' he said. 'One was a very old man. The other was a comparatively young fellow in a shabby suit who paid in advance. He left the day *after* Wheeler was shot *before* we were looking for anyone in the hotel, and long enough afterwards to dispel any suspicions on the part of the staff.'

The pain in my head disappeared. I felt my shoulders tightening up. 'Did they get a description? Was it . . .'

'No. No description. He was of medium build. He was in town to see a specialist to have some work done on a tooth. Most of his face was covered by a bandage.'

I said another four-letter word.

'It was a good enough reason for his being without baggage. Besides, he had the money to pay in advance.'

'It could have been Clyde,' I breathed. My throat was on fire.

'It could have been almost anybody. If you think Clyde is the one behind all this, let me ask you one thing. Do you honestly think he'd handle the murder end by himself?'

'No,' I said with disgust. 'The bastard would pay to have it done.'

'And the same thing for that deal at the arena.'

I smacked the arm of the chair with my fist. 'Nuts, Pat! That's only what we surmise. Don't forget that Clyde's been in on murder before. Maybe he has a liking for it now. Maybe he's smart enough not to trust anybody else. Let's see how smart he can get. Let's let it hang just a few days longer and see if he'll hang himself.'

'Days are important, Mike.'

I didn't like the look on his face. 'Why?'

'The D.A. didn't believe my story about being with you. He has his men out asking questions. It won't take them very long to get the truth.'

'Oh God!'

'The pressure is on the lad. The kind of pressure he can't ignore. Something's going to pop and it may be your neck and my job.'

'O.K., Pat, O.K.! We'll make it quicker then, but how? What the hell are we going to do? I could take Clyde apart, but he'd have the cops on my neck before I could do anything. I need some time, damn it. I need those few days!'

'I know it, but what can we do?'

'Nothing. Not a damn thing . . . yet.' I lit another butt and glared at him through the smoke. 'You know, Pat, you can sit around for a month in a room with a hornet, waiting for him to sting you. But if you go poke at his nest it'll only be a second before you're bit.'

'They say if you get bitten often enough it'll kill you.'

I stood up and tugged my coat on. 'You might at that. What are your plans for the rest of the evening?'

Pat waited for me by the door while I hunted up my hat. 'Since you've gotten my schedule all screwed up I have to clean up some work at the office. Besides, I want to find out if Rainey's two pals have been found yet. You know, you called it pretty good. They both disappeared so fast it would make your head swim.'

'What did they do about the arena?'

'They sold out . . . to a man who signed the contracts and deeds as Robert Hobart Williams.'

'Dinky . . . Clyde! I'll be damned.'

'Yeah, me too. He bought it for a song. Ed Cooper ran it in the sports column of the *Globe* tonight with all the nasty implications.'

'I'll be damned,' I said again. 'It tied Rainey in very nicely with Clyde, didn't it?'

Pat shrugged. 'Who can prove it? Rainey's dead and the partners are missing. That isn't the only arena Clyde owns. It now appears that he's a man quite interested in sporting establishments.'

We started out the door and I almost forgot what I came for. Pat waited in the hall while I went back to the bedroom and pulled out the dresser drawer. The Luger was still there, wrapped in an oily rag inside a box. I checked the clip, jacked a shell into the chamber and put it in half-cock.

When I slid it into the holster it fitted loosely, but nice. I felt a lot better.

The snow, the damned snow. It slowed me to a crawl and did all but stop me. It still came down in lazy fashion, but so thick you couldn't see fifty feet through it. Traffic was thick, sluggish, and people were abandoning their cars in the road for the subway. I circled around them, following the cab in front of me and finally hit a section that had been cleared only minutes before.

That stretch kept me from missing Velda. She had her coat and hat on and was locking the door when I stepped out of the elevator. I didn't have to tell her to open up again.

When she threw her coat on top of mine I looked at her and got mad again. She was more lovely than the last time. I said, 'Where you going?'

She pulled a bottle out of a cabinet and poured me a stiff drink. It tasted great. 'Clyde called me. He wanted to know if this was "later" '

'Yeah?'

'I told him it might be.'

'Where does the seduction take place?'

'At his apartment.'

'You really have that guy going, don't you? How come he's passing up all the stuff at the Inn for you?'

Velda looked at me quickly, then away. I reached for the bottle. 'You asked me to do this, you know,' she said.

I felt like a heel. All she had to do was look at me when I got that way and I felt like I was crawling up out of a sewer somewhere. 'I'm sorry, kid. I'm jealous, I guess. I always figured you as some sort of a fixture. Now that the finance company is taking it away from me I get snotty.'

Her smile lit the whole room up. She came over and filled my glass again. 'Get that way more often, Mike.'

'I'm always that way. Now tell me what you've been doing to the guy.'

'I play easy to get but not easy to get at. There are times when sophistication coupled with virtue pays off. Clyde is getting that look in his eyes. He's hinting at a man-and-mistress arrangement with the unspoken plan in mind of a marriage licence if I don't go for it.'

I put the glass down. 'You can cut out the act, Velda. I'm almost ready to move in on Clyde myself.'

'I thought I was the boss,' she grinned.

'You are . . . of the agency. Outside the office I'm the boss.' I grabbed her arm and swung her around to face me. She was damned near as tall as I was and being that close to her did things to me inside that I didn't have time for. 'It took me a long time to wise up, didn't it?'

'Too long, Mike.'

'Do you know what I'm talking about, Velda? I'm not tossing a pass at you now or laying the groundwork for the same thing later. I'm telling you something else.'

My fingers were hurting her and I couldn't help it. 'I want you to say it, Mike. You've played games with so many women I won't be sure until I hear you say it yourself. Tell me.'

There was a desperate pleading in her eyes. They were asking me please, please. I could feel her breath coming faster and knew she was trembling and not because I was hurting her. I knew something was coming over my face that I couldn't control. It started in my chest and overflowed in my face when the music in my head began with that steady beat of drums and weird discord. My mouth worked to get the words out, but they stuck fast to the roof of my mouth.

I shook my head to break up the crazy symphony going on in my brain and I mumbled, 'No . . . no. Oh, good God, I can't, Velda. I can't.'

I knew what the feeling was. I was scared. Scared to death and it showed in my face and the way I stumbled across the room to a chair and sat down. Velda knelt on the floor in front of me, her face a fuzzy white blur that kissed me again and again. I could feel her hands in my hair and smell the pleasant woman smell of cleanliness, of beauty that was part of her ; but the music wouldn't go away.

She asked me what had happened and I told her. It wasn't that. It was something else. She wanted to know what it was, demanded to know what it was and her voice came through a sob and tears. She gave me back my voice and I said, 'Not you, kid . . . no kiss of death for you. There've been two women now. I said I loved them both. I thought I did. They both died—but not you, kid.'

Her hands on mine were soft and gentle, 'Mike . . . nothing will happen to me.'

My mind went back over the years—to Charlotte and Lola.

'It's no good, Velda. Maybe when this is all over it'll be different. I keep thinking of the women who died. God, if I ever have to hold a gun on a woman again I'll die first, so help me I will. How many years has it been since the yellow-gold hair and the beautiful face was there? It's still there and I know it's dead, but I keep hearing the voice. And I keep thinking of the dark hair too . . . like a shroud. Gold shrouds, dark shrouds. . . .'

'Mike . . . don't. Please, for me. Don't . . . no more.'

She had another drink in my hand and I poured it down, heard the wild fury of the music drown out and give me back to myself again. I said, 'All over now, sugar. Thanks.' She was smiling, but her face was wet with tears. I kissed her eyes and the top of her head. 'When this is settled we'll take a vacation, that's what we'll do. We'll take all the cash out of the bank and see what the city looks like when there's not murder in it.'

She left me sitting there smoking a cigarette while she went into the bathroom and washed her face. I sat there and didn't think of anything at all, trying to put a cap over the raw edges of my nerves that had been scraped and pounded too often.

Velda came back, a vision in a tailored grey suit that accentuated every curve. She was so big, so damn big and so lovely. She had the prettiest legs in the world and there wasn't a thing about her that wasn't beautiful and desirable. I could see why

Clyde wanted her. Who wouldn't? I was a sap for waiting as long as I had.

She took the cigarette from my mouth and put it in her own. 'I'm going to see Clyde tonight, Mike. I've been wondering about several things and I want to see if I can find out what they are.'

'What things?' There wasn't much interest in my words.

She took a drag on the cigarette and handed it back. 'Things like what it is he holds over people's heads. Things like blackmail. Things like how Clyde can influence people so powerful they can make or break judges, mayors or even governors. What kind of blackmail can that be?'

'Keep talking, Velda.'

'He had conferences with these big people. They call him up at odd hours. They're never asking . . . they're always giving. To Clyde. He takes it like it's his due. I want to know those things.'

'Will they be found in Clyde's apartment, baby?'

'No. Clyde has them . . . ' she tapped her forehead, 'here. He isn't smart enough to keep them there.'

'Be careful, Velda, be damn careful with that guy. He might not be the pushover you think he is. He's got connexions and he keeps his nose too damn clean to be a pushover. Watch yourself.'

She smiled at me and pulled on her gloves. 'I'll watch myself. If he goes too far I'll take a note from that Anton Lipsek's book and call him something in French.'

'You can't speak French.'

'Neither can Clyde. That's what makes him so mad. Anton calls him things in French and laughs about it. Clyde gets red in the face, but that's all.'

I didn't get it and I told her so. 'Clyde isn't one to take any junk from a guy like Anton. It's a wonder he doesn't stick one of his boys on 'im.'

'He doesn't, though. He takes it and gets mad. Maybe Anton has something on him.'

'I can picture that,' I said. 'Still, those things happen.'

She pulled on her coat and looked at herself in the mirror. It wasn't necessary ; you can't improve on perfection. I knew what it was like to be jealous again and tore my eyes away. When she was satisfied with herself she bent over and kissed me. 'Why don't you stay here tonight, Mike?'

'Now you ask me.'

She laughed, a rich, throaty laugh and kissed me again. 'I'll shoo you out when I get in. I may be late, but my virtue will still be intact.'

'It had damn well better be.'

'Good night, Mike.'

' 'Night, Velda.'

She smiled again and closed the door behind her. I heard the elevator door open and shut and if I had had Clyde in my hands I would have squeezed him until his insides ran all over the floor. Even my cigarette tasted lousy. I picked up the phone and called Connie. She wasn't home. I tried Juno and was ready to hang up when she answered.

I said, 'This is Mike, Juno. It's late, but I was wondering if you were busy.'

'No, Mike, not at all. Won't you come up?'

'I'd like to.'

'And I'd like you to. Hurry, Mike.'

Hurry? When she talked like that I could fly across town.

There was an odd familiarity about Juno's place. It bothered me until I realized that it was familiar because I had been thinking about it. I had been there a dozen times before in my mind, but none of the eagerness was gone as I pushed the bell. Excitement came even with the thought of her, a tingling thrill that spoke of greater pleasures yet to come.

The door clicked and I pushed it open to walk into the lobby. She met me at the door of Olympus, a smiling, beautiful goddess in a long, hostess coat of some iridescent material that changed colour with every motion of her body.

'I always come back, don't I, Juno?'

Her eyes melted into the same radiant colour as the coat. 'I've been waiting for you.'

It was only the radio playing, but it might have been a chorus of angels singing to form a background of splendour. Juno had prepared Olympus for me, arranging it so a mortal might be tempted into leaving Earth. The only lights were those of the long waxy tapers that flickered in a dancing yellow light, throwing wavy shadows on the wall. The table had been drawn up in the living-room and set with delicate china, arranged so that we would be seated close enough to want to be closer, too close to talk or eat without feeling things catch in your throat.

We spoke of the little things, forgetting all the unpleasantness of the past few days. We spoke of things and thought of things we didn't speak of, knowing it was there whenever we were ready. We ate, but the taste of the food was lost to me when I'd look at her in that sweeping gown that laughed and danced in the rising and falling of the lights. The cuffs of her sleeves were huge things that rose halfway to her elbows, leaving only her hands visible. Beautiful, large hands that were eloquent in movement.

There was a cocktail instead of coffee, a toast to the night ahead, then she rose, and with her arm in mine, the short wisps of her hair brushing my face, took me into the library.

Cigarettes were there, the bar set was pulled out and ice frosted a crystal bowl. I put my crumpled pack of Luckies alongside the silver cigarette-box to remind me that I was still a mortal, took one and lit it from the lighter she held out to me.

'Like it, Mike?'

'Wonderful.'

'It was special, you know. I've been home every minute since I saw you last, waiting for you to come back.'

She sat next to me on the couch and leaned back, her head resting on the cushion. Her eyes were beginning to invite me now. 'I've been busy, goddess. Things have been happening.'

'Things?'

'Business.'

One of her fingers touched the bruise on the side of my jaw. 'How'd you get that, Mike?'

'Business.'

She started to laugh, then saw the seriousness in my face. 'But how . . .'

'It makes nasty conversation, Juno. Some other time I'll tell you about it.'

'All right, Mike.' She put her cigarette down on the table and grabbed my hand. 'Dance with me, Mike?' She made my name sound like it was something special.

Her body was warm and supple, the music alive with rhythm, and together we threw a whirling pattern of shadows that swayed and swung with every subtle note. She stood back from me, just far enough so we could look at each other and read things into every expression. I could only stand it so long and I tried to pull her closer, but she laughed a little song and twisted in a graceful pirouette that sent the gown out and up around her legs.

The music stopped then, ending on a low note that was the cue to a slow waltz. Juno floated back into my arms and I shook my head. It had been enough . . . too much. The suggestion she had put into the dance left me shaking from head to foot, a sensation born of something entirely new, something I had never felt. Not the primitive animal reflex I was used to, not the passion that made you want to squeeze or bite or demand what you want and get it even if you have to fight for it. It made me mad because I didn't know what it was and I didn't like it, this custom of the gods.

So I shook my head again, harder this time. I grabbed her

by the arm and heard her laugh again because she knew what was going on inside me and wanted it that way.

'Quit it, Juno. Damn it, quit fooling around. You make me think I want you and I lose sight of everything else. Cut it out.'

'No.' She drew the word out. Her eyes were half closed. 'It's me that wants *you*, Mike. I'll do what I can to get you. I won't stop. There's never been anyone else like you.'

'Later.'

'Now.'

It might have been now, but the light caught her hair again. Yellow candlelight that changed its colour to the gold I hated. I didn't wait to have it happen to me. I shoved her on the couch and reached for the decanter in the bar set. She lay there languidly, waiting for me to come to her and I fought it and fought it until my mind was my own again and I could laugh a little bit myself.

She saw it happen and smiled gently. 'You're even better than I thought,' she said. 'You're a man with the instincts of some jungle animal. It has to be when *you* say so, doesn't it?'

I threw the drink down fast. 'Not before,' I told her.

'I like that about you, too, Mike.'

'So do I. It keeps me out of trouble.' When I filled the glass I balanced it in my hand and sat on the arm of the couch facing her. 'Do you know much about me, Juno?'

'A little. I've been hearing things.' She picked one of her long cigarettes out of the box and lit it. Smoke streamed up lazily from her mouth. 'Why?'

'I'll tell you why I'm like I am. I'm a detective. In spirit only, now, but I used to have a ticket and a gun. They took it away because I was with Chester Wheeler when he used my gun to commit suicide. That was wrong, because Chester Wheeler was murdered. A guy named Rainey was murdered too. Two killings and a lot of scared people. The one you know as Clyde is a former punk named Dinky Williams and he's gotten to be so big nobody can lay a finger on him, so big he can dictate to the dictators.

'That isn't the end of it, either. Somebody wants me out of the way so badly they made a try on the street and again in my apartment. In between they tried to lay Rainey's killing at my feet so I'd get picked up for it. All that . . . because one guy named Chester Wheeler was found dead in a hotel room. Pretty, isn't it?'

It was too much for her to understand at once. She bit her thumbnail and a frown crept across her face. 'Mike . . .'

'I know it's complicated,' I said. 'Murder generally *is* complicated. It's so damn complicated that I'm the only one

115

looking for a murderer. All the others are content to let it rest as suicide . . . except Rainey, of course. That job was a dilly.'

'That's awful, Mike! I never realized . . .'

'It isn't over yet. I have a couple of ideas sticking pins in my brain right now. Some of the pieces are trying to fit together, trying hard. I've been up too long and been through too much to think straight. I thought that I might relax if I came up here to see you.' I grinned at her. 'You weren't any help at all. You'll probably even spoil my dreams.'

'I hope I do,' she said impishly.

'I'm going some place and sleep it off,' I said. 'I'm going to let the clock go all the way around, then maybe once more before I stir out of my sack. Then I'm going to put all the pieces together and find me a killer. The bastard is strong . . . strong enough to twist a gun around in Wheeler's hand and make him blow his brains out. He's strong enough to take me on in my own joint and nearly finish it for me. The next time will be different. I'll be ready and I'll choke the son-of-a-bitch to death.'

'Will you come back when it's over, Mike?'

I put on my hat and looked down at her. She looked so damn desirable and agreeable I wanted to stay. I said, 'I'll be back, Juno. You can dance for me again . . . all by yourself. I'll sit down and watch you dance and you can show me how you have fun on Olympus. I'm getting a little tired of being a mortal.'

'I'll dance for you, Mike. I'll show you things you never saw before. You'll like Olympus. It's different up there and there's nothing like it on this earth. We'll have a mountain-top all to ourselves and I'll make you want to stay there for ever.'

'It'd take a good woman to make me stay anywhere very long.'

Her tongue flicked out and left her lips glistening wetly, reflecting the desire in her eyes. Her body seemed to move, squirm, so the sheen of the house-coat threw back the lithe contours of her body, vivid in detail. '*I* could,' she said.

She was asking me now. Demanding that I come to her for even a moment and rip that damn robe right off her back and see what it was that went to make up the flesh of a goddess. For one second my face must have changed and she thought I was going to do it, because her eyes went wide and I saw her shoulders twitch and this time there was woman-fear behind the desire and she was a mortal for an instant, a female crouching away from the male. But that wasn't what made me stop. My face went the way it did because there was something else

116

again I couldn't understand and it snaked up my back and my hands started to jerk unconsciously with it.

I picked up my butts and winked good night. The look she sent me made my spine crawl again. I walked out and found my car half buried in a drift and drove back the street of lights where I parked and checked into a hotel for a long winter's nap.

CHAPTER TEN

I SLEPT the sleep of the dead, but the dead weren't disturbed by dreams of the living. I slept and I talked, hearing my own voice in the stillness. The voice asked questions, demanded answers that couldn't be given and turned into a spasm of rage. Faces came to me, drifting by in a ghostly procession, laughing with all the fury the dead could command, bringing with their laughter that weird, crazy music that beat and beat and beat, trying to drive my senses to the farthermost part of my brain from which they could never return. My voice shouted for it to stop and was drowned in the sea of laughter. Always those faces. Always that one face with the golden hair, hair so intensely brilliant it was almost white. The voice I tried to scream with was only a hoarse, muted whisper saying, 'Charlotte, Charlotte . . . I'll kill you again if I have to! I'll kill you again, Charlotte!' And the music increased in tempo and volume, pounding and beating and vibrating with such insistence that I began to fall before it. The face with the golden hair laughed anew and urged the music on. Then there was another face, one with hair a raven-black, darker than the darkness of the pit. A face with clean beauty and a strength to face even the dead. It challenged the golden hair and the music, commanding it to stop, to disappear for ever. And it did. I heard my voice again saying over and over, 'Velda, thank God! Velda, Velda, Velda.'

I awoke and the room was still. My watch had stopped and no light filtered in under the shade. When I looked out the sky was black, pinpointed with the lights of the stars that reflected themselves from the snow-covered street below.

I picked up the phone and the desk answered. I said, 'This is Hammer in 541. What time is it?'

The clerk paused, then answered, 'Five minutes to nine, sir.'

I said thanks and hung up. The clock had come mighty close to going around twice at that. It didn't take me more than ten minutes to get dressed and checked out. In the restaurant that adjoined the hotel I ate like I was famished, took time for a slow smoke and called Velda. My hand trembled while I waited for her to answer.

I said, 'Hello, honey, it's Mike.'

'Oh . . . Mike, where have you been? I've been frantic!'

'You can relax, girl. I've been asleep. I checked into a hotel

118

and told them not to disturb me until I woke up. What happened with you and Clyde? Did you learn anything?'

She choked back a sob and my hand tightened around the receiver. Clyde was dying right then. 'Mike . . .'

'Go on, Velda.' I didn't want to hear it but I had to.

'He almost . . . did.'

I let the phone go and breathed easier. Clyde had a few minutes left to live. 'Tell me,' I said.

'He wants me in the worst way, Mike. I—I played a game with him and I was almost sorry for it. If I hadn't gotten him too drunk . . . he would have . . . but I made him wait. He got drunk and he told me . . . bragged to me about his position in life. He said he could run the city and he meant it. He said things that were meant to impress me and I acted impressed. Mike . . . he's blackmailing some of the biggest men in town. It's all got to do with the Bowery Inn.'

'Do you know what it is?'

'Not yet, Mike. He thinks . . . I'm the perfect partner for him. He said he'd tell me all about it if . . . if I . . . oh, Mike, what shall I do? What shall I do? I hate that man . . . and I don't know what to do!'

'The lousy bastard!'

'Mike . . . he gave me a key to his apartment. I'm going up there tonight. He's going to tell me about it then . . . and make arrangements to take me in with him. He wants me, Mike.'

A rat might have been gnawing at my intestines. 'Shut up! Damn it, you aren't going to do anything!'

I heard her sob again and I wanted to rip the phone right off the wall. I could barely hear her with the pounding of the blood in my head. 'I have to go, Mike. We'll know for sure then.'

'No!'

'Mike . . . please don't try to stop me. It isn't nearly as . . . serious as what you've done. I'm not getting shot at . . . I'm not giving my life. I'm trying to give what I can, just like you . . . because it's important. I'm going to his apartment at midnight and then we'll know, Mike. It won't take long after that.'

She didn't hear me shout into the phone because she had hung up. There was no stopping her. She knew I might try to, and would be gone before I could reach her.

Midnight. Three hours. That's all the time I had.

It wasn't so funny any more.

I felt in my pocket for another nickel and dialled Pat's number. He wasn't home so I tried the office and got him. I told him it was me without giving my name and he cut me off with a curt hello and said he'd be in the usual bar in ten minutes if I wanted to see him. The receiver clicked in my ear as he hung up. I stood there and looked at the phone stupidly.

The usual bar was a little place downtown where I had met him several times in the past and I went there now. I double-parked and slid out in front of the place to look in the windows, then I heard, 'Mike . . . Mike!'

I turned around and Pat was waving me into my car and I ran back and got in under the wheel. 'What the hell's going on with you, Pat?'

'Keep quiet and get away from here. I think there's been an ear on my phone and I may have been followed.'

'The D.A.'s boys?'

'Yeah, and they're within their rights. I stopped being a cop when I lied for you. I deserve any kind of an investigation they want to give me.'

'But why all the secrecy?'

Pat looked at me quickly, then away. 'You're wanted for murder. There's a warrant out for your arrest. The D.A. has found himself another witness to replace the couple he lost.'

'Who?'

'A local character from Glenwood. He picked you out of the picture file and definitely established that you were there that night. He sells tickets at the arena as a sideline.'

'Which puts you in a rosy red light,' I said.

Pat muttered, 'Yeah. I must look great.'

We drove on around the block and on to Broadway. 'Where to?' I asked.

'Over to the Brooklyn Bridge. A girl pulled the Dutch act and I have to check it myself. Orders from the D.A. through higher headquarters. He's trying to make my life miserable by pulling me out on everything that has a morgue tag attached to it. The crumb hopes I slip up somewhere and when I do I've had it. Maybe I've had it already. He's checked my movements the night I was supposed to have been with you and is getting ready to pull out the stops.'

'Maybe we'll be cellmates,' I said.

'Ah, pipe down.'

'Or you can work in my grocery store . . . while I'm serving time, that is.'

He said, 'Shut up. What've you got to be cheerful about?'

My teeth were clamped together, but I could still grin. 'Plenty, kid. I got plenty to be cheerful about. Soon a killer will be killed. I can feel it coming.'

Pat sat there staring straight ahead. He sat that way until we reached the cutoff under the bridge and pulled over to the kerb. There was a squad car and an ambulance at the wharf side and another squad car pulling up when Pat got out. He told me to sit in the car and stay there until he got out. I promised him I'd be a good boy and watched him cross the street.

He took too long. I began to fidget with the wheel and chain-smoked through my pack of butts. When I was on the last one I got out myself and headed towards the saloon on the corner. It was a hell of a dive, typically waterfront and reeking with all the assorted odours you could think of. I put a quarter in the cigarette machine, grabbed my fresh deck and ordered a beer at the bar. Two guys came in and started talking about the suicide across the street.

One was on the subject of her legs and the other took it up. Then they started on the other parts of her anatomy until the bartender said, 'Jeez, cut it out, will ya! Like a couple of ghouls ya sound. Can the crap.'

The guy who liked the legs fought for his rights supported by the other one and the bartender threw them both out and put their change in his pockets. He turned to me and said, 'Ever see anythin' like that? Jeez, the dame's dead, what do they want of her now? What ghouls!'

I nodded agreement and finished my beer. Every two minutes I'd check my watch and find it two minutes later and start cursing a slimy little bastard named Clyde.

Then the beer would taste flat.

I took it as long as I could and got the hell out of the saloon and crossed the street to see what was taking Pat so long. There was a handful of people grouped around the body and the ambulance was gone. The car from the morgue had taken its place. Pat was bending over the body looking for identification without any success and had the light flashed on her face.

He handed one of the cops a note he fished out of her pocket and the cop scowled. He read, 'He left me.' He scowled some more and Pat looked up at him. 'That's all, Captain. No signature, no name. That's all it says.'

Pat scowled too and I looked at her face again.

The boys from the morgue wagon moved in and hoisted the body into a basket. Pat told them to put it in the unidentified file until they found out who she was.

I had a last look at her face.

When the wagon pulled away the crowd started to break up and I wandered off into the shadows that lined the street. The face, the face. Pale white to the point of transparency, eyes closed and lips slightly parted. I stood leaning up against a plank wall staring at the night, hearing the cars and the trolley rattle across the bridge, hearing the cacophony of noises that go to make up the voice of the city.

I kept thinking of that face.

121

A taxi screamed past and slid to a stop at the corner. I backed up and a short fat figure, speaking in guttural English, shoved some bills in the driver's hand and ran to the squad cars. He spoke to the cop, his arms gesticulating wildly; the cop took him to Pat and he went through the same thing again.

The crowd that had turned away turned back again and I went with them, hanging on the outside, yet close enough so I could hear the little fat man. Pat stopped him, made him start over, telling him to calm down first.

The fat man nodded and took the cigarette that was offered him, but didn't put it in his mouth. 'The boat captain I am, you see?' he said. 'The barges I am captain of. We go by two hours ago under the bridge and it is so quiet and peaceful then I sit on the deckhouse and watch the sky. Always I look up at the bridge when I go by. With my night-glasses I look up to see the automobiles and marvel at such things as we have in this country.

'I see her then, you understand? She is standing there fighting and I hear her scream even. She fights this man who holds his hand over her mouth and she can't scream. I see all this, you understand, yet I am not able to move or do a thing. On the barge we have nothing but the megaphone to call with. It happens so fast. He lifts her up and over she goes into the river. First I thought she hit the last barge on the string and I run and shout quickly, but it is not so. I must wait so long until I can get somebody to take me off the barge, then I call the police.

'The policeman, he told me here to come. You were here. The girl has already been found. That is what I have come to tell you. Understand?'

Pat said, 'I understand all right. You saw this man she fought?'

The guy bobbed his head vigorously.

'Could you identify him?'

Everyone's eyes were on the little guy. He lifted his hands out and shrugged. 'I could tell him from someone else . . . no. He had on a hat, a coat. He lifted the girl up and over she goes. No, I do not see his face for I am too excited. Even through the night-glasses I could not see all that so well.'

Pat turned to the cop next to him. 'Take his name and address. We'll need a statement on it.'

The cop whipped out a pad and began taking it down. Pat prompted him with questions until the whole thing was straight then dismissed the batch of them and started asking around for other witnesses. The motley group hanging around watching didn't feel like having any personal dealings with the police department for any reason at all and broke up in a hurry. Pat got that grim look, muttered something nasty and started across the street to where I was supposed to be.

I angled over and met him. 'Nice corpse,' I said.

'I thought I told you to stay in the car. Those cops have you on their list.'

'So what? I'm on a lot of lists these days. What about the girl?'

'Unidentified. Probably a lovers' quarrel. She had a couple of broken ribs and a broken neck. She was dead before she hit the water.'

'And the note . . . did the lover stuff that in her pocket before he threw her overboard?'

'You have big ears. Yes, that's what it looks like. They probably argued previously, he invited her for a walk, then gave it to her.'

'Strong guy to mess her up like that, no?'

Pat nodded. I opened the door and he got in, sliding over so I could get behind the wheel. 'He had to be to break her ribs.'

'Very strong,' I mused. 'I'm not a weak sister myself and I know what it's like to come up against one of those strong bastards.' I sat there and watched him.

A look of incredulity came over his face. 'Now wait a minute. We're on two different subjects, feller. Don't try to tell me that he was the same . . .'

'Know who she was, Pat?'

'I told you she was unidentified at present. She had no handbag, but we'll trace her from her clothes.'

'That takes time.'

'Know a better way?'

'Yeah,' I said. 'As a matter of fact I do.' I reached behind the seat and dragged out an envelope. It was crammed with pictures and I dumped them into my lap. Pat reached up and turned on the overhead light. I shuffled through them and brought out the one I was looking for.

Pat looked a little sick. He glanced at me then back to the picture. 'Her name is Jean Trotter, Pat. She's a model at Anton Lipsek's agency. Several days ago she eloped.'

I thought he'd never stop swearing. He fanned out the pictures in his hand and squinted at them with eyes that blazed not as the fires of hell. 'Pictures! Pictures! Goddamn it, Mike, what are we up against? Do you know what that burned stuff was that you found in Emil Perry's house?'

I shook my head.

'Pictures!' he exploded. 'A whole mess of burned photographs that didn't show a thing!'

The steering-wheel started to bend under my fingers. I

jammed my foot on the starter and roared away from the kerb. Pat looked at the picture again in the light of the dash. His breath was coming fast. 'We can make it official now. I'll get the whole department on it if I have to. Give me a week and we'll have that guy ready to face a murder trial.'

I glowered back at him. 'Week, hell!—all we have is a couple of hours. Did you trace that piece of fabric I gave you?'

'Sure, we traced it all right. We found the store it came from . . . over a year ago. It was from a damn good suit the owner remembered selling, but the guy had no recollection for faces. It was a cash transaction and he didn't have a record of the size or any names and addresses. Our killer is one smart Joe.'

'He'll trip up. They all do.'

I cut in and out of the traffic, my foot heavy on the accelerator. On the main drag I was lucky enough to make the lights and didn't have to stop until I was in front of the Municipal Building. I said, 'Pat, use your badge and check the marriage bureau for Jean Trotter's certificate. Find out who she eloped with and where she was married. Since I can't show my nose you'll have to do this on your own.'

He started out of the car and I handed him the photograph. 'Take this along in case you have to brighten up a memory or two.'

'Where'll you be?'

I looked at my watch. 'First I'm going to see what I can get on the girl myself. Then I'm going to stop a seduction scene before it starts.'

Pat was still trying to figure that one out when I drove off. I looked in the rear-vision mirror and saw him pocket the photograph and walk away up the street.

I stopped at the first drugstore I came to and had a quarter changed into nickels, then pushed a guy out of the way who was getting into the booth. He was going to argue about it until he saw my face then he changed his mind and went looking for another phone. I dropped the coin in and dialled Juno's number. I was over-anxious and got the wrong number. The second time I hit it right, but I didn't get to speak to Juno. Her phone was connected to one of those service outfits that take messages and a girl told me that Miss Reeves was out, but expected home shortly. I said no. I didn't want to leave a message and hung up.

I threw in another nickel and spun the dial. Connie was home. She would be glad to see me no matter what the hour was. My voice had a rasp to it and she said, 'Anything wrong, Mike?'

'Plenty. I'll tell you about it when I get there.'

I set some sort of a record getting to her place, leaving behind me a stream of swearing-mad cab drivers who had tried to hog the road and got bumped over to the side for their pains.

A guy had his key in the downstairs door so I didn't have to ring the bell to get in. I didn't have to ring the upstairs bell either, because the door was open and when Connie heard me in the hall she shouted for me to come right in.

I threw my hat on the chair, standing in the dull light of the hall a moment to see where I was. Only a little night light was on, but a long finger of bright light streamed from the bedroom door out across the living-room. I picked my way round the furniture and called, 'Connie?'

'In here, Mike.'

She was in bed with a couple of pillows behind her back reading a book. 'Kind of early for this sort of thing, isn't it?'

'Maybe, but I'm *not* going out?' She grinned and wiggled under the cover. 'Come over here and sit down. You can tell me all your troubles.' She patted the edge of the bed.

I sat down and she put her fingers under mine. I didn't have to tell her something bad had happened. She could read it in my eyes. Her smile disappeared into a frown. 'What is it, Mike?'

'Jean Trotter . . . she was murdered tonight. She was killed and thrown off the bridge. It was supposed to look like suicide, but it was seen.'

'No!'

'Yes.'

'God, when is this going to stop, Mike? Poor Jean! . . .'

'It'll stop when we have the killer and not before. What do you know about her, Connie? What was she like . . . who was this guy she married?'

Connie shook her head, her hair falling loosely around her shoulders. 'Jean . . . she was a sweet kid when I first met her. I—I don't know too much about her, really. She was older than the teen-age group, of course ; but she modelled clothes for them. We . . . never did the same type of work, so I don't know about that.'

'Men . . . what men did she go with? Ever see them?'

'No, I didn't. When she first came to work I heard that she was engaged to a West Point cadet, then something happened. She was pretty broken up for a while. Juno made her take a vacation and when she came back she seemed to be all right, though she didn't take much interest in men. One time at an office party she and I were talking about what wolves some men are and she was all for hanging every man by his thumbs and making it a woman's world.'

'Nice attitude. What changed her?'

'Now you've got me. We sort of lived in different parts of the world and I never saw too much of her. I know she had a good sum of money tied up in expensive jewellery she used to wear and there was talk about a wealthy student in an upstate college taking her out, but I never inquired about it. As a matter of fact, I was very surprised when she eloped like that. True love is funny, isn't it, Mike?'

'Not so funny.'

'No, I guess not.'

I put my face in my hand, rubbing my head to make things come out all right. 'Is that all . . . everything you know about her? Do you know where she was from or anything about her background?'

Connie squinted at the light and raised her forefinger thoughtfully. 'Oh! . . . I think . . .'

'Come on, come on . . . what?'

'I just happened to think. Jean Trotter wasn't her right name. She had a long Polish name and changed it when she became a model. She even made it legal and I cut the piece out of the paper that carried a notation about it. Mike . . . over there in the dresser is a small leather folder. Go get it for me.'

I slid off the bed and started through the top drawer until Connie said, 'No . . . the other one, Mike.'

I tried that one, too, but couldn't find it. 'Damn it, Connie, come over here and get it, will you!'

'I can't.' She laughed nervously.

So I started tossing all her junk to the floor until she yipped and threw back the covers to run over and make me stop. Now I knew why she didn't want to get out of bed. She was as naked as a jaybird.

She found the folder in the back of a drawer and handed it to me with a scowl. 'You ought to have the decency to close your eyes, at least.'

'Hell, I like you like that.'

'Then do something about it.'

I tried to look through the folder, but my eyes wouldn't stand still. 'For Pete's sake, put something on, will you!'

She put her hands on her hips and leaned towards me, her tongue sticking out. Then she turned slowly, with all the sultry motion she could command, and walked to the clothes closet. She pulled out her fur coat and slipped into it, holding it closed around her middle. 'I'll teach you,' she said. Then she sat in a low boudoir chair with her legs crossed, making it plain that I could look and be tempted, but that was all, brother, that was all.

When I went back to pawing through the folder she let the coat clip open and I had to turn my back and sit down. Connie laughed ; but I found the clipping.

Her name had been Julia Travesky. By order of the court she was now legally Jean Trotter. Her address was given at a small hotel for women in an uptown section. I stuffed the clipping in my wallet and put the folder in the dresser drawer. 'At least it's something,' I said. 'We can find out the rest from the court records.'

'What are you looking for, Mike?'

'Anything that will tell me why she was important enough to kill.'

'I was thinking . . .'

'Yeah?'

'There are files down at the office. Whenever a girl applies for work at the agency she has to leave her history and a lot of sample photos and press clippings. Maybe Jean's are still there.'

I whistled through my teeth and nodded. 'You've got something, Connie. I called Juno before I came up, but she wasn't home. How about Anton Lipsek?'

Connie snorted and pulled the coat back to bare her legs a little more. 'That drip is probably still sleeping off the drunk he worked up last night. He and Marion Lester got crocked to the ears and they took off for Anton's place with some people from the Inn about three o'clock in the morning. Neither of them showed up for work today. Juno didn't say much, but she was plenty burned up.'

'Nuts! Who else might have the keys to the place, then?'

'Oh, I can get in. I had to once before when I left my pocket-book in the office. I kissed the janitor's bald head and he handed over his passkey.'

The hands of my watch was going around too fast. My insides were beginning to turn into a hard fuzzy ball again. 'Do me a favour, Connie. Go up and see if you can get that file on her. Get it and come right back here. I have something to do in the meanwhile and you'll be helping out a lot if you can manage it.'

'No,' she pouted.

'Cripes, Connie, use your head! I told you . . .'

'Go with me.'

'I can't.'

The pout turned into a grin and she peeked at me under her eyelashes. She stood up, put a cigarette between her lips, and in a pose as completely normal as if she had on an evening gown, she pushed back the coat and rested her hands on her hips and swayed over until she was looking up into my face.

I had never seen anything so unnaturally inviting in all my life.

'Go with me,' she said, 'then we'll come back together.'

I said, 'Come here, you,' and grabbed her as naked as she was and squeezed her against my chest until her mouth opened. Then I kissed her good. So good she stopped breathing for long seconds and her eyes were glazed.

'Now do what I told you to do or you'll get the hell slapped out of your hide,' I said.

She lowered her eyes and covered herself up with the coat. The grin she tried so hard to hide slipped out anyway. 'You're the boss, Mike. Any time you want to be my boss, don't tell me. I'll know it all by myself.'

I put my thumb under her chin and lifted her face up. 'There ought to be more people in this world like you, kid.'

'You're an ugly so-and-so, Mike. You're big and rough just like my brothers and I love you ten times as much.'

I was going to kiss her again and she saw it coming. She shed that coat and flew into my arms and let her body scorch mine. I had to shove her away when it was the one thing I didn't want to do, because it reminded me that soon something like this might be happening to Velda and I couldn't let it happen.

The thought scared the hell out of me. It scared me right down to my shoes and I was damning the ground Clyde walked on. I practically ran out of the apartment and stumbled down the stairs in my haste. I ran to the corner and into a candy store where the owner was just turning out the lights. I was in the phone-booth before he could tell me the place was closed and my fingers could hardly hold the nickel to drop it in the slot.

Maybe there was still time, I thought. God, there had to be time. Minutes and seconds, what made them so important? Little fractions of eternity that could make life worth living. I dialled Velda's number and heard it ring. It rang a long time and no one answered, so I let it go on ringing and ringing and ringing. It rang for a year before she answered it. I said it was me and she wanted to hang up. I shouted, and she held it, and cautiously, asked me where I was.

I said, 'I'm nowhere near your place, Velda, so don't worry about me pulling anything funny. Look, hold everything. Don't go up there tonight . . . there's no need to now. I think we have the thing by the tail.'

Velda's voice was soft, but so firm, so goddamn firm I could have screamed. She said, 'No, Mike. Don't try to stop me. I know you'll think of every excuse you can, but please don't

128

try to stop me. You've never really let me do anything before and I know how important this is. Please, Mike . . .'

'Velda, listen to me.' I tried to keep my voice calm. 'It isn't a stall. One of the agency girls was murdered tonight. Things are tying up. Her name was Jean Trotter . . . before that she was Julia Travesky. The killer got her and . . .'

'Who?'

'Jean . . . Julia Travesky.'

'Mike . . . that was the girl Chester Wheeler told his wife he had met in New York. The one who was his daughter's old school chum.'

'What!'

'You remember. I spoke of it after I came back from Columbus.'

My throat got dry all of a sudden. It was an effort to speak. 'Velda, for God's sake, don't go up there tonight. Wait . . . wait just a little while,' I croaked.

'No.'

'Velda . . .'

'I said no, Mike. I'm going. The police were here earlier. They were looking for you. They want you for murder.'

I think I groaned. I couldn't get the words out.

'If they find you we won't have a chance, Mike. You'll go behind bars and I couldn't stand that.'

'I know all about that, Velda. I was with Pat tonight. He told me. What do I have to do—get on my knees? . . .'

'Mike! . . .'

I couldn't fight the purpose in her voice. Good Lord, she thought she was helping me and I couldn't tell her differently! She thought I was trying to protect her and she was going ahead at all costs! Oh, Lord, think of a way to stop her, I couldn't! She said, 'Please don't bother to come up, Mike. I'll be gone, and besides, there are policemen watching this building. Don't make it any harder for me, please.'

She hung up on me. Just like that. Damn it, she hung up and left me cooped up in that two-by-four booth staring at an inanimate piece of equipment. I slammed the receiver back in the hook and ran past the guy who held the pull cord of the light in his hand, ready to turn it out. Lights out. Lights out for me too.

I ran back to the car and started it up. Time. Damn it, how *much* time? Pat said give him a week. A while ago I needed hours. Now minutes counted. Minutes I couldn't spare just when things were beginning to make sense. Jean Trotter . . . she was the one Wheeler met at that dinner meeting. She was the one he went out with. But Jean eloped and got out of the picture very conveniently and Marion Lester took over the

129

duty of saying Wheeler was with her, and Marion Lester and Anton Lipsek were very friendly.

I needed a little talk with Marion Lester. I wanted to know why she lied and who made her lie. I'd tell her once to talk, and if she wouldn't I'd work her over until she'd be glad to talk, glad to scream her guts out and put the finger on the certain somebody I was after.

CHAPTER ELEVEN

I TRIED hard to locate Pat. I tried until my nickels were spent and there wasn't any place else to try. He was out chasing a name that didn't matter any more and I couldn't find him at the time when I needed him most. I left messages for him to either stay in his office or go home until I called him and they promised to tell him when, and if, he came in. My shirt was soaked through with cold sweat when I got finished.

The sky had loosened up again and was letting more flakes of snow sift down. Great. Just great. More minutes wasted getting around. I checked the time and swore some big curses then climbed in the car and turned north into traffic. Jean Trotter and Wheeler. It all came back to Wheeler after all. The two were murdered for the same reason. Why . . . because he saw and recognized her as an old friend? Was it something he knew about her that made him worth killing. Was it something she knew about him?

There was blackmail to it, some insidious kind of blackmail that could scare the pants off a guy like Emil Perry and a dozen other big shots who couldn't afford to leave town when it pleased them. Photographs. Burned photographs. Models. A photographer named Anton Lipsek. A tough egg called Rainey. The brains named Clyde. They added.

I laughed so loud my chest hurt. I laughed and laughed and promised myself the skin of a killer. When I had the proof I could collect the skin and the D.A., the cops and anybody else could go to hell.

I had to park a block away from the Chadwick Hotel and walk back. My coat collar was up around my face like everyone else's and I wasn't worried about being seen. A patrolman swinging a night stick went by and never gave me a tumble. The lobby of the hotel was small, but crowded with a lot of faces taking a breather from the weather outside.

The Mom type at the desk gave me a smile and a nasal hello when I went to the desk. 'I'd like to see Miss Lester,' I said.

'You've been here before, sonny. Go ahead up.'

'Mind if I use your phone first?'

'Nah, go ahead. Want me to connect you with her room?'

'Yeah.'

She fussed with the plugs in the switchboard and triggered

her button a few times. There was no answer. The woman shrugged and made a sour face. 'She came in and I didn't see her go out. Maybe she's in the tub. Them babes is always taking baths anyway. Go on up and pound on her door.'

I shoved the phone back and went up the stairs. They squeaked, but there was so much noise in the lobby nobody seemed to mind. I found Marion's room and knocked twice. A little light was seeping out from under the door so I figured the clerk had been right about the bath. I listened, but I didn't hear any splashing.

I knocked again, louder.

Still no answer.

I tried the door and it opened easily enough.

It was easy to see why she couldn't answer the door. Marion Lester was as dead as a person could get. I closed the door quietly and stepped in the room. 'Damn,' I said, 'damn it all to hell!'

She had on a pair of red satin pyjamas and was sprawled out face down. You might have thought she was asleep if you didn't notice the angle of her neck. It had been broken with such force the snapped vertebra was pushed out against the skin. On the opposite side of the neck was a bluish imprint of the weapon. When I put the edge of my palm against the mark it almost fitted and the body was stone-cold and stiff.

The only weapon our killer liked was his strong hands.

I lifted the phone and when the clerk came on I said, 'When did Miss Lester come in?'

'Hell, she came in this morning drunk as a skunk. She could hardly navigate. Ain't she there now?'

'She's here now, all right. She won't be going out again very soon either. She's dead. You better get up here right away.'

The woman let out a muffled scream and started to run without bothering to break the connexion. I heard her feet pounding on the stairs and she wrenched the door open without any formalities. Her face went white to grey then flushed until the veins of her forehead stood out like pencils. 'Lawd! Did you do this?'

She practically fell into a chair and wiped her hand across her eyes. I said, 'She's been dead for hours. Now take it easy and think. Understand, think. I want to know who was up here today. Who called on her or even asked for her. You ought to know, you've been here all day.'

Her mouth moved, the thick lips hanging limp. 'Lawd!' she said.

I grabbed her shoulders and shook her until her teeth rattled A little life came back into her eyes. 'Answer me and stop looking foolish. Who was up here today?'

Her head wobbled from side to side. 'This tears it, sonny. The joint'll be ruined. Lawd, there goes my job!' She buried her face in her hands and moaned foolishly.

I slapped her hands away and made her look at me. 'Listen. She isn't the first. The same guy that killed her killed two others and unless he's stopped there's going to be more killing. Can you understand that?'

She nodded dumbly, terror creeping into her eyes.

'All right ; who was up here to see her today?'

'Nobody. Not nobody at all.'

'Somebody was here. Somebody killed her.'

'H—how do I know who killed her?'

'I didn't say that. I said somebody was here.'

She pulled her thick lips together and licked them. 'Look, sonny, I don't take a count of who comes and goes in this place. It's easy to get in and it's easy to get out. Lotsa guys come in here.'

'And you don't notice them?'

'No.'

'Why?'

'I ain't . . . I ain't supposed to.'

'So the dump's a whore-house Nothing but a whore-house.'

She glared at me indignantly, the terror fading. 'I ain't no madam, sonny. It's just a place where the babes can stay with no questions asked, is all. I ain't no madam.'

'Do you know what's going to happen around here?' I said. 'In ten minutes this place will be crawling with cops. There's no sense running because they'll catch up with you. When they find out what's going on . . . and they will . . . you'll be up the creek. Now, you can either start thinking and maybe have a little while to get yourself a clear story to offer them or you can take what the cops have to hand out. What will it be?'

She looked me straight in the eye and told me the God's honest truth. 'Sonny,' she said, 'if my life depended upon it I couldn't tell you anything different. I don't know who was in here to-day. The place was crawling with people ever since noontime and I read a book most of the day.'

I felt like I fell through a manhole. 'O.K., lady. Maybe there's somebody else who would know.'

'Nobody else. The girls who clean the halls only work in the morning. The guests take care of their own rooms. Everyone who lives here is a regular. No overnighters.'

'No bellboys?'

'We ain't had 'em for a year. We don't need 'em.'

I looked back at the remains of Marion Lester and wanted to vomit. Nobody knew a thing. The killer had no face. Nobody saw him. They felt him and didn't live to tell about it.

Only me. I was lucky, I got away. First the killer tried to shoot me. It didn't work. Then he tried to lay murder in my lap and that didn't work either. Then he tried an ambush and slipped up there. I was the most important one in the whole lot.

And I couldn't make a target of myself because there wasn't time to play bait.

I looked at Marion and talked to the woman who sat there trembling from head to foot. 'Go on downstairs and put me through to the police department. I'll call them from here, but I won't be here when they come. You can tell them the same thing you told me. Go on, beat it.'

She waddled out, her entire body bearing the weight of the calamity. I held the phone to my ear and heard her call the police. When the connexion was through I asked for Homicide and got the night man. I said, 'This is Mike Hammer. I'm in the Chadwick Hotel with a dead woman. No, I didn't kill her, she's been dead for hours. The D.A. will want to hear about it so you better call him and mention my name. Tell him I'll drop by later. Yeah, yeah. No I won't be here. If the D.A. doesn't like that, it's just too damn bad. Tell him I said that, too. Goodbye.' I walked downstairs and out the front door with about a minute to spare. I was just starting up my car when the police came up with their sirens wide open, leading a black limousine that skidded to a halt as the D.A. himself jumped out and started slinging orders around.

When I drove by I beeped the horn twice, but he didn't hear it because he was too busy directing his army. Another squad car came up and I looked it over hoping to see Pat. He wasn't with them.

My watch said twenty minutes to twelve. Velda would be leaving her apartment about now. My hands were shaking when I reached for a Lucky and I had to use the dashboard lighter to get it lit, a match wouldn't hold still. If there was any fight left inside me it was going fast, draining out with each minute, and in twenty minutes there wouldn't be a thing left for me, not one damn thing.

I stopped at a saloon and pulled the phone book from its rack and fingered through the L's until I came to Lipsek, Anton. The address was right on the fringe of the Village in a section I knew pretty well. I went back to the car and crawled down Broadway.

Twenty minutes. Fifteen now, tempus fugit. Tempus fugits fast as hell. Twelve minutes. It started to snow harder. The wind picked it up and whipped the stuff into parallel, oblique lines across the multicoloured lights that lined the street. Red lights. I made like I was skidding and went through. Cars honked and I cursed back, telling them to be quiet. The gun

134

under my arm was burning a hole in my side and my finger under the glove kept tightening up expectantly.

Fourteenth street went by and two cabs were bumper-locked in the middle of the road. I followed a pick-up truck on to the pavement and off again to get around them. A police whistle blew and I muttered for the cop to go to the devil and kept on my way behind the truck.

Five minutes. My teeth were making harsh, grinding noises I could feel through my jaw. I came to my street and pulled into a parking space. Another minute went by while I oriented myself and followed the numbers in the right direction. Another two minutes went by before I found it.

Three minutes. She should almost be there by now. The name on the bell read, ANTON LIPSEK, ESQ., and some kid had written a word under it. The kid had my sympathy. I felt the same way myself. I pushed the bell and heard it tinkle some place upstairs.

Nothing happened. I pushed it again and kept my finger on it. The tinkling went on and and on and still nothing happened. I pushed one of the other bells and the door clicked open. A voice from the rear of the first floor said, 'Who is it?'

'Me,' I said. 'I forgot my key.'

The voice said, 'Oh . . .O.K.' and the door closed. Me, the magic password. Me, the sap, the sucker, the target for a killer. Me, the stupid bastard who was going around in circles while a killer watched and laughed. That was me.

I had to light a match at every door to see where I was. I found Anton's on the top floor with another Esq. after it. There was no sound and no light, and when I tried the knob it was locked.

I was too late. I was too late all around. It was five after twelve. Velda would be inside. The door would be closed and the nuptial couch laid. Velda would know all about it the hard way.

I kicked the door so hard the lock snapped and the door flew open. I kicked it shut the same way and stood there hoping the killer would come at me out of the darkness, hoping he'd run right into the rod I held in my fist. I prayed that he'd come, listened hard hoping to hear him. All I heard was my own breathing.

My hand groped for the wall switch and found it, bathing the place with a brilliant white light. It was some place. Some joint. The furniture was nothing but wooden porch furniture and the lamps were rigged up from discarded old floodlights. The rug on the floor must have been dragged out of an ash can.

But the walls were worth a million dollars. They were hung with canvases painted by the Masters and must have been genuine, otherwise their lavish frames and engraved brass nameplates were going to waste. So Anton had money and he didn't spend it on dames. No, it went into pictures, something with a greater permanent value than money. The inscriptions were all in French and didn't mean a thing to me. Although the rest of the room was littered with empty glasses and cigarette butts, not a speck of dust nested on the frames or the pictures, and the brass plates had been recently polished.

Could this be Anton's reward for wartime collaboration? Or was it his own private enterprise?

I picked some of the trash out of the way and prowled around the apartment. There was a small studio filled with the usual claptrap of a man who brings his work home with him, and adjoining, a tiny darkroom. The sinks were filled and a small red light burned over a table. That was all there was to it. I would have left, but the red light winked at me from a reflected image in a shiny bit of metal against the wall and I ran my hand over the area.

It wasn't a wall, it was a door. It was set flush with the wall and had no knob. Only the scratch on the concealed hinge showed me where it was. Some place a hidden latch opened it and I didn't waste time looking for it. I braced my back against the sink and kicked out as hard as I could.

Part of the wall shook and cracked.

I kicked again and my foot went through the partition. The third time I had made a hole big enough to crawl into. It was an empty clothes closet that faced into another apartment.

Here was where Anton Lipsek lived in style. A wall had separated two worlds. There was junk lying around here, just the evidence of a recent and wild party. One side was a bar, stocked to the hilt with the best that money could buy. The rest of the room was the best that money could buy, too. There were couches and tables that didn't come from any department store and they matched the drapes and colour scheme perfectly. Someone with an eye for good taste had done a magnificent job of decorating. Someone like an artist-photographer named Anton Lipsek. The only thing out of place were the cheap prints that were framed in bamboo. They belonged outside with the junk. Anton was as cracked as the Liberty Bell.

Maybe.

There were other rooms, a whole lot of rooms. Apparently he had rented two apartments back to back and used the dark-room as a secret go-between. There was a hall that led into three beautiful bedrooms, each with its own shower stall and toilet. Each bedroom had ash trays filled with cigarette butts, some plain, some stained with lipstick. In one room there

136

were three well-chewed cigar stubs squashed out in a glass coaster beside the bed.

Something was wrong. There had to be something wrong. I would have seen it if my mind wasn't twisted and dead. The whole thing was as unnatural as it was possible to be. Why the two apartments? Why the one place crawling with dirt and decorated with a fortune in pictures and the other lavish in furnishings and nothing else?

Anton was a bachelor. Until recently he didn't mess with women, so why all the bedrooms? He wasn't so popular that he was overloaded with guests. I sat on the edge of the bed and shoved my hat back on my head. It was a nice bed, soft, firm and quiet. It made me want to lean back and sleep for ever to wash the fatigue from my mind. I lay back and stared at the ceiling.

It was a white ceiling with faint lines criss-crossing in the calcimine. My eyes followed the lines to the wall where they disappeared into the moulding. Those lines were like the tracks the killer went. They started at no place and went everywhere, disappearing just as effectively. A killer who was strong as he was vicious.

I stared at the moulding some more then picked out the pictures that hung over the bed and stared at them. They were funny little pictures painted on glass—seascapes, with the water a shimmering silver. The water had tiny palms. I got up off that bed slowly and looked at the lines criss-crossing it too, reflecting the cracks in the ceiling.

My breath was hot in my throat and my eyes must have been little slits. I could feel my nails bite into my palms. The water was shiny and silver because the water part was a mirror. It made a lovely, decorative picture.

Lovely, but very practical. I tried to wrench the frames loose, but they were screwed into the wall. All I could do was swear and claw at the damn things and it didn't do any good. I ran back through the living-room, opened the door of the closet and wiggled through the hole in the wall. The splinters grasped at my coat and held me back until I smacked at them with my hand.

The pictures. Those beautiful canvases by the Old Masters. They were worth a million as they stood and they had another million dollars' worth behind them. I grabbed the one with the two nudes playing in the forest and lifted it from the hook. It came away easily and I had what I was looking for.

On the other side a hole had been cut into the wall and I saw the little seascape in its frame on the other side. The shore line and the sky were opaque under the paint, but where the glass had been silvered you could see everything that went on in the room.

What a blackmail set-up that was! One-way glass set above a bed! Oh, brother!

It took me about ten seconds to locate the camera Anton used. It was a fancy affair that would take shots without missing a single detail of expression. It had been tucked in a cabinet along with a tripod whose legs were still set at the proper level to focus the camera into the bedroom.

I threw it all on the floor and hauled out everything else that was in the cabinet. I was looking for pictures, direct evidence that would be hanging evidence. Something that would give me the big excuse when I pumped a slug into his guts.

It was simple as hell now, as simple as it could ever get. Anton Lipsek was using some of the girls to bait the big boys into the bedroom. He took pictures that set him up for life. It was the best kind of blackmail I could think of. The public could excuse anything else, but coarse infidelity, no.

Even Chester Wheeler fitted it. He was money, big money. He was in town alone and a little bit drunk. He walked into the trap; but he made one mistake that cost him his life. He recognized the girl. He recognized her as a girl that went to school with his daughter. The girl got scared and told Anton, so Anton had to see to it that Wheeler died. But the girl was still scared and eloped, grabbing the first guy who was handy. She did fine until the killer caught up with her again and didn't take any chances with her getting so scared she *would* talk.

Yeah, it all was so simple now. Even Marion. Anton was afraid of me. The papers had it down that I was a cop and my ticket had been lifted. If I had never shown my face around neither Jean nor Marion would have died, but it was too late to think of that now. Anton made Marion pick up the story and say she was the one who went out with Wheeler, but she gave it an innocent touch that couldn't be tracked down. It should have stopped there.

What happened? Did Marion get too big for her pants and want a pay-off for the story she told? Sure, why not? She was in this thing. When those pictures turned up her face would be there. All she could lose would be her character and her job, but if she had something on somebody too, she didn't stand to lose a thing. So she died. Pretty! You bet your life it was!

I started to grin and my breath came fast through my teeth. Even right back to the beginning it checked. It didn't start from the night Wheeler died, it started a few days before, long enough to give the killer time to register in the hotel and take Wheeler at a convenient moment. I was just there by accident. I was a witness who didn't matter because I was out cold, and if I had been anybody else but me it made the killing so much the better. Whisky-drunk and out like a light with no memory

138

of what happened. The cops would have tagged me and I would have tagged myself.

All the killer forgot was my habit of keeping that .45 loaded with six shots. He took back the extra slug and shell case and overlooked that one little item. If the killer had sense enough to go through my pockets he would have found a handful of loose shells and replaced that one bullet that went into the mattress.

But it only takes one mistake to hang a guy. Just one. He made it.

The killer must have been scared witless when he found out I was a cop. He must have known I'd been looking to get my ticket back, and he must have gone even further . . . he'd want to know what I was like. He'd check old papers and court records and ask questions, then he'd *know* what I was like. He'd know that I didn't give a damn for a human life any more than he did. I was just a little bit different. I didn't shoot anything but killers. I loved to shoot killers. I couldn't think of anything I'd rather do than shoot a killer and watch his blood trace a slimy path across the floor. It was fun to kill those bastards who tried to get away with murder and did sometimes.

I started to laugh and I couldn't stop. I pulled the Luger out and checked it again when it didn't need it. This time I pulled the trigger off half-cock and let it sit all the way back ready to nudge a copper-covered slug out of the barrel and into a killer's face.

It was later than ever, late enough to make my blood turn cold as ice. I had to make myself stop thinking. I couldn't look for those pictures and think too.

If ever a room got torn apart, this was it. I ripped and I smashed and I tore looking for those damn photographs and there wasn't a damn thing to see except some unexposed plates. I pulled the room apart like Humpty Dumpty and started on the darkroom when I heard the steps outside.

They came from the hall that led into the good apartment, the one with the bedrooms. The key turned in the lock and the door opened. For one second I had a glimpse of Anton's face, a pale face suddenly gone stark white, then the door slammed shut and the feet pounded down the stairs.

I could have killed myself for leaving the lights on when they had been out!

My coat caught on the sink and ripped. It caught again when I crawled through the hole in the partition. I ripped it loose and felt it tear clear up to the collar. I screamed my rage and took plaster and lath with me when I burst through.

Damn that son-of-a-bitch, he was getting away! I twisted

139

the lock and tumbled into the hall without bothering to close the door. I heard feet slamming on the stairs and the downstairs door smash shut. I started down the steps and fell. I ran and fell again and managed to reach the bottom without breaking any bones. All over my body were spots that would wait until later to hurt, raw spots that stuck to my clothes with my own blood.

My gun was in my hand when I ran out on the street and it was nothing more than a useless weight because Anton's car was screaming up the street towards the intersection.

How important can a guy get? What does he have to do to please the fates that hamstring him every inch of the way? I saw the red dot of his tail-light swing to the right as a cruising cab cut him off. I heard the grinding of metal and the shouts of the drivers and Anton Lipsek was up on the pavement trying to back off.

It was too far to run, too much of a chance to take. I wheeled and dashed into the alleyway that passed between the buildings and leaped for the fence at the end and pulled myself over. I climbed in my car and turned the key, felt the motor cough and catch, and I said a prayer that the snow under the wheels would hold long enough for me to get away.

The fates laughed a little and gave me a push. I pulled away from the kerb and sped down the street. Just as I turned the corner Anton drove across the pavement and back into the street while the cab driver ran after him waving his arms and yelling at the top of his lungs. I had to lean on my horn to get out of the way.

Anton must have heard the horn because he stepped on the gas and the big, fat sedan he was using leaped ahead like it had a rocket on it. That sedan was the same one that was used as a gun platform when I was shot at on Thirty-third Street. Rainey. I hope he was burning in hell where he belonged. He did the shooting while Anton drove.

I was glad to see the snow now. It had driven the cars into garages and the cabs to the kerbs. The streets were long funnels of white stretched out under the lights. I was catching up to him and he stepped down harder on the pedal. Red lights blinked on and were ignored. The sedan started to skid, came out of it safely and tore ahead.

Now he could get scared. Good and scared. He could sit there behind the wheel with the spit drooling out of the corner of his mouth and wonder why he couldn't get away. He would curse that big, fat sedan and ask it why the hell it couldn't shake an old rattletrap like mine. Anton could curse and he'd never know about the oversized engine under my hood. I was only fifty yards away and coming closer.

The sedan tried to make a turn, yawed into a skid and slammed against the kerb. It seemed to come out of it for a moment and my stomach suddenly turned sour because I knew I'd never make it if I tried it too. This time the fates laughed again and gave me Anton. They gave me Anton with a terrible crash that threw the sedan into the wall of a building and left it upside down on the pavement like a squashed bug.

I drove my heel into the brake and did a complete circle in the street. I backed up and stopped in the middle of the road and ran to the sedan with my gun out.

I put the gun back and grunted some obscene words. Anton was dead. His neck was topped with a bloody pulp that used to be a head. All that was left were his eyes and they weren't where they were supposed to be. The door was wrenched open and I took a quick look around, hoping to find what I was after.

The only thing in the car was Anton. He was a couple of bucks worth of chemicals now. One of the dead eyes watched me go through his pockets. When I opened his wallet I found a sheaf of five-hundred-dollar bills and a registered mail receipt. There was a pencilled notation on it that said 'Sent Special Delivery' and it was dated this morning.

It was addressed to Clyde Williams.

Then it wasn't Anton after all . . . it was Clyde. That ratty little punk *was* the brains. Clyde was the killer and Velda was with him now. Clyde was the brains and the killer and Velda was trying to pump a guy who knew every angle.

I was an hour and a half too late.

Time had marched on. It marched on and trampled me underfoot into the mud and slime of its passing. But I could get up and follow it. I could catch up with that lost hour and a half and make it give back what it had stolen, by God!

People were screaming at me from the windows when I jumped in my car. From down the block came the low wailing of a siren and a red eye that winked on and off. The screaming came from both directions then, so I cut down a side street and got out of their path. Somebody was sure to have grabbed my licence number. Somebody was sure to relay it to the police and when they found out it was me the D.A. would eat his hat while his fat head was still in it. Suicide, he had said. He gave his own personal opinion that Chester Wheeler had been a suicide.

Smart man, our D.A., smart as a raisin on a bun.

The sky agreed with a nod and let loose more tiny flakes of snow that felt the city out and called for reinforcements. There was still a mile to go and the snow was coming down harder than ever. My fate snickered.

CHAPTER TWELVE

I CHECKED the address on the mail receipt against the one on the apartment. They both read the same. The building was a yellow-brick affair that towered out of sight into the snow, giving only glimpses of the floors above.

A heavy blue canvas canopy sheltered the walk that led into the lobby, guarded by a doorman in an admiral's uniform. I sat in the car and watched him pace up and down, flapping his arms to keep him warm. He took the admiral's hat off and pressed his hands against his cauliflowered ears to warm them and I decided not to go in the front way after all. Guys like him were too eager to earn a ready buck being tough.

When I crossed the street I walked to the next building until the snow shielded me, then cut back to the walk that took me around the rear. A flight of steps led down to a door that was half open and I knocked on it. A voice with a Swedish accent called back and an old duck with lip whiskers that reached to his ears opened the door and said, 'Ya?'

I grinned. The guy waited. I reached in my pocket and pulled out a ten-spot. He looked at it without saying anything. I had to nudge him aside to get in and saw that the place was part of the boiler room in the basement. There was a table under the solitary bulb in the place and a box drawn up to it. I walked over to the table and turned around.

The old boy shut the door and picked up a poker about four feet long.

I said, 'Come here, pop.' I laid the ten on the table.

He hefted the poker and came over. He wasn't looking at the ten-spot. 'Clyde Williams. What's his apartment number?'

Whatever I said made his fingers tighten around the poker. He didn't answer. There wasn't time to be persuasive. I yanked out the Luger and set it next to the ten. 'Which one, pop?'

His fingers got tighter and he was getting ready to take me. First he wanted to ask a question. 'Why you want him?'

'I'm going to break him in little pieces, pop. Anybody else that stops me might get it too.'

'Poot back your gun,' he said. I shoved it in the holster. 'Now poot back your money.' I stuck the ten in my pocket. He dropped the poker to the floor. 'He is the penthouse in. There is elevator in the back. You use that, ya? Go break him, ya?'

I threw the ten back on the table. 'What's the matter, pop?'

'I have a daughter. She was good girl. Not now. That man . . .'

'O.K., pop. He won't bother you again. Got an extra key for that place?'

'No penthouse key.' The ends of his whiskers twitched and his eyes turned a bright blue. I knew exactly how he felt.

The elevator was a small service job for the tradesmen delivering packages. I stepped in and closed the gate, then pressed the button on top marked 'UP.' The cable tightened and the elevator started up, a slow tedious process that made me bite my lip to keep from yelling for it to hurry. I tried counting the bricks as they went by, then the floors. It dragged and dragged, a mechanical object with no feeling for haste. I wanted to urge it, lift it myself, do anything to hurry it, but I was trapped in that tiny cubicle while my watch ticked off the precious seconds.

It had to stop some time. It slowed, halted and the gate rattled open so I could get at the door. My feet wanted to run and I had to force them to stand still while I turned the handle and peered out into the corridor.

There was a stillness about the place you would expect in a tomb, a dead quiet that magnified every sound. One side of the hall was lined with plate-glass windows from ceiling to floor, overlooking a city asleep. Only the safety light over the elevator showed me the hall that stretched along this enclosed terrace to the main hall farther down. I let the door close softly and began walking. My gun was in my hand and cocked, ready to blast the first person I saw into a private hell of their own. The devil didn't get any assistants because the hall was empty. There, around the bend, was a lobby that would have overshadowed the best room in the executive mansion, and all it was used for was a waiting-room for the elevator.

On the walls were huge framed pictures, magnificent etchings, all the gimmicks of wealth. The chairs were of real leather, enough of them to seat twenty people. On the end tables beside the chairs were huge vases of fresh-cut roses that sent their fragrance through the entire room. The ash trays were sterling silver and clean. Beside each ash tray was a sterling silver lighter. The only incongruous thing was the cigar butt that lay right in the middle of the thick Oriental rug.

I stood there a moment taking it all in, seeing the blank door of the elevator that faced the lobby, seeing the ornate door of the apartment and the silver bell that adorned the opposite wall. When I stepped on the rug there was no sound of my feet except a whisper that seemed to hurry me forward, until I stood in front of the door wondering whether to shoot the lock off or ring the bell.

Neither was necessary. Right on the floor close to the sill was a small gold-plated key and I said thanks to the fate that was standing behind me and picked it up. My mouth was dry as a bone, so dry that my lips couldn't pull over my teeth when I grinned.

Velda had played it smart. I never thought she'd be so smart. She had opened the door and left the key there in case I came.

I'm here, Velda. I came too late, but I'm here now and maybe somehow I can make it all up to you. It didn't have to be this way at all, but I'll never tell you that. I'll let you go on thinking that you did what was right ; what you had to do. You'll always think you sacrificed something I wanted more than anything else in the world, and I won't get mad. I won't get mad when I want to slap the hell out of the first person that mentions it to me, even if it's you. I'll make myself smile and try to forget about it. But there's only one way I can forget about it and that's to feel Clyde's throat in my hand, or to have him on the end of a gun that keeps going off and off until the hammer clicks on an empty chamber. That way I'll be able to smile and forget.

I turned the key in the lock and walked in. The door clicked shut behind me.

The music stole into the foyer. It was soft music, deep music with a haunting rhythm. The lights were low, deliberately so to create the proper effect. I didn't see what the room was like ; I didn't make any attempt to be quiet. I followed the music through the rooms unaware of the splendour of the surroundings, until I saw the huge phonograph that was the source of the music and I saw Clyde bending over Velda on the couch. He was a dark shadow in a satin robe. They both were shadows there in the corner, shadows that made hoarse noises, one demanding and the other protesting. I saw the white of Velda's leg, the white of her hand she had thrown over her face, and heard her whimper. Clyde threw out his arm to toss off the robe and I said, 'Stand up, you stinking bastard!'

Clyde's face was a mask of rage that turned to fear in the single instant he saw me.

I wasn't too late after all. I was about one minute early.

Velda screamed a harried 'Mike!' and squirmed upright on the couch. Clyde moved in slow motion, the hate . . . the unbounding hate oozing out of him. The skin of his face was drawn tight as a bowstring as he looked at her.

'Mike, you said. You know him then! It was a frame!' He

spoke every word as though it was being squeezed out of him.

Velda came out of the couch and under my arm. I could feel her trembling as she sobbed against my chest. 'She knows me, Dinky. So do you know me. You know what's going to happen now?'

The red hole that had been his mouth clamped shut. I lifted Velda's face and asked, 'Did he hurt you, kid?'

She couldn't speak. She shook her head and sobbed until it passed. When it was over she mumbled, 'Oh, Mike . . . it was awful.'

'And you didn't learn a thing, did you?'

'No.' She shuddered and fumbled with the buttons of her suit coat.

I saw her handbag on the table and pointed to it. 'Did you carry that thing with you, honey?'

She knew I meant the gun and nodded.

'Get it,' I said.

Velda inched away from me, loath to leave the protection of my arm. She snatched the bag and ripped it open. When she had the gun in her hand I laughed at the expression on Clyde's face. 'I'm going to let her kill you, Dinky. I'm going to let Velda put a slug in you for what you tried and for what you've done to other girls.'

He stuttered something I didn't get and his lower lip hung away from his teeth. 'I know all about it, Dinky. I know why you did it and how you did it. I know everything about your pretty little blackmail set-up. You and Anton using the girls to bring in the boys who counted. When the girls had them in bed Anton took the pictures and from then on you carried the ball. You know something, Dinky . . . you got a brain. You got a bigger brain than I've ever given you credit for.

'It just goes to show you how you can underrate people. Here I've been figuring you for a stooge and you're the brain. It was clever as hell the way you killed Wheeler, all because he recognized one of the kids. Maybe he was going to have his little affair kept quiet, but you showed up with the pictures and wanted the pay-off. He wired for five grand and handed it over, didn't he? Then he got sore and got in touch with Jean Trotter again and told her who he was. So Jean ups and tells you, which put the end to Wheeler.'

Clyde looked at me speechlessly, his hands limp at his sides.

'That really started things. You had Wheeler planned for a kill and Wheeler grabbed my gun and tried to hand it to you. Only two things stump me. What was it you had planned for Wheeler before he reached for my rod and gave you the bright idea of suicide? And why kill Rainey? Was it because

145

he wasn't the faithful dog you thought he was? I have an idea on that . . . Rainey missed his first try at me on the street and you gave him the whip, hard enough so that Rainey got sore and made off with the dough he got for the photos from Emil Perry. You went out there to the arena to kill him and spotted me. You saw a nice way to drop it in my lap and promised the two witnesses a six-gun pay-off unless they saw it your way.

'Brother, did you get the breaks. Everything went your way. I bet you even have a dandy alibi rigged up for that night. Velda told me you were out until midnight . . . supposedly at a conference. It was enough time, wasn't it?'

Clyde was staring at the gun in my hand. I held it at hip level, but he was looking right down the barrel. Velda's was aimed right at his stomach.

'What did you do with Jean, Clyde? She was supposed to have eloped. Did you stash her away in a rooming-house somewhere planning to get rid of her? Did she read the papers and find out about Rainey and break loose until you ran her down and tossed her over the bridge? Did Marion Lester put the heat on you for cash when she had you over the barrel until she had to be killed too?'

'Mike . . .' he said.

'Shut up. I'm talking. I want to know a few things, Clyde. I want to know where those pictures are. Anton can't tell me because Anton's dead. You ought to see his head. His eyes were where his mouth was supposed to be. He didn't have them so that puts it on you.'

Clyde threw his arms back and screamed. Every muscle of his face contorted into a tight knot and the robe fell off his shoulders to the floor. 'You aren't hanging murder on me, you shamus! I'm not going to hang for any murder, not me!'

Velda grabbed my arm and I shrugged her off. 'You called it, Clyde. You won't hang for any murder, and you know why? Because you're going to die right here in this room. You're going to die and when the cops come I'll tell them what happened. I'll tell them that you had this gun in your hand and I took it away from you and used it myself. Or I can let Velda do it and put this gun in your hand later. It came from overseas . . . nobody will ever trace it to me. How do you like those apples, Clyde?'

The voice behind me said, 'He don't like 'em, mister. Drop that gun or I'll give it to you and the broad both.'

No, it couldn't happen to me again. Not again. Please, God, not this time. The hard, round snout of a gun pressed against my spine. I dropped the Luger. Velda's hit the floor next to it. Clyde let out a scream of pure joy and staggered across the room to fall on it. He didn't talk. He lifted that rod by the

146

butt and slashed it across my jaw. I tried to grab him and the barrel caught me on the temple with a jolt that dropped me to my knees. The voice with the gun took his turn and the back of my head felt like it flew to pieces.

I don't know how long I lay there. Time didn't mean a thing any more. First I was too late, then I was early, now I was too late again. I heard Clyde through the fog ordering Velda into another room. I heard him say to the guy, 'Drag him in with her. It's soundproof in there, nobody'll hear us. I'll fix him good for this when I get through with her. I want him to watch it. Put him in a chair and make him watch it.'

Then there were hands under my arms and my feet dragged across the floor. A door slammed and I felt the arms of a chair digging in the small of my back. Velda said, 'No . . . oh, God! . . . NO!'

Clyde said, 'Take it off! All of it!' I got my eyes open. Clyde was standing there flexing his hands, his face a picture of lust unsatisfied. The other guy stood to one side of me watching Velda back away until she was against the wall. He still had the gun in his hand.

They all saw me move at the same time. My heart hammered me to my feet and I wanted to kill them both. Clyde rasped, 'Shoot him if he tries anything.' He said it knowing I was going to try it anyway, and the guy brought the gun up.

There was only a single second to see it happen. Clyde and the guy had their eyes off Velda just long enough. Her hand went inside her suit jacket and came out with a little hammerless automatic that barked a deadly bark and the guy with the gun grabbed his stomach and tried to swear.

The pain in my head wouldn't let me stand. I tried to reach her and fell, seeing Clyde grab her arm and wrestle for the rod even as I was dragging myself towards the snub-nosed revolver that was still clutched in the other guy's hand.

Velda screamed, 'Mike . . . get him! *Mike!*' She was bent double trying to hold on to the gun. Clyde gave a wrench and she tumbled to the floor, her jacket ripping wide open. Velda screamed again and the gun clattered across the floor. Clyde wouldn't have had time to get it before I reached the other one and he knew it. He swore obscenely and ran for the door and slammed it shut after him. A bolt clicked in the lock and furniture was rammed against it to block the way. Then another door jarred shut and Clyde was gone.

Velda had my head in her lap rocking me gently. 'Mike, you fool, are you all right? Mike, speak to me.'

'I'm O.K., kid. I'll be fine in a minute.' She touched the cuts on my face, healing them with a kiss. Tears streamed down her cheeks. I forced a grin and she held me tighter. 'Shrewdie,

147

a regular shrewdie, aren't you?' I fingered the straps of the miniature shoulder holster she was wearing under the ruins of her jacket. 'You'll do as a partner. Who'd ever think a girl would be wearing a shoulder rig?'

She grinned back and helped me to my feet. I swayed and held on to the chair for support. Velda tried the door, rattling the knob with all her strength. 'Mike . . . it's locked! We're locked in.'

'Damn it!'

The guy on the floor coughed once and twitched. Blood spilled out of his mouth and he gave one final, convulsive jerk. I said, 'You can put a notch on your gun, Velda.'

I thought she was going to get sick, but that animal look screwed her face into a snarl. 'I wish I had killed them both. Mike, what are we going to do? We can't get out.'

'We have to, Velda. Clyde . . . '

'Did he . . . is he the one?'

My head hurt. My brain was a soggy mass that revolted against thought. 'He's the one. Try that door again.' I finally picked the gun up off the floor and stood with it in my hand. It was almost too heavy to hold.

'Mike . . . that night that Rainey was killed . . . Clyde was at a conference. I heard them talking about it in the Bowery Inn. He was there.'

My stomach heaved. The blood was pounding in my ears. I put the gun to the lock and pulled the trigger. The crack of it sent it spinning out of my hand. The lock still didn't give. Velda repeated, 'Mike . . .'

'I heard you, goddamn it! I don't care what you saw or what anybody said. It was Clyde, can't you see that? It was Clyde and Anton. They had the pictures and . . .'

I stopped and stared at the door. 'The pictures . . . Clyde's gone after those pictures. If he gets them he'll have the protection he needs and he'll get out of this sure as grass grows in the springtime!'

I found the gun and levelled it at the lock, pulling the trigger until the room reeked with the fumes of burned powder. Damn his soul! Those pictures . . . they weren't in Anton's apartment and they weren't here . . . the outside door had slammed shut too fast to give him time to pick anything up on the way. That left only one other place, the agency office.

Thinking about it gave me the strength I needed to bash it with my shoulder until it budged. Velda pushed with me and the furniture on the other side moved. We leaned against the dead weight, harder, working until the cords stood out in our necks. Something toppled from the pile and the door moved back far enough to let us out.

148

There was utter silence.

I threw the revolver on a chair and picked the Luger off the floor and stuffed it under my arm. I waved my thumb to the phone. 'Call Pat. Try until you get him and if you can't, call the D.A.'s office. That'll get action quick enough. Make them put out a call for Clyde and we might be able to stop him in time.' I half-ran, half-stumbled to the door and held it open. Velda shouted something after me that I didn't hear and I scrambled out to the lobby. The elevator pointer was at the bottom floor, the basement. But the service car was still in place. It took its own, agonizing time about going down and I stopped it at the main hall and ran out the front. The admiral gave me a queer look, tried to grab me and got a fist in the mouth. He lost me in the snow before he could get up, but I could hear him yelling as I got in my car. I was two blocks away from the apartment building when the first squad car shot by. I was five blocks farther on when I remembered that Connie had gone up to the office that night.

I got that funny feeling back in my stomach again and jammed my foot down on the throttle and weaved across town so I could intersect Thirty-third Street without wasting a minute.

When I came to the cemetery of buildings I slowed down and parked. A light was on behind the entrance doors and an old fellow sat under it reading a paper. He was just checking his turnip watch when I pulled the door open. He shook his head and waved for me to go away.

I kicked the door so hard it shook violently. The old guy threw his paper down and turned the lock. 'It's too late. You can't go in. We closed up half-hour ago. Not even late visitors. Go on, scram.'

He didn't get a chance to close it on me. I rammed it with the heel of my hand and stepped inside. 'Anybody been here in the last few minutes?'

His head jerked nervously. 'Ain't been nobody here for over an hour. Look, you can't come in, so why don't you . . .'

Clyde hadn't shown up. Hell, he had to come here! He should be here! 'Is there another way in this place?'

'Yes, the back way. That's locked up tight. Nobody can get in that way unless I unbolt it. Look, mister . . .'

'Oh, keep quiet. Call the cops if you want to.'

'I don't understand . . . what you after?'

I let him have the nastiest look I could work up. 'A killer. A guy with a gun.'

He swallowed hard. 'Nobody's been in . . . you're kidding, ain't you?'

'Yeah, I'm kidding so hard it hurts. You know who I am,

Mac? My name is Mike Hammer. The cops want me. The killer wants me. Everybody wants my skin and I'm still walking around loose. Now answer my question—who was in here tonight.'

This time he gulped audibly. 'Some . . . a guy from the first . . . floor. He came back and worked. A few people from the insurance came in. Some others were with Roy Carmichael when he came in. They got some likker out of the office and left. I saw some others standing around the register later. Maybe if you looked there . . .'

'Sure, he wrote his name down. Take me upstairs, pop. I want to get in the Anton Lipsek Agency.'

'Oh, say now! Young girl went in there while back. Nice kid. Sure I let her in there. Don't remember seeing her come back. Must've been making my rounds.'

'Take me upstairs.'

'You better use the self-service elevator . . .'

I shoved him in one of the main cars and he dropped his time clock. He glared at me once and shut the door. We got out and walked down the hall to the office and my gun was in my hand. This time there wouldn't be anybody coming up behind me.

The light was on and the doors were open, wide open. I went in running with my gun waist-high and covered the room. The watchman was wheezing in the doorway, bug-eyed with fright. I combed the rooms until the place was lit up like it was a working day. There were dressing-rooms and minor offices, closets for supplies and closets for clothes. There were three neat darkrooms and one not so neat. I found the room I was looking for branching off a layout studio.

I found it and I opened the door and stood there with my mouth open to let me breathe up all the insane hatred that was stored up in my chest.

Connie was lying in the middle of the room with her eyes wide open. Her back had been bent to form a 'V' and she was dead.

The room was ceiling high with storage cabinets, covered with dust that revealed its infrequent use. The drawer of one of those cabinets gaped wide open and a whole section of folders had been removed.

I was too late again.

The watchman had to hold on to me to keep from fainting. He worked his mouth, trying to keep his eyes from the body. He made slobbering noises and shouted his fear and he held on tighter. He was still holding my arm when I kneeled down to look at Connie.

No marks, just that look of incredible pain on her face. The

150

whole thing had been done with one swift, clean stroke. I opened her fingers gently and lifted out the piece of shipping tag she had clutched so tightly. The part that was left said, 'To attach magnifier to screen . . .' the rest had been torn off. In the dust of the floor was the outline of where a crate had stood. Another fine line in the dust showed where the same crate had been tipped on end and dragged out in the hall. There were no marks after that and no crate either.

I left the door open and went back to the foyer, the little watchman blubbering behind me. After I tried a half-dozen combinations in the switchboard I got an outside wire. I said, 'Give me the police.' The watchman sat down and trembled while I told the desk man at the precinct station where to look for a body. When I hung up I steered the little guy back to the elevator and made him run me down to the basement.

It was just what I had expected. The door that was supposed to have been bolted so tightly to keep people out was swinging wide where a killer had gotten out.

The watchman didn't want to be left alone, and begged me not to go. I shoved him away and walked up the stairs and around the building.

I knew where the killer was hiding now.

CHAPTER THIRTEEN

THE snow that had tried so hard to block me wasn't something to be fought any longer. I leaned back against the cushions of the car in complete relaxation and had the first enjoyable cigarette I'd had in a long time. I sucked the smoke down deep into my lungs and let it go reluctantly. Even the smoke looked pretty as it drifted out the window into the night.

Everything was so white, covering up so much filth. Nature doing its best to hide its own. I drove slowly, carefully, staying in the tracks of the cars ahead. When I turned on the radio I heard my name mentioned on the police broadcast band and turned the dial until I had some late music.

When I reached my destination I backed in between two cars and even went to the trouble of locking the door like any good citizen would who expects to go home and to bed for the rest of the night. There were a few lights on in the apartment building, but whether they came from the one I wanted or not, I couldn't tell.

I took one last drag on the butt and flipped it into the gutter. It lay there a moment fizzling before it went out. I walked in the lobby and held my finger on the buzzer until the door clicked, then I walked in.

Why hurry? Time had lost its value. My feet took each step carefully, one after the other, bringing me to the top. I walked straight down the hall to the door that stood open and said, 'Hello, Juno.'

I didn't wait for her answer. I brushed right past her and walked inside. I walked through the room and pulled chairs from their corners. I walked into the bedroom and opened the closet doors. I walked into the bathroom and ripped the shower curtain down. I walked into the kitchen and poked around the pantry.

My hands were ready to grab and my feet were ready to kick and my gun was ready to shoot. But nobody was there. The fires began in my feet and licked up my body until they were eating into my brain. Every pain that had been ignored up to this moment gave birth to greater pains that were like teeth ripping my flesh apart. I held the edge of the door and spun around to face her with all that pain and hatred laid bare on my face.

My voice was a deadly hiss. 'Where is he Juno?'

152

The hurt that spoke to me from her eyes was eloquent. She stood there in a long-sleeved gown, her hands clutching her throat as my madness reached her. 'Mike! . . .' that was all she could say. Her breasts rose under the gown as her breath caught.

'Where is he, Juno?' I had the Luger in my hand now. My thumb found the hammer and dragged it back.

Her lips, her beautiful lips quivered and she took a step away from me. One step then another until she was standing in the living-room. 'You're hiding him, Juno He came here. It was the only place the crazy bastard could come. Where is he?'

Ever so slowly she closed her eyes, shaking her head. 'Oh, please, please, Mike. What have they done to you? Mike . . .'

'I found Connie, Juno. She was in the storeroom. She was dead. I found the files gone. Clyde might have had just enough time to get in and tear those files out after he killed Connie. I found something else, the same thing she found. It was part of a shipping ticket for a television set. That was the set you were supposed to deliver to Jean Trotter, but you knew she wasn't going to need that so you had it stacked in the storeroom until you could get rid of it. You were the only one who knew it was there . . . until tonight. Did Clyde find it and take it away so you wouldn't get tied into this?'

Her eyes opened wide, eyes that said it wasn't true, not any part of it. I didn't believe them. 'Where is he, Juno?' I brought the gun up until it pointed at a spot midway between those laughing, youthful breasts under the gown.

'Nobody is here, Mike. You saw that. Please . . .'

'Seven people are dead, Juno. Seven people. In this whole crazy scheme of things you have a part. It's a beautiful scheme though, hand-tailored to come apart whenever you try to get a look at it. Don't play games with me, Juno. I know why they were killed and how they were killed. It was trying to guess *who* killed them that had me going in circles. Your little blackmail cycle would have remained intact. Just one of those seven would have died if I hadn't been in the room with Wheeler that night. Who knew that I'd do my damndest to break it open?'

She watched me, her hands still at her throat. She shook her head and said, 'No, Mike, no!' and her knees trembled so she fought to keep her balance. It was too much. Juno reached out her hand to steady herself, holding the back of the chair. Slowly, gracefully even now, she sat down on the edge of it, her lower lip between her teeth.

I nodded yes, Juno, yes. The gun in my hand was steady. The hatred I had inside me bubbled over into my mouth and spilled out. 'I thought it was Anton at first. Then I found a mail receipt to Clyde. Anton had sent him some pictures. The Bowery Inn was a great place to draw the girls. It was designed specifically for that. It got the girls and with them the suckers.

'Who let the girls there in the first place, Juno? Who made it a fad to hang out down there where Clyde could win at his gambling tables and insure his business with photos that gave him the best coverage in the world. Did you do that, Juno? Did Clyde have a crush on you at one time and figure a good way of being able to stay in business? Was it Clyde who saw the possibilities of getting blackmail evidence on the big shots? Or was it you? It wasn't Anton, for sure. That goon had rocks in his head. But he co-operated, though, didn't he? He co-operated because he saw a way to purchase all those expensive paintings he had in his place.'

Her eyes were dull things, all the life gone from them. She sat with her head down and sobbed, one hand covering her face.

I spat the words out. 'That's the way it was, all right. It worked fine for a while. Clyde had his protection and he was using it for all he was worth. But you, Juno . . . you wanted to go on with it. It wasn't so hard to do because money is easy to like. You were the brains of the outfit . . . the thinking brains. Clyde was the strong-arm boy and he had his little army to help him out.'

I stopped and let it sink in. I waited a full minute.

'Juno! . . . '

She raised her head slowly. Her eyes were red, the mascara streaking her cheeks. 'Mike . . . can't you . . .'

'Who killed them all, Juno? Where is he?'

Her hands dropped to her lap, folded across her stomach in despair. I raised the gun. 'Juno!' Only her eyes looked at me. 'I'm going to shoot you, Juno, then I'm going to go out and get him all by myself. I'm going to shoot you where it will hurt like hell and you won't die quickly . . . if you don't tell me. All you have to do is tell me where I can find him and I'll give him the chance to use his hands on me like he tried to do before and like he did to some of the others. Where is he, Juno?'

She didn't speak.

I was going to kill her, so help me God! If I didn't she could fake her way out because I was the only one who knew what had happened. There wasn't a single shred of evidence against her that could be used in court and I knew it. But I could kill her. She had a part in this! The whole thing was her doing and she was as guilty as the killer!

The gun in my hand wavered and I clamped down on the

154

butt to keep it lined up. It was in my face; I could feel it. She could see it. The poison that is hate was dripping out of me and scoring my face. My eyes burned holes in my head and my whole body reeled under the sickening force that pulled me towards her.

I pointed the gun at her head and sighted along the barrel and said, 'My God, I can't!' because the light was in her hair turning it into a halo of white that brought the dead back to life and I was seeing Charlotte's face instead of hers.

I went crazy for a second. Stark, raving mad. My head was a throbbing thing that laughed and screamed for me to go on, bringing the sounds out of my mouth before I could stop it. When the madness went away I was panting like a dog, my breath coming in short, hot gasps.

'I thought I could do it. I thought I could kill you, Juno. I can't. Once there was another woman. You remind me of her. You've seen me when I was hating something . . . I was hating her. I loved her and I killed her. I shot her in the stomach. Yeah, Juno . . . I didn't think it would be this much trouble to kill another woman, but it is.

'So you don't die tonight. I'll take you down to the police and do what I said. Go on, sit there and smile. You'll get out of it, but I'm going to do everything I can to see that you don't.'

I stuck the gun back under my arm and reached for her hand. 'Come on, Juno. I have a friend on the Force who will be happy to book you on my word, even if it means his job.'

She came out of the chair.

Then all hell broke loose. She grabbed my arm and a fist smashed into my nose and I staggered back. There wasn't time to get my hands up before I crashed into the wall, stunned. A devil had me by the throat and a knee came up into my groin. I screamed and doubled over, breaking the grip on my neck. Something gave me the sense to lash out with my feet and the next second she was on top of me clawing for my eyes.

I jerked my head away feeling the skin go with it and brought my fist up and saw it split her nose apart. The blood ran into her mouth and choked off a yell. She tried to get away, fought, kicked and squirmed to get away, but I held on and hammered until she rolled off me.

She didn't stay off. The room echoed with a torrent of animal noises and my arm was wrenched back in a hammer-lock that pulled me completely off my feet. A knee went into my spine and pushed, trying to split me in half. My madness saved me. It flowed into my veins giving me the strength for a tremendous, final effort that hurled me out of her arms and tumbled her in front of me. She came back for another try and

I leaped in to meet her and got my hands on her clothes to jam her in close.

But she twisted away and there was a loud whispering tear of cloth and the gown came away in my hands. Juno went staggering across the room stark naked except for the high-heel shoes and sheer stockings. She rammed an end table, her hands reaching for the drawer, and she got it open far enough for me to see the gun she was trying to get at.

I had mine out first and I said harshly, 'Stand still, Juno!'

She froze there, not a muscle in that beautiful body moving. I looked at all that white bare skin, seeing it in contrast with the shoes and the stockings. Her hands were still on the drawer and inches away from the gun. She didn't have to be told that it couldn't be done.

I let her stand in that position, that ridiculous, obscene position while I lifted the phone off its hook. I had to be sure of just one thing. I went through Information and gave her an address, and I heard Clyde's phone ring. It took a little persuasion to get the cop off the line and Velda on it. I asked her one question and she answered it. She said Clyde was down in the basement out cold. The janitor had gotten him with a poker for some reason or other when he tried to get out. Clyde had never been near the office! She was still asking questions when I hung up.

It was all over now. I had found out *why*, I had found out *how*, now I knew *who*. The dead could go back to being dead for ever.

I said, 'Turn around, Juno.'

No dancer of ballet could have been more poised. Juno balanced delicately on tiptoe and stared at me, the devils of the pit alive in her eyes. The evil of murder was a force so powerful that I could feel it across the room. Juno, queen of the goddesses, standing naked before me her skin glistening in the light.

Tomorrow I'd get my licence back from the D.A. with a note of apology attached. Tomorrow Ed Cooper would have his scoop. Tomorrow would be tomorrow and tonight was tonight. I looked across Olympus and stared at Juno.

'I should have known, Juno. It occurred to me every time you rolled those big beautiful eyes at me. I knew it every time you suggested one of your little love games, then got scared because you knew you didn't dare go through with it. Damn it, I knew it all along and it was too incredible to believe. Me, a guy who likes women, a guy who knows every one of their stunts . . . and I fall for this. Yeah, you and Clyde had a business arrangement all right. You had a lot more than that, too. Who kept who, Juno? Are you the reason why Velda went

156

over so big with Clyde? God, what an ass I was! I should
have caught it the day you hauled me into that village joint
for dinner. There was a Lesbian who followed you into the
ladies' room. I bet she could have kicked herself when she
found out you were no better than she was. It was a part that
fitted you to perfection. You played it so well that only the
ones who didn't dare talk knew about it. Well, Juno, I know
about it. Me. Mike Hammer, I know all about it and I'll talk.
I'll tell them you killed Chester Wheeler because he got mad
enough to try to expose the girl who framed him, and you
killed Rainey because he tried to clip you out of some dirty
dough, and Jean Trotter died for knowing the truth, and
Marion Lester for the same reason. You couldn't have anybody knowing a truth that could be held over your head. Then
Connie died because she discovered the truth when she found
that television set in the storeroom and knew you never delivered it because Jean Trotter was no more married than you
were. Yeah, I'm going to talk my fool head off, you slimy
bastard, but first I'm going to do something else.'

I dropped the Luger to the floor.

It was too impossible for her to comprehend and she missed
her chance. I had the Luger back in my hand before she could
snatch the gun out of the drawer. I forgot all my reservations
about shooting a woman then. I laughed through the blood on
my lips and brought the Luger up as Juno swung around with
eyes blazing a hatred I'll never see again. The rod was jump-
ing in my hand, spitting nasty little slugs that flattened the
killer against the wall with periods that turned into commas as
the blood welled out of the holes. Juno lived until the last shot
had ripped through flesh and intestines and kicked the plaster
from the wall, then died with those rich, red lips split in a
snarl of pain and fearful knowledge.

She lived just long enough to hear me tell her that she was
the only one it could have been, the only one who had the
time. The only one who had the ability to make her identity a
bewildering impossibility. She was the only one who could
have taken that first shot at me on Broadway because she
tailed me from the minute I left the house. She was the one
all the way around because the reasons fit her perfectly as well
as Clyde and Clyde didn't kill anybody. And tomorrow that
was tomorrow would prove it when certain people had their
minds jarred by a picture of what she really looked like, with
her short hair combed back and parted on the side.

Juno died hearing all that and I laughed again as I dragged
myself over to the lifeless lump, past all the foam rubber
gadgets that had come off with the gown, the inevitable falsies
she kept covered so well along with nice solid muscles by

157

dresses that went to her neck and down to her wrists. It was funny. Very funny. Funnier than I ever thought it could be. Maybe you'd laugh, too. I spit on the clay that was Juno, queen of the gods and goddesses, and I knew why I'd always had a resentment that was actually a revulsion when I looked at her.

Juno was a queen, all right, a real, live queen. You know the kind.

Juno was a man!

THE END

THE LAST COP OUT *by* MICKEY SPILLANE

Gillian Burke—known as Gill—had been the toughest, biggest and most effective cop in New York. That was until the Mob decided he was getting too dangerous and pulled the strings which got him dishonourably removed from the force.

But—even disgraced—Gill was still the only cop who knew how the Mob operated, and when their top operators began to be put violently out of business Gill was persuaded—by a frightened district attorney—to put his badge back on and find the killer.

His investigation had hardly begun when he became involved with a cop's daughter—Helen—who was on the syndicate's payroll, and Helga, a luscious Swedish blonde who made her living out of love. But even with such delightful diversions Gill found himself trapped in one of the bloodiest vendettas of all time, pitted against a faceless assassin whose sole aim was destruction. . . .

0 552 09577 X—45p   T193

THE MAN WHO RAISED HELL
by RICHARD SALE

KEYHOLD

It operated on an international scale, its victims were the world's richest men with a secret to hide or a weakness that could be exploited. Its income was incalculable, its methods unscrupulous and its demands inescapable. Any victim who failed to comply with its requirements finished up a corpse with a single identifying characteristic—a simple piece of pasteboard in flaming scarlet, embossed with the promise 'Good Until Death'.

And Sam Carson, greenhorn spy, commandeered decoy for the U.S. National Security agency and accountable to the President only, was the next 'client' of the organisation that no security force had been able to penetrate or destroy . . .

0 552 09111 1—50p   T75

A SELECTED LIST OF CRIME STORIES
FOR YOUR READING PLEASURE

All these books are available at your bookshop or newsagent: or can be ordered directly from the publisher. Just tick the titles you want and fill in the form below.

CORGI BOOKS. Cash Sales Department, P.O. Box 11, Falmouth, Cornwall.

Please send cheque or postal order, no currency. U.K. and Eire send 15p for first book plus 5p per copy for each additional book ordered to a maximum charge of 50p to cover the cost of postage and packing. Overseas Customers and B.F.P.O. allow 20p for first book and 10p per copy for each additional book.

NAME (Block letters)..

ADDRESS ....

(APRIL 75) ....

While every effort is made to keep prices low, it is sometimes necessary to increase prices at short notice. Corgi Books reserve the right to show new retail prices on covers which may differ from those previously advertised in the text or elsewhere.

KU-375-385

TEACH YOURSELF BOOKS

BEE-KEEPING

D. Sinclair
Killiemuller
Kirgussie

This book provides a clear and concise introduction to the art of keeping bees. It covers the many aspects of apiarism, including how to set up a hive, swarming and swarm protection, honey production, feeding and the diseases of bees. Although intended primarily for the beginner, this practical guide should also be of value as a source of reference to the more experienced bee-keeper.

This book is "definitely practical in its approach and is a handy book of reference which will provide the answers to most of the questions that normally confront the beginner in bee-keeping during the initial stages of his apprenticeship. It also contains information that will be of great value during many succeeding seasons."

Higher Education Journal

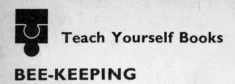

Teach Yourself Books

BEE-KEEPING

Lt.-Col. A. Norman Schofield, C.B.E., LL.M.
Solicitor

Illustrations by
W. W. Newman, M.Inst.C.E., F.S.I.

ST. PAUL'S HOUSE WARWICK LANE LONDON EC4

First printed   *1943*
Third edition   *1958*
Fourth edition   *1971*
Second impression *1973*

Copyright © 1958, 1971
The English Universities Press Ltd.

All rights reserved. No part of this publication may
be reproduced or transmitted in any form or by any
means, electronic or mechanical, including
photocopy, recording, or any information storage
and retrieval system, without permission in writing
from the publisher.

ISBN 0 340 05520 0

Printed in Great Britain for The English Universities Press Ltd, by
C. Tinling & Co., Ltd, London and Prescot.

FOREWORD

Bee Research Laboratory,
Rothamsted Experimental Station,
Harpenden, Herts.

MR. NORMAN SCHOFIELD has done me the honour of asking me to criticise the manuscript of this little book, and to write a short foreword.

In the past it has unfortunately been only too easy to criticise to their disadvantage many of the books on bee-keeping, since their authors often appeared to be ignorant of the advances in bee research, which had already been made at the time the books were written. What is worse, some of the authors of the past appear merely to have taken a few text-books on bee-keeping, and having selected what they considered to be best in each, to have copied it almost verbatim, thus perpetuating mistakes. Frequently, the results have been a mere re-hash, and often inferior ones, of earlier works.

Mr. Schofield has, I am glad to say, done no such thing ; he has written an easily readable little book, based on his own practical experience as a bee-keeper, and I am convinced that the expert as well as the beginner will find something of value here.

I am very pleased to find that many of the old fallacies such as the idea that bees must be coddled with much packing in the winter, and that cane-sugar obtained from sugar-beet is harmful to bees, are conspicuous by their absence. Mr. Schofield will, I am sure, agree that the following words of Pope, which I recently saw quoted in a Bee Journal, give excellent advice to modern bee-keepers :

" Be not the first by whom the new is tried,
Nor yet the last to lay the old aside."

C. G. BUTLER

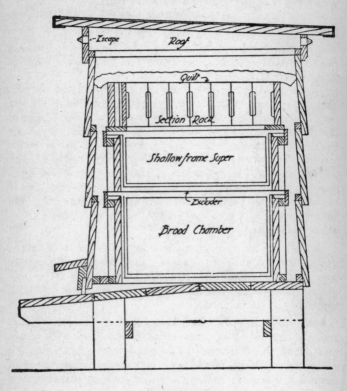

Escape   Roof

Quilt

Section Rack

Shallow frame Super

Excluder

Brood Chamber

THE W.B.C. HIVE

PREFACE TO FIRST EDITION

DURING the present war the value of sugar, and commodities containing sugar, have been more appreciated by the general public than in years of peace.

It is not surprising therefore that many thousands have turned to the most ancient means of producing sweetening material, namely, the keeping of the honey-bee. There are those who imagine that this is a simple matter to which they may readily turn a hand. Experience will show that a great deal of care is essential for, as in most practices, success will only be achieved by patience and perseverance.

There are those, too, who embark upon bee-keeping as a means to an end, namely, the production of honey for honey's sake, and who regard the bees as being the medium.

The true bee-keeper is the man who will see that his bees receive the best possible attention, who sees that they have always plenty of food, and who keeps them free from disease. He will reap his reward in much greater measure than the man who takes from the bees their last ounce of honey.

Unless the reader has no other object than the production of honey he should refrain from bee-keeping and leave these valuable creatures to those who will care for them.

It becomes an absorbing hobby to those who put a real interest in it, as do all studies of nature. It provides scope for the handyman. It can become a profitable hobby if due care is taken. It does not interfere with normal holidays and it can be carried on by the townsman just as well as the countryman, although the townsman has the disadvantage of travelling to his bees. Little ground is necessary, and only a small capital expenditure.

There is no more contentious subject matter amongst bee-keepers than bees, Many readers may disagree with many of my ideas. I should be grateful to have their views and the results of any experiments they may have carried out.

This book is intended to be an elementary guide to bee-keeping. Many of the finer practices are purposely omitted for fear of confusing the beginner. There are many advanced books on this matter to which the reader can readily refer—most public libraries contain a good number of them.

My sincerest thanks are due to Dr. C. G. Butler, of Rothamsted, for reading through the manuscript and for his suggestions and corrections. Also my thanks are due to Mr. Newman, also a bee-keeper, for his excellent drawings.

I must not forget to thank my good friend, Mr. F. Farquharson, of Watford, for all he has taught me.

A. NORMAN SCHOFIELD

The White House,
   Hempstead Road,
      Watford.
         Nov., 1943.

PREFACE TO THE FOURTH EDITION

SINCE the publication of the earlier Editions I have received a great many letters from readers who have sent me their views on many matters. Certain errors in those Editions have now been rectified as a result of these letters.

This correspondence has been extremely helpful and I hope has improved this little book.

I refer to what is a comparatively new discovery in Chapter IV, dealing with the selection by the bees them-selves of the sex of the resultant bee developed from the eggs laid by the queen. This may cause a great deal of controversy, but if in the end it leads to the truth, then it will have been worthwhile introducing it here.

Again I welcome observations and criticisms.

A. NORMAN SCHOFIELD

Southampton,
   March 1970.

TABLE OF CONTENTS

ix

LIST OF ILLUSTRATIONS

PLATES

Between pages 80 and 81

ILLUSTRATIONS IN TEXT

CHAPTER I

THE PURPOSES OF BEE-KEEPING

Honey

FROM time immemorial man has pursued the art of bee-keeping with the primary object of securing honey for food. Until the introduction of sugar derived from the sugar cane and sugar beet, it was the only known method of sweetening. To-day, the honey bee is used almost entirely as a producer of food.

As a food, honey has a very high market value and it is generally understood that it is one of the most easily assimilated of foodstuffs. Many ardent bee-keepers claim that it has virtues almost reaching the romantic. It is, however, used extensively in the making up of medicines, particularly for those prescribed for the throat, probably because of its syrup-like nature and the claim that it is an excellent antiseptic.

It is at all times a very welcome addition to the table.

Wax Production

A most valuable by-product of honey is beeswax. The story of its production is told elsewhere in this book. This product is of very great importance to the bee-keeper and it cannot be too strongly emphasised that not one scrap of it should be discarded by the bee-keeper. It should be stored in a tin so that the wax moth which is destructive of wax comb cannot destroy it. Later it should be melted down and clarified and sold to the manufacturers of wax foundation.

Shown later is a diagram of a solar wax extractor. Pieces of old comb are placed inside and the lid closed down. The sun's rays have a greenhouse effect and the heat generated melts the wax (see *Fig. 25*).

Natural History Study

For the naturalist and the student of natural history, the honey bee offers a fascinating study. Many people who commence bee-keeping for the purpose of producing honey soon become captivated with the study of the lives of the insects from which they reap such a sweet harvest. A great deal of knowledge has been recorded in recent years by bee-keepers, particularly since the introduction of the movable frame hive, and many of the mysteries to which ancient bee-keepers attached superstitions are normal and regular happenings in the hive.

Pollination of Blossoms

Apart from the production of honey, the pollination of blossoms is a most important role of the honey bee. Some experts, in particular Doctor Butler, of Rothamsted, assert that the production of honey is only secondary compared with the value of the honey bee as a pollinator of blossoms. Zander's original estimate was that the financial value of pollination was ten times the value of honey. It has now been established beyond all doubt that the yield of fruit from orchards having hives of bees exceeds many times those without. Whilst there are many, many insects, and indeed the elements of wind and rain which act as pollinators, none are so consistent and subject to such control as the honey bee. Orchard trees, however, are not pollinated by the wind at all. This has been shown by experiment at the John Innes Horticultural Institute.

Farmers and seedsmen have now come to realise the value of the honey bee as a pollinator of such crops as white clover, sanfoin, lucerne, the brassica family and the like. It has been discovered in the case of red clover that under favourable conditions the bees will visit it every third or fourth day for, on account of the shortness of their tongues they are unable to reach the nectar until it rises sufficiently in the flower for them to reach it.

Therefore, for the fruit grower, hives of bees are essential. It has been recommended that one hive to the acre of fruit trees is adequate to ensure complete pollination.

Breeding for Sale

This side of bee-keeping is the most commercial and at the present time very profitable. A stock of bees, with care, can be trebled or quadrupled in a season if honey is not worked for, and this will show a gross profit of from ten to fifteen pounds per hive, which is seldom, if ever, obtained from honey-producing hives.

CHAPTER II

THE COLONY OF BEES

A COLONY of bees consists of a hive containing combs, a Queen bee, a large number of worker bees and a number of drones.

The hive may be one of many types, but the beginner is well advised to purchase equipment of a standard type and to purchase all future supplies of the same standard. In this way, all his equipment will be inter-changeable, which is a most important thing. This cannot be too strongly emphasised. The standards which are in the commonest use in this country are British Bee-keepers Association Standards.

There are three principal kinds of hives in use in this country. (a) The straw skep hive, (b) the W.B.C. double-walled hive, and (c) the single-walled National hive.

The Straw Skep Hive

This hive has many advantages and many disadvantages over the modern movable frame hive, but the disadvantages far outweigh the advantages.

It is, however, cheap for it costs about ten shillings, it is light and easily moved from place to place. This was found convenient in the old bee-keeping days when transport was difficult and when bees were taken to the heather after the field flowers had died down. It produces swarms which are of value for stock increases. It can be "supered," a process which is later described. It certainly produces honey, for Pettigrew, in his "Handy Book of Bees," 1875 records that a Mr. Jack, of Wilshaw, had a straw hive and its swarms which, at the end of the season, weighed 474 lbs. A conservative estimate of the honey which could have been obtained from those straw hives was 300 lbs. Many modern bar-frame hive operators may wonder at these results, but these and others are recorded in that book.

Straw hives are useful when the bees are required for pollination only.

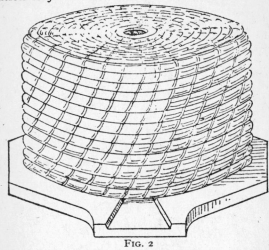

FIG. 2
The Straw Skep Hive

The colony which has become established in a straw skep may be transferred to a bar frame hive by placing the skep on top of a standard brood chamber as shown in Plate I. The queen will ultimately lay in the new brood chamber in the bars fitted there. When she is found " below " a queen excluder (see page 27 and *Fig.16*) should be put between the skep and the brood chamber.

The brood chamber is that part of the hive where the queen lays her eggs and the young brood are reared (see *Figs. 4* and *5*).

Straw hives, **however,** do not permit of complete control in management. They may harbour disease and be a danger to other stocks. If, however, the bee-keeper is bent upon a complete study of his subject, he should keep one stock in a straw hive in his apiary. On account, however, of the present serious position with regard to bee diseases, in particular foul brood, it is not recommended that the skep should be the normal method of housing a colony of bees.

The skep in this drawing is made of straw bound by split cane and stands on a hive board. It has a flat crown and a hole in the centre. This enables a small crate of section boxes to be placed over the crown hole and when the bees gather honey they take it up through the crown hole and store it in the section boxes. This is called supering.

A crate of section boxes is shown in *Fig. 26*.

The W.B.C. Doubled-walled Hive

This hive bears the initials of one *W*illiam *B*roughton *C*arr, its inventor. This has now become the most popular of all hives. The main feature of this hive is that the outer walls and the brood chamber are separated by an air space which ensures the hive being perfectly dry. Bees only prosper in dry hives. They can tolerate the coldest of winters if dry, but cold and damp are fatal. A note on keeping hives dry is given in the chapter dealing with the wintering of bees.

From the diagram of this hive (ante, at page vi), it will be noticed that the brood chamber is placed on a stoutly constructed wooden stand. On the stand outside the brood chamber is placed the outer wall, this is built up in tiers, the bottom of one fitting on top of, but on the outer side of the one below. These tiers are called " lifts." These lifts fit on each other like slates or tiles to prevent the rain from getting inside. The whole is covered in with a roof which either slopes from the centre outwards or from front to back. The latter is preferred as it ensures the rain being kept clear of the entrance to the hive. It is also easier to make and has a very smart appearance (see also *Fig. 3* showing the outward appearance of a W.B.C. hive).

The brood chamber is of B.B.K.A. standard measurements and is designed to hold 10 B.B.K.A. standard brood frames and a division board. This board is a desirable fitting, as it ensures that all the standard frames fit snugly together. The frames hold the wax foundation and are to be seen in *Figs. 6* and *10*. If the frames do not fit correctly together, the bees build comb between the frames and at right-angles to the frames. This is called brace comb and

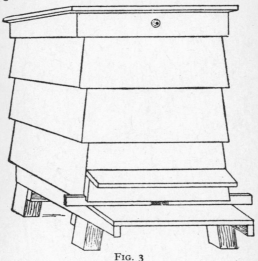

FIG. 3
The Outer Structure of a W.B.C. Hive

is a great nuisance when manipulation of the hive is in progress. Further, if the combs are not set snugly together, the bees are apt to build drone comb in the frames. When manipulating a hive, this board is first taken out and the space left in the brood chamber enables the frames to be eased and lifted out more readily and without crushing any bees.

In the diagram of the W.B.C. hive (frontispiece) will

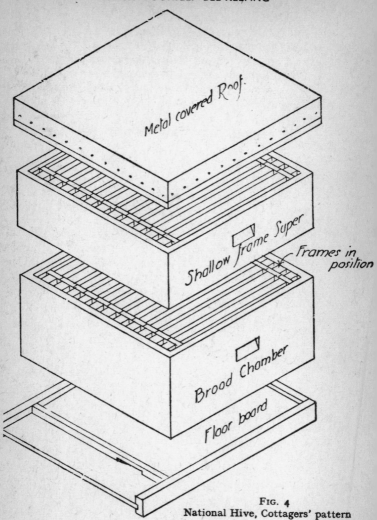

FIG. 4
National Hive, Cottagers' pattern

be noticed another chamber over the brood chamber. This chamber is constructed so as to hold a number of shallow frames in which is stored the honey. This chamber or crate is called a " super " or shallow frame crate.

In place of this super or in addition to it may be placed a crate of sections if the production of section honey is required (see *Fig. 26*).

Again, it should be emphasised that if the beginner decides upon the W.B.C. hive, he should ensure that all the outside lifts are interchangeable.

The National Hive

The characteristic of this hive is that it is single walled only. That is, the walls of the brood chamber form the only protection between the bees and the outside atmosphere. It has proved to be perfectly satisfactory, provided that the hive is kept dry. It is cheaper than the W.B.C. hive, both initially and in the long run, and it is more economical than the double-walled types. The National hive holds eleven brood frames in its brood chamber, it has less parts than the W.B.C. and is more readily portable, and for this reason, is ideal for use for those bee-keepers who place their bees on the heather.

The single-walled hive can be purchased in a cheaper form known as the Cottagers' hive (*Fig. 4*). This hive is placed on a stand. A wide drain pipe set into the ground is most suitable, as its smooth surface prevents mice and other pests from entering the hive. Its great disadvantage is the risk of damp entering the hive.

Fig. 5 shows a National Hive with a deep cover. In winter time when the super is off it acts as a double wall to the brood chamber.

The Brood Frame

As has already been described, the brood chamber in B.B.K.A. standard has 10 brood frames. *Fig. 6* shows a standard brood frame.

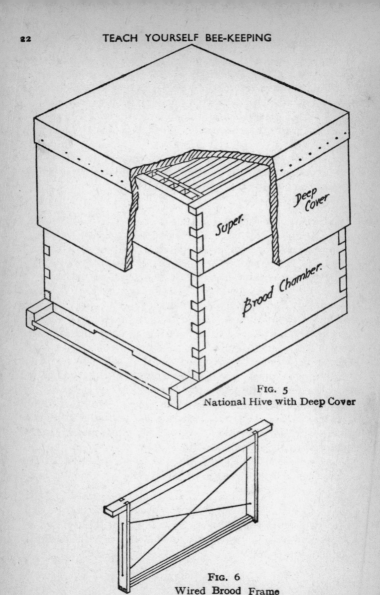

FIG. 5
National Hive with Deep Cover

FIG. 6
Wired Brood Frame

The measurement of the top bar is 17 ins. long, $\frac{7}{8}$ in. wide, and $\frac{3}{8}$ in. thick,

The side bars have an overall length of $8\frac{1}{2}$ ins. and the bottom bar has an overall length of 14 ins. Both side and bottom bars are $\frac{7}{8}$ in. wide and $\frac{3}{4}$ in. thick.

At the ends of the top bars, " metal ends " are fitted.

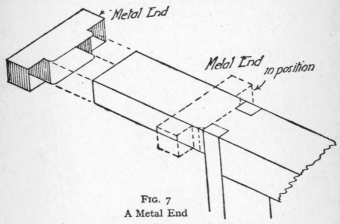

Fig. 7
A Metal End

These metal ends are designed to ensure that the frames are accurately spaced, for the bees build their brood comb $\frac{7}{8}$ in. thick from face to face with an intervening space between of $\frac{5}{8}$ in. This makes the metal end $1\frac{1}{2}$ ins. wide. Wider metal ends, 2 ins. wide, are sometimes fitted to standard shallow frames used for the production of extracted honey, and the use of these is described in the chapter on honey production.

Foundation

The invention of this material manufactured from pure beeswax is one of the greatest boons to bee-keepers. This material consists of a thin sheet of beeswax impressed mechanically with the forms of the bases of the cells of honeycomb and the bases of the cell walls. This is sold in sheets of the correct sizes to fit in the wooden brood frames, shallow frames and section boxes. For brood frames, " worker foundation " is supplied. This ensures that the bees are induced to build worker cells in the brood chamber to the exclusion of drone cells. It should here be pointed out that it is a great disadvantage to have too many drone cells in the brood chamber for too many drones are said to encourage swarming and, as they are not honey gatherers, consume large quantities of honey which might otherwise be stored.

Bees, however, will not always draw out the worker foundation as worker cells. Sometimes they draw out the foundation part worker and part drone. The intermediate cells are called transition cells (see *Fig. 8*).

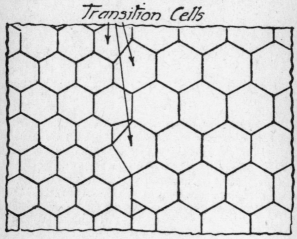

FIG. 8
Transition Cells

For shallow frames " drone foundation " is recommended, because the bees do not often store pollen in drone cells (see Plate 2, page 35), but honey only, and when honey is stored in drone cells it is more readily extracted than from worker cells. In natural surroundings bees build drone cells in which to store honey. It should be pointed out, however, that when drone foundation is used in the supers a queen excluder is absolutely essential. There are other disadvantages in the use of drone combs. Sometimes the bees hesitate to go into drone combs until the queen has laid eggs in them. This is frustrated if a queen excluder is used. Further they cannot be used as food storage combs for winter. There are those who think

The Correct Way   The Incorrect Way

FIG. 9

The Correct and Incorrect Way of Fixing Foundation

that the use of a queen excluder outweighs the advantages of drone cells for the storage of honey. It certainly is a great help to have drawn out worker combs in shallow frames to form an addition to the brood nest. On the whole drone combs for supers are preferable.

There are approximately 28·87 worker cells to the square inch ; each cell being approximately 1/5 in. in diameter. The cells are hexagonal in shape, two sides of the cells are vertical. This is important to remember for if the foundation is inserted with two sides horizontal, the bees will break down the foundation and build more drone cells than the bee-keeper desires. This causes delay and waste of effort on the part of the bees. *Fig. 9*, ante, shows the correct way up of foundation and also the incorrect way.

Drone cells are larger than worker cells, being approximately $\frac{3}{4}$ in. diameter. There are 18·48 cells to the square inch.

Foundation should be made from pure beeswax. Any

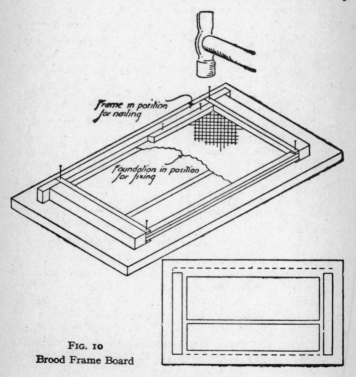

FIG. 10
Brood Frame Board

foundation which is adulterated with any other material should be refused by the bee-keeper.

Foundation used for sections is made of the finest selected beeswax and is much thinner than for brood or shallow frame foundation. It is cut in squares 4⅜ in. each way, ready to fit into the sections.

Mr. Newman has devised a special board for ensuring that the frames when nailed together are absolutely square. The beginner would be wise to make one of such boards (see *Fig. 10*).

Queen Excluder

This is the name of a device which is placed over the brood chamber and which permits the worker bees to pass through but not the Queen. The Queen, being larger in the thorax than the workers, is therefore kept " downstairs " in the brood chamber, and does not lay any eggs in the supers. This is particularly desirable where sections are being worked—for in that case the honey must not be contaminated by breeding in the honeycomb which is to be eaten.

The excluders are made either of zinc with slots cut in it, as shown in *Fig. 16*, or are made of wire held firmly by separators. (*Fig. 17*.) The principal pattern in use is called the Waldron excluder, and this pattern is generally thought to be a very great advance on the zinc types.

The excluder is laid on the top of the brood frames, the slots in the excluder being laid at right-angles to the brood frames. The excluder covers the whole of the brood frames. Over the excluder the shallow frame crate or the section crate is set and over the crate the quilt.

It is essential for the bee-keeper to take great care with queen excluders. If the zinc type is used care should be taken to ensure that the zinc separating the slots does not become broken or buckled otherwise the queen will find her way through. Also with the Waldron excluder care should be taken to ensure that none of the wires are bent or the queen will also get through.

The Quilt

This is a piece of fabric. Some people use ticking or linen, but deck chair canvas or sail cloth proves as satisfactory as any.

Over the quilt is placed one or two dry clean sacks or one or two thicknesses of carpet under-felting.

Many bee-keepers prefer to use a clearer board all the year round. (*Fig. 20.*) The author himself has tried both canvas and clearer boards and much prefers the latter. In winter the clearer board dispenses with the necessity for bee passages referred to in Chapter X.

PURCHASING BEES

Purchasing a Stock

The beginner is advised to take the advice of any experienced bee-keeper in selecting a stock of bees.

The best type of stock to buy is an established stock on 10 brood frames, with a Queen born the year before. A Queen is thought to be at its best in the second year. The purchaser should insist that the stock is to B.B.K.A. standard. The standard is as follows :—

Two-thirds of the number of combs in the colony should contain brood.

All combs to be well covered with bees and in each stock a fertile Queen must be present.

To purchase a stock is the most expensive method, but if honey is required in the first year, this is the surest way of obtaining it. It costs about £6-0-0.

The other ways of starting are as follows :—

Purchasing a Swarm

The advantages of purchasing a swarm are :—

(*a*) It is comparatively cheap. It costs about £3-0-0.

(b) If fed with warm syrup, the swarm becomes quickly established.

(c) There is an uncanny " urge " in a swarm to establish itself rapidly and produce a surplus for winter stores. If it is an early swarm, i.e., a May or early June swarm, a surplus is assured if the season is good.

The disadvantages of purchasing a swarm are :—

(a) It is always problematical how a swarm will develop. The Queen may be past her prime and the stock prove useless as honey producers.

(b) If the swarm is from an unknown source, the characteristics of the bees are uncertain and may prove savage or diseased.

Purchasing a Nucleus

A nucleus is a small stock of bees having a fertile Queen of the current year. The advantages of this way are :—

(a) This is a cheaper way than purchasing a full stock.

(b) The purchaser is assured of a young Queen.

(c) The purchaser knows the source and characteristics of his bees.

The disadvantages are :—

(a) The improbability of obtaining surplus honey in the current year.

(b) The cost of feeding up the nucleus to enable it to live through the winter.

The best advice is to purchase a full stock on at least eight frames in the month of May. In this way, with careful treatment in swarm prevention, the bee-keeper is assured of a surplus of honey in his first year.

CHAPTER III

HOW TO WORK FOR SURPLUS HONEY

IT must be impressed upon the beginner that the worker bees produce honey and that the more bees there are the more honey is likely to be produced.

Spring Stimulation

The first step to take to ensure a successful season is to winter the stock well and carefully. Then Spring comes and early Spring sunshine causes the bees to fly. When this time arrives it is the signal for the bee-keeper to take the first step in a definite plan.

In the last week in March in the South of England, and in the second or third weeks of April in the North of England, Spring stimulation should be started.

Spring stimulation consists of two matters :
(*a*) Stimulative feeding.
(*b*) Brood spreading.

There are many views in regard to feeding. Some say that a cake of candy placed over the feed hole and constantly renewed, is all that is necessary in the Spring. That certainly is an easy and troubleless method but it is not the most effective.

An established method and one which has proved very satisfactory is by giving the bees a cupful of warm thin syrup through the slow feeder. The slow or bottle feeder is shown in this diagram.

This dose should be given every second day. If too much syrup is given, the bees will spend their energies storing the syrup. The idea in giving them this syrup is to make them believe the honey flow has started. They then start feeding the Queen, who lays eggs in proportion to the amount of feeding she receives. The feeding should be kept up until the early blossoms appear and provide the nectar to take the place of the artificial food.

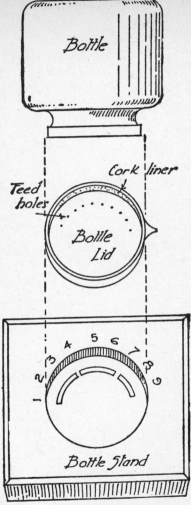

FIG. 11
Slow or Bottle Feeder

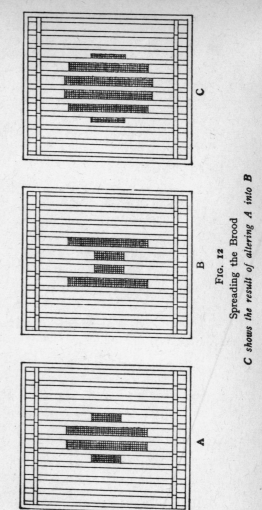

FIG. 12

Spreading the Brood

C shows the result of altering A into B

The usual accepted formula for Spring syrup is 1 pint of water to 1 lb. of sugar. Some give as a suitable recipe 2 pints of water to 1 lb. of sugar.

Dr. Butler, of Rothamsted, has recently been carrying out experiments on very thin syrup indeed, and it is understood with favourable results. The author, hearing Dr. Butler on this matter, tried feeding by a rapid feeder a pint of warm syrup daily of 1 lb. of sugar to 10 pints of water. The stock did extremely well, producing 92 lbs. of surplus honey in the 1942 season which, in the Home Counties, was not regarded as a very good season.

However, it should be clearly understood that too much sugar may prevent the Queen from laying because of the consequent filling up of the cells.

It is known that bees require a considerable amount of water when they are breeding, and feeding very dilute syrup to them saves them many chilly journeys in search of water in the early Spring mornings.

It is also known that the length of the life of a bee bears a direct reverse ratio to the amount of flying time. Therefore, if you can save bees a lot of flying time by feeding water to them, you will ultimately obtain more nectar collecting from your bee population.

On a warm sunny day about seven days after you start this thin syrup feeding, take a look at your bees. You will probably find a certain amount of sealed brood but a larger proportion of grubs and eggs. If you find large patches of eggs and grubs, you may be quite satisfied that your stimulative feeding is having effect.

Spreading the Brood

Having stimulated the Queen to activity with satisfactory results, it is now possible to extend the activities of the Queen. There are two conditions precedent to brood spreading and they must be adhered to very rigidly; otherwise, it may prove disastrous.

First, the weather must not be too cold or raw. Preferably, the third week in April must be reached.

Secondly, the hive must contain a large number of young bees to ensure good cover for the combs.

These two conditions are important and must be observed ; otherwise, the brood may become chilled and die.

The Queen in Spring lays her eggs in the centre of the cluster of bees. .

It will be noticed from the diagram (brood chamber " A ") that the two centre combs have more brood in them than the combs adjoining them on either side. Now place the outer combs in the centre, as in brood chamber " B," and the effect is to encourage the Queen to lay in this fresh accommodation, resulting in brood chamber " C." After a week, move the other outer combs to the middle and a similar stimulation will be given to the Queen. As the bees hatch out, the brood will spread even further. Keep on bringing in the outer combs if the weather continues fair and warm, until all the combs are filled with brood. Do not get over enthusiastic too early in the season with this hazardous method of stimulation and on no account should any combs which have no brood in them be put in the centre of the brood until at least the second week in May. If this method of stimulation proves successful, be sure to give the bees plenty of space for storing honey, otherwise the stock will be so strong that it will swarm at the earliest opportunity. The other methods of swarm control should also be carried out. These are enumerated later. If the beginner is in any doubt he should avoid this practice and the risks it entails.

Spring Cleaning

Whilst all this Spring stimulation is proceeding, an opportunity should be taken on a warm fine day to clean up the interior of the hive.

One very good way of doing this is to prepare a spare

hive and brood chamber and move the stock to one side and place the spare hive and brood chamber exactly where the stock previously stood. Then take out each brood frame in turn, examine each carefully for the effects of wax moth, or excessive amounts of drone cells in the combs. Scrape each frame clean of all unnecessary comb and propolis. Smear the metal runners in the br od chamber with vaseline and then place each frame in the new brood chamber in exactly the same order as in the old chamber. Take away the old hive and brood chamber and clean them up ready to deal with the next stock. Remove any combs which have an excessive number of drone cells. You want workers not drones (see Plate II).

Reference is made here to the use of vaseline. This is most desirable for it prevents the bees from cementing the metal ends together with propolis. It will be found later that any bar can be lifted out without the necessity of using a hive tool, chisel or screw-driver for loosening the bars. The absence of " jarring " has a marked effect on the bees and they are much more docile when vaseline is used.

Cleanliness in a hive is very important and it is a great help in resisting bee diseases. The " dirty " bee-keeper loses the respect of his fellow bee-keepers who come to regard his apiary as a source of danger to the district.

Propolis is described at page 48.

Capacity of Brood Chamber

As already stated, the B.B.K.A. standard brood chamber has ten standard brood frames, but this is considered by many to be too small. Experience has generally shown this to be so in many districts and with the best and modern strains of bees.

If Queens are prolific breeders it is estimated that they may lay anything up to 3,000 eggs per day, and as one brood comb has approximately 5,000 cells, i.e., including both sides of the comb, there is approximately one and a half days work in each comb, bearing in mind that not all the cells on each side of the comb are filled with eggs. As has been stated elsewhere, worker bees take 21 days from egg to bee—one and a half into 21 goes 14 times. Therefore, at the height of the season, 14 frames would appear to be required.

Many bee-keepers use two brood chambers of 10 brood frames in each, one placed above the other, but a brood chamber together with a crate of shallow frames having worker foundation proves most suitable. It is found that a normal Queen will keep these combs fully occupied with brood rearing.

There is a rational argument against too large a brood chamber and it is that too much effort can be wasted by the bees in rearing so large a stock to the detriment of honey production.

It is certainly true that at the height of the honey flow, if there are two or three cold days, large stocks consume an enormous amount of stored honey.

Many bee-keepers who use a brood chamber and shallow frames for breeding, discard the Queen excluder completely, especially when sections are being worked. But if this is drone, done foundation should not be used for the upper shallow frames in case the Queen should find her way up there and fill the drone cells with eggs. Queens do not particularly like section boxes for breeding and they remain below in the more spacious apartments. The absence of a Queen excluder is certainly an advantage to the worker bees, who very often refuse to work sections if there is a Queen excluder below the section crate.

Having now developed through stimulative feeding a strong stock, the bee-keeper must take very good care that the strength of his stock does not defeat his object.

Honey Storage by Bees

If there is not sufficient room for honey storage, the bees will follow their natural instinct and swarm. A separate chapter deals with the question of swarm prevention, but it is desirable to set out here briefly the ways to prevent swarming :—

(a) Having a young Queen.

(b) Have sufficient space for breeding.

(c) Have sufficient space for honey storage.

(d) Eliminate as many drones as possible.

(e) Inspect periodically, at least every 10 days, to remove any Queen cells, and, if necessary, give more room for honey storage.

Therefore, as soon as the brood combs appear to have their upper cells drawn out with new white wax, the bee-keeper must without delay give more room for honey storage.

Remove the quilt and place the Queen excluder on top of the brood chamber or, if brood chamber and shallow combs are used for breeding, then on top of the shallow combs. Over the Queen excluder place the new crate of shallow combs and over the shallow combs place the quilt.

Sometimes, it is found that the bees are somewhat slow in making use of these combs, particularly if they are frames with new foundation. The bees can readily be encouraged by placing a feeder of warm syrup over the feed hole in the quilt, or by splashing the new combs with a liberal quantity of sugar syrup. The bees will then rise very quickly and use the syrup to make the wax needed to draw out the foundation.

In many districts where the early fruit blossoms are in abundance, it is not unusual to get a little surplus honey provided the stock is a strong one and the combs are already drawn out.

Where foundation is used instead of combs, it will be found that those in the centre of the crate are drawn out first. It is a great advantage to have all the combs drawn out in readiness for the main honey flow. The bee-keeper is therefore advised to watch the combs and as the centre ones are drawn out, to move them outwards and place the outside combs in the middle and so on until all the combs are fully drawn out.

Before all the combs are drawn out, a considerable quantity of uncapped honey is found to be stored. If the weather continues favourable, the bees will begin to cap over the honey. They will not, however, cap over the honey until it is of the right consistency, that is, in such a state that it will not ferment.

As soon as one-third of the total surface of supers is capped over, the bee-keeper must place another super on the hive ; otherwise, the bees may swarm. This is the way in which the super should be placed on the hive. Take off the partly filled super and place the new super on top of the Queen excluder and then place the partly-filled super on top of the empty one. The reason for this is that bees naturally build their combs from the roof downwards, and will continue from the top super downwards to the brood chamber.

The bees in their travels up to the top super become accustomed to the new super and are soon seen preparing the combs to receive their store of honey. So long as the bees go on storing honey, so the bee-keeper should continue adding supers.

Some people say it is desirable to leave the honey on the hive until the end of the honey flow. This is not advised when sections are being worked because even though the combs are filled and sealed, the bees continue to walk over the surface of the combs and they become discoloured or " travel-stained," and this makes them less appetising and of a reduced market value.

CHAPTER IV

THE OCCUPIERS OF THE HIVE

AT the height of the season, that is in the months of June and July, the bee-hive contains a very heavy population indeed. Estimates vary as to the number of bees contained in a colony, but in a normal colony somewhere between 40,000 and 60,000 bees occupy a hive. Of these, there is one Queen only, a few hundred drones, and the remainder are worker bees. (*Fig. 13.*)

Taking these bees in order, we come first to the Queen.

The Queen Bee

A great deal of mystery surrounds the Queen, and

Drone Queen Worker

FIG. 13

enquiring strangers to the craft of apiculture invariably are anxious to see the Queen bee. She is the only genuine female in the hive, and is controlled by the workers and does not in any way rule the hive. She is born from a special cell known as the Queen cell. (*Fig. 14.*) This cell, the size and shape of a medium acorn, hangs downwards in the hive. The cell is formed by the bees of a mixture of beeswax and pollen, and is made semi-porous to enable the Queen to have air before hatching out. After the cell is formed, the workers usually themselves place in the cell an egg which has been laid by the Queen in a worker cell. Dr. Caird recorded having seen a Queen lay an egg in a Queen cell (*Bee World* 16, p. 69). It is quite understandable that she herself will hesitate to lay the egg for a newcomer who will ultimately take her place in the hive. The workers immediately place in the cell along with the egg a white creamy substance which is called by bee-keepers, "royal jelly." This " Royal Jelly " has been found to have invigorating and tonic qualities. It is now produced by some pharmaceutical chemists in a palatable medicinal form, particularly in France. When the egg hatches on the third day, the grub which emerges from the egg feeds on this special food for a period of five days. It then spends a day spinning a cocoon, after which it rests for a further two days.

Fig. 14

Queen Cells

On the next day, the eleventh, it is transformed from a larvae into a nymph, and after three days as a nymph it emerges as a virgin Queen bee. The emergence of a Queen is a matter over which she has little control. The control is exercised by the workers, who only permit the Queen to emerge either to replace an old Queen who has passed her usefulness as an egg layer or to replace a Queen who has left with a swarm. It therefore takes 14 days to rear a Queen from the egg to the Queen herself. After leaving her cell, from which she is released by the worker bees, who lift the cap from the cell, she walks about the hive without

any ceremony.   After a few days, she goes out of the hive
on the first available fine day on her first flight.   The
length of time she remains in the hive depends to a very
great extent on weather conditions.   Fine weather is
essential.   The drones in the hive and neighbouring drones
fly in front of the hive containing the virgin Queen, and
she comes out on the landing board of the hive.   Eventually
she takes her first flight.   Observers say that she hovers in
front of the hive to establish her location and then flies
upwards into the sky, followed by any drones which may
then be flying.   Dr. Butler believes that the Queen makes
several orientation flights before making her mating flight.

Coition between drone and Queen takes place in mid-air,
and results in the immediate death of the drone, for his
gential organs are torn out by the queen.   She then returns
to the hive, still having the drone's organs attached.   She is
welcomed by the workers, who immediately commence to
feed the queen lavishly and remove the drone's organs.   The
author has seen a virgin queen leave the hive, circle round
many times, and fifteen minutes later return with the
drone's organs attached.   In a few days the Queen commences to lay eggs, somewhat spasmodically at first, until
later she lays at a very great rate.   It is generally accepted
that in her prime, that is in her second year, she lays at the
rate of 2,000 to 3,000 eggs a day.   The Queen is a handsome
insect ; a long and graceful abdomen, but with short wings
which fold neatly over her back.   The laying power of the
Queen is one of the marvels of the hive.   For months on
end she will lay at a great rate, and her useful life lasts
roughly four years, but for honey production, experienced
bee men do not keep the Queens for more than two years
at the longest.   It must, however, be borne in mind that
during the coldest part of the Winter, the Queen either
ceases to lay altogether or her laying is reduced to a very
minimum   The bees, however, when the days lengthen
towards the middle of February, begin to feed the Queen

with more food, and she lays a little more frequently in the centre of the winter cluster. It is at this stage that a cake of candy over the hole in the quilt will provide the necessary supply of food to ensure the safe arrival of the young·bees, which are so important at this stage to the future welfare of the hive. As the weather becomes warmer, so the Queen expands her laying until at the end of April she becomes the prolific layer she continues to be until mid-August. At the end of this period of the year her laying is curtailed by the bees, who feed her less generously, because at this season of the year the honey flow is ending.

The reader is referred to the chapter on swarming for further information regarding this most interesting creature.

The Drone

This is the male bee. The control of his life is in the hands of the worker bee. His birth is restricted in numbers by the worker. He is principally fed by the workers. He remains indoors during any but the best of weather, and when his functional services are no longer required, and when the honey flow draws to a close he is killed by the workers.

In the early Spring the workers gather in nectar from the Spring flowers, and the urge for colonisation enters into the hive. After ensuring stores for the future occupants of the hive, the workers then commence to build drone cells. Many of these may already exist in the combs in the brood chambers from the previous year. If they do not, the workers will break down some worker comb and rebuild it as drone comb. This conversion usually takes place in the worker comb, which is not of good quality, namely that at the bottom of the comb. These cells are usually made in the lower half of the comb, and are easily distinguished by their size, being larger than the worker cells. The Queen is then induced to lay eggs in these cells. The Queen lays an egg precisely similar in appearance to any other egg she lays, but the result is a male. How it is done has never been satisfactorily explained The author in 1944 had the privilege of discussing this matter with a research student at the Hebrew University, Jerusalem. Her theory is that all the eggs laid by a queen are identical but that the sex of the resultant bee is determined by the quantity of Vitamin E which is supplied by the bees themselves in the food which they feed to the grub.

If her theory is correct—and the author feels sure it is from experiments which he has carried out both before and since meeting this student in Jerusalem—then one of the mysteries of the hive will at last have been solved.

A theory which has often been expounded is that the queen lays the appropriate egg for the cell. It is clear that there is more room in the drone cell in which the Queen can lay, and it is supposed by some that the act of the Queen laying an egg in a worker cell in a somewhat restricted position brings the egg into contact with the seminal fluid of the drone, which she constantly retains in her abdomen. It is also true that the virgin or unmated Queen which lays eggs lays nothing but male eggs, and so it must be assumed that the drone's mating has the effect of enabling the Queen to lay female eggs in addition to male eggs. Incidentally a laying worker bee, of which more is said elsewhere, being unfertilised, lays none but male eggs.

The egg laid in the drone cell hatches out at the end of the third day, and the larvae or grub is fed for six days by the workers. Three days are spent by the larvae in spinning a cocoon. Four days are taken to transform the larvae to the nymph stage, and the drone remains in the nymph stage for seven days, and on the 24th day it hatches out and comes out of the cell by its own efforts. Drones are often helped out of their cells by the workers and some are of opinion that this is usually the case. The capping of the drone cell is very readily distinguished by its domed appearance. The crown of each cell is raised fully 1/16th of an inch above the cell walls. It will be seen that the drone emerges from its cell on the 24th or 25th day after the egg is first laid. The drone remains in the hive at least 5 days before emerging for its first flight. But he may not be fully mature until 14 days old. This should be borne in mind when queen rearing. The drone can easily be distinguished in its flight by the noise it makes. Drones have never been seen to alight on flowers to help themselves to nectar, for they have not the organic faculties for carrying back honey to the hive. Although they make this noise in flight, which is somewhat alarming to the beginner, the drones have no stings. There are two points of view concerning drones some think that the bee-keeper should endeavour to curtail the number of drones in the hive, for they are said to have two ill effects. One, they consume honey which would otherwise be stored, and the other, that their presence in large numbers encourages the workers to prepare to swarm. This is particularly important, for if large stores are to be worked for it is essential that swarms should not be allowed to leave the hive. The other view is that drones are natural to a colony of bees and assist by generating much needed warmth. On the matter of swarm prevention the reader is referred to the chapter on swarming.

The Worker Bee

The worker bee is one of the most interesting, instructive and useful of all insects. By sex it is an undeveloped female. The grounds for this assertion are, first, that the worker is born of the same variety of egg as a Queen. An egg from a worker cell or even a hatched out grub from a worker cell may be placed by the bee-keeper in a Queen cell and a perfectly normal Queen will emerge. Secondly, in the event of a stock being without a Queen for a length of time, the bees will feed up workers as they do a Queen and the workers will commence to lay, but, alas, only male eggs and all the offspring are drones.

It is supposed that these converted workers can only lay an egg every other day or so. Laying workers result from a shortage of brood and a consequent absence of work for the nurse bees and not necessarily by any concerted action by the bees themselves.

Workers are only produced from eggs laid by a Queen after she has been fertilised. It is a source of great satisfaction to the bee-keeper who has been Queen rearing when he sees a patch of eggs and grubs in worker cells, but more so when he sees that the cells are covered with the characteristic cappings of worker cells. These cappings are very slightly raised above the surrounding cell walls and are made of beeswax and pollen and are khaki- or coffee-coloured.

When the Queen is fertilised by the drone, the seminal fluid from the drone is stored by the Queen in a small sac in her abdomen, and when she lays eggs her abdomen is curved so that as the egg is about to pass out it comes into contact with this seminal fluid which enters a small hole in the egg, called the micropyle, and the egg then becomes fertile.

The eggs, when laid, hatch out on the third day into minute pearly white grubs, and are then fed by the bees for five days, after which they spend two days spinning a cocoon, and remain at rest for a further two days. The transformation from larvae to nymph takes a further day. The last stage is a seven-day period in the nymph state until, on the 21st day after egg laying, the young worker bee hatches out. It emerges from the cell by its own effort, and these young bees can often be seen biting their way out through the cappings. They appear fluffy and young. The older bees appear sleek and glossy in comparison with the young ones. For the first day or so young bees spend their time feeding and becoming accustomed to their surroundings. They then enter upon their duties as nurse bees. They feed the grubs with " pap," which is a mixture of honey, pollen and water. Young bees are believed to feed the older grubs first and cannot feed the younger ones until the pollen they eat has developed their brood food glands. They feed also the Queen and help the foraging bees unload their burdens until, about the ninth or tenth day after birth, they emerge for a " sunning " on the landing board of the hive. At the height of the day, young bees can be seen on the landing board running about in circles and then " taking off " for their first flight, which consists in hovering in front of the hive. When a number of young bees do this it often stimulates the preliminary stages of emergence of a swarm. Suddenly the " party " ceases, and the bees return to their domestic duties.

Between 14 and 21 days after birth, the worker bee commences to work out of doors, but they commence as early as the sixth day if the foraging bees have been lost by the hive being moved. This work consists of water carrying, pollen and propolis gathering, and nectar gathering. These tasks are all tasks of bringing in to the hive. But there are important tasks of carrying from the hive, namely, the scavenging duties. These include the cleaning of the hive, the removal of any dead bees, and the removal of the faeces of the Queen, drones and young bees. Bees are the cleanest of insects. The hive is always sweet smelling except when diseased. They will never allow anything dead to remain in the hive if they have the power to remove it. If they are unable to remove anything from the hive they cover it with a coating of propolis, which is a sweet-smelling bee glue obtained from the sticky buds of trees. Mice and snails have been known to enter hives and die there and have been found to have been completely covered and sealed by the bees with propolis. As an example of their cleanliness, let the bee-keeper uncap some sealed drone cells. Hardly before he has completed replacing the covers of the hive the bees can be seen dragging the white corpses out on the landing board. The author has seen a worker bee get on top of the corpse and wrap its legs round it and with great effort take off with a burden much heavier than itself and fly upwards and away from the hive, and when about twenty yards away drop its burden and return to the hive. Again, one of the duties of the worker is to clean out and polish the interior of the cells in readiness for new eggs from the Queen.

The collecting duties of the bees are the principal duties of practical interest to the bee-keeper, particularly the collecting of nectar.

Pollen

Pollen collected by the bees is obtained from most flowers and catkins. It is the fertilising dust of flowers, it is usually found in large quantities on the summits of the anthers. The flowers depend in many cases for their fertilisation on the visit of pollinating insects. Nature provides encouragement to the bees by giving the flowers bright and gay colours, attractive perfumes and, not the least of attractions, nectar. When gathering pollen bees will pass from flower to flower of the same varieties. They will pass over attractive looking flowers to find flowers of the same variety as those they have just visited. This appears to be Nature's way of ensuring the continuance of existing species of flowers instead of producing innumerable hybrids. The pollination of flowers is now regarded by agriculturalists as the primary duty of the honey bee. Fruit growers are recommended by experts to have at least one hive of bees to the acre of fruit trees. The complete pollination by honey bees not only produces more fruit but it produces fruit of correct shape. Lob-sided apples, for instance, are almost unknown in an apple orchard correctly populated with bees. The Ministry of Agriculture, realising the value of the honey bee, recommends fruit growers to avoid the use of arsenical sprays when the trees are in flower.

The bees gather the pollen in their baskets, which are technically called "corbiculae." The bees pack the pollen in these baskets, which are on their hind legs. They pack in each hind leg a quantity of pollen about the size of a mustard seed. The pollen varies in colour according to the flower visited. For example, dandelion produces golden yellow pollen, poppy black, willow herb saxe blue, apple pale green, mignonette carrot colour, and so on. One of the interesting pastimes of the bee-keeper is to watch the bees at their work and watch what flowers are being visited and to discover whether nectar or pollen is being carried and to study the colour of the pollen. Although the bees are so particular in selecting the same flowers for collecting the same variety of pollen, yet, when they return to the hive, they pack away the pollen into cells regardless of colour. When a pollen cell is opened a large variety of colours can be seen in the same cell.

Pollen is called bee bread, and it is used by the nurse bees to feed the grubs which hatch out of the eggs. They masticate the pollen along with honey and produce a creamy liquid. Pollen provides the protein which provides the bodies of the bees with replacement of tissue.

The bees usually store pollen in the outer combs of the brood chamber, usually the one next to the outermost comb.

It is important when creating new stocks, as described elsewhere, that stores containing pollen should be provided to ensure that the new stocks are not handicapped for lack of essential foods.

Propolis

The word propolis means "before the city," or an outwork in defence. Before the introduction of the modern hive, bees were accustomed to close up the entrance of the straw hives with this substance, leaving apertures through which they left and entered the hive. This was done by them to prevent the intrusion of their enemies, in particular, according to Huber, to exclude the " Sphinx Atropos," commonly known as the death's head moth.

Propolis is a gum which is collected from the buds of trees and is used by the bees to stop up all cracks and loose parts in the hive. It is an extremely pleasant smelling gum, and it has a similar smell to vanilla. Propolis may become a nuisance, particularly when the bees use large quantities of it to seal the tops of movable frames to the brood chamber. This nuisance can be overcome if the beekeeper will use vaseline on the underside of the lugs of the frames and on the metal ends on the lugs. The bees collect this material and pack it in their pollen bags. Drones do not possess these corbiculae, and therefore are unable to collect either pollen or propolis.

The trees principally visited by the bees for this substance are the poplar, pine and horse chestnut. Bees have been found to collect bitumen from roadways and use this for the same purpose as the natural product.

Hives containing large quantities of this material are usually those placed under large trees. The motion of the roots of the trees in high winds causes the bees to secure the interior of the hive, and particularly the movable parts. Some species of bees, particularly Caucasians, use this material in large quantities.

Nectar

This substance is secreted from the the nectaries of flowers. This secretion is one of Nature's ways of attracting the pollenising insect. As the bee travels from flower to flower in search of this sweet liquid, its body comes into contact with the pollen. This is carried from flower to flower, reaching ultimately the ovaries of the visited flowers. Bees visiting flowers which are self-pollinating shake the pollen from the anthers on to the stigmas.

The bees suck the nectar from the flowers. It then

passes through the oesophagus into the honey sac, which is the storage organ of the honey bee. Before being collected by the bee, nectar is a dilute solution of cane and other sugars in water. It also contains aromatic substances, which provide the flavour and aroma of the finished honey. The sugar content varies considerably. The sugar content depends to a very great extent upon weather conditions, e.g., the humidity of the atmosphere rather than upon plant species. For instance, nectar from an apple-tree at 8 a.m. on any given day may have a concentration of 15 per cent. but at 3 p.m. on the same day may have a concentration of 30 per cent. This change is due to the evaporation of water leading to the concentration. Some flowers produce a 50 per cent. content, whilst others are recorded as producing less than 20 per cent. sugar content.

When the honey sac is full, the bee returns to the hive and regurgitates the nectar into the cells, where it accumulates. Sometimes the bee is in such a hurry to return to nectar collecting that it regurgitates the nectar to a nurse bee, who takes it up and then takes it and deposits it in the honey cell. When the nectar reaches the honey cell it has become a weak solution of grape sugar. The heat of the hive reduces the water content to such an extent that fermentation is impossible. When the water content has been reduced to the required standard, the bees will cap over the cell with a wax capping.

The secretion of nectar from the flowers varies generally according to the temperature of the day. It is usually supposed, for example, that it requires a temperature of 70° to produce the secretion of nectar in the common wild white clover.

The secretion is also affected by the rainfall. A long period of drought reduces the water content of the nectar and sometimes stops it completely.

The substantial secretion of nectar from a variety of blooms at one time is known as a honey flow. This occurs with spring blossoms, fruit blossoms, clover, lime blossoms and heather. It is most important that the bee-keeper should get his stock up to strength for each of these honey flows. They will not all occur in the same district, and the beginner should investigate the flora in his district so that he may prepare his stocks accordingly.

It is desirable, where the bee-keeper desires to separate his various grades of honey, that he should watch for the honey flows of the various flowers. For instance, when the apple and hawthorn are in bloom together, the bee-keeper should extract the sealed honey produced. This honey is considered by some to be the most delicious of all English honey.

The bees gather considerable quantities of honey from the sycamore and gooseberry, which are usually in bloom together. This honey is green, but is not considered of very high quality. The clover bloom provides a very fine quality honey which is very pale and produces a very attractive and finely granulated white honey. It is the most popular of English honeys.

The lime tree produces very large quantities of honey, but this crop is very fickle, starting about the first or second week in July and terminating at the end of July. Those who rely on this crop are often frustrated by a wet July, but when the weather is favourable surpluses of upwards of 75 lb. per hive from this source alone are not uncommon. The honey is pale green, and has a faint flavour of peppermint. It is a very pleasant honey indeed.

The main flow in moorland country is from the heather. This occurs in August, and produces a dark, thick and very popular honey. The demand for this honey is very great, and commands a price approximately 50 per cent. over other honey.

Other flora produce large quantities. Mustard and

charlock produce a pale honey which granulates quickly. The willow herb, which grows profusely where woodlands have been cleared, produces a very pale honey as clear as water. Lucerne, field beans, catmint (nepeta) and Michaelmas daisies are flowers which produce large quantities of honey.

Water

Bees gather large quantities of water for use in the hive, particularly to manufacture food with which to feed the young grubs. This at one time was, and still is, by some bee-keepers wrongly called " chyle " food. This term was originally applied to the brood food when it was believed that this was regurgitated from the " ventriculus " or " chyle stomach " of the worker. This is now known to be incorrect. It is known that one of the three pairs of salivary glands—the brood food glands—produce the brood food and that regurgitation from the ventriculus is physically impossible. They also collect this water for their own consumption, and for the consumption of the nurse bees which have not yet left the hive. Some experts state the quantity to be as high as a quart per day at the height of the season. However much it may be, it is essential that the bee-keeper should see that there is ample water available near to the hive. A water fountain can be made with a jam jar and a piece of grooved wood. This jar should be replenished daily, and kept at least 25 feet away from the hive, otherwise the bees will go to a much greater distance to obtain supplies.

The flying time spent in collecting water from a distance is of supreme importance. If this can be reduced, more is the time available for nectar gathering. Experiments have been carried out with great success by putting a rapid feeder over the hole in the quilt in the hive and keeping this replenished. It is quite surprising the amount of water which the bees will consume. It is recommended that one teaspoonful of salt should be added to each gallon of water. This is a mineral which the bees seem to appreciate.

Honeydew

In hot dry weather, bees collect this substance from the leaves of trees. It is only in hot dry weather that the bees are attracted by it. In normal summer weather, the bees will collect nectar from flowers in preference to it, but if there is a prolonged dry period, then the flow of nectar decreases and the bees then resort to honeydew.

In this dry weather the aphides which live on the underside of the leaves of certain trees, such as the sycamore, oak and plum, suck out the sap from the leaves and secrete a sweet sticky substance, and this is what the bees collect. This sticky liquid often falls to the ground and in dry weather can be seen in spots on pavements. The lower leaves of trees are often made shiny with drops of it which have dried on their upper surfaces. Motorists purposely avoid leaving their cars under such trees on account of the sticky drops which fall.

It is a rank-tasting substance, dark in appearance and, strangely enough, is stored by bees in cells separately from the honey. It can be detected in the comb by holding it up to the light. Before the combs are extracted, as described later in the chapter on The Honey Harvest, each cell which appears black, on being held up to the light, can be uncapped and swilled out with a fountain pen filler, so that the rest of the honey is not spoilt by this substance.

CHAPTER V

EQUIPMENT

IN order to carry out effectively simple bee-keeping, the following equipment is necessary.

(1) Hive

Different types of hives have been described elsewhere, but the beginner is advised to purchase or make the National or the W.B.C. hive. Whichever he buys or makes, he must continue with the same standards in order that his equipment can be interchangeable. This cannot be too strongly emphasised. An apiary having varieties of equipment cannot be efficient, and inefficiency in this way can only be overcome by expense. If the bee-keeper wishes to pay his way he must standardise.

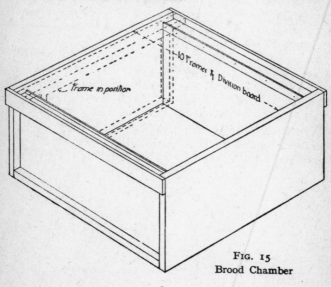

FIG. 15
Brood Chamber

(2) Brood-chamber

For the W.B.C. hive this must be of the B.B.K.A. standard to hold 10 standard brood-frames and one division board, the standard brood-frames having 1½ inch metal ends. (*Fig.* 15). For the National hive, 11 brood-frames are necessary.

(3) Brood-frames

The standard B.B.K.A. brood-frames should be purchased to complete the brood chamber equipment. Even though the bee-keeper purchases a stock on brood-frames he should have in reserve always 10 spare brood-frames, in case he picks up a stray swarm or forms a nucleus of his own. (See *Fig.* 6.)

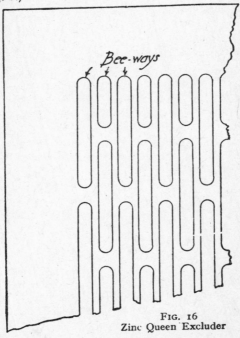

FIG. 16
Zinc Queen Excluder

(4) Wax foundation for brood-frames

This should be purchased only according to requirements, as it deteriorates on keeping in that it loses both its colour, aroma and softness. Bees take much more readily to new wax foundation. However, the beginner should have sufficient sheets of foundation to meet any emergency. Nothing is more tantalising than to lose a swarm through lack of a little additional equipment. Eleven sheets of medium foundation weigh $1\frac{1}{2}$ lbs.

(5) Queen Excluder

This is essential when extracted honey is being worked for. There are three recognised types of Queen excluder, all of which work on the same principle.

(a) The sheet zinc excluder with long slots stamped out of it. This is the type in most common use, principally on account of its cheapness. (*Fig. 16.*)

(b) The Waldron wire excluder. This is reputed to have a distinct advantage over the zinc excluder in that it provides more bee spaces than the zinc one and allows of less interruption with the ventilation of the hive. It certainly has an advantage over the unmounted zinc excluder, in that it is so constructed that the obstructing wire is raised a bee-space over the brood-frames. This affords the maximum opportunity for the bees to make their way into the supers. (*Fig. 17.*)

(c) The Burgess wood and wire excluder. This consists of alternate strips of wood and strands of wire. It has the advantage of the greater grip which bees have on wood compared with wire. They are easily able to make their way up to the supers for this reason.

One matter which should be borne in mind by the bee-keeper is that when laying the Queen excluder over the tops of the brood-frames, the slots or apertures in the Queen excluder should lie at right-angles to the tops of the brood-frames, although this is not so important in the case of the Waldron excluder.

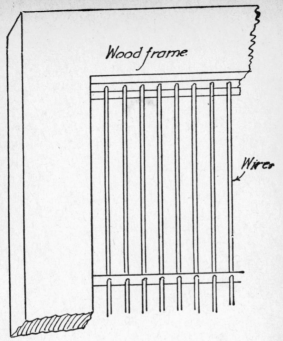

Wood frame

Wires

FIG. 17
Waldron Queen Excluder

(6) Shallow frame rack

This rack consists of 10 extracting or shallow storage combs, in the case of the National hive 11 combs. These should be fitted with drone foundation for three very good reasons.

(*a*) Bees in the wild store most of their surplus in drone comb. The author, as an experiment, recently used a brood-comb in the upper chamber when "demareeing." The lower half of the brood-comb had many drone cells in it. The lower half of the comb was cut away and during the honey flow the bees rebuilt the comb and every new cell was a drone cell except the transition cells which joined the new comb to the upper worker cells.

(*b*) Bees do not usually store pollen in drone comb.

(*c*) Honey is more readily extracted from drone comb as there is less wax surface to which the honey adheres in proportion to the amount of honey as compared with worker cells, and therefore proportionately less adhesion of honey.

Two of these racks will probably be required, particularly if there is good bee pasturage in the district. Alternatively, if sections are to be worked for, then it is desirable that two section racks complete with sections and foundations be acquired. The racks will last permanently, although the sections will have to be replaced annually.

(7) Quilts, Ticking and Felting

A sheet of ticking, sailcloth or deck-chair canvas, the size of the top of the brood-chamber, is required to act as a cover next to the bees, and this should be surmounted with two or three thicknesses of carpet under-felting or two clean, dry sacks would do instead.

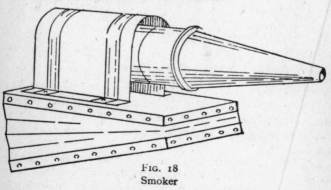

Fig. 18
Smoker

(8) Smoker

This is a necessity, especially to the beginner. It gives

one a feeling of confidence when approaching a hive to feel that one is armed with an instrument which will subdue bees. (*Fig. 18.*) In time, however, the bee-keeper will discard this instrument, particularly during the honey flow, as the effect of smoke on bees is to make them gorge themselves with honey. Occasionally the bees acquired do require the smoker with which to subdue them.

(9) Carbolic Cloths

Two of these cloths, the size being slightly larger than that of the brood chamber top, are very useful. They should be soaked in a 10 per cent. solution of Jeyes' fluid or carbolic acid, and kept moist in a tin. The reason for and the use of these cloths, which are commonly called stink cloths, is described in the chapter on Subduing of Bees.

(10) Feeder

There are many types of feeders, and they are used for a variety of purposes, but the one of most service to the bee-keeper is the rapid feeder. Although this is comparatively inexpensive, it can be dispensed with to curtail expenditure. A very convenient makeshift alternative is a piece of perforated zinc placed over the feed hole in the quilt and a 2 lb. jam jar, the mouth of which is covered with muslin. (See *Fig. 30.*)

(11) Perforated Zinc

A piece of this material 6 inches square, which is useful for wintering and for the makeshift feeder, should be purchased for each hive.

(12) Veil

This is a necessity. There are two principal types :—

(*a*) Fine black cotton netting which can be purchased from any draper. A yard 36 inches wide is sufficient.

(*b*) The wire veil. This is much more durable and

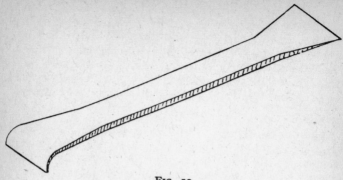

FIG. 19
The Hive Tool

cheaper in the long run. Further, it gives better protection.

(13) Hive Tool

A very handy thing to have, but it is not a necessity. A blunt, old wide chisel will serve equally as well. This is used for levering open various parts of the hive which have been glued together with propolis. (*Fig. 19.*)

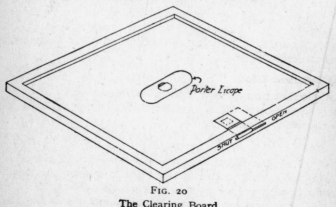

FIG. 20
The Clearing Board

(14) Clearing Board

This board, sometimes called a bee escape board, is desirable but not essential. The super can be cleared with stink rags, as described elsewhere in the chapter on Subduing of Bees. If, however, the bee-keeper intends to keep more than one stock, he should purchase or make one of these. (*Fig. 20.*) These are often called " Porter Board."

Diagram 21 shows the detail of the Porter Bee Escape,

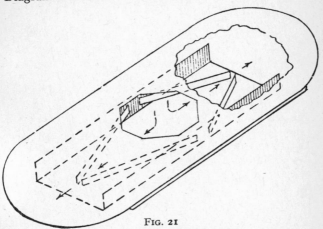

Fig. 21

Details of the Porter Escape

which is set in the middle of the clearing board.

There are many other items of equipment which may be purchased, but they are not necessities. If the bee-keeper will join the local association, he will almost invariably have the advantage of hiring for a nominal sum the Association's extractor and ripener. And here a word to those who borrow this equipment. Do please scald out this equipment before returning. Take the extractor to pieces, scald each part, and wipe dry. Scald out and wipe dry the barrel and reassemble, and remember that it will last much longer if it is cared for. So many who borrow the extractor never dream of taking it to pieces—a simple operation—to clean it properly. Honey has certain natural acids in it, and these, in a very short time, will penetrate the tinned surface of these implements and rust will ensue.

To summarise, here is a table showing what equipment is essential and what desirable.

Essential Equipment.	*Desirable, but not Essential.*
Hive.	Rapid Feeder.
Brood-chamber.	Bottle Feeder.
Brood-frames.	Wire Veil.
Wax Foundation.	Clearing Board.
Queen Excluder.	Straw Skep.
2 Shallow-frame Racks.	Spare Hive.
Ticking Quilt.	Spare Brood-frames and
Smoker.	Foundation.
Perforated Zinc.	Hive Tool.
Veil.	

CHAPTER VI

SWARMING AND SWARM PREVENTION

THIS is a perfectly natural propensity of all stocks of bees. It is the only natural method of perpetuating this species of insect. The bee-keeper, however, does not desire the bees to spend their energy in colonising—for that is what swarming is—but rather to direct it into the storage of surplus honey.

It has been found by long experience that the bee-keeper can exercise considerable control over the swarming instinct, apart from the selection of supposed " non-swarming " varieties of bees.

The first signs of swarming can be detected with fair accuracy. In the early Spring, when the first blossoms provide the bees with nectar, breeding of worker bees proceeds with increasing speed, and storage of surplus nectar commences. It is then that the bee-keeper takes the first step in swarm prevention. This step is to provide the bees with more storage room. This action of the bee-keeper may delay the swarming impulse, for the bees now have more room in which to operate. But the natural impulse cannot be frustrated for long. The bees realise, presumably from instinct, that when they swarm they must leave behind males who will fertilise the queen whom they will never see, but who will be born when they have left the hive. They again, by instinct, know that the males take longer to be created than Queens. They therefore show the next sign of swarming by building a number of drone cells, and at this stage they will even break down a number of worker cells and rebuild drone cells in their places. This diagram shows worker cells on the left and drone cells on the right, with transition cells between the two. (*Fig. 8.*) This should be watched by the bee-keeper. He can handicap them in their intentions by ensuring that all the combs upon which the bees winter are as free from drone cells as is possible. When the bees have capped over these drone cells, the bee-keeper should uncap them so as to expose the sealed larvae or nymphs. The bees will then not tolerate these exposed corpses in the hive, and within a very few moments can be seen hauling them out of the hive, flying away with them, and dropping them in the distance. This is regarded by some as a bad practice and not tending to prevent swarming but the author finds in practice that it is effective. This action defers the progress of the creation of drones for several days. When destroying the drones in this way, the bee-keeper should search very carefully indeed for queen cells, and if any should be found, they should be cut away from the combs in which they are built. At least every 10 days the hive should be inspected for signs of queen cells, all of which should be ruthlessly removed.

Weather conditions may also help the bee-keeper. Rain will also prevent bees swarming, but here the bee-keeper should be warned. When bees are kept indoors in the early part of the year, they often rapidly build queen cells in readiness for the fine weather to come. If, however, the weather remains bad for any length of time, the bees may give up the idea of swarming and destroy the queen cells and their occupants.

If the bee-keeper is unable to prevent a swarm and the weather is favourable, the swarm will emerge. Those who have seen a swarm emerge from a hive will agree that it is one of the most astonishing of phenomena in nature, and this is what is seen. A number of bees will hover in front of the hive facing the hive. Among these will be seen a large number of drones creating their boisterous noise. This noise is said by some to stimulate the impulse of swarming. Those who have observed the interior of an observation hive say that the queen ceases to lay and can be seen hurrying about the hive from comb to comb. Eventually she comes out on to the landing board. Meanwhile thousands upon thousands of bees have poured out of the hive. The appearance of the mouth of the hive resembles boiling treacle. There seems no end to the exodus. They crowd the landing board and the front of the hive and take off into the air, swirling round and creating an alarming noise. Gradually the centre of the swirling crowd of bees moves away from the hive and becomes more compact. The queen has left the landing board and taken to the air for at least the second time in her life, the first being her mating flight. Whilst this is stated here the writer cannot with certainty say that she never leaves except on these two occasions. That appears to be the general opinion of many. On the contrary it may be that she may take a trip on her own. Since the publication of the first edition the author has received many letters which satisfy him that Queens do in fact make excursions after the mating flight. Hives are often found to be queenless without any apparent reason. It may be that the Queen has either been destroyed by the bees or else has taken an occasional flight and not returned having either lost her direction or having been destroyed by birds.

Suddenly there will be noticed on the branch of a shrub or tree a small knot of bees which grows very rapidly as the flying bees settle. The cluster varies in size according naturally to the number of bees which leave the hive. It is, however, very common for swarms to be about the size of a Rugby football, and to weigh five to six pounds. There are between 3,500 and 4,000 bees to the pound, and therefore a swarm of five pounds weight approximates 20,000 bees. Bees weigh heavier when swarming as they fill themselves with honey before leaving the hive. The Queen is in this mass. If she leaves and flies away, the bees will follow her.

This swarm may hang on the tree for as long as 48 hours, but this depends principally upon the weather. The bee-keeper is advised to take the swarm as early as possible.

A day or two before the swarm emerges the stock has sent out scouts to find a suitable new home. This they find, investigate it, and prepare it for the swarm. They then return to the hive and when the swarm emerges and

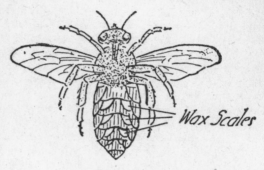

FIG. 22
Worker Bee with Wax Scales

has settled down from the excitement of swarming, lead the swarm to its new home. It is therefore desirable to skep the swarm as early as is possible.

Also whilst the bees are clustering in this mass they become hot and commence to sweat the wax through the eight glands on their abdomens in readiness for the new home they are going to furnish with honeycomb. *Fig. 22* shows an enlarged drawing of a worker bee with the wax scales on the underside of the abdomen.

Here follows a description of the method of taking a swarm.

How to take a Swarm

At first the prospect of capturing 20,000 bees appears formidable, and a little courage is needed by the beginner. However, properly protected, the bee-keeper will come to no harm. The veil should be worn, and gloves also, particularly if the bees are in a difficult situation. A man should either put his socks over his trouser leg bottoms or wear cycle clips or gum boots. A woman should wear slacks or jodhpurs, and her arms should be covered. A golf jacket is admirable. Bees do not like rough woollen clothes, and will often attack the bee-keeper who wears them. They also appear to dislike navy blue clothing. This protection should be used by the beginner to prevent him being badly stung. Later he will get over the fear of being stung and should discard all except the veil.

It is not always necessary to use a veil when taking a swarm but the beginner should do so.

Before the bees come out of the hive in the swarm they consume considerable quantities of honey. This makes the bees content and less likely to sting the bee-keeper. There are some writers who say that they consume enough honey to last them three days, but it is quite impossible for a bee when active to consume sufficient honey to last it for three days.

To take a swarm, the equipment needed is a white cloth 4 to 5 feet square, a straw skep [see *Fig. 2*] or an open wooden box about 15 inches square and one foot deep.

Spread the white cloth on the ground in the shade near to the swarm ; take the skep or box, and hold it mouth upwards immediately under the swarm. Take hold of the branch on which the swarm is hanging and give it one or two firm shakes so that the swarm, or the greater part of it, falls into the skep or box. The skep or box should then be carried into the shade, and placed mouth downwards in the centre of the sheet. Take two stones about two inches thick or two pieces of wood and place them under one side of the skep or box so as to allow the bees to come in or out. If the Queen is in the skep or box then the bees will remain with her there. If not, the bees will come out and fly back to where she may be, or if the Queen is lost they will return to the hive. Stand by for a few minutes, and it will be noticed that the remaining bees on the tree will join the swarm in the skep or box.

The skep should be sheltered from the sun and left until the late afternoon. If the bee-keeper wishes to allow this swarm to start a new stock, he will prepare a hive in readiness to hive it, or he may wish to return the swarm to the hive. There is always a risk that the swarm may leave the hive before evening and many bee-keepers hive their swarms straight away.

Hiving the Swarm

The following is the method of hiving the swarm. First prepare a hive in the following way. Have a brood-chamber with 10 brood-frames with foundation fixed—or for preference ten drawn out brood-combs and a division board. Place this on a hive floor board and raise the front of the brood-chamber about one inch by means of small wedges of wood. Cover the brood-frames with a quilt having a feed hole in it. In front of all this and sloping up to the hive place a large board.

Go to the swarm at dusk. Remove the stones or small blocks of wood, take hold of all four corners of the white cloth and tie them over the top of the skep or box and carry the whole and stand it on the board sloping up to the brood-chamber. Untie the white sheet and so arrange it that one edge almost reaches the entrance of the brood-chamber. Level out the sheet so that it lies flat on the board. Take hold of the skep or box firmly with both hands and raise it a little over a foot from the white cloth and with one sharp jerk throw the contents downwards on to the cloth, retaining hold of the skep or box. A firm throw will invariably dislodge the whole mass of bees.

This seething mass will then turn their heads uphill, as it is the natural tendency of bees to crawl uphill, and some will approach the entrance of the hive. These then come out of the entrance, face the hive, turn up their tails and fan their wings very quickly, exposing a white speck at the point of the abdomen. This white speck is the scent gland. The fanning bees at the entrance to the hive blow the scent towards the mass of bees, thus directing them to their new home. Then the stampede starts. Look for the Queen and you will see her enter, Once she has entered, all the others will follow.

When all the bees have entered the brood-chamber the wooden wedges should be removed and the outer walls and roof of the hive should then be placed round and over the brood-chamber. The feeder, for preference a rapid feeder, which should have been placed over the feed hole in the quilt and be filled with warm syrup of a strength of 1 lb. of sugar to a pint of water before the swarm is hived. This is most important for two reasons. First, the bees need food to enable them to produce wax to use in the drawing out of the comb. The sooner the comb is drawn out the more quickly will the Queen commence laying. Whatever is used by the way of sugar at this time will be amply repaid. It is truly an example of " casting bread upon the waters." The supply of syrup should be kept up for a few days until it is observed that the bees are well established, then take away the feeder and place on top the queen excluder and a super, as the bees which have swarmed store very rapidly after the foundation is drawn out.

The second reason for feeding is to secure that the bees remain in their hive and do not abscond. Many a beginner has discovered that the bees have flown, and upon enquiry from an experienced hand has learnt once and for all of his reason for disappointment.

Hunger Swarms

Occasionally a bee-keeper is called to remove a swarm of bees of unknown origin.

The bees may appear vicious and restless. If the time is very early spring or late in the season, a hunger swarm should be suspected. The method of dealing with this is to take a skep or box and smear it inside with honey. Shake the swarm into the skep, and place a feeder immediately on top of the skep and leave it overnight. The swarm should only be hived when it has become more docile. To avoid any wasted effort, the bees can quite properly be left to winter in the skep provided they are well fed. In the early spring the skep should be placed on top of a brood-chamber filled with brood-frames fitted with foundation. The bees will gradually work their way down into the brood-frames, filling the skep with honey in natural honeycomb. [See Plate I.]

How to prevent Swarming

(1) Selection of Stock

The swarming instinct is stronger in some strains of bees than in others. Therefore the first step towards swarm prevention is to acquire a stock from a breeder whose bees are not prone to swarming. Many dealers advertise bees as " non-swarming." This is a misnomer, for all strains of bees will swarm if uncontrolled.

It has been stated earlier that bees show signs of swarming in advance of that event.

(2) Destruction of drone cells

The bee-keeper should examine the hive early in the spring to see whether the combs have many drone cells.

If any combs have a large number of these, they should be removed and new brood frames fitted with worker foundation. In any event three combs out of ten should be replaced each year, so those having most drone cells should be removed. If the Queen has laid eggs in drone cells it is almost certain that the bees intend that there shall be plenty of prospective mates for the Queens which the workers will rear in queen cells. The bee-keeper should uncap any drone cells which are sealed over. The cells can readily be identified as they are larger than the worker cells and have a dome shaped capping. An ordinary pocket knife is all that is necessary. Within a few moments the bees will have removed the white corpses of the drone nymphs from the hive. If all capped drone cells are removed, it is almost certain that the bees will start again to produce drones, but the process of swarming will have been deferred for a week or two.

(3) Removal of Queen cells

Shortly after the Queen lays in drone cells the workers will commence to build Queen cells. How long after can approximately be determined as follows. A drone is ready for function as a mate for a Queen when it is 14 days old. A Queen is ready for mating when it is approximately 4 days old. Therefore the drone must be born at least 10 days before the Queen. A Queen takes approximately 15 days to mature from the time of laying the egg. Therefore the Queen cell is charged with an egg five days before the birth of the drone. As it takes a day or so to construct the Queen cell, it can be regarded as certain that if drone cells are allowed to progress beyond 14 days the bees will start to make Queen cells.

Again, the Queen cells, when seen, should be neatly cut out with the pocket knife. They are easily seen. They hang down from any place on the comb or even from the wooden frame, but particularly do they hang from the bottom half of the comb. Frequently the bees cluster round them and hide them from the bee-keeper's view. The bees can be brushed away with a goose feather or blown on by the bee-keeper. The bees do not like human breath, and run away quickly, exposing the naked comb, and any Queen cells can readily be seen. All Queen cells are not shaped like a complete acorn. In the early state of construction they have the appearance of acorn cups. These should also be excised. Great care must be taken to ensure that all Queen cells are removed, for if one is left the stock will probably swarm just as if there were many.

The bee-keeper must inspect his hives for Queen cells at least every seven days.

(4) Provision of more room

The removal of drone and Queen cells only delays the swarming impulse, whereas if these steps are combined with other measures they become really effective. The first of these is the provision of more room. This enables the bees to spend their energies on building up their stores in the newly created accommodation.

The bees can be given more room in two distinctly different ways. The simpler method is to place a crate of shallow combs immediately above the brood-chamber, placing the Queen excluder in between the brood-chamber and the shallow combs. The bees will proceed to fill these with honey instead of filling the brood-frames which crowds out the bees. Some bee-keepers lift up the brood-chamber and place a crate of shallow combs of worker cells under the brood-chamber. This has its disadvantages in that the bees proceed to store honey in the brood-frames and to commence breeding in the shallow combs. It is doubtful whether the bee-keeper is ever able to extract this honey without it becoming contaminated with brood.

However, the bee-keeper who practises this latter method should only place the shallow crate below the brood-chamber where the Queen is a good layer, then he should also place a shallow crate over the brood-chamber. Very soon the queen will make full use of the laying accommodation, and if the season is good, will rapidly fill the supers.

(5) The Demaree system of swarm control

In the year 1892, a certain Mr. Demaree wrote to the *American Bee Journal* setting out his system of swarm control when the object of the bee-keeper was honey production. It is a system now widely practised in this country and its popularity is due to its simplicity and its general success. However, if carried out as suggested by the originator, it is a dirty method of honey production for reasons explained later. It is, however, an excellent method of producing natural stores in brood sized combs, useful for helping out weak stocks and providing winter feed.

This is the system. First go through each comb of the stock and remove all Queen cells in whatever state of development. Take out all combs with the exception of one having brood and place them in a clean prepared second brood-chamber, which is to be the upper storey. The brood-frame containing the Queen should be retained in the original brood-chamber. The number of brood-frames in the second chamber should be made up to ten in number and a division board fitted at one end. Likewise, the original brood-chamber should be filled up with brood-frames. More progress will, of course, be made if the added brood-frames have drawn out comb. Again, a division board should be fitted to this brood-chamber, and care should be taken to see that it is fitted at the same end as the one fitted in the second brood-chamber. Now place a Queen excluder over the first brood-chamber and over this place the second brood-chamber. In this way the Queen has a completely new brood-chamber in which to lay and continues laying at a rapid rate. Meanwhile, all the bees in the brood-combs above are hatching out rapidly and these young bees provide the Queen with a constant supply of nurse bees. All the cells in the upper storey will be vacated within twenty-one days of the operation being carried out. The hive will have an enormous population with a Queen laying rapidly. If there has been a honey flow most of the cells in the upper storey will have been filled with honey as soon as they are vacated by the emerging bees. If the honey flow still continues the combs in the upper storey should be extracted and the operation repeated. Dr. Butler has discovered what he considers to be an improvement on this system. He always places a shallow super complete with combs between the brood-chambers at the first operation.

The advantages of this system are, first, that the Queen is never cramped for laying room and therefore one of the predisposing causes of swarming is removed ; and secondly, that the system provides a large stock of bees for honey collection.

The disadvantages are first, that unless the operation is repeated after 21 days there is every possibility of the hive being so crowded that swarming is merely postponed and the swarm may leave at the height of the honey flow. Secondly, the honey produced is regarded by some as " dirty honey." It has been stored in cells where grubs have developed into nymphs and left their excreta behind and nymphs turned into bees in their turn having left their outer skins behind. They say it is not honey which a clean bee-keeper would eat himself and therefore he should not sell it to the public. This particular objection may perhaps be negatived when we are told by observers that during a good honey flow the field bees usually place the honey they have collected in the first available cell in the brood-chamber often on top of an egg or even a young larva. One very helpful letter which the author received after the publication of the first edition read as follows :—

"It is surely silly to call honey from brood-combs 'dirty.' The bees would be apt to be poisoned themselves (they would naturally be more liable to suffer than animals like ourselves not nearly related to them) if that were so. They do use old brood-combs for storage, in a wild state ; and natural selection would long ago have eliminated the habit if the honey was really 'dirty.' Do you eat sausages ? If so, is not that habit worse ? The vast bulk of commercial honey is produced in old brood-combs."

Thirdly, there is one danger which is not always explained about this system—and that is that unless every care is taken to prevent Queen cells maturing in the upper storey after the transfer to it of brood, a Queen may hatch out which cannot get through the excluder which may result in either a swarm emerging after all or the virgin Queen becoming a drone layer, as she is unable to get out of the hive to become fertilised. Therefore it is essential that after two or three days the bee-keeper should go through the upper storey and cut out any Queen cells which may have been formed in the interim. This is most important and should be repeated after a period of seven days.

There are those who think that if the Queen cells are cut out of the upper storey that the bees cannot place a young enough grub or egg in the upper storey. The writer's experience shows that they will fetch eggs from the lower storey even 10 days later.

This system is often used when the bee-keeper desires to increase his stocks, for in the upper storey the bees will often after the operation has been carried out make a large number of Queen cells. These can be made into nuclei which will be helped on rapidly by the large number of young bees which will shortly hatch out.

(6) Clipping the Queen's Wings

This is a method which is intended to prevent swarming by prohibiting the Queen from leaving the hive. There are two principal methods of carrying this out. First, the Queen should be located on a comb and whilst moving about should have one wing clipped by cutting with scissors half way along the wing. The second method is by picking up the Queen by the wings with the right hand then take hold of her with the thumb and first finger of the left hand by the thorax. Then one wing should be clipped halfway along. Both these methods have a grave element of risk and danger for damage to the Queen will probably have harmful results upon the progress of the stock.

FIG. 23
Clipping the Queen's Wings

This method of swarm control does not prevent the swarming instinct for the swarm will emerge in just the same way as a natural swarm except that the Queen will not leave as she will be unable to fly. The bees then return to the hive when they find she is absent from the swarm. It may be however that the Queen has fallen from the landing board of the hive and unless careful watch is made she may be lost. However, if the bee-keeper sees the swarm emerge and finds the Queen on the landing board of the hive and returns the Queen and bees to the hive he should then take steps to overcome the swarming instinct by removing all Queen cells and giving the bees more room for honey storage.

(7) Artificial Swarms

The chief danger of swarming is that the swarm will be lost, and the chief disadvantage of swarming is that the stock is so reduced in strength that it is rendered virtually useless as a honey producer. If, therefore, the stock shows continued intentions of swarming it is desirable that the bee-keeper should form an artificial swarm. This has two main advantages, one that the bee-keeper's stocks are increased, the other that the swarm having been created artificially the urge to swarm dies.

This is how it is done. About the middle of a bright warm day when the bees are flying well, get a second empty hive and place it on the stand of the hive to be operated upon, removing that, the parent hive, to a distance of two or three yards. Then open up the parent hive, find the Queen and place the brood comb on which she is found into the brood-chamber of the new hive. Take from the parent hive also two other brood-combs containing stores of honey and pollen and place one at each side of the one containing the Queen. Then fill up the new brood-chamber with brood frames, having either drawn out comb or foundation. Similarly fill up the three spaces created in the parent stock with brood frames. Thus the new stock has a laying Queen and a number of young bees on the brood-combs along with the Queen. The bees which are out flying and collecting stores will return to the old stand and join the old Queen. Not a bee need be lost in the process. Now this is what happens to the parent stock. The bees finding that they have lost their Queen will proceed to make Queen cells if they have not already done so and will in time hatch out a Queen, but time may be saved by the introduction of a new Queen or by inserting a ripe Queen cell in the brood-chamber.

If this process is carried out in May or early June there is no reason why each stock should not build up sufficiently to take a useful part in the July honey flow and they will most certainly be ready for the August heather honey flow.

To assist the artificial swarm to make rapid progress they should be fed with a pint of warm stimulating syrup every other night for 10 days and the system of brood-spreading described in the chapter on spring stimulation should be carried out. If the bee-keeper is only able to provide foundation for the brood-frames instead of drawn out comb then a little more syrup should be given. This helps them to build the comb on the foundation more rapidly thus giving the Queen more room in which to lay.

If the bee-keeper desires still further to increase his stock he may repeat this procedure, using the parent hive again after a four weeks rest, being sure first of all that there is a reasonable quantity of brood and particularly newly laid eggs left behind, otherwise the parent stock will be rendered Queenless.

(8) Ventilation

One of the causes of swarming is congestion in the hive. Congestion causes heat and absence of air suitable for the bees to breathe. Therefore in hot weather it is desirable to see that the hive is kept as cool as possible and given extra air. The hive should normally be placed where it can be shaded from the mid-day sun, but in very hot weather the entrance to the hive should be shaded, but so as not to obstruct the entrance to the hive. The brood-chamber should be lifted on small blocks of wood about three-quarters of an inch thick and the roof of the hive lifted by putting two laths of wood on the top of the top lift and resting the roof on the laths. In this way there will be a through draught of air. As the weather cools the parts of the hive should be replaced otherwise the bees will remain indoors when they might be out collecting winter stores.

(9) The Snelgrove Method

This method of swarm control has proved itself to be the greatest boon to bee-keepers. It is an advance and elaboration upon the Demaree system, and those who practise it according to instructions are wholly satisfied with its results.

It would be unfair to Mr. Snelgrove to describe the system in detail in these pages and the reader is strongly advised to buy Mr. Snelgrove's book, " Swarm Control."

The exclusion of young bees from the brood chamber and returning them by a simple device is the principle on which Mr. Snelgrove works. His contention is that a super-abundance of young bees in the brood chamber is one of the principal factors in creating the swarming impulse.

His system works more readily with the National hive than with the W.B.C., although it can be worked with the latter.

The only additional equipment required is a board which is placed over the super but under the original brood chamber. This board has an area of wire cloth inserted which enables the top queenless stock to have the same smell as that underneath. This is important as it ensures the ready return of flying bees to the bottom stock from the top stock. By a simple system of opening and closing three pairs of entrances in the frame work of this special board foraging bees leave the top stock. Later the entrance is shut and the entrance into the lower stock opened, and so the foragers from the top stock augment the bottom stock which then becomes a powerful honey getter. The other two pairs of doors are similarly put into operation.

It is an almost foolproof system and admirably suited for out apiary stocks.

In time, naturally, unless prevented the top stock will hatch out a Queen which may be used for re-queening the parent stock.

These are the ways recognised which assist in swarm prevention.

Let Alone Bee-keeping

In the face of the current systems of swarm control there has grown up the cult of " Let Alone " bee-keeping. Once spring cleaning has taken place those who carry out this system of leaving matters alone in the brood chamber never interfere. They contend that constant interference disturbs the bees and that provided you give the bees plenty of room in which to breed and plenty of room to store, you will in the end obtain better results.

The author recently spoke to a lady who has always been a let alone bee-keeper even to the extent of her saying that she had never seen a queen bee in over 40 years' bee-keeping.

The author said ; " You must get a large number of swarms." " Yes " the lady replied, " but I get an awful lot of honey."

PLATE I.

Transferring an established stock of bees from skep to
standard brood-chamber. The Queen when found in
brood-combs should be prevented from going back into skep
by a queen excluder.

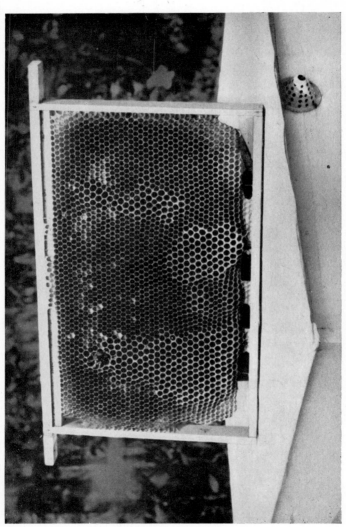

PLATE II.

A bad brood-comb. Combs like this should be taken from the hive, melted down and fitted with

PLATE III.

Protection against stings: wire net veil, gauntlet gloves
and cycle clips on trousers.

The correct way to hold a comb, i.e., vertically over the
hive. Note lift on left being used as a rest for comb.

The incorrect way of holding a comb. The comb should
not be held horizontally and should be held over the hive

PLATE IV.

CHAPTER VII
HONEY PRODUCTION

HAVING, presumably, succeeded in saving the bees from leaving the parent hive, the bee-keeper will proceed to carry out his main object, namely, that of honey production.

It will be recollected that one of the principal ways of preventing swarms is to give more room. This is to enable the bees to store their honey in the room provided rather than in the brood-chamber. As the honey begins to accumulate in the super, naturally there is much less room for the bees. This must be remembered by the bee-keeper. As the honey becomes sealed, that is, covered with a white wax capping, the bees start to fill up the other cells. Usually the bees fill up the centre combs first. When these centre combs are almost filled they should be lifted and placed on the outsides and the remainder moved to the centre. In this way the bees are kept active with work always in front of them. When the first super is a little over half full, a second super should be provided. There is a right and wrong way of putting this on the hive. First have the second super complete with 10 shallow frames fitted with drone foundation or with combs already drawn out. The roof and outer lifts should be removed leaving the brood-chamber accessible. If possible the bees should not be smoked as this makes them consume honey. If, however, they are fractious, three puffs should be made with the smoker at the entrance to the hive. The existing partly filled super should then be slowly levered up with the greatest gentleness for rough handling disturbs the bees more than anything else. Before lifting the super, after loosening it, give it a slight twist in a circular movement so that when lifted it does not bring away with it any brood-frame which may have become attached by brace-comb. The super should then be lifted off and placed on top crossways on one of the lifts. A carbolic cloth should then be laid over the exposed Queen excluder which lies on top of the brood-frames. Next the empty super should be held immediately over the carbolic cloth. Care should be taken to ensure that the direction of the shallow frames should be the same as the brood-frames. The idea in placing the carbolic cloth on the top of the brood-frames is to drive the bees down to prevent them becoming restive and being crushed. Pull the carbolic cloth smartly away and gently lower the new super until it fits exactly on the brood-chamber top. Then replace the partly filled super, brushing away any bees which may be adhering to the bottom of the crate with a goose feather. Do this very gently, and brush the bees into the empty shallow frame crate. Close the hive down gently so as to avoid any further disturbance of the bees. The new crate is placed under the partly filled one in order to make the bees accustomed to the new crate when passing through to the old crate which they are in process of completing. An inspection a few days later will show that the bees are busy working on the new combs. They will in fact have commenced to draw out the wax foundation, or if combs already drawn out are supplied there will be signs of honey being deposited in the centre combs. When the clover is in full flower about the third week in June, honey will be stored more rapidly than before and the top super will be completed. If the season is good the top super will soon be filled. This should be removed, when about two-thirds of the cells are capped. The uncapped honey to all intents is ripe at this stage and a great saving in honey will be effected by relieving the bees from capping the remaining cells. The shallow frames should then be extracted and returned to the hive underneath the other crate of shallow frames next to the brood-chamber. When this is done the opportunity should be taken to place the unfilled combs in the centre of the other shallow frame crate.

Dr. Butler is of opinion that the effect of a carbolic cloth is that it subdues bees in exactly the same manner as smoke, that is, it makes them fill their honey stomachs with honey But the writer's experience is that as soon as the carbolic cloth is placed on the brood-frames the bees run away from it without making any attempt to fill up with honey. On one occasion the writer had a powerful carbolic cloth on the hive and left it too long and it drove the whole stock out of the hive. Unfortunately the Queen was lost, so powerful cloths are no longer used by the writer.

It is convenient at this juncture to describe the effect of using wide metal ends on the lugs of the shallow frames.

These wide metal ends should be fitted when the foundation is drawn out almost to the fullest extent when the 1½ inch metal ends are used. The wide ends are 2 inches wide and therefore they permit the comb being drawn out quarter of an inch on each face of the comb. The internal measurement of a shallow frame crate is usually 16 inches and therefore only eight shallow frames with two inch metal ends can be inserted instead of ten having the narrow metal ends. A shallow comb with narrow metal ends when completely full produces approximately 2¾ lbs. of honey, but a shallow comb having wide metal ends produces about 4¼ lbs. of honey. The comparisons are therefore 10 shallow frame combs at 2¾ lbs. each equals 27½ lbs., and 8 shallow frame combs at 4¼ lbs. of honey each equals 36 lbs. Thus showing that the eight with wide metal ends hold more than ten with the narrow ends.

It is recognised that wax requires many times its weight of honey to produce. In consequence eight frames which have only a total of 16 faces to be capped as against 20 faces of the frames having narrow ends certainly afford a great saving of honey which would otherwise be used in producing wax.

There are those who argue that it is difficult to extract

honey from the combs that are drawn out so wide, but the answer to that is that if drone foundation is used for these combs the honey comes out very easily.

The two advantages of using wide metal ends are ; first that it is more economical in that only eight frames are needed instead of ten, a saving of 20 per cent. on shallow frames alone, and secondly, a greater amount of honey is produced because there is a saving in wax cappings.

The Honey Harvest

To the bee-keeper whose aim is honey production, this is the climax of his years' work. Assuming that as the bees have stored their honey in the combs provided, and the bee-keeper has continued to provide more storage space as and when inspections of the hive have justified it, the time will come when he should remove the surplus stores. As stated earlier, some bee-keepers believe in the removal of surplus as and when it is completely sealed over and replacing the frames taken out by frames fitted with foundation or with combs already drawn out. The principal argument against this is that it is better to allow the honey to remain in the hive and mature in the comb. There does not appear in any of the books which have been written on this subject any reasoned argument as to why sealed honey should acquire any more virtue after it has been sealed. There are however several very good arguments why it should be taken from hives piecemeal. Here are the principal reasons. The capital outlay is much less for if combs are extracted during the honey flow and then replaced in the hive they are virtually in constant use instead of being used as storage only. One of the pleasures of bee-keeping for honey production is to acquire the different varieties of honey. In many districts the early spring blossoms, particularly in woodland districts where wild cherry is abundant, sealed surplus of delightful honey can be obtained but only in limited quantities.

A bee-keeper having say three hives may average from this source perhaps two sealed combs of two and a half pounds each net weight, thus producing fifteen pounds of spring honey. Later, following the apple and hawthorn, the sycamore and gooseberry, the clover, lime and heather. In districts where a surplus is obtained from mustard charlock and the brassicas it is most important that extraction is carried out piecemeal as honey from these sources granulates very quickly and it is far better that granulation should take place in the jar than in the comb.

The man who would store all until the end of the lime and clover and then extract altogether, has an admixture which may be pleasant but which lacks the characteristic of the individual flavours.

One important advantage of extracting piecemeal is that when the combs are put back into the hive they are already fully drawn out and in addition are wet with honey which makes them readily acceptable by the bees for refilling.

In wooded districts there is the danger of honeydew, which if extracted with the bulk may result in a spoilt season's work. The chief danger in leaving all on the hive is the danger of losing the surplus either by robbing or inclement weather. Robbing, described elsewhere, is often the cause of the loss of not only the surplus stores but also of the bees themselves. Inclement weather at the close of the honey season has produced many a heart-broken bee-keeper. A fortnight of wet weather and as much as 30 to 40 pounds has been known to be consumed by the bees, but if the bee-keeper has taken his surplus he can tide over the wet period by feeding his bees with sugar syrup.

A disadvantage of extracting piecemeal is that extracting is often a messy business. Also when extracting takes place a certain amount of waste takes place by honey adhering to the sides and wire frames of the extractor.

The same amount of waste takes place for 50 frames as for 5, so that the more times during the season the extractor is used the more the total waste.

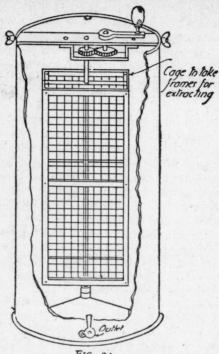

FIG. 24
Simple Honey Extractor

Extracting Honey

There are many admirable mechanical extractors on the market and they vary in price according to their size and capacity. No small bee-keeper need go to the trouble of purchasing one if he is a member of his local bee-keepers association. Most bee-keepers associations own an extractor and a ripener. The principle upon which most extractors work is that the combs have the surface cappings cut off and are placed in the extractor, the honey being extracted by centrifugal force. Other extractors operate by having the frames placed in the cage of the extractor at right angles to the outer drum, the drum rotating and the honey being extracted by suction. The honey is thrown on the sides of the drum. It then runs down and is drained out of the bottom through a treacle tap.

Cleanliness is essential if the bee-keeper is to suceed in marketing his surplus honey for nothing is more likely to discourage customers from future purchases than honey having a dirty appearance.

Therefore, before commencing, scour out the extractor and ripener and all its parts with copius quantities of hot water. Wipe it out and set it before a warm fire to dry out thoroughly.

It is most important that before any honey is uncapped or exposed in any other way that the room in which the work is to be done should be made proof against bees and wasps ; otherwise large numbers will enter and impede the work. Never attempt to extract out of doors as the risk is not worth what the consequences will probably be.

It is unwise to expose any honey or syrup near any apiary otherwise robbing will probably ensue.

Next, take the crate of combs awaiting extraction and clear away from each frame any loose propolis. Hold the frame up to the light to see if there are any dark looking cells. Bees store honeydew in cells on its own and do not often mix it with honey. Remove any cells containing pollen with the point of the knife. Pollen does spoil honey.

A note on honeydew appears earlier in this book.

It may be that the dark cell contains pollen which the bees store for feeding the young bees. In no circumstances should this substance be allowed to become mixed with the honey as it will spoil its taste, making the honey taste strong and powdery. Any honey so contaminated should be fed back to the bees and they will distil it afresh. If the bee-keeper follows the advice given earlier and uses drone foundation in his extractor frames he will certainly avoid the pollen trouble as bees do not often store pollen in drone cells (see Plate II). Some readers have written the author saying they have found pollen in drone cells but the author has never seen it. There are two ways of dealing with honey-dew. First, if these dark cells are capped over the cappings should not be disturbed but the rest of the cappings over the normal honey should be removed and the frame is then ready for extraction. When extracted, the cappings over honeydew should be removed, the honeydew washed out with a syringe of warm water and the comb placed back in the hive. The second way is first to uncap and wash out the honeydew with a fountain pen filler, then to uncap the remainder and extract. The bees will then clean it up.

This is the simplest method of uncapping extractor combs. First, have ready a carving knife, a large jug of boiling hot water and a large meat dish or large pie dish. Stand the frame vertically in the dish, holding one lug in the left hand and the other lug standing in the dish. Then lean the frame away from you at an angle of 30 degrees. Take the carving knife, which should have been in the hot water for a few moments, in the right hand, wipe it and commence to cut the cappings by bringing the knife upwards in a sawing motion. It will be noticed that immediately under the capping wax there is a thin air space. In course of time you will become more expert and the knife will cut through this space very easily with the result that the whole capping will be cut away at one attempt with little or no honey adhering. Don't be easily discouraged and keep the knife blade hot, otherwise the comb will be injured by dragging. If you notice any dragging and collapsing of cells, stop the cutting and pick out the damaged broken away part and start again.

The uncapping should be repeated on the other side of the comb and when both sides are done the comb should be placed immediately in the extractor making sure that the wire net in the extractor is placed on the outside of the comb. This wire net is used in order to prevent the comb collapsing when the extractor is working.

It will be found that holding the frame at an angle of 30 degrees away from you will result in the wax capping falling away from the uncapped cells into the dish.

The extractor uses centrifugal force to extract the honey. The combs should all be fixed in the cage with the lugs in the corresponding position, in other words, when the combs are in the cage the lug ends or top of the frames should not be adjoining each other. This ensures that the cells of each comb are all pointing in a similar direction. The combs should be of approximately even weight to stop the extractor from wobbling when in action. The extractor should then be rotated slowly and it will soon be seen if it is being rotated in the correct direction. It should be rotated so that the cage is moving in the direction which is opposite to that in which the cells adjoining the wire net are facing.

After it is apparent that the operation is succeeding stop the extractor, take out and reverse the frames one by one so that the unextracted side faces outwards. Turn slowly for approximately the same number of turns as were given to the first side. It is important that the extractor should not be turned rapidly whilst either side of the comb is full of honey or the combs will break. The speed of the extractor may be increased in inverse proportion to the amount of honey left in the combs. The combs after being completely extracted should be put back in the hives. If, however, it is not intended to work for any more honey the frames should be placed in a crate and put back in the hive but over a Porter board which is illustrated earlier in this book. After they are placed on the hive the slide of the Porter board should be placed in the " open " position and left like that for about a week. In the meantime, the bees will have cleaned out the combs and taken down any remaining honey and stored it in the combs below the Porter board. The slide in the board can then be moved into the " shut " position.

In the next 24 hours the bees remaining in extracted combs will have joined the rest of the stock, making their way through the escape in the board. The combs can then be removed and stored for the winter.

" Ripening " the Honey

This is the generally accepted, although erroneous, term for storing honey prior to bottling. The ripener is a cylindrical container made from tinned sheet iron having a funnel filter at the top and a treacle tap at the bottom. When the honey is whisked out of the combs in the extractor it flies off the combs in small particles and often small pieces of wax go with it. The honey settles at the bottom of the extractor and is filled with minute bubbles and small fragments of wax. It is therefore run out of the extractor into the ripener and allowed to stand for several days before bottling. The filter at the top of the ripener is removable. It consists of a funnel with a gauze at its base. This gauze is only small enough to catch large particles of foreign matter so it is necessary for some other filtering medium to be put there in addition. A double thickness of muslin is adequate to catch smaller particles of wax, etc. This should be tied on the outside of the funnel. There is usually a flange round which it can be tied.

The honey is then run from the extractor into the ripener through the filter. This is rather a slow process, but it is well worth while. Nothing looks worse to a critical eye than cloudy honey with particles of dirt either suspended in it or lying at the bottom of the jar, and such honey never wins prizes even when granulated for dirt shows up even then. In spite of every care taken in cleanliness it is surprising to see the quantity of foreign matter which the filter will collect.

The honey should now be allowed to stand in the ripener for several days in a reasonably warm place. This enables the minute bubbles in the extracted honey to rise to the surface. Do not be in too great a hurry to bottle the honey otherwise disappointment will follow in that a scum of bubbles will appear in the top of the jar and so spoil the general appearance of the honey. So people run their honey straight into jars from the ripener. It is a matter of choice.

Wax Capping

The wax cappings may be dealt with in several ways. In the days when mead was more frequently drunk as a beverage the cappings and the adhering honey were steeped in water which was then allowed to ferment. Some bee-keepers place the pie dish which they have used to collect the cappings into a slow oven. This melts the wax which floats in a liquid form on the surface of the honey. The whole is then allowed to cool, the wax sets hard, is then cracked and the honey poured through the filter. This has disadvantages in that the heating of honey reduces its aroma. It may, too, become overheated in the oven and be ruined. Further, as the wax melts, a certain amount of pollen which is mixed with wax cappings comes into contact with the honey and tends to spoil it. The most satisfactory method of daeling with it is to place the whole of it in the top of the filter after having passed all the other honey through first. In two or three days time, the cappings will be almost drained clear of honey. They can then be washed in a little clear water which should be fed back to the bees. In this way not any honey is lost or spoilt.

Use may be made of a Solar Wax Extractor (see *Fig. 25*).

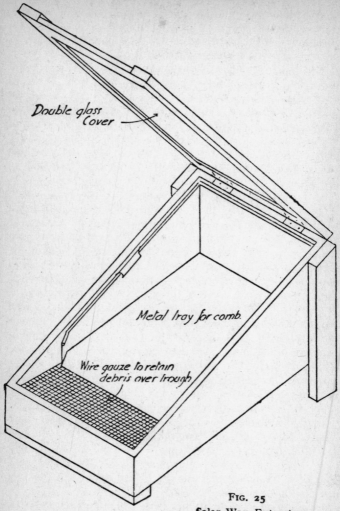

Double glass Cover

Metal tray for comb.

Wire gauze to retain debris over trough

FIG. 25
Solar Wax Extractor

The sun's rays are used to melt the wax capping with this simple device.

Extracting Unsealed Honey

Bees do not seal over their honey until it is mature. By that it is meant that the honey will not be sealed until the surplus moisture has been evaporated from the honey.

There are two main objections to the use of unsealed honey and particularly to its sale. First, it is low in sugar content compared with sealed honey as it has too great a proportion of water in it and if sold the seller is liable to be charged with selling " to the prejudice of the Purchaser." Secondly, it is highly probable that it will ferment. Therefore, if you have any combs which are partly unsealed, extract the unsealed honey first and feed it back to the bees, for preference to a hive which is finishing off sections. Extracting unsealed honey is very simple. It means that you do not uncap the sealed honey but merely put the combs into the extractor as they are and the sealed honey will remain in the comb for extraction later.

Bottling Honey

After the extracted honey has remained in the ripener for a few days, it will be noticed that there is a scum of very fine bubbles on the top. This is perfectly pure and can be skimmed off with a warm spoon and used in the household. The honey is then ready for bottling. For household use, ordinary jam jars are quite adequate but for the sale of the surplus attractive jars help considerably in securing a market. These jars are of two types. The " tall " and " squat " screw top pound and half pound jars. The squat jars have the tendency to make the honey look a little darker and for show purpose are not very popular in consequence. Special jars with burnished aluminium caps are available for those who intend to compete at the show bench. Squat jars are much more popular with consumers as they may be used more readily on the table and are becoming more popular at shows.

Great care should be taken to see that jars contain the correct amount of honey. If you sell a jar as a 1 lb. jar, that jar should contain 1 lb. Tricks of the trade unfortunately have already stepped in and jars which hold only 14 ozs. have been introduced and take cover under the term " reputed

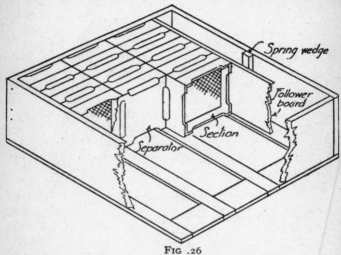

FIG .26
Details of a Section Crate

1 lb. jars." Weigh one or two jars empty and weigh them full and if all your jars are standard you will soon know how far up to fill them. It is better to err on the generous side rather than spoil your future clientele.

Don't sell all your surplus to one customer, the more people who buy your honey the greater will be the demand in the next season. Ask your regular customers to return their jars when placing their next order and a considerable sum will be saved in this way.

Section Honey

Section honey is a popular but hazardous method of producing honey.

There are many stocks of bees which will not for some reason or other take kindly to sections. In many cases it is found that rather than work on sections the bees will avoid completely the additional storage space which the bee-keeper places at their disposal, and will swarm particularly so if the first super placed over the brood-chamber consists of a crate of sections.

The usual section crate for a standard hive consists of 21 sections. There are three rows of seven in a row. The wooden section boxes are purchased in the flat in cases of 100. Great care must be taken in the assembling of the sections. It is desirable to make a " matrix " box into which the section can be folded. This box is made very easily. It is made just large enough to hold a section but has the top and one side missing. Take one flat section box, moisten the wood at the back of the grooves and fold over two of the sides at the grooves and slide into the matrix box leaving the split top with the dovetailed end upright. Take a sheet of thin wax foundation which is also purchased in packages of 100 and slide it into the grooves on the inside of the section box, making sure that the foundation is vertical and correct as shown in *Fig. 9*. Then fold over the split top and secure the dovetailed ends. After having done one crate in this way, set the sections with the split tops upwards in three rows of seven, each three being separated by a metal separator. These metal separators are used to prevent the sections being joined together with bracecomb. Bracecomb is honeycomb built by bees to tie together comb which is more than a bee space ($\frac{5}{8}$ths of an inch) apart. Bracecomb is often built by the English black bee which incidentally is usually a good section worker and makes a very white capping.

The best time to place a crate of sections on the hive is when the honey flow is well under way and a crate of shallow frames is almost filled with sealed honey. The bees will then have to pass through the sections in order to reach the shallow frames and in this way become accustomed to them. An inspection about seven days afterwards should be made to see if the foundation is being drawn out by the bees and at the same time an inspection should be made to discover any queen cells. If none of the section foundation is drawn out and Queen cells are discovered, one can be pretty certain that rather than use the sections they intend to swarm. In this case the section rack should be removed and the Queen cells also and a crate of shallow frames inserted in place of the section rack. Care should be taken to see that this stock does not continue with its swarming impulse by using the methods described in an earlier chapter.

A stock, however, will probably be found which will accept a rack of sections. If the honey flow is on then it is astonishing with what rapidity the bees fill the section boxes. It is no uncommon thing for a stock to complete a rack of 21 sections fully filled and capped over in one week. More often the process is slower. When several sections are seen to be capped over, remove the rack, take out the completed sections, move those already started to the middle of the rack and fill up the blank spaces with fresh section boxes and return the rack to the hive.

It is desirable when working for section honey to take away the sections as soon as they are sealed over because if they are left in the hive for any appreciable period after sealing they become " travel stained," that is, they become darkened in colour with the constant walking over by the bees. This makes them less attractive for the market.

Towards the end of the normal honey flow it is desirable to collect from the hives with sections all those which are nearly complete and place them in one rack on the best hive. If necessary, extract the partly filled sections and feed back the honey together with the washing of the cappings of the shallow bars, care being taken to do this at night-time and by means of a rapid feeder. In this way many sections will be completed which would otherwise be quite useless to market. Those which are extracted can be packed away with care for preference in a biscuit tin and used either in the following year or for the heather honey flow. If used in the following year they will be readily accepted by the bees who will start with partly drawn out combs which is such an advantage.

If the combs are used for heather honey they will in all probability be completed. The advantage of drawn out comb in honey production cannot be too strongly stressed.

It is a well-known fact that it is useless to hope to make a real success of extracted heather honey if the combs are to be retained for further use. Even when drone comb is used and the comb is put into the extractor warm it is a most arduous task, unless the extractor is power driven. So, for the average bee-keeper who seeks heather honey, the section is the better proposition. Heather for the purposes of this paragraph means, of course, Ling Heather (Calluna Vulgaris) and not Bell Heather (Erica Cinerea) the honey from the latter being readily extracted.

Sending stocks of bees to the heather is not a very difficult matter, many associations organise collective transport and arrange for suitable " out apiaries." The secretary of your local association will give you details of the arrangements which are available for its members.

The advantage of sending bees to the heather is that the honey season is prolonged, the bee-keeper receives an added return on his outlay and heather honey always commands a higher price than other varieties.

There are several well known hints regarding heather honey production. They are briefly as follows. Don't place the hive in a valley on the moors where mists hang about or near heather growing on damp boggy land. Don't place your hives too near to those of others. You may pass on disease from your bees to the hives of others or you may find your bees infected by theirs. In any case too many bees in one locality tends to reduce the total amount of honey obtained from each hive, although saturation point is not reached unless there are very large numbers of hives.

The wax on heather honey is usually much whiter than on other honey and this makes it the more attractive as a marketable honey.

It is reputed that bees do not winter well on heather honey, therefore, when the bees are brought back they should be fed well with sugar syrup. For details of the method of feeding see the chapter on Winter Feeding.

In the South bees winter quite well on heather honey.

Skep Honey

At one time this was the principal source of honey production in this country. The method of obtaining the honey was both cruel and uneconomic.

The skeps which were heaviest were held over burning sulphur so that the fumes killed the bees which dropped, dead, out of the hive.

The combs which were left were cut out and outer combs were used as comb honey and the brood combs containing honey were bruised and broken, put in a muslin bag and hung over a container in front of a warm fire. This method resulted in the destruction of the entire stock of bees, the honey comb and the brood-comb and, further, the honey which was obtained was anything but pure, it being in part obtained from that stored in brood-comb where the faeces of the larvae had accumulated.

Later the process of driving bees out of skeps was adopted, with the result that the bees at any rate survived, although the combs were ruined.

The method of driving bees is as follows. Have available a spare skep with or without comb. Give a puff or two of smoke into the skep with bees. Too much smoke is undesirable. Turn the skep of bees upside down and place the spare skep over the exposed bees. Raise the front of the empty skep to an angle of 30 degrees and fix it in that position with driving irons. These irons are about 1 foot long and have spikes at either end, both at right-angles to the main iron and two of these are stuck into the skeps to keep them in position. The operator then beats the lower skep repeatedly with the palms of both hands for about five minutes. The bees object very much to this disturbance and quit their home and run up into the empty skep. It may be necessary to continue this procedure for longer than five minutes until all the bees have gone up. The new skep should then be placed on the stand of the old skep and fed with sugar syrup until there are sufficient stores for the winter. Fortunately, the present method of procuring extracted honey is simpler in some ways and much more hygienic.

Casual Honey

Occasionally a bee-keeper is asked to remove a stock of bees from the eaves of a house or some such place, where they are unwanted.

Sometimes phenomenal quantities of honey are obtained from these sources, dependent upon the number of years that the bees have been in occupation. The writer himself has tackled one of such stocks and six hours work produced 16 pailfulls of sealed honeycomb and one nucleus stock cut out of the brood-combs. The mass of combs measured 4 feet 6 inches across, were 2 feet 6 inches tall, tapering off to 6 inches. The main stock was left behind, together with about one-third of the total quantity of honey.

Certain experience was obtained which is worth recording. A great deal of honey was cut away in the comb without disturbing the bees to any great extent, but once disturbed they became extremely vicious, and even the best protection failed to stop dozens of stings. The bees, in large numbers, made for the hurricane lamp used.

The smoker was used extensively for several minutes on end and then the work proceeded with less interference. It was found helpful to have a few quarter of an hour breaks. This seemed to have the effect of settling the bees down again.

The honey collected was mostly granulated, having been stored in the comb for a considerable length of time. The comb was spotlessly clean and was all drone cell except those cells containing pollen. This confirmed the view that all storage combs should be fitted with drone foundation, as bees make drone comb for storage in their natural state.

The honeycomb collected in this way can either be packed away in tins or reduced to " run honey." As it was granulated in this case, it was put into a clean pail and put into a copper half filled with boiling water. After an hour the honey had melted out of the comb and the wax had also melted. The pail was taken out of the copper and set on one side to cool. The wax, solidified, was lifted off in a cake and the honey run through the filter into the ripener. Later, this was run off into jars and has proved a very good honey indeed.

Some of the meltings down were spoiled by some comb containing pollen contaminating the rest, but this was useful in supplying winter storage for another stock. The comb should have been held up to the light and the pollen would have been identified and could have been eliminated.

The nucleus was made by cutting out of the brood-comb pieces the size of an ordinary standard brood-frame and were inserted the correct way up in empty brood-frames and kept in position by each being tied round with red tape. Care was taken to ensure that there were freshly-laid eggs in one comb and all went well. The old stock was left in the roof with substantial stores and will be available for honey gathering later on.

CHAPTER VIII

INCREASE OF STOCKS

THE bee-keeper must know how to increase the number of his stocks, for there are seasons when disease overcomes some and in some years stocks die out through lack of winter stores.

In due time and from experience the bee-keeper will learn which is his best all round stock and from this best stock he should provide the Queens which are to populate his other hives.

There are five main ways of increasing stocks. First, collecting swarms; secondly, Artificial Swarms; thirdly, Formation of Nucleus Stocks; fourthly, Nucleus Swarms; and lastly by the utilisation of a number of stocks.

Collecting Swarms

This method is most precarious. Modern bee-keepers deprecate the practice of swarming. The accumulation of large stocks of surplus honey cannot be expected from hives which swarm however early in the season that may occur. Also, unless the bee-keeper is available at all times to deal with the swarm, his efforts in encouraging the stock to swarm may be lost as the swarm may abscond in his absence. If, however, the bee-keeper intends to rely on casual swarms his chance is even more precarious. He may collect a number which may or may not be useful. One thing is certain and that is that he will have no idea of the characteristics of his bees until the end of the season. He may be blest with good fortune and yet he may acquire diseased stocks which may infect his others and so be a danger to his apiary and those of his neighbours.

There are in many parts of the country "bee-men" who are called in to remove swarms. They hive them in skeps, boxes and derelict hives. They collect a certain amount of skep honey and occasionally section honey by placing a crate of sections on the box or skep. They care nothing about the welfare of the bees and are unaware of their possible diseased condition. Such men are a source of danger to the community of bee-keepers. Don't in any circumstances buy bees from such bee-keepers.

The principle objections to collecting swarms are that the bee-keeper collects bees whose swarming propensity has been proved and that a swarm usually consists of old bees with an old Queen.

Artificial Swarms

This is by far the simplest, convenient and most effective way of increasing stocks but should be carried out early in the season if surplus honey is to be expected. One great advantage is that the Queen who will operate in the artificial swarm for the rest of the season is the Queen whose characteristics are already known.

The following preparations are necessary to make a real success of the operation. First stimulate the stock which you intend to operate upon. This stock is called the parent stock. There are two methods of stimulation as described earlier under the heading of " Spring Stimulation." Briefly this consists of stimulation which it will be remembered is carried out in two ways:— stimulative feeding and brood spreading. The feeding should be commenced about the first and second weeks in April and the capped honey on the centre brood-combs should be uncapped or bruised so that the bees will use these stores and fill the empty cells with brood. A regular quantity of thin warm syrup should also be given. If these instructions are carried out with care it will be found that the stock will be extremely strong by the first week in May. It will be full of bees and brood and it may be found that there are signs of Queen cells.

Preparing a strong stock is the first important step to the sucess of the whole operation.

Have ready an empty hive with the brood chamber ready to receive the artificial swarm. It should be empty and ten spare brood-frames should be available to fill up the blanks which will be created in the parent stock and also to act as brood-frames for the artificial swarm.

Lift the parent stock about four feet to one side and place the new hive in the exact position of the parent hive. Open up the parent hive and find the Queen. Take the brood-frame on which the Queen is and place it in the new hive. Take a comb of sealed brood, too, with the adhering bees and place it next to the Queen. Then take two frames containing honey and pollen but no brood or eggs. These are usually found on the outer combs of the parent hive. Place one on each side of the two frames already in the new hive. Fill up the remaining space in the new hive with the spare brood-combs three on each side of those already put in the new hive. This will make the full complement of 10 brood-combs in the new hive. Place a quilt over the 10 brood-combs and pack the hive down and leave it alone for several days. Now as to the parent hive. The frames containing brood should now be placed together. It will be remembered that four frames were removed so that it will be necessary to place the last four spare frames in the parent hive. These should be put on the outsides, two on each side. The hive should then be closed down. The parent stock should be fed for a few days as much of its reserve stores have been removed to the new hive. Also, the bees which remain in the parent hive are young bees and have not yet become foragers.

The result of this operation is that the flying bees will return to their original situation and join their own original Queen. They will soon assist the Queen to build up the new stock. The young bees will soon hatch out of the sealed brood and will act as nurse bees, leaving their empty cells ready to receive the Queen's eggs. The bees in this time will build up to produce a strong stock and will all being well produce surplus honey the same season. The parent stock in the meantime will have realised the loss of their Queen and will proceed forthwith to make a number of Queen cells using the eggs which the parent Queen had laid in worker cells. In due course a virgin Queen will be hatched out and after a lapse of about four weeks from the operation the stock will begin to build up again and will be strong enough to produce surplus honey. One big advantage will be apparent, that is, the parent stock having been reduced at a time when swarming was imminent will have lost its swarming instinct for the season. Another advantage is that the parent stock will go forward to the following season with a new Queen.

Formation of Nucleus Stocks

Again as in the case of artificial swarms only strong stocks should be used and the method of stimulating described earlier should again be carried out. The operator should in the case of forming a nucleus wait until a little later in the season than in the case of making an artificial swarm, the reason for this being that in the case of an artificial swarm a strong swarm with existing brood, flying bees and a laying Queen is able to carry itself on just as well as if it were a natural swarm, whereas in the case of a nucleus there is no Queen to carry on the laying and a great deal less number of flying bees to forage for and build up the stores.

The operation is carried out as follows. Prepare a spare hive ready to receive the nucleus or alternatively a nucleus hive. The illustration of a nucleus hive shown here is a very useful part of a bee-keeper's equipment and every bee-keeper should make or acquire one capable of holding four or five brood-frames.

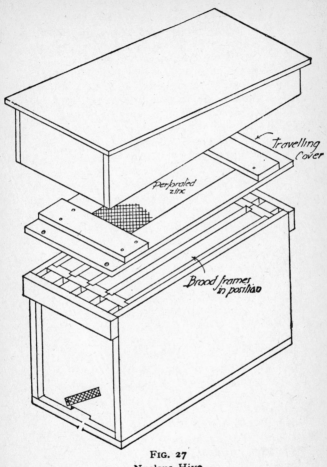

FIG. 27
Nucleus Hive

If a spare hive is used and it is the intention to have the brood-frames at right angles to the entrance then two division boards will be necessary but if the brood-frames are placed parallel with the entrance, usually called the warm way, then only one division board will be necessary.

First place the hive to receive the nucleus about two yards away from the parent hive and have all the equipment ready before opening up the parent hive. The equipment should include four spare brood-frames filled with worker foundation or preferably with the foundation already drawn out; a quilt and extra felting or sacking to keep the nucleus extra warm.

Next open up the parent hive at the height of a fine day when many of the flying bees are out foraging, leaving the young bees on the combs, and find the Queen. This is most important as the Queen must not go with the nucleus but remain with the parent stock. Find two brood-combs each containing eggs which are freshly laid and place these combs with the adhering bees into the spare hive together with two combs of stores which are usually found to be the outside combs of the parent hive. These should be placed one on either side of the two combs containing eggs. They should then be packed down by placing a division board on either side of the four combs if the combs are placed at right angles to the entrance, but if they are placed parallel with the entrance then they should all be placed at the front of the brood-chamber with a division board at the back. Great care should be taken not to jar the brood-combs when moving them from one hive to another. If this happens the bees, which are mostly young bees, will fall off the brood-combs. If insufficient bees are in the nucleus then a comb or two from the parent hive should be shaken in until the four combs are well covered, special care again being taken to ensure that the Queen of the parent hive is not in the nucleus. They should then be covered with a quilt having a feeder hole cut in the top; a rapid feeder should be placed over the whole and a supply of warm syrup should be given daily to the nucleus to ensure that it will not perish of hunger. It should again be emphasised that whatever is given to the bees at this stage by way of syrup will be amply repaid by a stronger stock later on. The entrance to the hive should be closed down to two inches and should be very lightly plugged with dry grass. This enables the bees to breathe through the grass but prevents their escape back to the parent hive. This should be removed after 48 hours during which time the bees will have lost their homing instinct and will regard the nucleus as their home.

When the bees discover that they are Queenless they will immediately commence to form Queen cells to create their new Queen. It will help matters very much if a Queen cell either from the parent stock or from another good stock can be inserted in the nucleus. Usually it will be accepted by the bees and they will continue to rear it to fruition. This means that valuable time will be saved if a sealed Queen cell is inserted. Recently, in early June, the writer opened a hive for a friend some seven miles from his apiary and discovered a number of excellent Queen cells sealed. As they were being cut away in any case to prevent swarming he placed one in a match-box and then in his waistcoat pocket to keep it warm and returned to his apiary, made a nucleus and inserted the ripe Queen cell in the nucleus by wiring it with tinned wire to one of the nucleus combs. Next day, on inspection, it was noted that the bees had annealed the cell to the comb with wax and had freshened up the appearance of the cell. The following day, on inspection, it was noted that the Queen had hatched out and was accepted by the bees who formed no other Queen cells. In a further ten days, eggs and unsealed brood were discovered. This nucleus did well and produced a small amount of surplus honey.

An excellent way of starting a nucleus going is to purchase a young fertile Queen from an apiary of repute. This arrives in a Queen travelling box [*Fig. 28*].

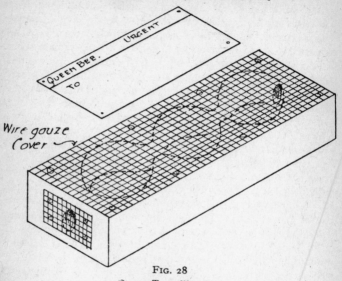

FIG. 28

Queen Travelling Box

Normally a nucleus if made before the end of **May** will build up to full strength before the honey season is over and may even produce surplus honey but the help that is given at the start both by careful feeding and the provision of a ripe Queen cell will be reflected in the final result.

Nucleus Swarms

There are two ways of carrying out this operation both of which in practice meet with equal success.

First method. Carry out the formation of a nucleus as described earlier but instead of packing the four brood-frames together and shielding them with division boards, place six brood-frames with either foundation or drawn out comb, for preference the latter and instead of putting the nucleus on a new stand put the parent hive at a distance and the nucleus on the stand of the parent hive.

In this way the nucleus will receive a large number of flying bees and build up very rapidly but the parent stock will be depleted rather heavily although by way of compensation will have a laying Queen and a fair number of young bees to help build up. If this process is adopted the parent stock should be fed also as the foraging bees to a great extent will have joined the nucleus.

Second method. In this case, two strong stocks are needed. A nucleus should be formed of two combs of eggs, and sealed brood and two combs of food from the parent hive. Six brood-frames with foundation or drawn out comb should be added. The first parent hive should remain on

FIG. 29
Wire Gauze Cage

its own stand but the second parent hive which is to supply the flying bees should be removed from its stand and moved at least 3 yards away and in its place should be put the nucleus. Thus it will be noted that the first parent hive supplies the eggs and sealed brood, but the second parent hive supplies the bees.

This is an extremely good method for both parent hives rapidly overcome their losses and the nucleus will forge ahead with the help it has received. Only the nucleus need be fed and then to only assist the bees to draw out the comb foundation.

A nucleus can always be strengthened by transposing the nucleus and the stock from which flying bees are to be taken, but when a nucleus has hatched out its Queen, a special precaution is necessary. Open the nucleus, find the Queen and place a wire gauze cage [*Fig. 29*] over her with two or three young bees with her. Add additional brood frames and transpose the nucleus and the other hive. The nucleus will receive the flying bees from the other hive which, in its turn, will receive the flying bees from the nucleus. After 48 hours the Queen will be accepted by the bees and should be freed from the cage. The young bees are encaged with Queen to ensure that there are bees to feed the Queen who may not be capable of feeding herself. A young Queen not in lay can certainly feed herself and there seems no reason why a Queen in lay could not do so, although admittedly she does not do so, being tended by the workers instead.

The great advantage of forming nuclei from strong stocks is that the bee-keeper is assured that because of their strain the nuclei will also prove themselves by becoming strong stocks, also that the withdrawal of part of the strength of strong stocks early in the season tends to overcome the swarming impulse before the main honey flow arrives.

Using a number of stocks

This method results in less drain on the parent and other hives than any other methods. Take, for example, five hives. Take two combs of eggs without bees from one, two combs of sealed brood without bees from the second, two combs of sealed brood without bees from the third, the same from the fourth, pack these with two combs with foundation one on either side, making ten combs in all.

Place the whole on the stand of the fifth stock, which is moved to one side. The stocks which are depleted have the blanks filled up with fresh combs or frames with foundation. In this way one hive supplies the eggs, three supply the sealed brood which will, in turn, supply the foraging and nurse bees for the new Queen and the fifth, which supplies the bees.

Within a very short time this will be a very strong stock indeed. There will be ample room for the new Queen to lay as all the sealed brood will have hatched out by the time the new Queen is laying. This stock is almost bound to produce surplus honey. The other stocks, too, will recover quickly and will scarcely appear to be affected by the operation. Almost certainly the swarming impulse will have been controlled for the season, particularly if the operation is repeated three weeks later, and another nucleus formed in a similar way.

This is the method usually adopted by bee-keepers who make stocks up for sale. It pays the beginner to purchase a stock of this type because he is assured of a young Queen in a stock which will prove a honey gatherer.

There is one other method which permits of an increase of stock and yet ensures a surplus honey yield. If in spite of all precautions taken by the bee-keeper a swarm emerges, he should follow the following instructions. It must, of course, be presupposed that one of the methods of swarm control which he has adopted is the supering of the parent stock. The swarm should be hived temporarily in a skep or box. A new hive should be prepared and placed immediately adjoining the parent stock. In the evening the swarm should be hived in the new hive and the super of the parent stock placed over the brood chamber. The parent stock should be closed down and fed as it will have lost the greater portion of its stores, and on the morrow will lose many more of its bees for reasons explained. At the height of the following day the parent stock should be removed some distance away and the new stock moved slightly so that it stands in a position which is just midway between where the two hives were placed the day before. In this way the swarm has added to it additional flying bees. It will be some time before all the foundation is drawn out on the ten frames in which the Queen will ultimately lay. During that time as all the bees are flying bees, a substantial amount of honey will be stored in the super. If this is done early in the season, the swarm will prove a good surplus honey producer.

The drawback to this method is that as the parent stock is very depleted owing to the departure of both the swarm and, later, the flying bees, it is a longer time recovering and cannot be expected to be a surplus honey producer. However it is a maxim among bee-keepers that one strong stock is worth two weak ones, and this practice is strongly advocated.

CHAPTER IX

THE FEEDING OF BEES

THIS can be classified into three principal groups. Spring or Stimulative Feeding, Summer Feeding and Autumn or Storage Feeding.

The purpose of feeding may, to the beginner, seem strange as bees are reputed to be producers of sweetness rather than consumers of it.

Spring Feeding

Spring feeding should not normally be necessary but in the present period of shortage of sugar it is not possible to feed adequately in the autumn to render spring feeding unnecessary.

Feeding at any time always stimulates foraging.

The purpose of Spring feeding is to encourage the bees to breed in greater numbers and at an earlier time than they would normally breed. Earlier in this book is a description of Spring feeding. Before supplying any syrup look down between the combs. Do not disturb the bees unless it is a warm day. See if there is any quantity of sealed stores particularly at the centre of the cluster. If this is visible uncap the sealed honey there either with a penknife or in some other way so that the hive is little disturbed. It is generally accepted that if bees are disturbed too greatly at this season that they frequently " ball " their queen. That is, they cluster round her so tightly that she is suffocated. The bees will clear up and use the honey in the cells which are uncapped and make ready the cells for the Queen for immediate use. Further use may be made of this method until it is seen that four or five combs are being used for breeding. Then comes the time for the stimulative feeding by the slow feeder. Although the recipe given below is generally accepted as correct, the bee-keeper is advised to try spring stimulation with the very thin syrup which the writer has by experiment shown to be very effective. In any case recipes vary to such an extent that the life or death of the bees does not appear to be materially affected.

Digges advises equal weights of water and sugar ; that is equivalent to 1¼ lbs. of sugar to each pint of water. The author of the Ministry of Agriculture's Bulletin No. 9 on Bee-keeping advises half a pint of water to every pound of sugar, that is 10 ozs. of water to 16 ozs. of sugar.

The amount which is given to a stock depends upon its strength and also upon the amount of the stores existing in the hive but the syrup of equal weights of water and sugar can be given at the rate of a cupful every other evening. An occasional inspection will show whether or not the bees are storing the syrup in the comb. If they are storing then cut down the supply of syrup and resort to brood spreading.

Spring feeding is the feeding which appears to show the best results. The stocks grow more rapidly and the stocks get into the condition for which the bee-keeper has been longing during the winter months.

Care should be taken to feed the bees only in the evening and to keep the entrance of the hive closed down to three inches. The sugar used must be clean white sugar. Brown sugar gives the bees dysentery. The sugar must not be burned when dissolving in the water. There are those who aver that beet sugar is unsuitable for feeding bees and that only cane sugar should be used. This is, of course, absurd, as both the sugar beet and the sugar cane produce identically the same chemical substance which chemists call " cane sugar." A reason for this belief may have arisen, for in the early stages of beet sugar production Barium salts were used in the refining process. Barium is a cumulative poison and although great care was taken some very small amounts may have escaped with the product. These amounts were not sufficient to do any serious harm to human life but it is possible that even a minute quantity of a Barium salt may have been harmful to bees.

Barium salts are not now used in the refining of beet sugar which may be the reason for the present beet sugar being quite harmless.

There are those too who say that the syrup must be boiled to sterilise it. This too is totally unnecessary. Is the nectar given up by the flowers boiled? Why should sugar fit for human consumption have to be boiled for bees? The only virtue in boiling the water is that the sugar dissolves the more readily in it. Some add vinegar, some salt and others even beer and wine. What a waste of good material!

Summer Feeding

Many bee-keepers fail to make use of summer feeding. There is very often after the early fruit blossoms an hiatus before the flowers commence their nectar flow. This means that any surplus which the bees may have stored from the early blossoms may be completely used up in maintaining the growing stock. Not only may they have used that up but may even throw out of their hive the immature nymphs and grubs. This occurs particularly if the weather is bad and the bees cannot forage. Then is the time that the judicious bee-keeper will feed his stock liberally so as to maintain his stock in a strong condition and even increase its strength for the honey flow which is to follow. Care, however, should be taken to ensure that the bees do not commence to store the sugar syrup in the supers. Some take the supers off when they find it necessary to begin summer feeding to avoid storing syrup in the combs, but this is unwise for almost without warning the honey flow starts and the bee-keeper may lose a few days of valuable honey gathering He may, too, by his action begin to crowd out his bees with the result that the swarming instinct may be roused with unhappy consequences.

To avoid any trouble whatever with the storage of sugar syrup in the supers the perfect bee-keeper should feed with pure honey diluted with one cupful of water to each pound of honey. They can store this if they wish in the supers without harm.

To those bee-keepers who intend to send their bees to the heather a word of warning is due. When taking off the honey at the end of the clover flow, that is during the third or fourth week in July, do not rob the bees of all their honey. The end of July and the early part of August is often a very treacherous time and the stock may be totally unfit for the heather unless sufficient stores are left or unless generous feeding is adopted. Always be generous with your bees; they are generous to the bee-keeper.

Again, when taking all the surplus honey off the hive at the end of the honey flow give the bees a little syrup and keep it up until the main autumn feed in September. If this is done, the bee-keeper is assured of a very strong stock for wintering.

The syrup recommended for summer feeding, 2 lbs. of sugar to 3 pints of water which is approximately the strength of nectar which is drawn from the flowers. Nectar varies in its water content from approximately between 50 per cent. to 80 per cent. water, but may vary even more than this.

Autumn Feeding

It is often incorrectly stated that the purposes of Autumn feeding are twofold, (a) to stimulate the bees to breed and so go through the winter a strong stock, and (b) to have sufficient stores to live through the winter.

The second only of these purposes is correct.   In support of (a) above, many experienced bee-keepers advise spreading the period of autumn feeding over a period of two to three weeks.   This is wrong and wasteful.   If the bee-keeper will only continue with an occasional small feed after the honey flow has ceased the stock will remain strong until the middle of September.   Then the autumn feed should be given as rapidly as possible and it will be found that the bees will seal it quickly, breeding will be restricted as the available cells will be filled with stores. At Rothamsted Experimental Station better results are obtained by completing Autumn feeding by the middle of September at the latest.   It should however be noted that Rothamsted is not a heather district.   The restriction of breeding at this stage is not undesirable if the stock is strong.   The writer recently made a feeder capable of holding ten pints of syrup.   This was emptied by the bees in two days, filled again, and emptied this time in three days.   An inspection later showed the combs very well filled with almost all the syrup sealed.   The stock wintered well, was expanded to 16 brood-combs in the Spring, a six frame nucleus was taken, then a four frame nucleus 14 days after and three weeks later it threw a 4¾ lbs. swarm and gave 16 lbs. of surplus honey.   This was all carried out in an experimental hive, details of which the writer proposes to record at some early date.

If the Autumn feed is given slowly the bees will believe a honey flow has started and breeding will be stimulated to an excessive amount and the stores intended for the winter will be consumed in feeding the grubs and young bees instead of being kept for winter feed.   The correct method is to keep the stock strong all the time and then give the Autumn feed rapidly.

Use a rapid feeder, the larger the better.   Feed if possible all your stocks at one time as this tends to avoid robbing.

The strength of syrup for winter feed should be greater

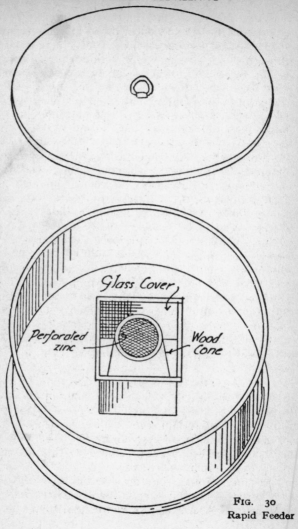

FIG. 30
Rapid Feeder

than for either Spring or Summer feeding. Two and a half pounds of sugar to one pint of water makes a very practical syrup. Some add oil of thyme and some chemicals to prevent fermentation but if a thick syrup is fed, and fed rapidly to a strong stock the bees will seal it over. Sealed syrup does not ferment; unsealed syrup may, but the bees will always consume the unsealed first before breaking into their stores.

Candy for Winter Feeding

This substance is an unnatural food for bees and should be used only as an emergency measure. To buy it is expensive, to make it is found difficult by many and its use is a sign that the bee-keeper has doubts as to whether he has given his bees sufficient winter stores. Some bee-keepers of wide experience state that rather than give candy to their bees they would prefer to put on the rapid feeder and give the bees a dose of thick warm syrup, the reason given is that candy is worked at by the bees continuously and that disturbs the hive, whereas a feeder full of syrup is taken down overnight and the bees settle down again to their winter conditions.

A recipe which has proved satisfactory is given here. Three pounds of sugar, half pint of hot water and half a teaspoonful of cream of tartar. Place the water in a pan, heat it and add the sugar gradually, stirring all the time to ensure that all the sugar dissolves and does not burn. However slightly burnt, the mixture as it is will be useless for the bees. Add the half a teaspoonful of cream of tartar. The whole should be brought to the boil and allowed to boil for two minutes. Then stand the pan in cold water until the contents of the pan begin to cloud. As soon as this cloudiness appears stir hard and pour into the containers. The containers should be made so as to contain about 1 lb. of the candy. They can be made of a section box glazed on one side. This has the advantage that an inspection without disturbing the bees can be made. If the bees have upon inspection removed the greater portion of the candy, another box can be placed over, say, half of the feed hole by moving the original box half way off the hole. When the first one is all used up, it should be removed and the second one made to cover the hole, or a third one to replace the first. This may be continued and fed to the bees so long as they continue to remove it. The weakness of this method is that the bees remove the candy before consuming their own stores and even store the candy in their combs after liquefying it. The result may be that when the Spring arrives, the hive is crowded with surplus food ; it is a waste from the point that the effort and the candy have been unnecessary. The alternative to candy feeding is to ensure that the bees are adequately fed before being bedded down for the winter. A good method of ensuring that bees have sufficient food is to inspect the hive during a warm day in the early part of October. If, on average, the ten bars of the brood-chamber hold more than half their cells filled with sealed stores then there is sufficient to see the stock through the winter. One brood-comb filled with sealed stores contains about five pounds weight of honey or syrup. Therefore ten half filled brood-combs contain approximately twenty-five pounds of stores, which is regarded by experts as enough to see the bees through the winter.

If on inspection it is found that there is a deficient quantity of stores, put on a rapid feeder and give the bees sufficient thick syrup to make up their requirements.

It is important to remember that it is much better to err on the generous side than to lose a stock of bees through starvation.

It has been found after long trial at Rothamsted that the best results are obtained if each colony is left 25–30 lbs. of natural stores in the Autumn and then are fed with an additional 5–10 lbs. of concentrated syrup as quickly as possible so that it is stored and not used for immediate consumption.   It is found that 35–40 lbs. of stores in all is quite sufficient to tide any colony over the non-productive months of the year without any further feeding whatsoever.   Some experienced bee-keepers think even this is inadequate and the beginner is advised to be generous with his bees.

CHAPTER X

WINTERING OF BEES

Bee Passages

A VERY important matter in winter in the hive is the ability of the bees to reach their stores. Many stocks have been known to perish through their inability to reach their stores. Three effective methods of dealing with the problem are employed. The crudest method is to cut a hole about 1 inch diameter at the top of each comb just where it joins the cross bar of the frame. In this way the bees can get through to any comb in the hive for stores. This is not a satisfactory method for the bees will repair the damage with drone cells to the disadvantage of the hive. The second method of making a free passage is the placing of two sticks about a foot long and $\frac{3}{8}$ of an inch in diameter about two inches apart across the top of the brood-frames. The quilt is laid across over the sticks and this makes a kind of long tent through which the bees can pass to any comb for stores. The third and very effective method is to use a Porter board. Remove the bee trap and cover the hole with a piece of glass or zinc gauze. The Porter board by being set in a frame permits of the passage of bees to any part of the hive. Some claim this to be the ideal winter cover for bees and in support state that in natural conditions bees live in holes in trees which have a wooden roof and that a cloth roof is less natural. The advantage of having a piece of glass over the bee escape hole is that an inspection can be made without disturbing the bees. The piece of glass has one disadvantage in that condensation is likely to occur and drops of water may drop on the bees. This they hate so that the zinc gauze is advised for preference. If it is found necessary to feed the bees either with candy or syrup, this can be done by sliding the piece of glass or zinc gauze to one side. The writer has used this method quite successfully and without loss of stocks. If the zinc gauze becomes clogged with propolis it should be removed and scraped clean at the end of October, then replaced and will probably not be clogged up until the Spring.

Winter Packing

Coincidental with winter feeding is the matter of packing bees down for the winter. There are many and varied views on this matter. Some bee-keepers make special boxes containing chaff or cork granules and place this immediately over the brood-chamber. Others pack lots of felt sacking and old clothes over the brood-chamber. But all that is really necessary is the ticking quilt, a square of carpet underfelting and a folded sack. Cold of itself does not kill bees in the winter. But cold and damp will kill them. It is therefore more important to ensure that the hive is kept dry than to see that the bee-hive is overpacked with blankets of all types.

It has been recommended that the feed hole flap in the quilt be turned back and the hole covered with a square of perforated zinc and that this should be covered with a blanket of felt. The object in this is to see that there is sufficient ventilation in the hive to ensure that it is kept completely dry. The writer followed this recommendation but discovered that the zinc perforations soon became completely sealed up with propolis and that the bees had even dragged the hairs of the felting through the perforations and made the holes one mass of propolis mixed with hair. The following Spring it was found impossible to remove the felt without also moving the zinc.

Very little more winter covering is needed than summer covering. The writer finds that summer cover plus a folded dry sack is sufficient.

Winter work in the Apiary

Apart from Autumn feeding and packing down for the winter, there are a good many other matters which require attention. This is the time of preparation for the Spring and later the honey flow.

Storage of combs. All the shallow combs should be inspected by holding up to the window or bright light for traces of the devastation of the wax moth, they should be scraped clean of propolis and brace comb. The metal ends should be cleaned up and the runners of the shallow bar rack should be well vaselined. The crates should be sealed top and bottom with newspaper after placing a few of the volatile crystals of Paradichlorobenzine, commonly called P.D.B., in each crate. This acts as a fumigant against wax moth in stored combs. The crates should then be packed one on top of the other and stored in a place with an even temperature. Each crate should be labelled as to its contents stating whether the combs are worker or drone foundation. These crates should not be opened until they are required for the hive in the Spring where they may be wanted at a moment's notice. If they are labelled, mistakes such as placing drone combs over the brood-chamber as additional breeding room will be avoided. Queen excluders should be scraped and placed in between the wrapped shallow frame racks. This has two advantages. First, it keeps the excluders perfectly flat and secondly, it prevents any mice which may get into the stack of crates from passing from one crate to the other.

The roofs of the hives should be inspected to see that they are watertight. Any showing signs of leaks should be repaired immediately and damp felts replaced by dry ones.

The hives should be tilted forwards by raising the rear legs of the hive about one inch. This ensures that any rain driven in or condensation formed within the hive can readily run out.

In exposed districts the danger from snow is a serious menace to bees. A warm sunny spell after a fall of snow entices the bees out. The reflection of the sunlight on the snow gives the bees the idea that the Spring has arrived at last. They fly out in large numbers but the cold is too much for them, they land on the snow, become numbed and die. It is therefore desirable to screen the entrance of the hive when snow is lying on the ground.

The metal parts of feeders should be smeared with vaseline to prevent rusting and stored away until required.

The lifts from the hives should be removed, the paint-work brushed down with a wire brush and each lift given a coat of paint. Care should be taken to see that the top edges of the lift are not painted as this may become slightly sticky in summer and may result in jolting the hive when manipulating. This will disturb the bees unnecessarily and may anger them.

Repairs to hives and equipment should be carried out in readiness for the oncoming season.

Winter is a useful time to make spare equipment. Whatever you make see to it that it is standard in size. All equipment should be interchangeable. Nothing is more upsetting than to find out halfway through the manipulation of a hive that the equipment one is about to use does not fit.

If you make a spare hive, make it exactly like the others you have. This is both practical and economical.

Some precautionary treatment against Acarine disease (see chapter on bee diseases) might with advantage be carried out. The " tube wick " method described should be put into operation in the Autumn of the year.

CHAPTER XI

GENERAL ADVICE AND POINTS OF ETIQUETTE

ALL bee-keepers should be members of the local association. There are many advantages in so doing. Usually the local association provides a group insurance scheme against bee diseases and an insurance scheme against third party liability. Many associations provide arrangements for sending bees to the heather. Indoor meetings and lectures of value are arranged for the winter months whilst visits to and demonstrations in notable apiaries are arranged in the summer. Many associations arrange a " mart and exchange " among their members, also bulk purchase schemes. Lists are kept of those having bees for sale and those requiring bees. They also arrange a marketing scheme for surplus honey and collect beeswax for transmission to foundation manufacturers.

If you keep your bees in your own garden be neighbourly to your neighbours. Remember that a comb or jar of honey occasionally will sweeten them and you will not be unwelcome when your swarms lodge in their apple trees.

Don't keep too many stocks of bees in a suburban garden. Two or three is a reasonable number and no-one can take exception to it, but 10, 15 or 20 would be unreasonable and likely to lead the bee-keeper into trouble with his neighbours. In any case, it is inadvisable to keep more than two or three stocks in the first season and afterwards any additional hives should be kept in an out apiary where supplies of nectar are in greater abundance than in populated districts.

Don't be afraid to enter your products in the local agricultural and horticultural shows. This has proved one of the best marketing mediums and a means of learning a great amount about the craft.

If you have produced surplus honey the previous summer and sold it, you will probably be asked by others if you have any to sell. Keep a list of the names and addresses of those people, you may need them as future customers if your apiary develops.

Always be willing to send samples of your bees to the agricultural centre when requested for tests for disease. This will help you and help all other bee-keepers in tending to prevent the spread of bee diseases. The Bee Department, Rothamsted Experimental Station, Harpenden, Herts., will help you if you are in any doubt.

If you develop a good strain of bees let your bee-keeping friends know when you have a spare Queen cell or nucleus. Never charge bee-keepers for Queen cells. If you improve the stocks of your neighbouring bee-keepers this will probably in the end help you to maintain your high quality, for who knows but that a drone from a neighbouring bee-keeper may fertilise your next virgin Queen.

Always be willing to look after the stocks of another bee-keeper if he is ill or called away on important business ; do not expect any reward for this, you yourself may need help some day.

If you are called in to remove a swarm from premises near another apiary, take the swarm, but before removing it go to the other bee-keeper to ascertain if he has lost it, and if that be the case the rightful owner should be allowed to hive the swarm. If, however, you are the rightful owner, you should proffer some good evidence that it is your swarm.

There is an ill-founded notion amongst bee-keepers that it is permissible to trespass in pursuit of their swarms. A case was, however, recently decided in the High Court from which it is clear that such notion is now without effect. Keep sweet with your neighbours and you will not meet with difficulty over trespass.

Some bee-keepers in the hope of catching stray swarms

leave exposed an empty hive but fitted with brood-chamber and old combs. This is "not done" amongst good bee-keepers because if a swarm from another beekeeper's hive should emerge and the scouts from the swarm find this desirable home, then the swarm may decamp before the rightful owner has time to hive it.

Manipulation of a Hive

When opening up a hive great care should be taken to ensure that the bees are as little disturbed as is possible. Naturally the apparent breaking up of their home does cause the bees a certain amount of distress and concern and this is shown in two ways. Either the bees will become angry and will fly out and attack the operator or they will make for the honey cells and gorge themselves. with honey. The latter they do as a matter of instinct, for they will need that honey if they are compelled to find a new home.

Rough handling of the hive makes bees angry and they will attack the operator.

The illustration, Plate III, shows the author's protection when handling strange or "active" bees.

This method of approach has been found most satisfactory by the writer. First, have everything you intend to use in the hive handy and immediately available. Light the smoker and give the hive three good puffs of smoke direct into the entrance. Then, without hurrying, remove the roof and the outer lifts so that the interior is easily accessible. Do not jolt or jar the hive in any way. Remove the blankets, raise a corner of the quilt and give a small puff of smoke into the exposed combs. Pull off very gently the quilt and usually the bees will have their heads stuck into the honeycomb. Then take a "stink cloth," that is a cloth soaked in a weak solution of carbolic, lysol or Jeyes' fluid, and cover the exposed brood-combs Leave it there for a few seconds and then remove it. The bees will be completely subdued. Take the hive tool or an old broad chisel and remove the division board by levering up the lugs. Take out the end comb nearest the division board, look and see if the Queen is on the comb. If not, thump the bees off the comb by holding the comb in the left hand by a lug and thumping the left hand sharply with the right fist. The bees may

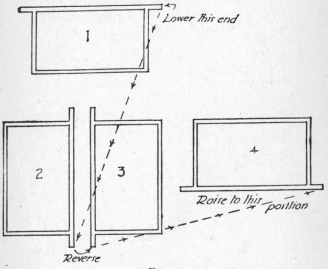

FIG. 31
Inspecting a Brood Comb

either be thumped on to the top of the brood-frame, or on to a board running up to the hive entrance, the latter for preference. Now place this outside comb on one side and lift up each comb in turn (see Plate IV, showing the comb resting across the walls of a lift). If you are in search of Queen cells it will be necessary to go through each comb with great care. There is a right and wrong way of turning combs over. Plate IV shows the correct method of inspecting a brood-comb and (Fig. 31) the correct methods of turning a comb over.

If whilst going through the brood-chamber it is found that the brood-bars stick to the runners in the brood-chamber, then smear the runner with vaseline and note the difference at the next manipulation. It will be found that the bees will not use propolis where there is vaseline and in consequence all sticking and the consequent jarring of the hive will be obviated.

Keep that part of the brood-chamber covered up which is not being manipulated; for preference use the stink rags. Care should also be taken always to hold the brood-bars over the brood-chamber when manipulating, the reason being that many young bees fall off and would otherwise be lost; also it is no uncommon thing for the Queen to fall. They all fall to safety as they fall in the brood-chamber (see Plate IV, showing this).

CHAPTER XII

DISEASES OF BEES

LIKE most other insects bees are liable to suffer from diseases ; some are mild and curable whilst others are malignant and deadly.

Bee diseases affect bees in two forms, namely, diseases of adult bees and diseases of brood.

Adult diseases are principally Acarine disease, Amœba disease and Nosema disease. Dysentery, most forms of Paralysis and Poisoning are not diseases but are complaints of the adult bee other than disease.

Amœba disease is very rare and does not seem to have occurred in this country in recent years. Nosema is widespread and fairly abundant and Acarine is both widespread and extremely abundant.

Acarine Disease

This disease in the early part of this century wrought untold havoc amongst the colonies of bees in this country. Bee-keepers became almost desperate about this plague which was alleged to have commenced in the Isle of Wight. Most people who have a scanty association with bee-keeping have heard of this dread disease. But science has mastered it and precautionary methods have been introduced which can now ensure the bee-keeper comparative freedom from this trouble.

The study of the anatomy of the bee will show that like other insects the bees have not got lungs as we understand them. Their breathing is confined to what is known as "tracheæ" which are a series of breathing tubes branching one from the other. The parasite, which is the cause of this disease, is called the "Acarapis Woodi" and from these names the term Acarine disease is derived.

This mite lives in the tracheæ of the thorax of the adult bee and is spread from bee to bee via the female of the species which when pregnant colonises by leaving its host and finding its way to a young bee less than 5 days old. It has been shown that it will find its way into Queen, drone and worker alike.

The female having found a new host proceeds to hatch out her young through the stages of eggs, larvae and adult. It is thought by some that the adults and the larvae feed upon the blood of the bee by sucking it through the tissues of the trachea although this is not yet proved. When they become sufficiently numerous they completely choke up these breathing tubes. This handicaps the bees in their flight and many die off through exhaustion during their absence from the hive and without the knowledge of the bee-keeper. This may show itself either in the fact that the stock fails to produce any stores of honey and also by the fact that the hive appears constantly weak.

The symptoms of the disease are :—

(1) *Crawling.* The bees find that they are too weak to fly and crawl out of the hive, fall to the ground and climb to the top of spikes of grass. This crawling should not be confused with the "dancing" of young bees on the alighting board. Neither should it be confused with an old bee returning after foraging with a heavy load. That bee can easily be distinguished by its shiny body and frayed wings. It is the bees which crawl *out* of the hive and drop off the landing board which give the tell-tale symptom. If there is what is described as mass crawling going on, that is bees crawling all over the ground round the hive then it is almost certain that the hive is badly infected.

(2) *Swollen abdomen.* For some reason said by some to be a form of poison which the mites return to the host when sucking its blood. the abdomen of the bee becomes

grossly distended and this symptom indicates an advanced stage of diarrhœa. This symptom does not always occur in an infected bee.

(3) *Laziness of bees*. If large numbers of adult bees are found loafing about the hive on a day when other stocks are out foraging then the bee-keeper should view it with suspicion and watch carefully for other symptoms. Laziness may also be associated with swarming which may take place within a day or two of laziness being apparent.

(4) *Dislocated wings*. Adult bees with this disease frequently appear crawling on the landing board of the hive unable to fly with their wings stuck out at odd angles.

There are other points of interest which may be given in regard to this disease.

The stocks affected dwindle rapidly and usually die out between one and two months although infected stocks may live for years.

It is thought that the disease is transferred from stock to stock by robber bees from an infected hive passing it on to the clean hives. Likewise " drifting bees," that is bees which enter the wrong hive, the hives being too close together. Natural swarms are a source of suspicion when they come from other places. Keep your eye on them for disease and never manipulate a strange swarm before operating upon " clean bees." Do it after and then wash your hands well.

The mite will not live very long when absent from its host and therefore it is quite safe to use the equipment of an infected hive after a period of say one month.

There are ways of avoiding this disease. The most important is to see that you do not buy bees from strange sources unless you are assured in writing that the apiary is free from disease. Do not place your bees near those of a " dirty " bee-keeper.

If in any doubt about your bees send a sample of them,

15 or 20, in a matchbox to the Rothamstead Experimental Station, Harpenden, Herts. No charge is made for a test. This station is very anxious to track down disease and you will be helping them as well as yourself.

These remarks apply to all bee diseases.

The Treatment of Acarine Disease.

The Frow Treatment.

About fifteen years ago Mr. R. W. Frow informed the bee-keeping world that he had discovered a cure for this disease. He had discovered a way of killing the mites without killing the bees. Dr. Rennie had already pointed out this as the way to succeed but to Mr. Frow has gone the due praise for the boon which his treatment has been to all bee-keepers. As a precaution against their colonies becoming victims serious bee-keepers always apply the treatment to prevent their stocks from becoming victims of the disease. The time may not be far distant when each bee-keeper will, in the interests of all other bee-keepers, be required by law to treat his bees annually. Sheep are dipped in a preventive dip : why not bees likewise ? This would almost eradicate the trouble.

The principle of Mr. Frow's treatment is simple. A volatile mixture is introduced into the hive and it permeates every nook and cranny even getting into the tracheae of the bees. There it does its deadly work on the live mites. It does not affect the eggs so that a further dose is necessary to dispatch them when they hatch out.

The prescription for the mixture which Mr. Frow has so generously made free to all is as follows :—

> Nitrobenzol or
> Oil of Mirbane ... 2 parts by volume.
> Safrol Oil ... ... 1 part by volume.
> Petrol ... ... 2 parts by volume.

Ordinary good quality petrol is all that need be used.

It should be thoroughly understood that this mixture

is poisonous and therefore should be handled with care.

There are two methods of treatment. One by lifting the front of the brood-chamber and slipping underneath a felt pad on which 20 minims of the liquid have been poured, and repeating the dose daily for six days to catch the mites which hatch out late. The other method of application is to put a pad of felt over the feed hole and so introduce the vapour from above. Either method is satisfactory.

Again, there is a difference of opinion as to the dose which should be given. Some say that a single dose of say 60 minims is as good as six doses of 20 minims. Both in practice have been found successful. The large dose seems to cover the hatching out period.

The treatment should be applied during the cold weather, November to February is a good time. The best time for application of the " Frow " or " Modified Frow " treatment has been found by most research laboratories to be in February or March as soon as possible after the bees have had a good cleansing flight. A measuring glass can be purchased from any dealer in bee-keeping appliances or a chemist. Multiple chemists have this treatment already made up with printed instructions as to its use.

The Oil of Wintergreen Treatment.

Experiments have been successfully carried out by introducing oil of wintergreen (methyl salicylate) into the hive. This is placed in a bottle between the combs at the back of the hive. One ounce of oil of wintergreen is placed in a bottle with a wick sticking up between the combs. This slow fumigation carries on until the bottle is empty.

There is at the present time a great shortage of safrol and there is not sufficient to meet the present demands of bee-keepers for treating the increased number of colonies of bees. An admirable substitute has been found in methyl salicylate (oil of wintergreen) for safrol. It has been found that if the proportion of nitrobenzine is increased the results are equally as effective as the original Frow recipe. Further, a substance known as Lingroin, which is a petroleum product, is quite suitable for this mixture.

The recipe for the substitute which is just as effective as the original Frow recipe is as follows :—

Methyl Salicylate
(Oil of Wintergreen) ... 2 parts by volume.
Nitrobenzine ... ... 6 ,, ,,
Lingroin ... ... 5 ,, ,,

Method of Application.

A pad of felt or flannel should be placed over the feed hole of the quilt covering the brood-chamber. If a crown board is used then over the feed hole in that board.

Seven doses of 30 minims (half a drachm) should be poured drop by drop over the pad. The doses should be administered alternate days taking a fortnight in all. But it is desirable to leave the pad on for a further two or three days. The pad should then be removed and the feed hole covered. The treatment is then ended.

Time of Application.

During February and March the bees will take their first cleansing flights. It is after these flights that the treatment should be given. If, however, it is known in the Autumn that the hive is infected the oil of wintergreen treatment described earlier should be administered during the winter.

If the beginner is in any doubt he should call in the local expert who will increase the dosage if that is found necessary.

Nosema Disease

This is not a very common disease in this country. It

is caused by an animal parasite which attacks the stomach of the bee called the chyle stomach. The parasite is called the " Nosema Apis " hence the term Nosema disease. It attacks the stomach lining, which it destroys, and the bee dies. The bees which are about to die resemble bees suffering from acarine disease. They crawl because they have not the strength to fly, but they fall off the landing board because they have no energy. They fall on their backs and die.

The disease attacks the workers, drones and the Queen. If the Queen is attacked it is doubtful if the stock will survive. But if the disease attacks the hive at the height of the season the rapid breeding will exceed the losses. The effect will be that it will remain a weak stock and the stock may recover. However, the losses will make the stock a poor honey producer.

The remedies for this disease.

All dead bees should be collected and burnt. The bees in severe cases should also be killed to prevent the spread of infection, the combs should be burnt, the hive scorched with a blow-lamp and the ground round the hive dug over and sprinkled with quicklime. This is to destroy the spores which are present in the discharged faeces of the infected bees.

Prevention of the disease may be effected by keeping all hives clean and the bees strong in numbers. Their drinking water should be watched. Queens and new stocks should only be obtained from *bona fide* sources.

Dysentery

This complaint which is not of itself a disease causes the bees to deposit their excrement within the hive. The excrement is dark in colour and cloudy, and offensive in smell. In the hive it is smeared on the combs, the walls and the floor. It is caused mainly by the bee-keeper through carelessness, and can be avoided. It is caused through incorrect feeding; feeding with glucose or brown sugar. Feeding too late in the Autumn so that the bees do not seal their stores, allows the unsealed stores to ferment and fermented honey gives the bees dysentery. Honeydew and honey containing too much dextrin will also cause this disease. If the hive is damp this is conducive to dysentery, particularly in the winter months. Sometimes, too, if the bees are confined to the hive they will develop this disease.

The treatment is to remove the soiled combs and to replace them with sealed stores, placing these in a clean brood-chamber. A cake of candy should be placed over the feed hole and the bees will soon recover.

It is wise for the bee-keeper to keep a comb or two of sealed natural stores on one side in case this disease should have to be dealt with. The hive should be kept warm and the bees left undisturbed.

Paralysis

Little is known of this disease. The symptoms are, first, the bees affected are shiny and hairless. When the dead bees are squeezed a watery liquid comes out. This has a bad smell. The live bees will be seen dragging out the dying bees. The stock may die out entirely, especially if the Queen is affected.

The remedies suggested are first raise the stock of bees higher from the ground so that affected bees cannot easily regain admission to the hive. Secondly, requeen the hive. Dusting the interior of the hive with flowers of sulphur and feeding the bees with syrup treated with thymol, as recommended by some, is not advised, as these substances may do more harm than good.

Poisoning

This is not really a disease of bees but this appears to be a suitable place to mention it. In fruit-growing districts when apple blossoms in particular are in bloom, it is the practice of the fruit-grower to spray his trees with certain arsenical preparations in order to deal with the pests on the trees. The bees gather the nectar containing the poison and return to the hive. They sometimes, too, gather water in the form of dew from the grass under the sprayed trees and this also is contaminated. Most of the bees will die before they reach the hive but they may return with pollen contaminated by the poison in which case other bees will be affected too. This, too, is the only known way in which brood becomes poisoned. The bee-keeper should tactfully approach the fruit-grower before the trees come into bloom and point out that the advice of the Ministry of Agriculture is that spraying before blossom is more effective than when the blossom is out. That is the only safe way to prevent what would otherwise cause " spring dwindling " among the bees.

Brood Diseases

The principal brood disease is Foul Brood. There are two distinct diseases, American Foul Brood, known as A.F.B., and European Foul Brood, known as E.F.B., each caused by different organisms.

American Foul Brood is unfortunately very prevalent in this country and every bee-keeper should do his best to take part in the campaign to eradicate it. The government have already taken steps to assist in its extermination by making an order imposing penalties for failing to deal with the complaint.

The cause of American Foul Brood is an organism known as " Bacillus Larvae " and is found in larvae affected by the disease.

The bee-keeper should constantly be on the watch for this disease. Every time a hive is examined a careful watch should be made. Look for the patches of brood and if there are a number of misses in the regular cappings look and see what is in the uncapped cells. Sealed brood usually occurs in blocks and a good number of uncapped cells give the first clue. Then see if any of the cell cappings are concave instead of the healthy convex cappings. Many of the cappings may be partially removed by the bees in their effort to get rid of the foetid contents of the cells. A recognised symptom is the foul smell emitted from the decaying larvae. Smell is not a safe guide as to the presence of foul brood. Some smell may or may not be present. In the case of A.F.B., the brood does not die until after it has been capped. In the case of E.F.B. the larvae are affected and die prior to sealing. Infected larvae have not got the pearly whiteness of healthy larvae. They appear flabby, yellowish brown and then turn slimey.

The disease is spread from hive to hive through robber bees and drifting bees. It can generally be prevented by the bee-keeper taking the following advice.

Always purchase bees from a known breeder of repute who can certify his apiary free from the disease.

Never feed your bees on "strange" honey.

Never purchase old combs for use in your apiary.

Never interchange combs in "doubtful" hives.

Always disinfect borrowed equipment before use and always disinfect it before returning it.

Always wash your hands after "handling" another's bees.

The safest treatment is destruction of the bees, combs and quilts and the scorching of the brood-chamber.

Neither A.F.B. nor E.F.B. can be cured by the use of any known drug or disinfectant.

The beginner should call in the expert whose name he can readily get from the local association's secretary.

He may advise two alternative methods of saving the stock, i.e., by shaking or by the artificial swarming method. But beginner, please do not try these cures without expert advice.

If the beginner will join the local association he will

enjoy the benefit of insurance against this disease and will not be the loser by the loss of the bees. The local association can obtain this cover by being affiliated to Bee Diseases Insurances Limited.

Remember always that if you do not deal with this disease you are a danger to the rest of the bee-keepers in your district. If in doubt call in the expert.

European Foul Brood

This disease is not so prevalent as the American variety. Its origin has now been definitely proved, the causal organism has recently been successfully cultured on an artificial medium. "Bacillus Pluton" is the cause of the trouble. Fortunately it is not so widespread as American Foul Brood. Although it is often present a foul smell is not necessarily associated with this disease. It all depends what secondary organisms are present in addition to the causal organism. The larvae die before they reach the pupa stage and emit a foul stench. The bees succeed in clearing out the dead larvae. In the case of American Foul Brood the larvae die after they reach the pupa stage and are capped over and the bees do not succeed in removing the dead in A.F.B. An excellent way of testing the difference between the two diseases is to take a matchstick and twist it in the dead matter in a cell. In the case of A.F.B., the matter will pull out in what is often described as ropiness, whereas with E.F.B., the matchstick comes away readily without pulling the dead matter out in a thin thread.

With A.F.B. the symptoms can be found at any time during the breeding season, whereas with E.F.B. the symptoms are usually found in the Spring but disappear as the season progresses.

Strong stocks always seem to be the best defence against bee diseases but unfortunately strong stocks are the very ones that are most likely to contract foul brood if it is present in the neighbourhood, as these are the colonies which, while being unlikely to be robbed on account of their strength, are most likely to rob out colonies weakened by foul brood.

Refrain from using borrowed equipment and do not buy bees in a doubtful market.

Cure for the disease has been professed by many but the beginner again is advised to call in the expert for advice.

In the absence of such advice destruction of the stock is the only way to eliminate the disease.

No cure or method of eliminating European Foul Brood from a colony of bees is known. Many laboratories have been attempting to find such a method for years and have also tested all methods suggested, all with complete lack of success. Total destruction is the only " cure " for European Foul Brood.

Addled Brood

This is a disease associated with the Queen and can readily be overcome by removing the Queen and replacing her with another Queen. The disease then disappears.

The symptoms are briefly as follows. The larvae usually, but not always, die in or before the pupal stage. That is after the cells have been sealed. This is one way of distinguishing it from foul brood. The cappings sink and the larvae have a shrivelled appearance as if ill-nourished and have a pungent acid smell which is unpleasant. The bees uncap these dead pupae and attempt to drag them out. Occasionally dead pupae are found on the alighting board outside the hive. These should be collected and sent to the Rothamsted Experimental Station for verification together with a complete comb. Sending a complete comb assists materially in the diagnosis of the complaint.

Chalk Brood

This disease is caused through a mildew or fungus.

Sealed brood only is affected. It is supposed to be more prevalent among the black varieties than amongst the yellow Italian varieties, although the writer has experienced it in a yellow stock. Curiously the drones are affected more than workers. The sealed larvae dry up and have the appearance of greyish mummified corpses. These are often seen near the entrance to the hive. This is not a serious disease and some well-known text-books say that it can usually be cleared by requeening, preferably with one of the yellow variety, but there is really no need to requeen at all. The colony if kept strong will probably overcome this disease itself in mild cases. In severe cases the bees should be transferred to a clean hive with new combs or foundation.

Chilled Brood

In addition to the troubles with brood caused through infection there are troubles caused through accident or through carelessness of the bee-keeper.

Manipulation of the hive too early in the season when the days are sunny but cold. This chills off the brood and the bees drag out the dead grubs and sometimes the dead sealed larvae. This puts the stock backward.

Similarly if the brood-nest is spread too rapidly there may not be enough bees to protect the brood and in consequence chilling occurs.

Starved Brood

In the early Spring when the brood nest is expanding a cold snap may come along which prevents the bees foraging. They will then use up stores and unless there are sufficient of these or candy or syrup provided the brood will die through lack of food. The bees then drag the corpses out and there is likelihood of the whole stock dying out. This may occur in the Autumn in which case the bees after dragging out their dead may leave the hive as a hunger swarm. Swarms in August onwards should always be suspected as being hunger swarms and taken with necessary caution.

Enemies of Bees

There are several enemies of bees each of which affect the stock in different ways.

The toad may sit on the landing board of the hive and pick up the bees as they land with their load. But they also pick up dead and perhaps diseased bees lying round the entrance so should not be discouraged.

Mice occasionally enter a hive in the winter and cause havoc. They can be prevented by a strip of Queen excluder being placed over the entrance.

Tits frequently tap at the entrance to hives in the winter time. The bees which are attracted to the entrance are picked off one by one by the tits.

Ants collect in the quilt of the hive and are a nuisance. They can be prevented from doing this if the four legs of the hive are stood in tins of old motor sump oil.

The same applies to earwigs although they can and will fly to the hive so that placing the hive legs in oil may not prevent all of these insects from getting into the hive.

The worst enemy to the hive is the wax moth. There are two species and they may do irreparable damage. They lay eggs in the comb and the grubs will eat very rapidly through a comb, soiling it with faeces. Great care should be taken with the storage of combs when they are not in use.

Hornets in other countries are a menace to bees. The author has seen in Palestine Arabs—who produce most of Palestine's honey—standing with large swatters by beehives swatting hornets in large numbers. Hornets even keep the bees indoors during the mid-day hours.

The best known method of fumigation to prevent wax

moth is the Paradichlora-benzine, commonly called
" P.D.B." and it is used in the following way :—

First, stack the brood-chambers and shallow frame supers
complete with the combs to be treated one above the
other. The space where the chambers meet should be
sealed over on the outside with strips of gummed paper so
that the effect is to allow a through draught of air. The
lowest brood-chamber should be placed on a sheet of newspaper which should be pasted up on the outer sides of the
brood-chamber.

Secondly, place an ounce or two of these crystals on a
saucer or plate on the top of the shallow frames in the top
crate, and cover the whole by pasting a sheet of newspaper
over the top, or by using a national roof as a cover.

P.D.B. crystals give off heavy volatile fumes and these
fumes will penetrate throughout the whole stack of
brood-chambers and crates.

If this is done in the Autumn and the P.D.B. crystals
replenished in January or February the combs will be
kept proof against wax moth.

Before using the brood-chambers or shallow bars, air
them in the open air for a few hours to get rid of the P.D.B.
fumes.

It is particularly important to note that in no circumstances should P.D.B. be used direct in the hive, otherwise
fatal results will follow.

APPENDIX

BOOKS OF REFERENCE

The reader is advised to take advantage of the opportunities of reading as much as he can about this absorbing subject and the following list of books is recommended for selection.

Author.		*Title.*
APIS CLUB	. .	Diseases of Bees.
BOFF, C.	. . .	How to Grow and Produce Your Own Food.
CHESHIRE, F. R.	.	Bees and Bee-keeping.
COWAN. T. W.	.	The Honey-bee.
COWAN, T. W.	.	British Bee-keepers' Guide Book to the Management of Bees in Movable-comb Hives, and the use of the Extractor.
DADANT, C. P.	.	Dadant System of Bee-keeping.
DIGGES, J. G.	. .	Practical Bee Guide.
EDWARDES, T.	.	Lore of the Honey-bee.
FABRE, J. H.	. .	Bramble-bees, and Others.
FRANÇON, J.	. .	The Mind of the Bee.
GILMAN, A.	. .	Practical Bee-breeding.
HASLUCK, P. N. (Ed.)		Bee hives and Bee-keepers' Appliances.
HEMPSALL, W. H.		Bee-keeping, New and Old.
HOOPER, M. M.	.	Commonsense Bee-keeping.
LAWSON, J. A.	.	Honeycraft in Theory and Practice.
MACE, H.	. . .	Book about the Bee.
MACE, H.	. . .	Modern Bee-keeping.
MACFIE, D. T.	. .	Practical Bee-keeping and Honey Production.
MAETERLINCK, M.	.	Life of the Bee.
MANLEY, R. O. B.	.	Honey Production in the British Isles.

PELLETT, F. C. . Productive Bee-keeping.

RENDL, G. . . . Way of a Bee.

ROOT, A. I. . . ABC and XYZ of Bee Culture.

SNELGROVE . . Swarm Control.

STEP, E. . . . Bees, Wasps, Ants and Allied Insects.

WEDMORE, E. B. . Manual of Bee-keeping for English-Speaking Bee-keepers.

WILLIAMS, C. . Story of the Hive.

INDEX